# Garfield ®
## Snack Pack
BY JIM DAVIS

# Volume Two

Ross Richie CEO & Founder • Joy Huffman CFO • Matt Gagnon Editor-in-Chief • Filip Sablik President, Publishing & Marketing • Stephen Christy President, Development • Lance Kreiter Vice President, Licensing & Merchandising
Phil Barbaro Vice President, Finance & Human Resources • Arune Singh Vice President, Marketing • Bryce Carlson Vice President, Editorial & Creative Strategy • Scott Newman Manager, Production Design • Kate Henning Manager, Operations
Spencer Simpson Manager, Sales • Sierra Hahn Executive Editor • Jeanine Schaefer Executive Editor • Dafna Pleban Senior Editor • Shannon Watters Senior Editor • Eric Harburn Senior Editor
Chris Rosa Editor • Matthew Levine Editor • Sophie Philips-Roberts Assistant Editor • Gavin Gronenthal Assistant Editor • Michael Moccio Assistant Editor • Gwen Waller Assistant Editor • Amanda LaFranco Executive Assistant
Jillian Crab Design Coordinator • Michelle Ankley Design Coordinator • Kara Leopard Production Designer • Marie Krupina Production Designer • Grace Park Production Design Assistant • Chelsea Roberts Production Design Assistant
Samantha Knapp Production Design Assistant • Elizabeth Loughridge Accounting Coordinator • Stephanie Hocutt Social Media Coordinator • José Meza Event Coordinator • Holly Aitchison Digital Sales Coordinator
Esther Kim Marketing Coordinator • Megan Christopher Operations Assistant • Rodrigo Hernandez Mailroom Assistant • Morgan Perry Direct Market Representative • Cat O'Grady Marketing Assistant • Breanna Sarpy Executive Assistant

**kaboom!**

**GARFIELD: SNACK PACK Volume Two, June 2019.** Published by KaBOOM!, a division of Boom Entertainment, Inc. Garfield is © 2019 PAWS, INCORPORATED. ALL RIGHTS RESERVED. "GARFIELD" and the GARFIELD characters are registered and unregistered trademarks of Paws, Inc. Originally published in single magazine form as GARFIELD 2018 VACATION TIME BLUES No.1 and GARFIELD 2018 TV OR NOT TV? No. 1. ™ & © 2018 PAWS, INCORPORATED. All rights reserved. KaBOOM!™ and the KaBOOM! logo are trademarks of Boom Entertainment, Inc., registered in various countries and categories. All characters, events, and institutions depicted herein are fictional. Any similarity between any of the names, characters, persons, events, and/or institutions in this publication to actual names, characters, and persons, whether living or dead, events, and/or institutions is unintended and purely coincidental. KaBOOM! does not read or accept unsolicited submissions of ideas, stories, or artwork.

BOOM! Studios, 5670 Wilshire Boulevard, Suite 400, Los Angeles, CA 90036-5679. Printed in China. First Printing.

ISBN: 978-1-68415-370-1 , eISBN: 978-1-64144-353-1

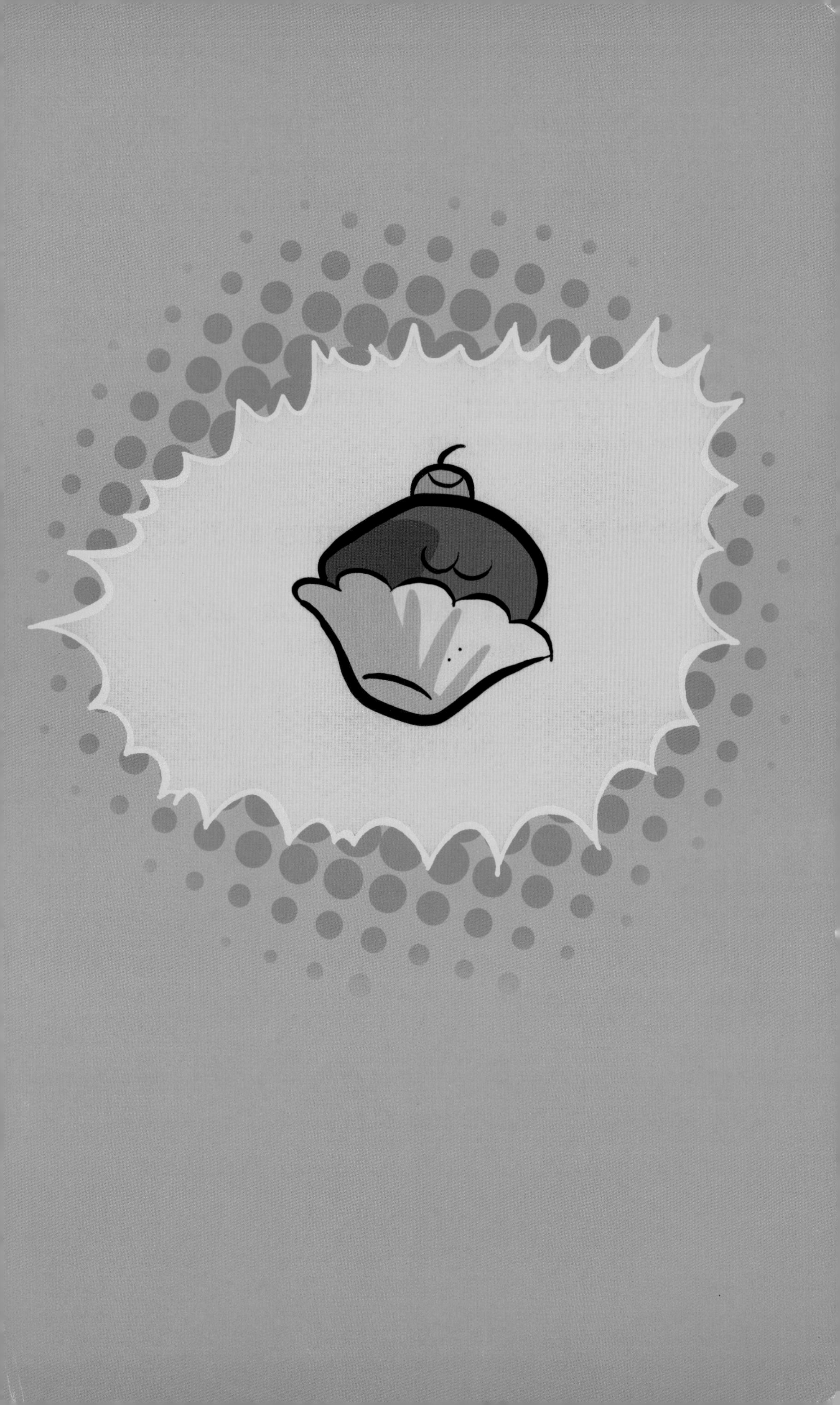

"SANDY SANDY"
WRITTEN BY MARK EVANIER
ILLUSTRATED BY ANTONIO ALFARO

"THE FALL SEASON"
WRITTEN BY MARK EVANIER
ILLUSTRATED BY DAVID ALVAREZ

"THE SUMMER OF THE
LASAGNA MONSTER"
WRITTEN BY SCOTT NICKEL
ILLUSTRATED BY DAVID DeGRAND

"COMEDY OF TERRORS"
WRITTEN BY SCOTT NICKEL
ILLUSTRATED BY ANTONIO ALFARO

COLORED BY LISA MOORE          LETTERED BY JIM CAMPBELL

COVER BY GARY BARKER AND DAN DAVIS
COLORED BY LISA MOORE

SERIES DESIGNER
GRACE PARK

COLLECTION DESIGNER
CHELSEA ROBERTS

EDITOR
CHRIS ROSA

SPECIAL THANKS TO JIM DAVIS AND THE
ENTIRE PAWS, INC. TEAM.

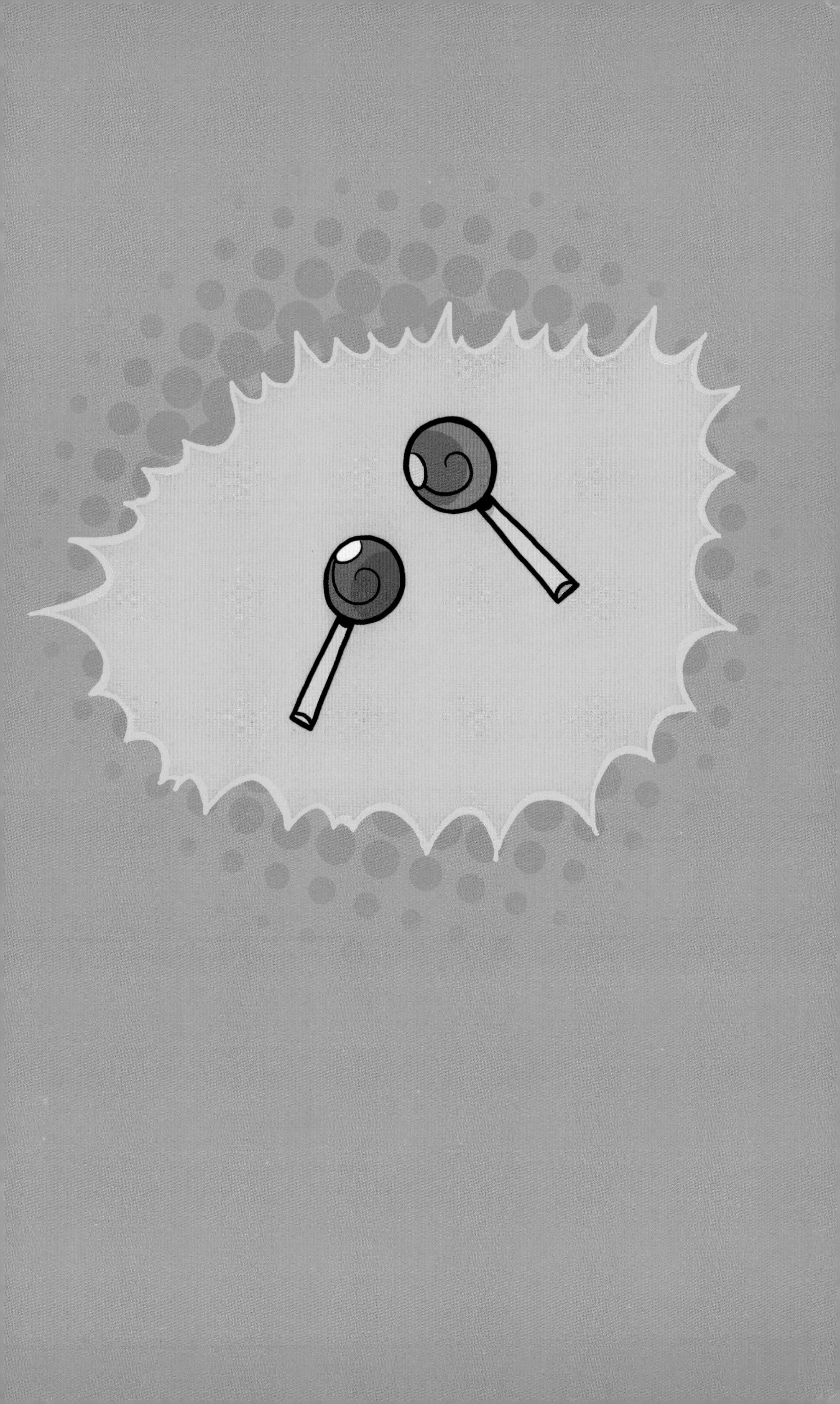

# Sandy
# Sandy

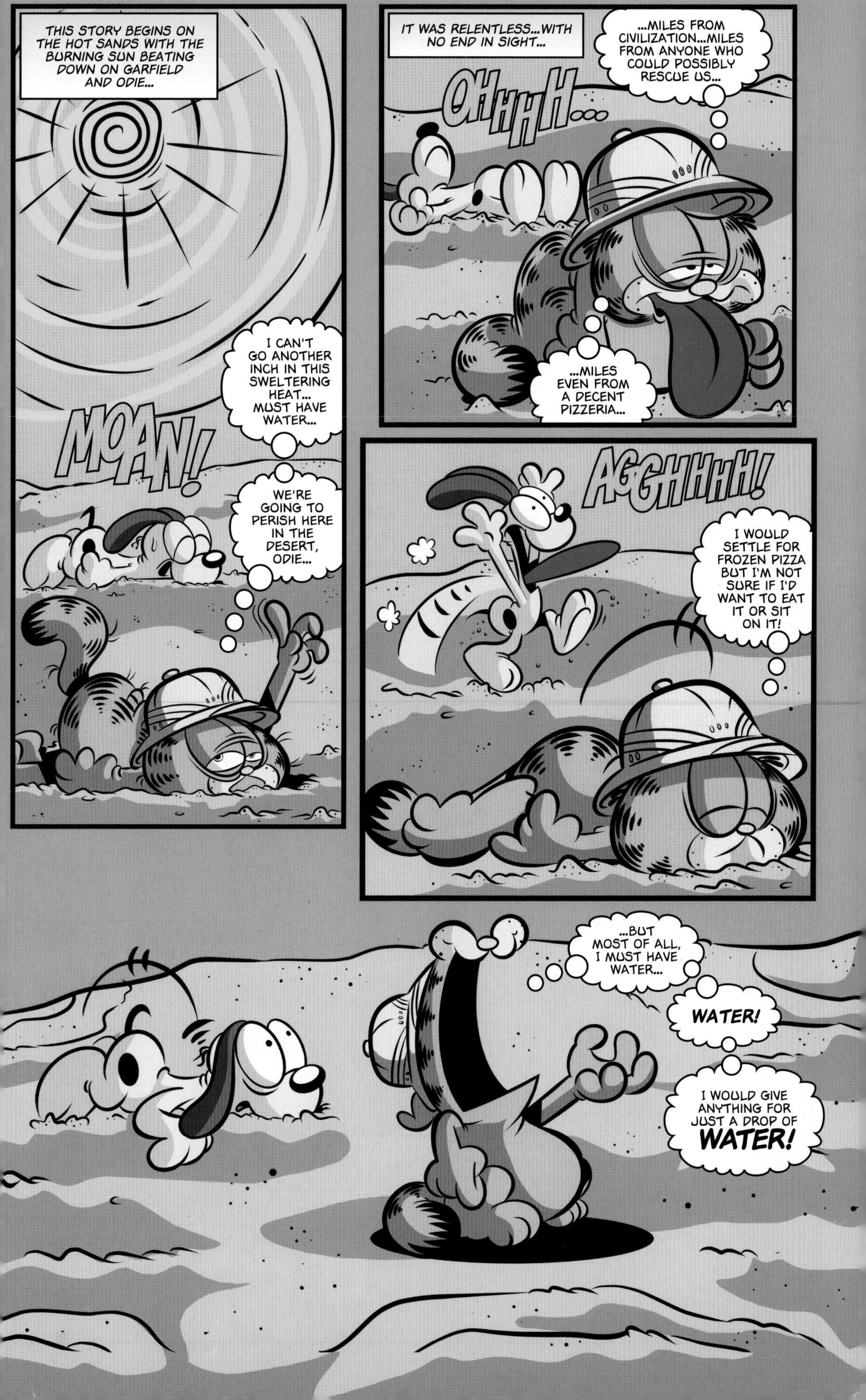

THIS STORY BEGINS ON THE HOT SANDS WITH THE BURNING SUN BEATING DOWN ON GARFIELD AND ODIE...
I CAN'T GO ANOTHER INCH IN THIS SWELTERING HEAT... MUST HAVE WATER...
MOAN!
WE'RE GOING TO PERISH HERE IN THE DESERT, ODIE...
IT WAS RELENTLESS...WITH NO END IN SIGHT...
...MILES FROM CIVILIZATION...MILES FROM ANYONE WHO COULD POSSIBLY RESCUE US...
OHHHH...
...MILES EVEN FROM A DECENT PIZZERIA...
AGGHHHH!
I WOULD SETTLE FOR FROZEN PIZZA BUT I'M NOT SURE IF I'D WANT TO EAT IT OR SIT ON IT!
...BUT MOST OF ALL, I MUST HAVE WATER...
WATER!
I WOULD GIVE ANYTHING FOR JUST A DROP OF WATER!

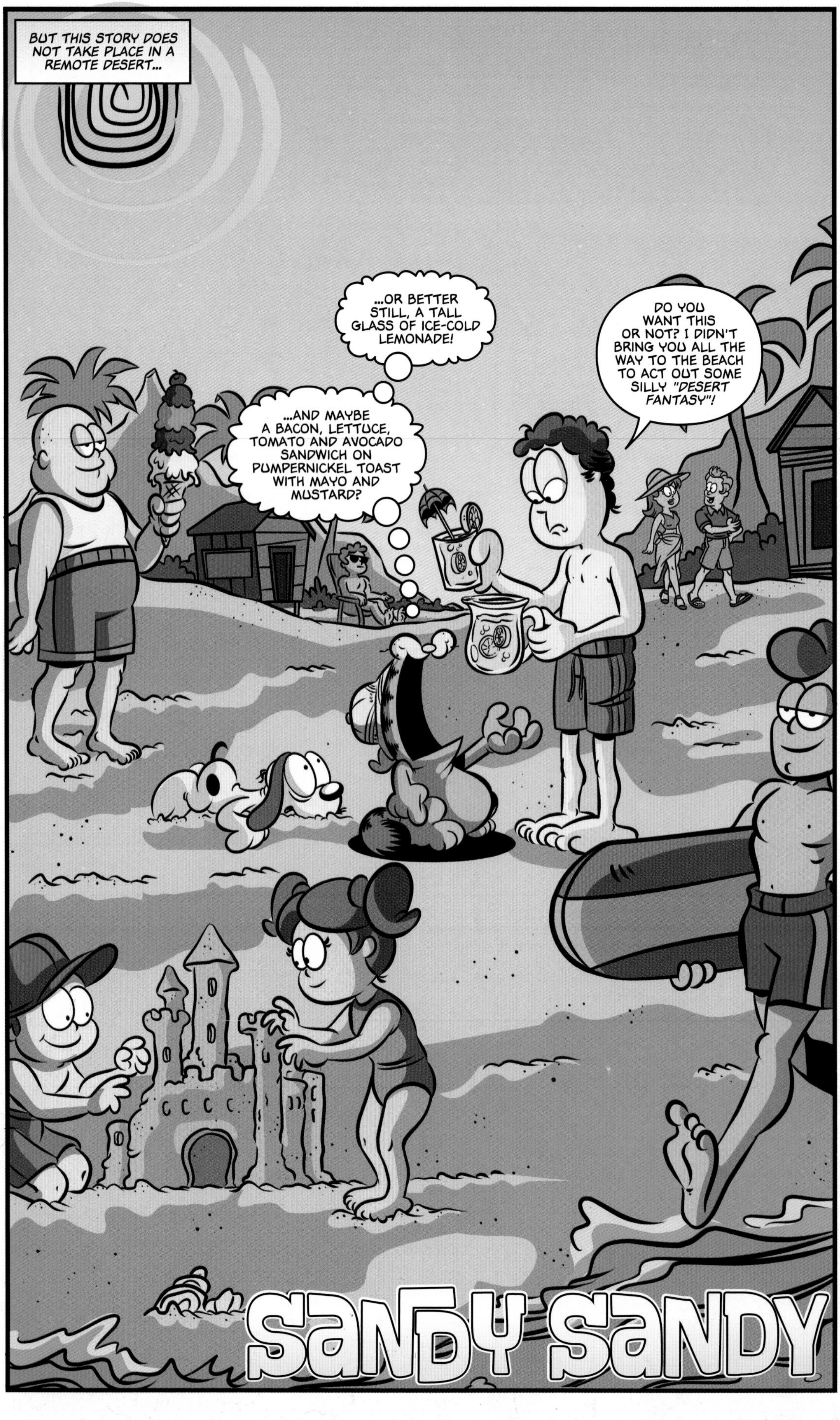

BUT THIS STORY DOES NOT TAKE PLACE IN A REMOTE DESERT...
...OR BETTER STILL, A TALL GLASS OF ICE-COLD LEMONADE!
...AND MAYBE A BACON, LETTUCE, TOMATO AND AVOCADO SANDWICH ON PUMPERNICKEL TOAST WITH MAYO AND MUSTARD?
DO YOU WANT THIS OR NOT? I DIDN'T BRING YOU ALL THE WAY TO THE BEACH TO ACT OUT SOME SILLY "DESERT FANTASY"!
SANDY SANDY

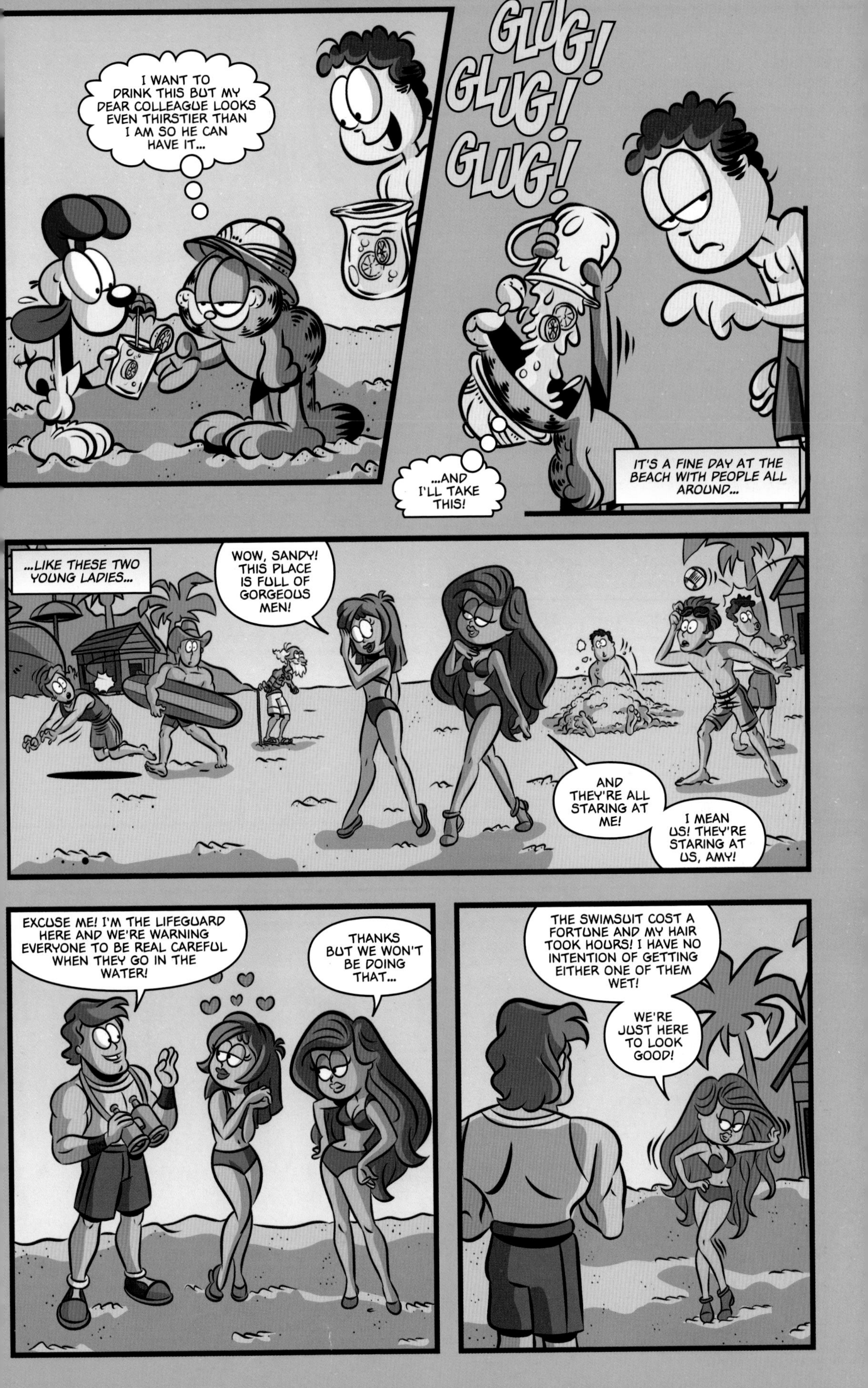
I WANT TO DRINK THIS BUT MY DEAR COLLEAGUE LOOKS EVEN THIRSTIER THAN I AM SO HE CAN HAVE IT...
GLUG! GLUG! GLUG!
...AND I'LL TAKE THIS!
IT'S A FINE DAY AT THE BEACH WITH PEOPLE ALL AROUND...
...LIKE THESE TWO YOUNG LADIES...
WOW, SANDY! THIS PLACE IS FULL OF GORGEOUS MEN!
AND THEY'RE ALL STARING AT ME!
I MEAN US! THEY'RE STARING AT US, AMY!
EXCUSE ME! I'M THE LIFEGUARD HERE AND WE'RE WARNING EVERYONE TO BE REAL CAREFUL WHEN THEY GO IN THE WATER!
THANKS BUT WE WON'T BE DOING THAT...
THE SWIMSUIT COST A FORTUNE AND MY HAIR TOOK HOURS! I HAVE NO INTENTION OF GETTING EITHER ONE OF THEM WET!
WE'RE JUST HERE TO LOOK GOOD!

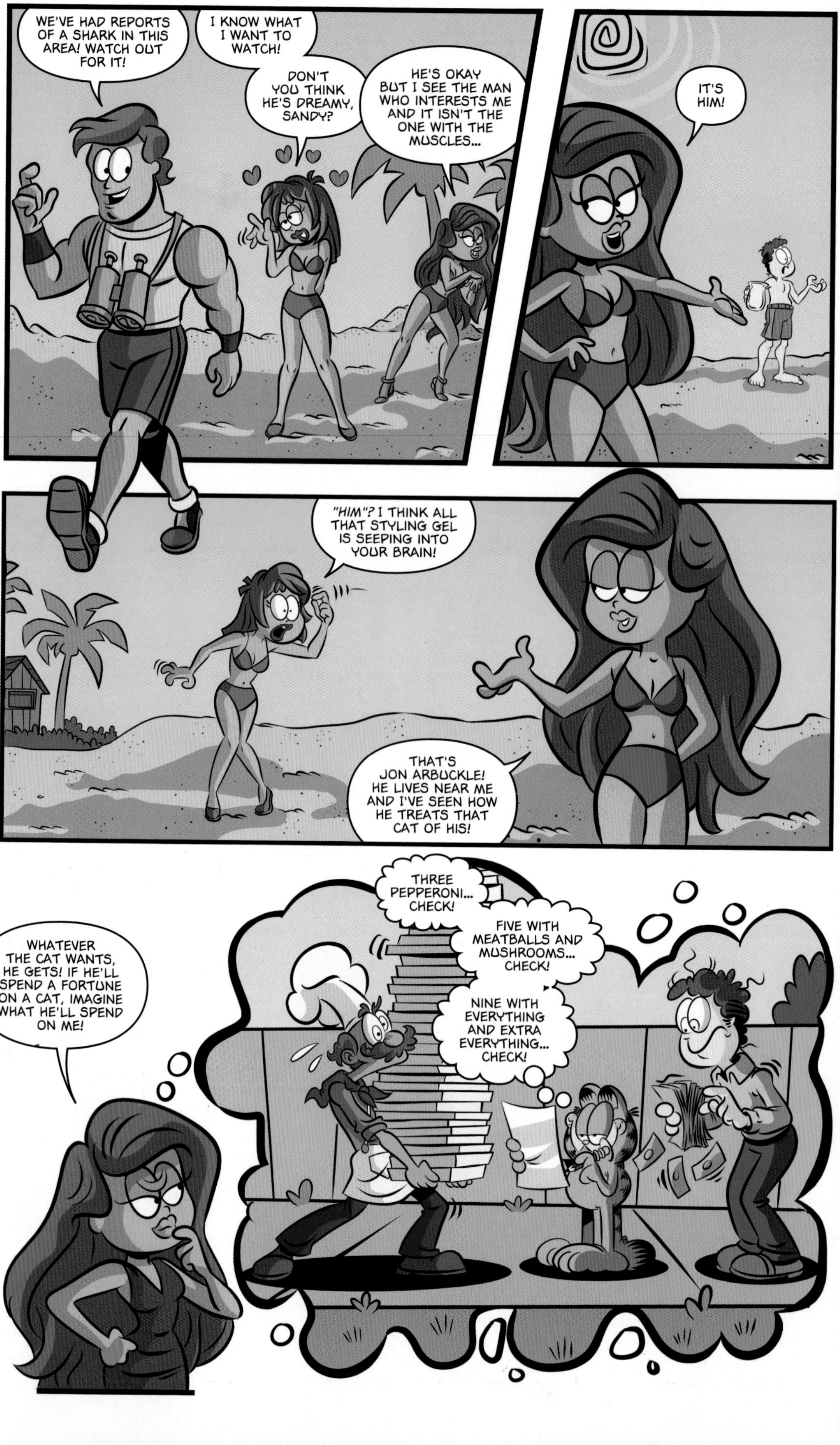
WE'VE HAD REPORTS OF A SHARK IN THIS AREA! WATCH OUT FOR IT!
I KNOW WHAT I WANT TO WATCH!
DON'T YOU THINK HE'S DREAMY, SANDY?
HE'S OKAY BUT I SEE THE MAN WHO INTERESTS ME AND IT ISN'T THE ONE WITH THE MUSCLES...
IT'S HIM!
"HIM"? I THINK ALL THAT STYLING GEL IS SEEPING INTO YOUR BRAIN!
THAT'S JON ARBUCKLE! HE LIVES NEAR ME AND I'VE SEEN HOW HE TREATS THAT CAT OF HIS!
WHATEVER THE CAT WANTS, HE GETS! IF HE'LL SPEND A FORTUNE ON A CAT, IMAGINE WHAT HE'LL SPEND ON ME!
THREE PEPPERONI... CHECK!
FIVE WITH MEATBALLS AND MUSHROOMS... CHECK!
NINE WITH EVERYTHING AND EXTRA EVERYTHING... CHECK!

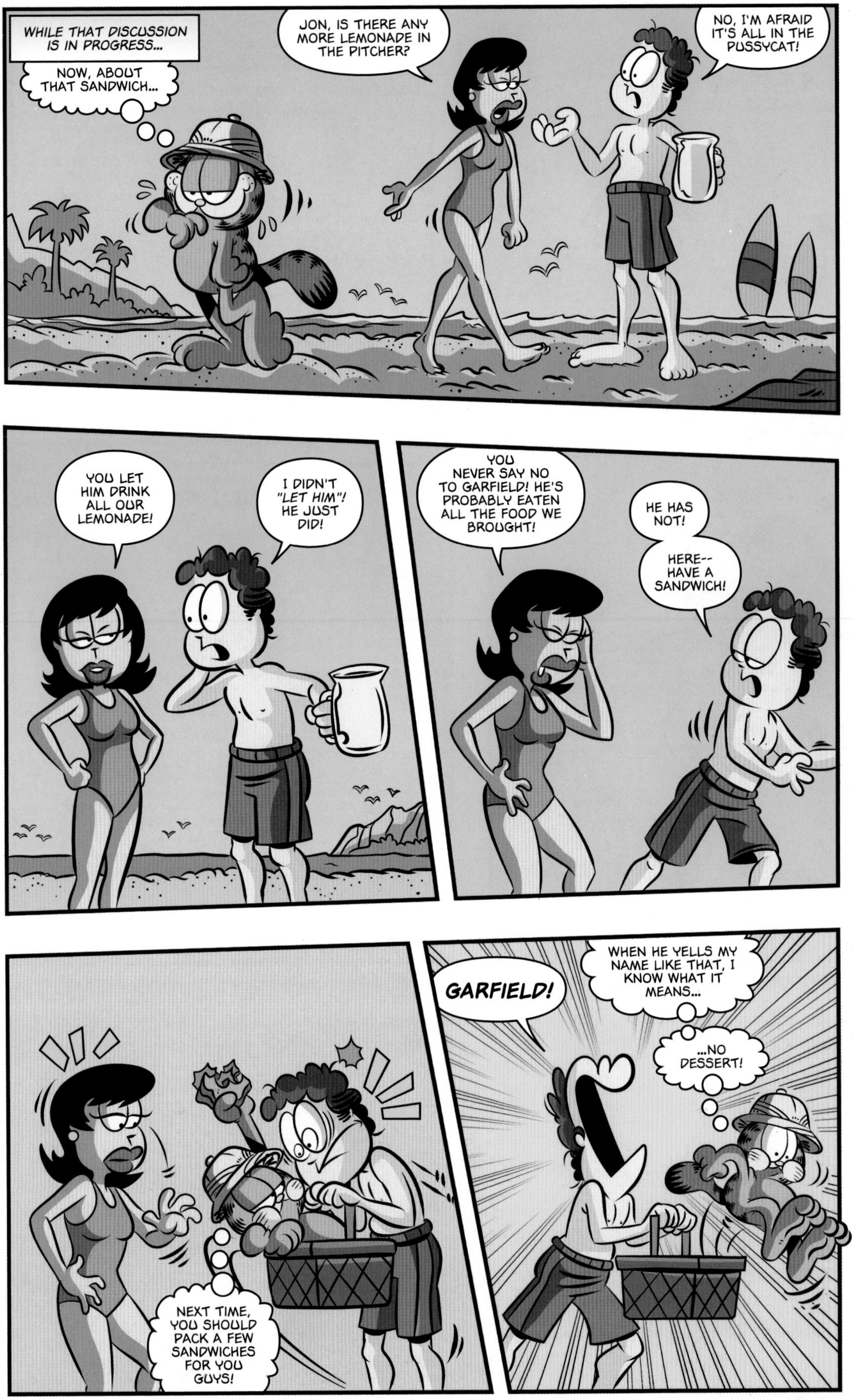
WHILE THAT DISCUSSION IS IN PROGRESS...
NOW, ABOUT THAT SANDWICH...
JON, IS THERE ANY MORE LEMONADE IN THE PITCHER?
NO, I'M AFRAID IT'S ALL IN THE PUSSYCAT!
YOU LET HIM DRINK ALL OUR LEMONADE!
I DIDN'T "LET HIM"! HE JUST DID!
YOU NEVER SAY NO TO GARFIELD! HE'S PROBABLY EATEN ALL THE FOOD WE BROUGHT!
HE HAS NOT!
HERE-- HAVE A SANDWICH!
NEXT TIME, YOU SHOULD PACK A FEW SANDWICHES FOR YOU GUYS!
GARFIELD!
WHEN HE YELLS MY NAME LIKE THAT, I KNOW WHAT IT MEANS...
...NO DESSERT!

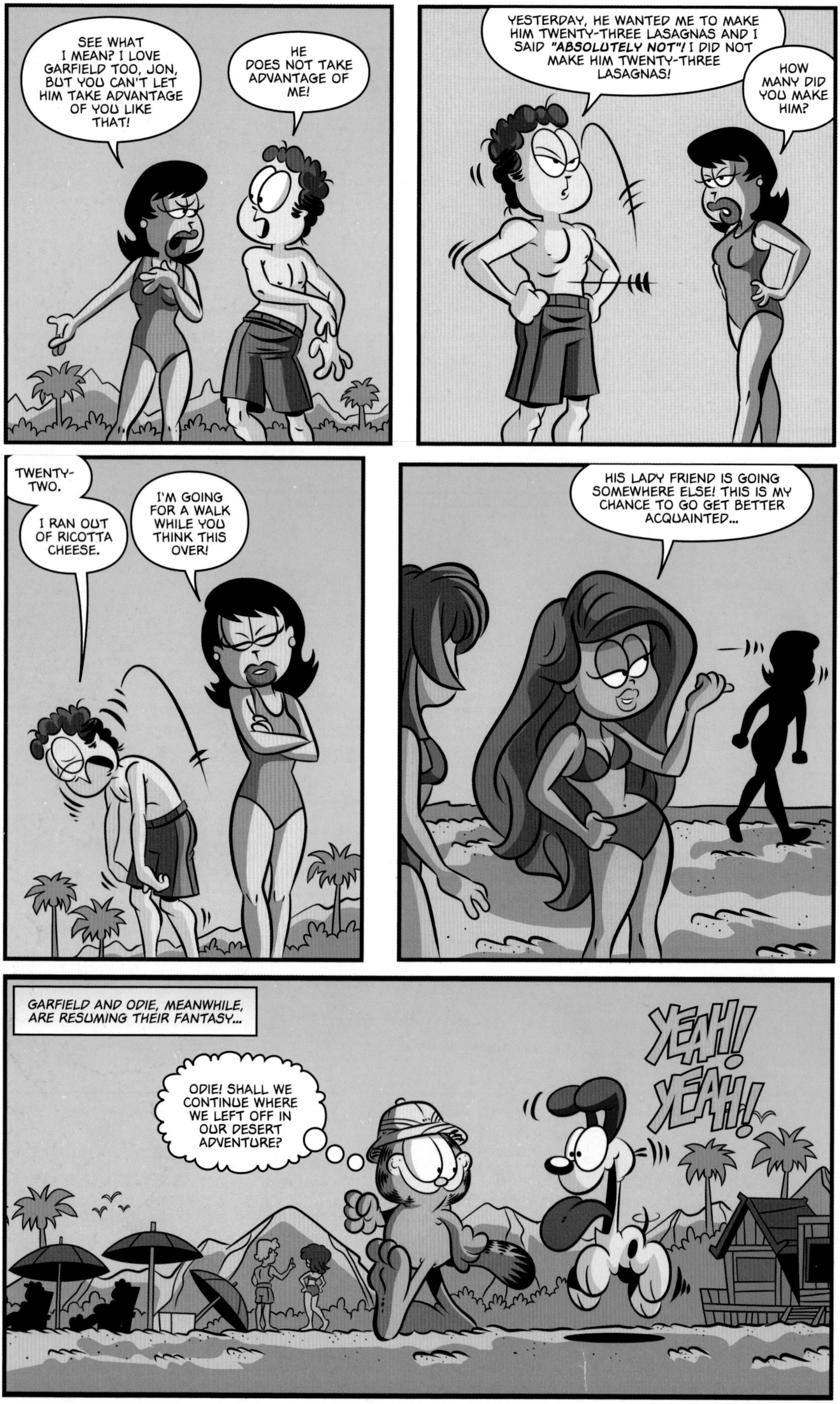
SEE WHAT I MEAN? I LOVE GARFIELD TOO, JON, BUT YOU CAN'T LET HIM TAKE ADVANTAGE OF YOU LIKE THAT!
HE DOES NOT TAKE ADVANTAGE OF ME!
YESTERDAY, HE WANTED ME TO MAKE HIM TWENTY-THREE LASAGNAS AND I SAID "ABSOLUTELY NOT"! I DID NOT MAKE HIM TWENTY-THREE LASAGNAS!
HOW MANY DID YOU MAKE HIM?
TWENTY-TWO.
I RAN OUT OF RICOTTA CHEESE.
I'M GOING FOR A WALK WHILE YOU THINK THIS OVER!
HIS LADY FRIEND IS GOING SOMEWHERE ELSE! THIS IS MY CHANCE TO GO GET BETTER ACQUAINTED...
GARFIELD AND ODIE, MEANWHILE, ARE RESUMING THEIR FANTASY...
ODIE! SHALL WE CONTINUE WHERE WE LEFT OFF IN OUR DESERT ADVENTURE?
YEAH! YEAH!

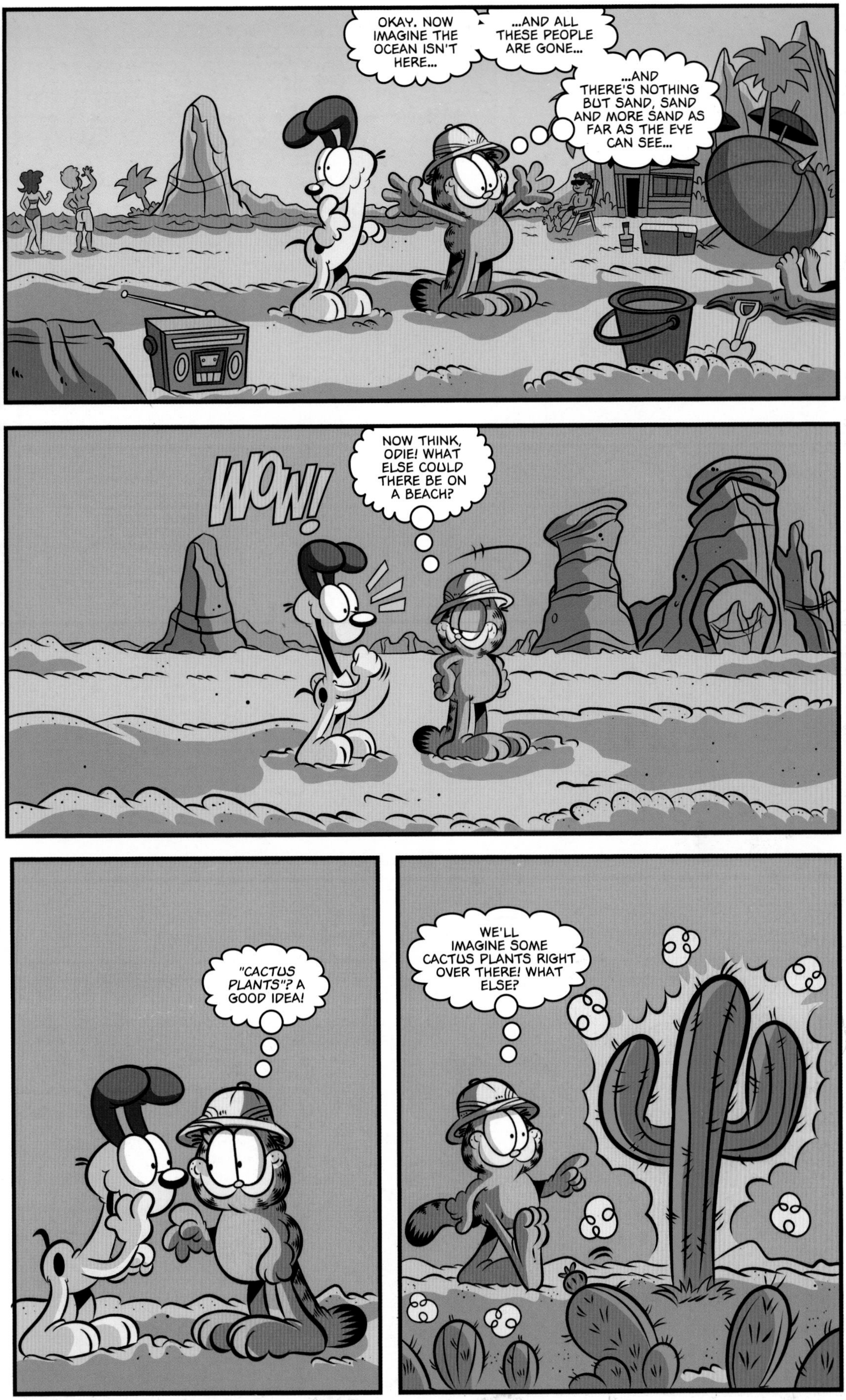
OKAY. NOW IMAGINE THE OCEAN ISN'T HERE...
...AND ALL THESE PEOPLE ARE GONE...
...AND THERE'S NOTHING BUT SAND, SAND AND MORE SAND AS FAR AS THE EYE CAN SEE...
WOW!
NOW THINK, ODIE! WHAT ELSE COULD THERE BE ON A BEACH?
"CACTUS PLANTS"? A GOOD IDEA!
WE'LL IMAGINE SOME CACTUS PLANTS RIGHT OVER THERE! WHAT ELSE?

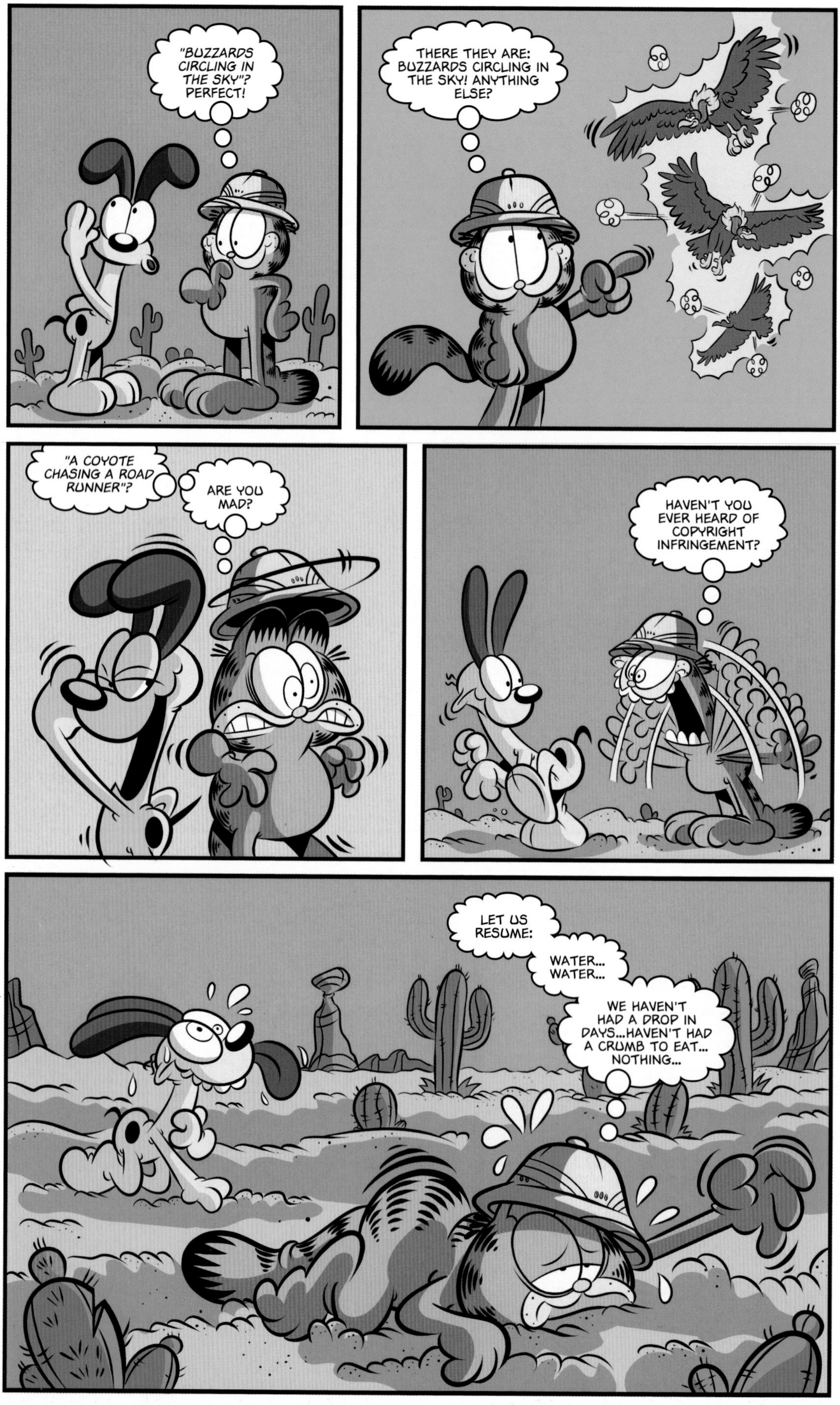
"BUZZARDS CIRCLING IN THE SKY"? PERFECT!
THERE THEY ARE: BUZZARDS CIRCLING IN THE SKY! ANYTHING ELSE?
"A COYOTE CHASING A ROAD RUNNER"?
ARE YOU MAD?
HAVEN'T YOU EVER HEARD OF COPYRIGHT INFRINGEMENT?
LET US RESUME:
WATER... WATER...
WE HAVEN'T HAD A DROP IN DAYS...HAVEN'T HAD A CRUMB TO EAT... NOTHING...

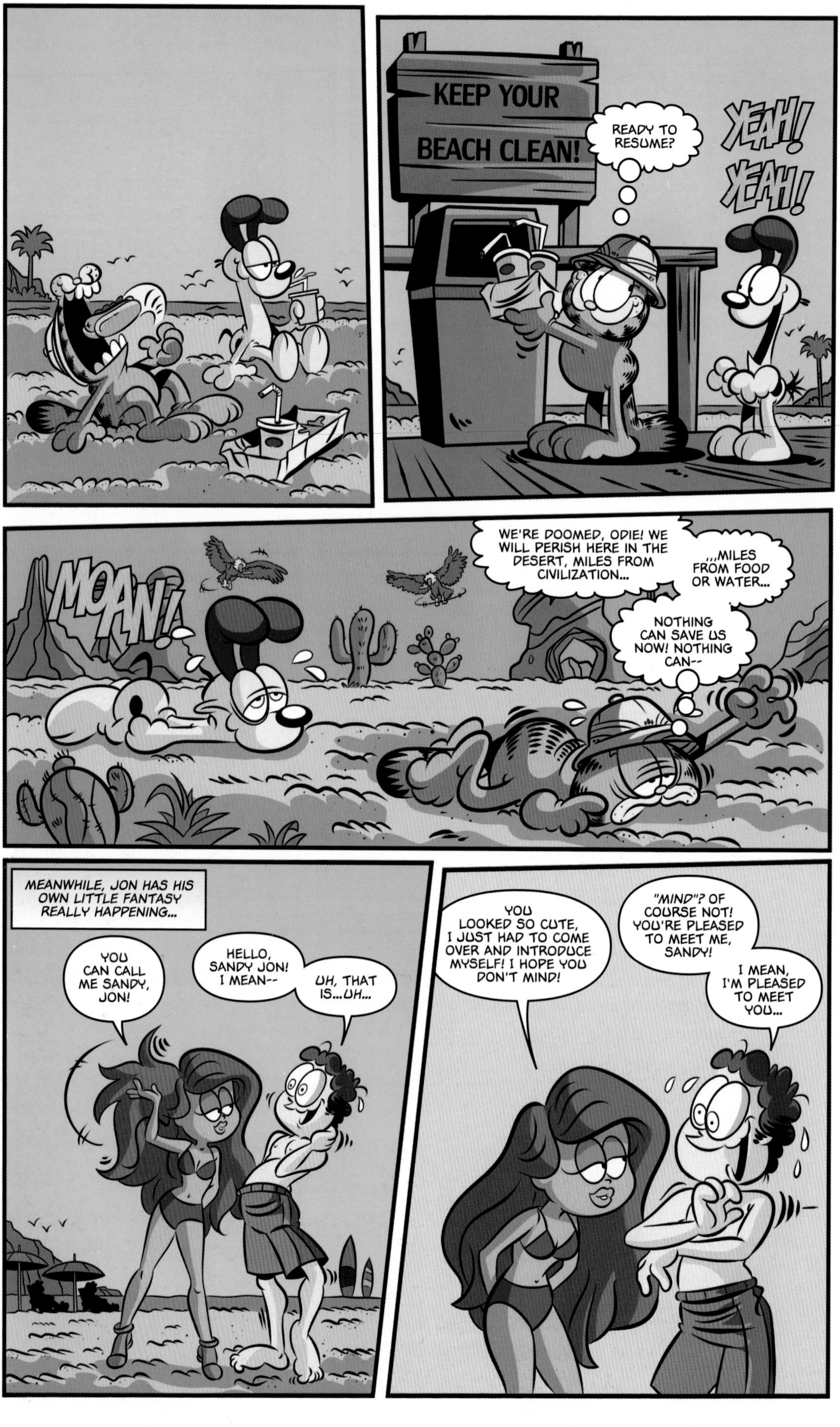
KEEP YOUR BEACH CLEAN!
READY TO RESUME?
YEAH! YEAH!
MOAN!
WE'RE DOOMED, ODIE! WE WILL PERISH HERE IN THE DESERT, MILES FROM CIVILIZATION...
...MILES FROM FOOD OR WATER...
NOTHING CAN SAVE US NOW! NOTHING CAN--
MEANWHILE, JON HAS HIS OWN LITTLE FANTASY REALLY HAPPENING...
YOU CAN CALL ME SANDY, JON!
HELLO, SANDY JON! I MEAN--
UH, THAT IS...UH...
YOU LOOKED SO CUTE, I JUST HAD TO COME OVER AND INTRODUCE MYSELF! I HOPE YOU DON'T MIND!
"MIND"? OF COURSE NOT! YOU'RE PLEASED TO MEET ME, SANDY!
I MEAN, I'M PLEASED TO MEET YOU...

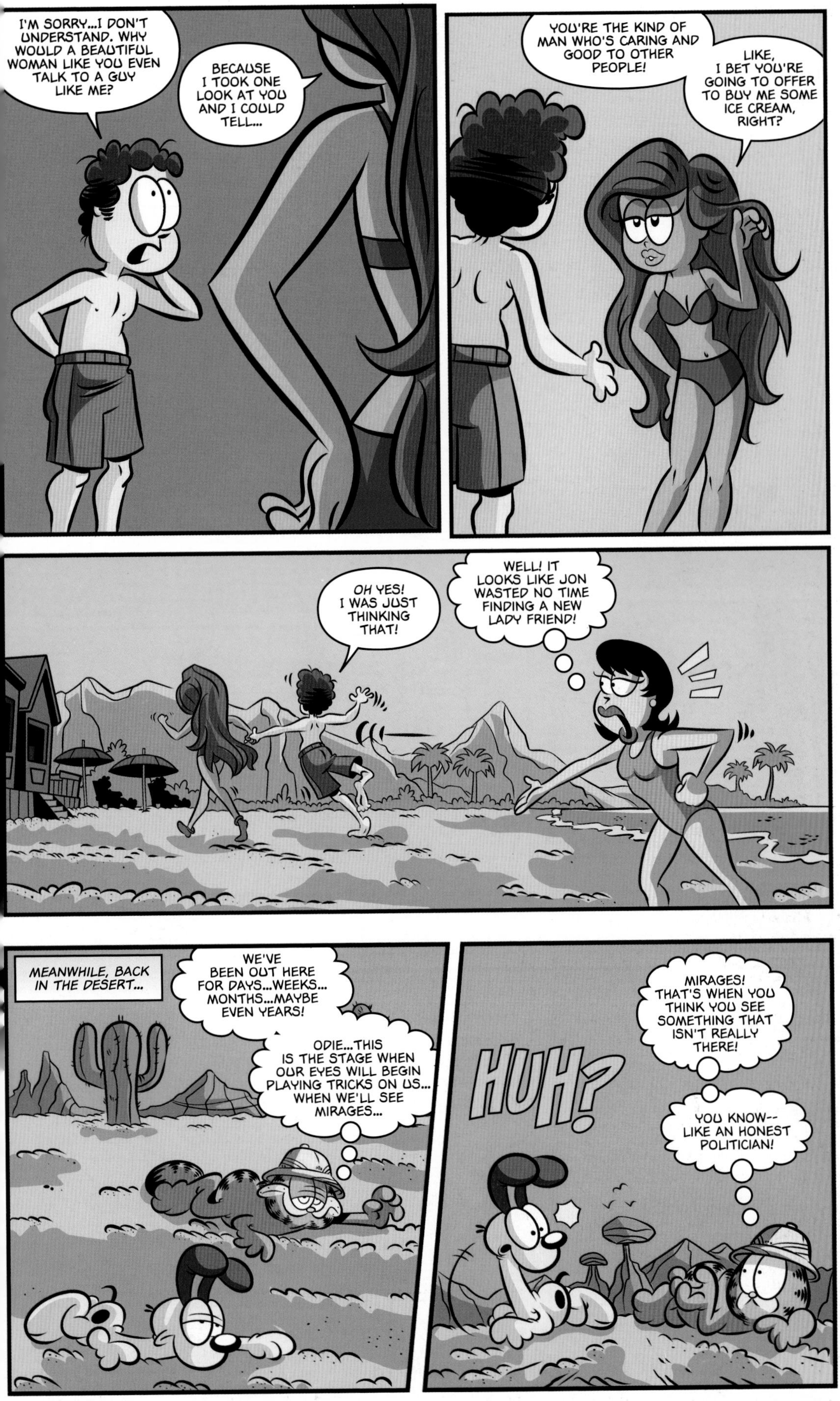
I'M SORRY...I DON'T UNDERSTAND. WHY WOULD A BEAUTIFUL WOMAN LIKE YOU EVEN TALK TO A GUY LIKE ME?
BECAUSE I TOOK ONE LOOK AT YOU AND I COULD TELL...
YOU'RE THE KIND OF MAN WHO'S CARING AND GOOD TO OTHER PEOPLE!
LIKE, I BET YOU'RE GOING TO OFFER TO BUY ME SOME ICE CREAM, RIGHT?
OH YES! I WAS JUST THINKING THAT!
WELL! IT LOOKS LIKE JON WASTED NO TIME FINDING A NEW LADY FRIEND!
MEANWHILE, BACK IN THE DESERT...
WE'VE BEEN OUT HERE FOR DAYS...WEEKS... MONTHS...MAYBE EVEN YEARS!
ODIE...THIS IS THE STAGE WHEN OUR EYES WILL BEGIN PLAYING TRICKS ON US... WHEN WE'LL SEE MIRAGES...
HUH?
MIRAGES! THAT'S WHEN YOU THINK YOU SEE SOMETHING THAT ISN'T REALLY THERE!
YOU KNOW--LIKE AN HONEST POLITICIAN!

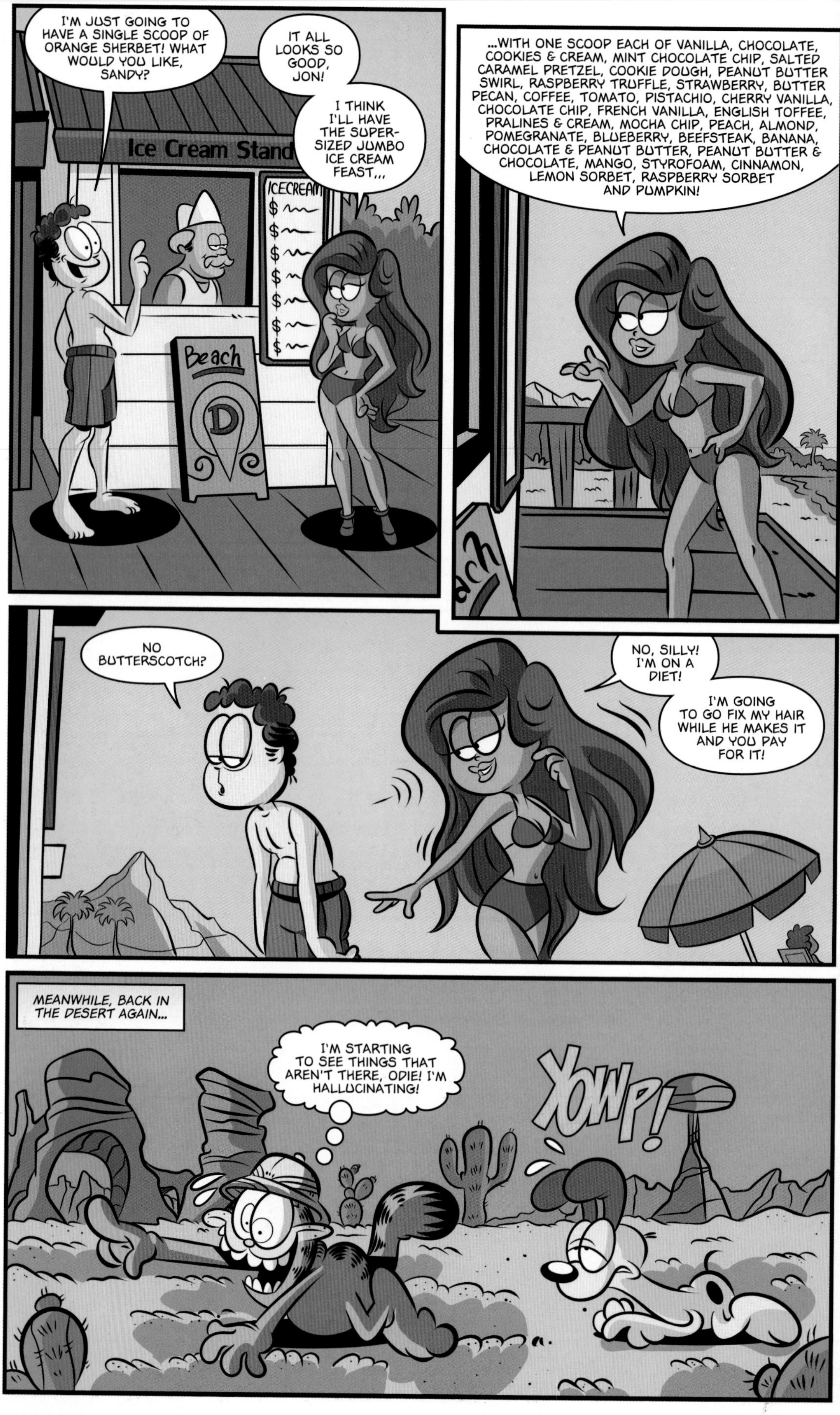
I'M JUST GOING TO HAVE A SINGLE SCOOP OF ORANGE SHERBET! WHAT WOULD YOU LIKE, SANDY?
IT ALL LOOKS SO GOOD, JON!
I THINK I'LL HAVE THE SUPER-SIZED JUMBO ICE CREAM FEAST,,,
Ice Cream Stand
ICECREAM
Beach
D
...WITH ONE SCOOP EACH OF VANILLA, CHOCOLATE, COOKIES & CREAM, MINT CHOCOLATE CHIP, SALTED CARAMEL PRETZEL, COOKIE DOUGH, PEANUT BUTTER SWIRL, RASPBERRY TRUFFLE, STRAWBERRY, BUTTER PECAN, COFFEE, TOMATO, PISTACHIO, CHERRY VANILLA, CHOCOLATE CHIP, FRENCH VANILLA, ENGLISH TOFFEE, PRALINES & CREAM, MOCHA CHIP, PEACH, ALMOND, POMEGRANATE, BLUEBERRY, BEEFSTEAK, BANANA, CHOCOLATE & PEANUT BUTTER, PEANUT BUTTER & CHOCOLATE, MANGO, STYROFOAM, CINNAMON, LEMON SORBET, RASPBERRY SORBET AND PUMPKIN!
NO BUTTERSCOTCH?
NO, SILLY! I'M ON A DIET!
I'M GOING TO GO FIX MY HAIR WHILE HE MAKES IT AND YOU PAY FOR IT!
MEANWHILE, BACK IN THE DESERT AGAIN...
I'M STARTING TO SEE THINGS THAT AREN'T THERE, ODIE! I'M HALLUCINATING!
YOWP!

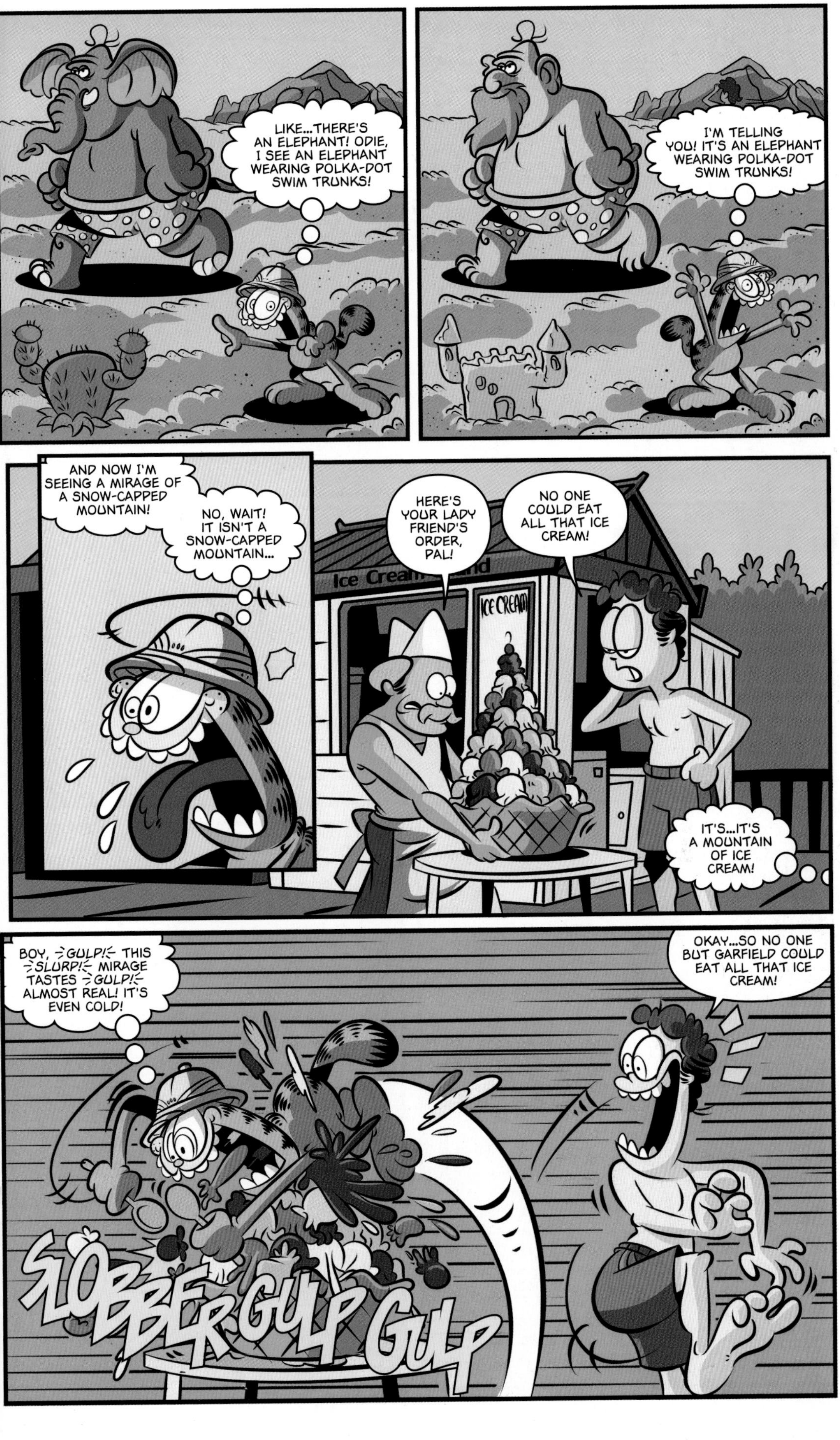
LIKE...THERE'S AN ELEPHANT! ODIE, I SEE AN ELEPHANT WEARING POLKA-DOT SWIM TRUNKS!
I'M TELLING YOU! IT'S AN ELEPHANT WEARING POLKA-DOT SWIM TRUNKS!
AND NOW I'M SEEING A MIRAGE OF A SNOW-CAPPED MOUNTAIN!
NO, WAIT! IT ISN'T A SNOW-CAPPED MOUNTAIN...
HERE'S YOUR LADY FRIEND'S ORDER, PAL!
NO ONE COULD EAT ALL THAT ICE CREAM!
ICE CREAM
IT'S...IT'S A MOUNTAIN OF ICE CREAM!
BOY, -GULP!- THIS -SLURP!- MIRAGE TASTES -GULP!- ALMOST REAL! IT'S EVEN COLD!
OKAY...SO NO ONE BUT GARFIELD COULD EAT ALL THAT ICE CREAM!
SLOBBER GULP GULP

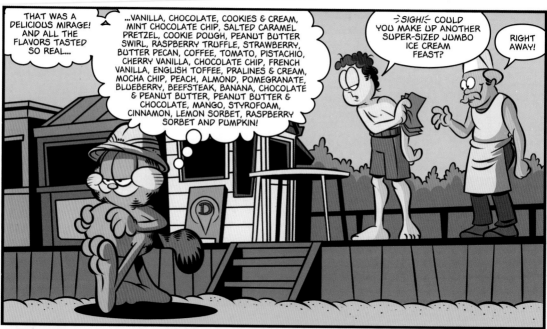

THAT WAS A DELICIOUS MIRAGE! AND ALL THE FLAVORS TASTED SO REAL...

...VANILLA, CHOCOLATE, COOKIES & CREAM, MINT CHOCOLATE CHIP, SALTED CARAMEL PRETZEL, COOKIE DOUGH, PEANUT BUTTER SWIRL, RASPBERRY TRUFFLE, STRAWBERRY, BUTTER PECAN, COFFEE, TOMATO, PISTACHIO, CHERRY VANILLA, CHOCOLATE CHIP, FRENCH VANILLA, ENGLISH TOFFEE, PRALINES & CREAM, MOCHA CHIP, PEACH, ALMOND, POMEGRANATE, BLUEBERRY, BEEFSTEAK, BANANA, CHOCOLATE & PEANUT BUTTER, PEANUT BUTTER & CHOCOLATE, MANGO, STYROFOAM, CINNAMON, LEMON SORBET, RASPBERRY SORBET AND PUMPKIN!

⸮SIGH!⸮ COULD YOU MAKE UP ANOTHER SUPER-SIZED JUMBO ICE CREAM FEAST?

RIGHT AWAY!

LOOK, ODIE! IT'S ANOTHER MIRAGE! AND IT'S A BEAUTIFUL ONE!

HUH?

IT'S AN OASIS! AN OASIS OF COOL, SHIMMERING, BLUE WATER!

YOWP!

LET US ENJOY THE OASIS, ODIE--THE COOL, SHIMMERING, BEAUTIFUL, REFRESHING OASIS!

UH-UH!

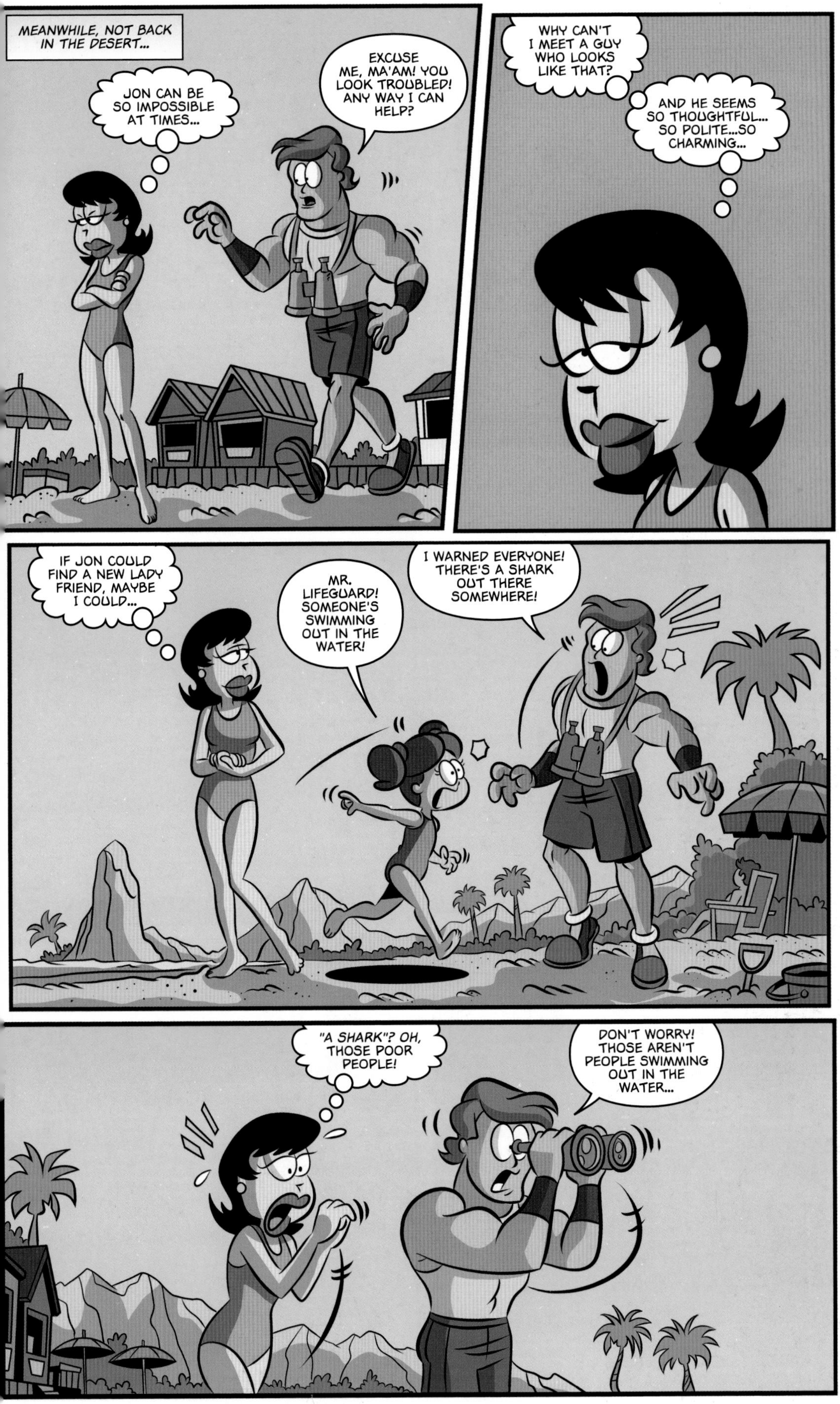
MEANWHILE, NOT BACK IN THE DESERT...
JON CAN BE SO IMPOSSIBLE AT TIMES...
EXCUSE ME, MA'AM! YOU LOOK TROUBLED! ANY WAY I CAN HELP?
WHY CAN'T I MEET A GUY WHO LOOKS LIKE THAT?
AND HE SEEMS SO THOUGHTFUL... SO POLITE...SO CHARMING...
IF JON COULD FIND A NEW LADY FRIEND, MAYBE I COULD...
MR. LIFEGUARD! SOMEONE'S SWIMMING OUT IN THE WATER!
I WARNED EVERYONE! THERE'S A SHARK OUT THERE SOMEWHERE!
"A SHARK"? OH, THOSE POOR PEOPLE!
DON'T WORRY! THOSE AREN'T PEOPLE SWIMMING OUT IN THE WATER...

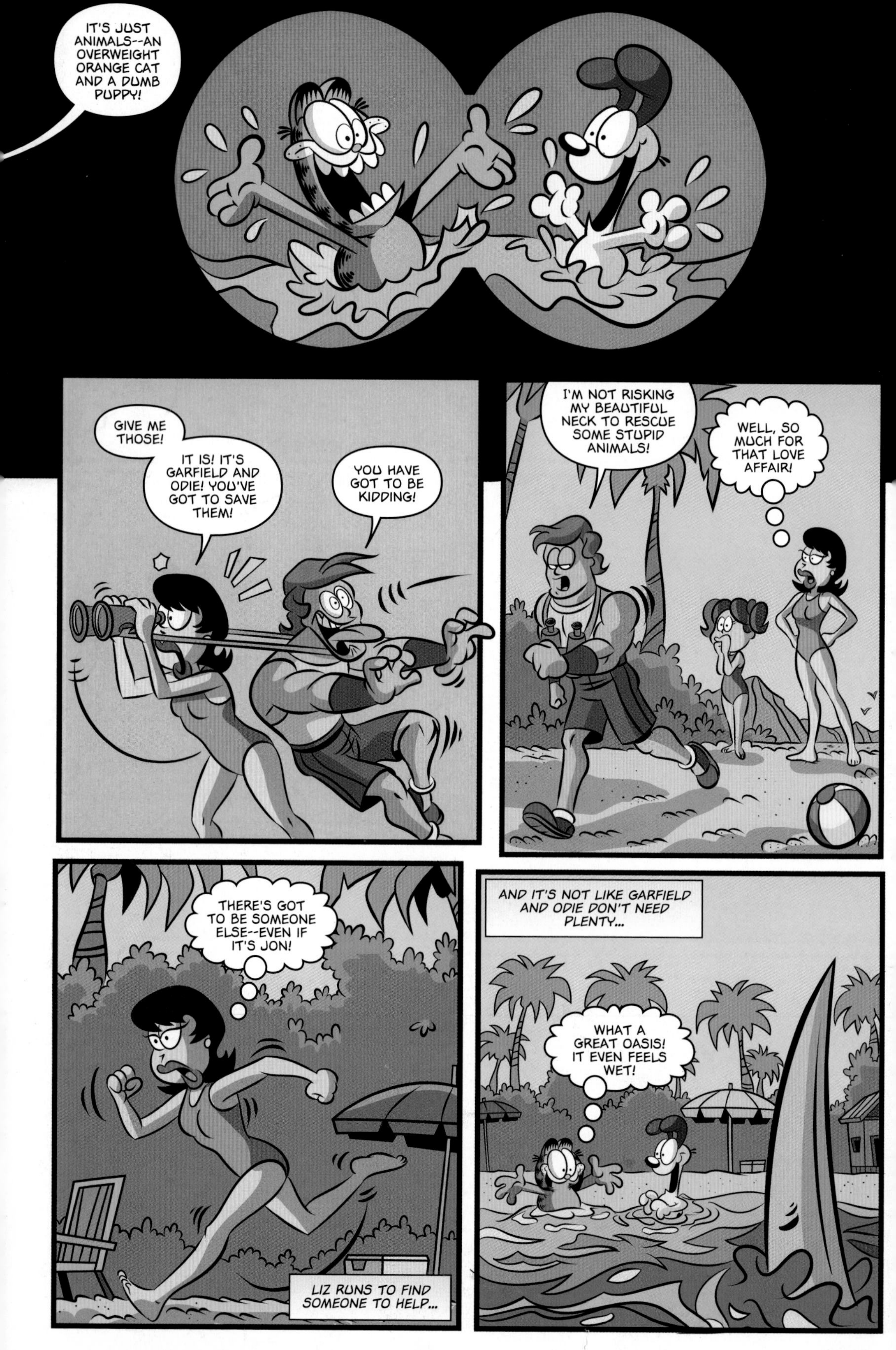
IT'S JUST ANIMALS--AN OVERWEIGHT ORANGE CAT AND A DUMB PUPPY!
GIVE ME THOSE!
IT IS! IT'S GARFIELD AND ODIE! YOU'VE GOT TO SAVE THEM!
YOU HAVE GOT TO BE KIDDING!
I'M NOT RISKING MY BEAUTIFUL NECK TO RESCUE SOME STUPID ANIMALS!
WELL, SO MUCH FOR THAT LOVE AFFAIR!
THERE'S GOT TO BE SOMEONE ELSE--EVEN IF IT'S JON!
LIZ RUNS TO FIND SOMEONE TO HELP...
AND IT'S NOT LIKE GARFIELD AND ODIE DON'T NEED PLENTY...
WHAT A GREAT OASIS! IT EVEN FEELS WET!

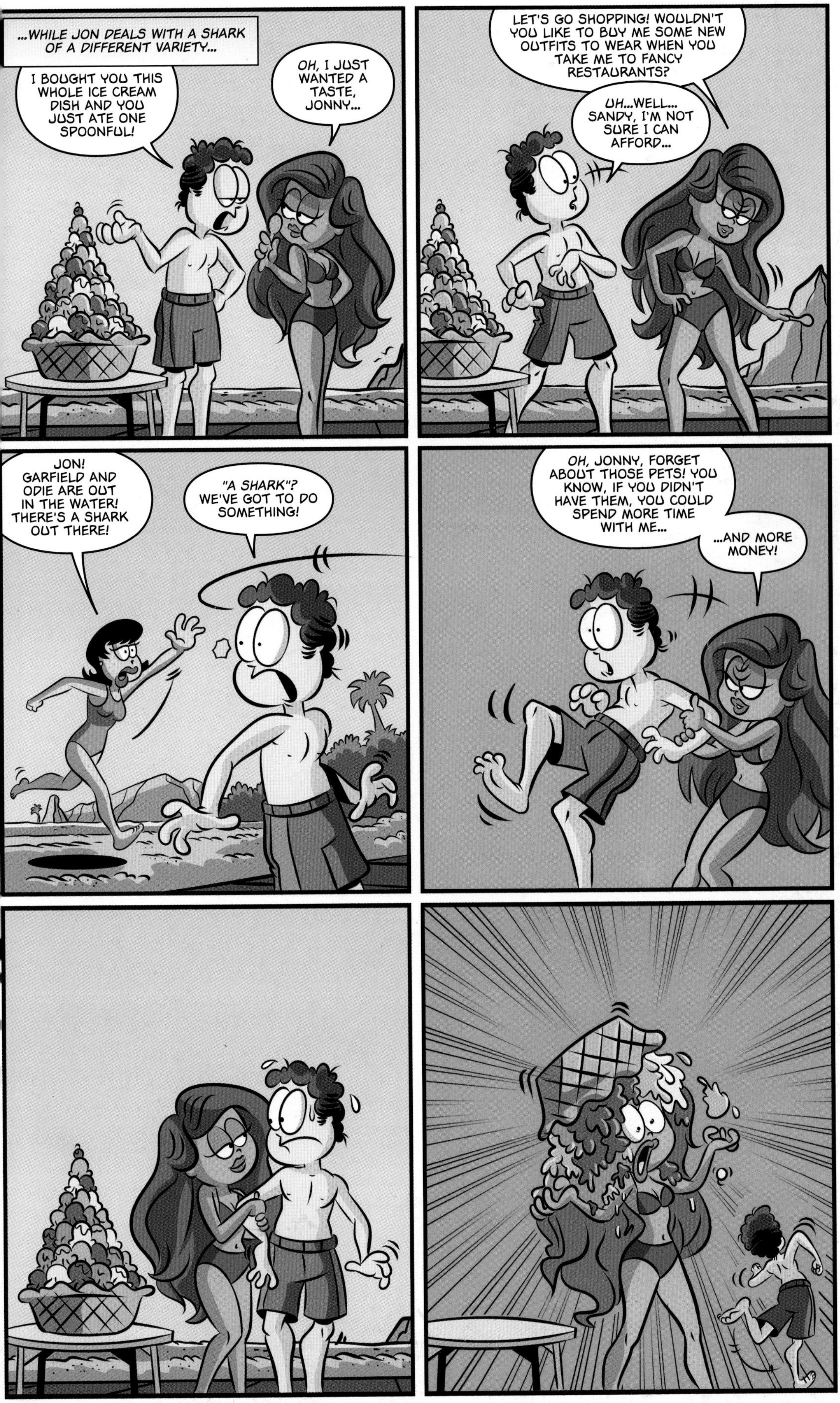
...WHILE JON DEALS WITH A SHARK OF A DIFFERENT VARIETY...
I BOUGHT YOU THIS WHOLE ICE CREAM DISH AND YOU JUST ATE ONE SPOONFUL!
OH, I JUST WANTED A TASTE, JONNY...
LET'S GO SHOPPING! WOULDN'T YOU LIKE TO BUY ME SOME NEW OUTFITS TO WEAR WHEN YOU TAKE ME TO FANCY RESTAURANTS?
UH...WELL... SANDY, I'M NOT SURE I CAN AFFORD...
JON! GARFIELD AND ODIE ARE OUT IN THE WATER! THERE'S A SHARK OUT THERE!
"A SHARK"? WE'VE GOT TO DO SOMETHING!
OH, JONNY, FORGET ABOUT THOSE PETS! YOU KNOW, IF YOU DIDN'T HAVE THEM, YOU COULD SPEND MORE TIME WITH ME...
...AND MORE MONEY!

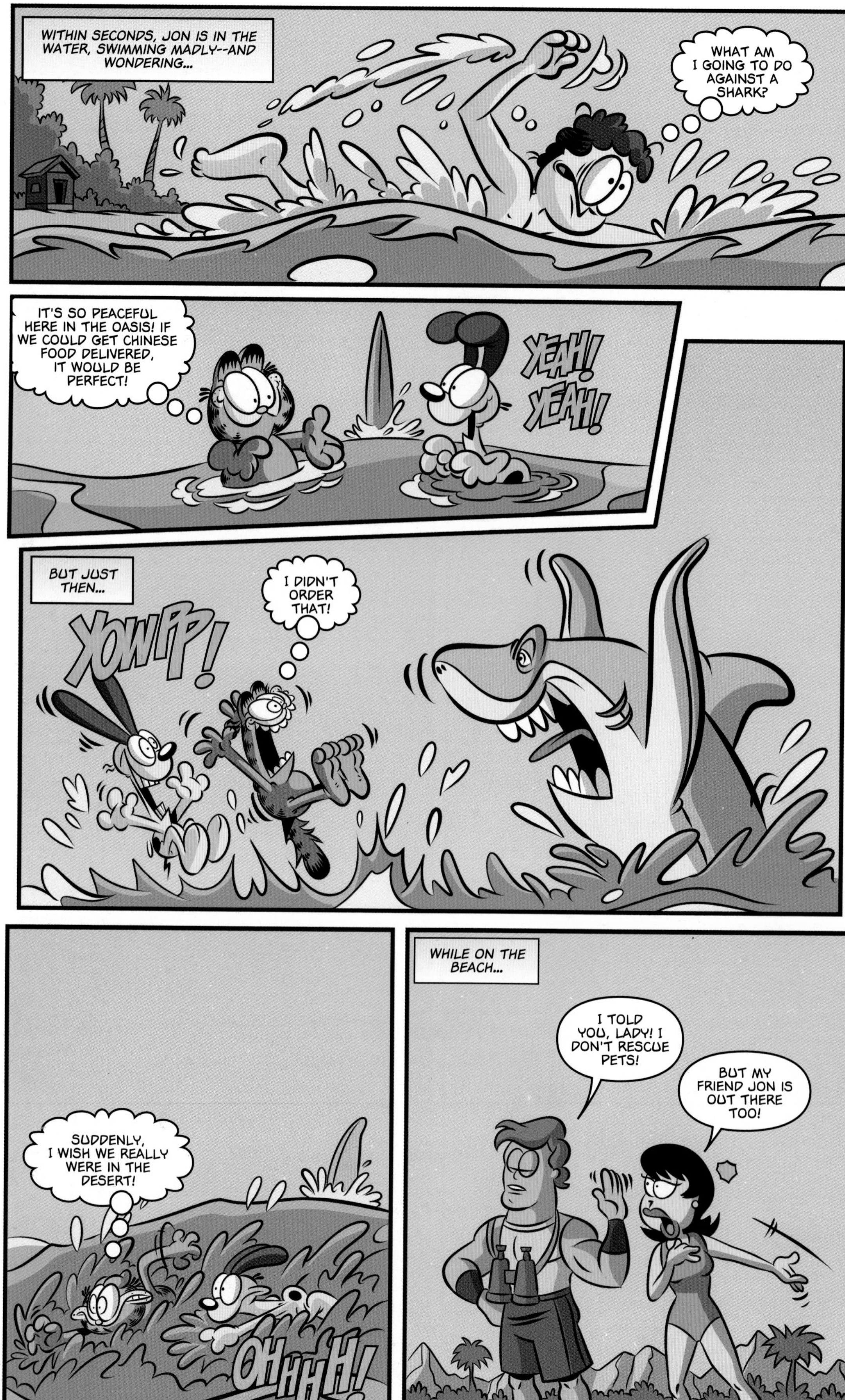
WITHIN SECONDS, JON IS IN THE WATER, SWIMMING MADLY--AND WONDERING...
WHAT AM I GOING TO DO AGAINST A SHARK?
IT'S SO PEACEFUL HERE IN THE OASIS! IF WE COULD GET CHINESE FOOD DELIVERED, IT WOULD BE PERFECT!
YEAH! YEAH!
BUT JUST THEN...
I DIDN'T ORDER THAT!
YOWPP!
SUDDENLY, I WISH WE REALLY WERE IN THE DESERT!
OHHHH!
WHILE ON THE BEACH...
I TOLD YOU, LADY! I DON'T RESCUE PETS!
BUT MY FRIEND JON IS OUT THERE TOO!

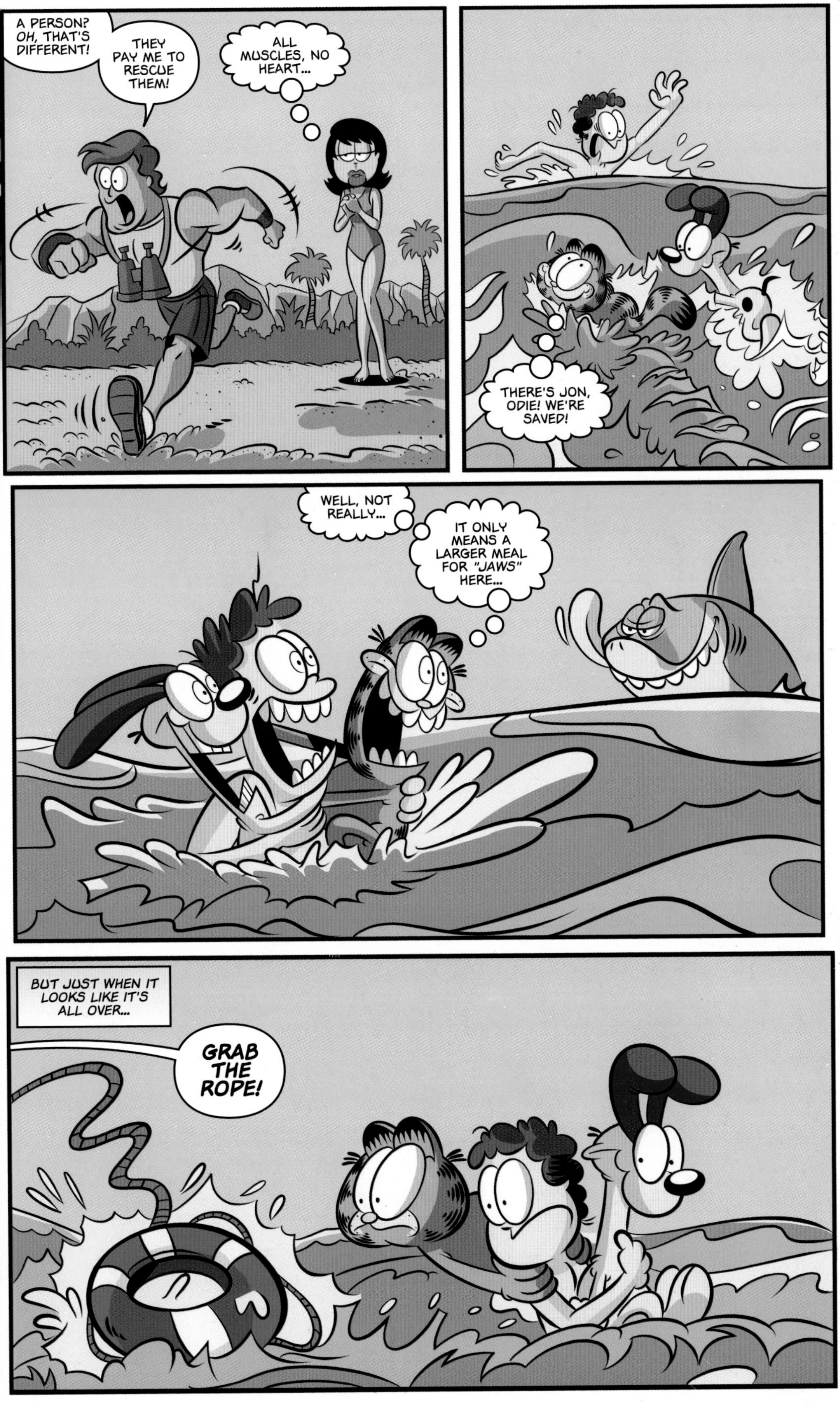

A PERSON? OH, THAT'S DIFFERENT!
THEY PAY ME TO RESCUE THEM!
ALL MUSCLES, NO HEART...
THERE'S JON, ODIE! WE'RE SAVED!
WELL, NOT REALLY...
IT ONLY MEANS A LARGER MEAL FOR "JAWS" HERE...
BUT JUST WHEN IT LOOKS LIKE IT'S ALL OVER...
GRAB THE ROPE!

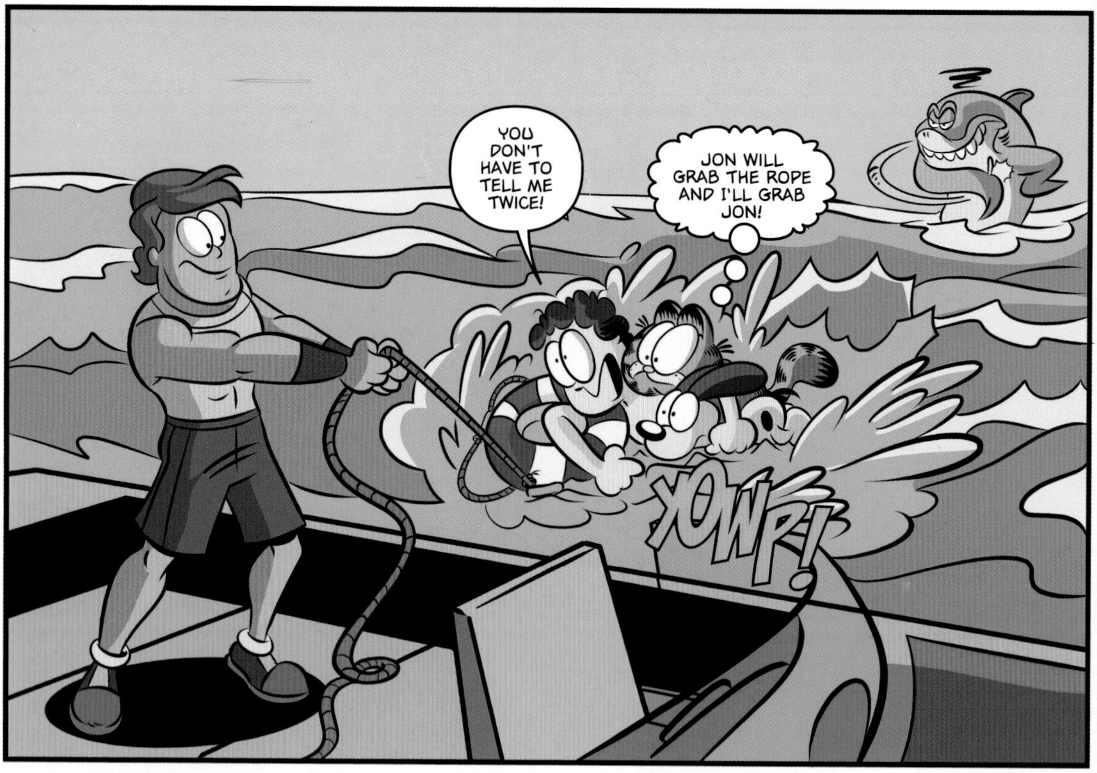
YOU DON'T HAVE TO TELL ME TWICE!
JON WILL GRAB THE ROPE AND I'LL GRAB JON!
YOWP!

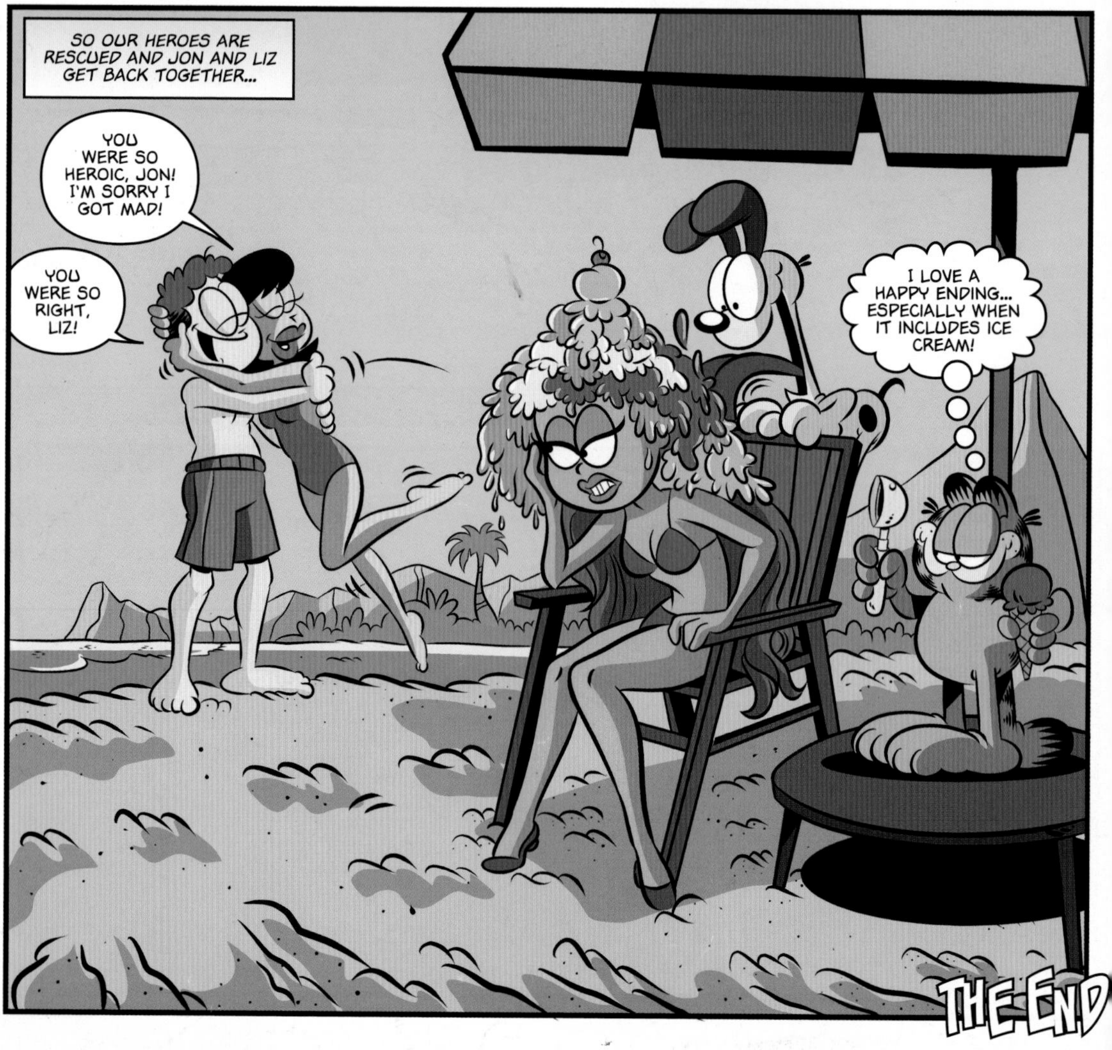
SO OUR HEROES ARE RESCUED AND JON AND LIZ GET BACK TOGETHER...
YOU WERE SO HEROIC, JON! I'M SORRY I GOT MAD!
YOU WERE SO RIGHT, LIZ!
I LOVE A HAPPY ENDING... ESPECIALLY WHEN IT INCLUDES ICE CREAM!
THE END

# Summer of the Lasagna Monster

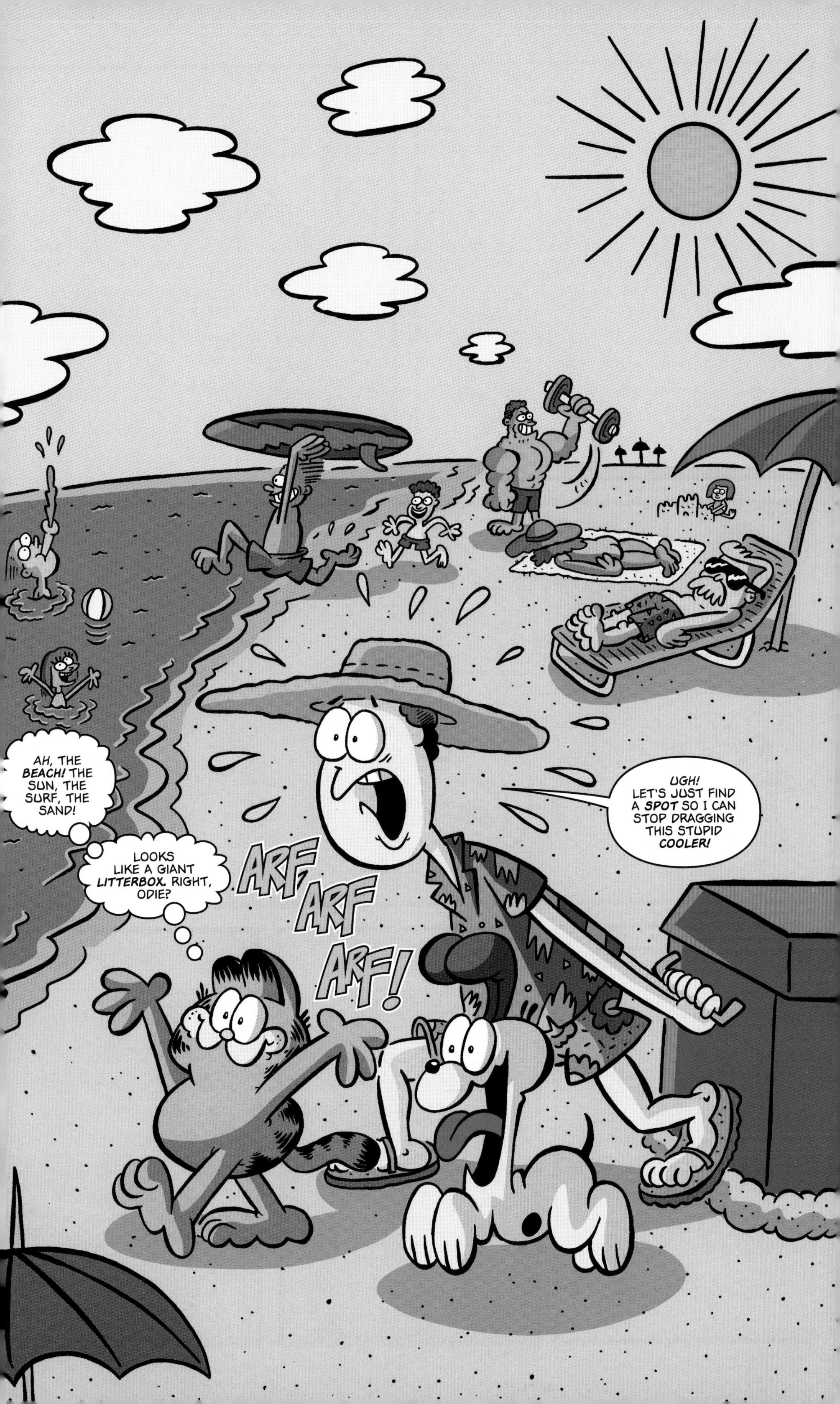

AH, THE BEACH! THE SUN, THE SURF, THE SAND!
LOOKS LIKE A GIANT LITTERBOX. RIGHT, ODIE?
UGH! LET'S JUST FIND A SPOT SO I CAN STOP DRAGGING THIS STUPID COOLER!
ARF ARF ARF!

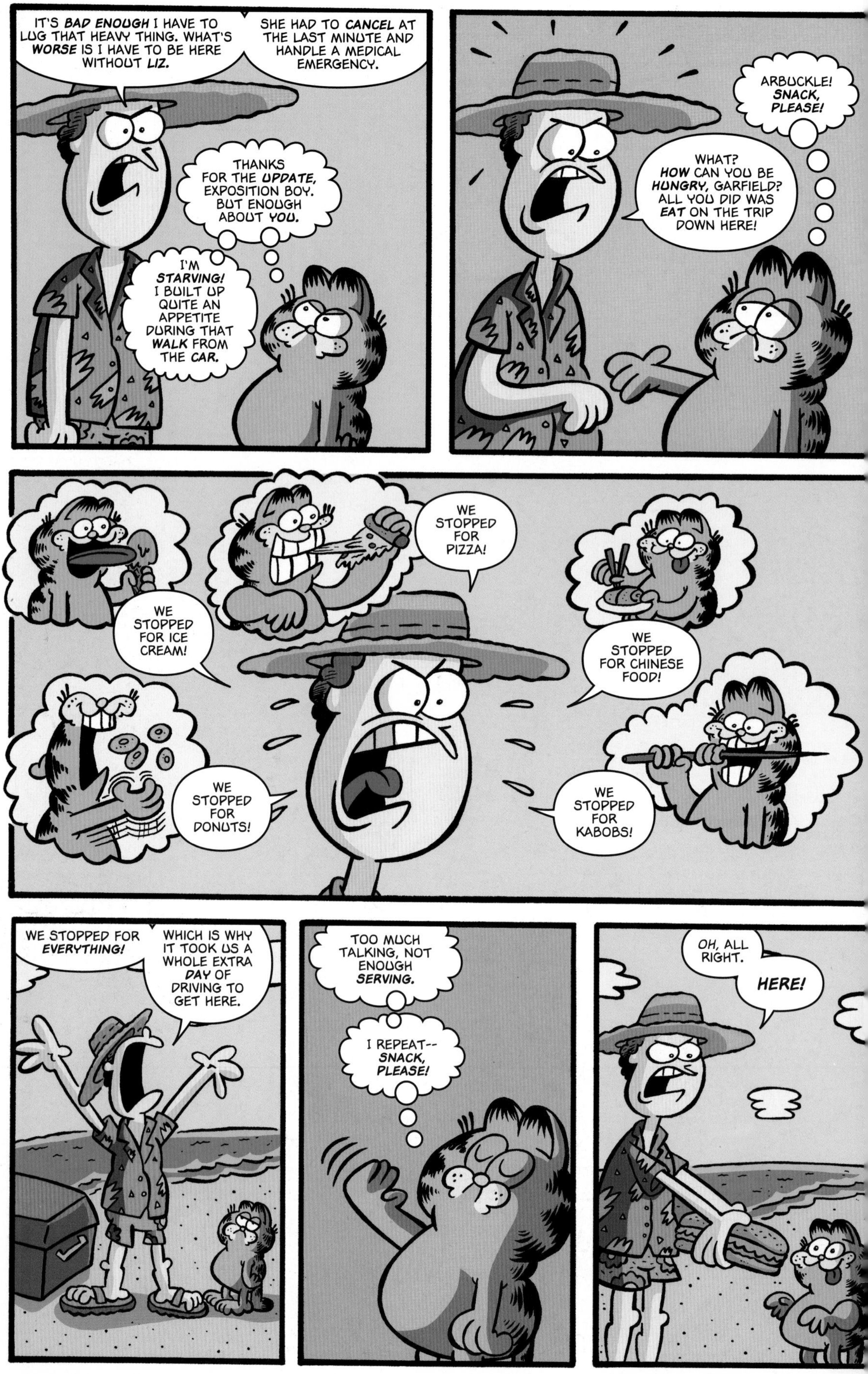
IT'S BAD ENOUGH I HAVE TO LUG THAT HEAVY THING. WHAT'S WORSE IS I HAVE TO BE HERE WITHOUT LIZ.
SHE HAD TO CANCEL AT THE LAST MINUTE AND HANDLE A MEDICAL EMERGENCY.
THANKS FOR THE UPDATE, EXPOSITION BOY. BUT ENOUGH ABOUT YOU.
I'M STARVING! I BUILT UP QUITE AN APPETITE DURING THAT WALK FROM THE CAR.
ARBUCKLE! SNACK, PLEASE!
WHAT? HOW CAN YOU BE HUNGRY, GARFIELD? ALL YOU DID WAS EAT ON THE TRIP DOWN HERE!
WE STOPPED FOR ICE CREAM!
WE STOPPED FOR PIZZA!
WE STOPPED FOR CHINESE FOOD!
WE STOPPED FOR DONUTS!
WE STOPPED FOR KABOBS!
WE STOPPED FOR EVERYTHING!
WHICH IS WHY IT TOOK US A WHOLE EXTRA DAY OF DRIVING TO GET HERE.
TOO MUCH TALKING, NOT ENOUGH SERVING.
I REPEAT-- SNACK, PLEASE!
OH, ALL RIGHT.
HERE!

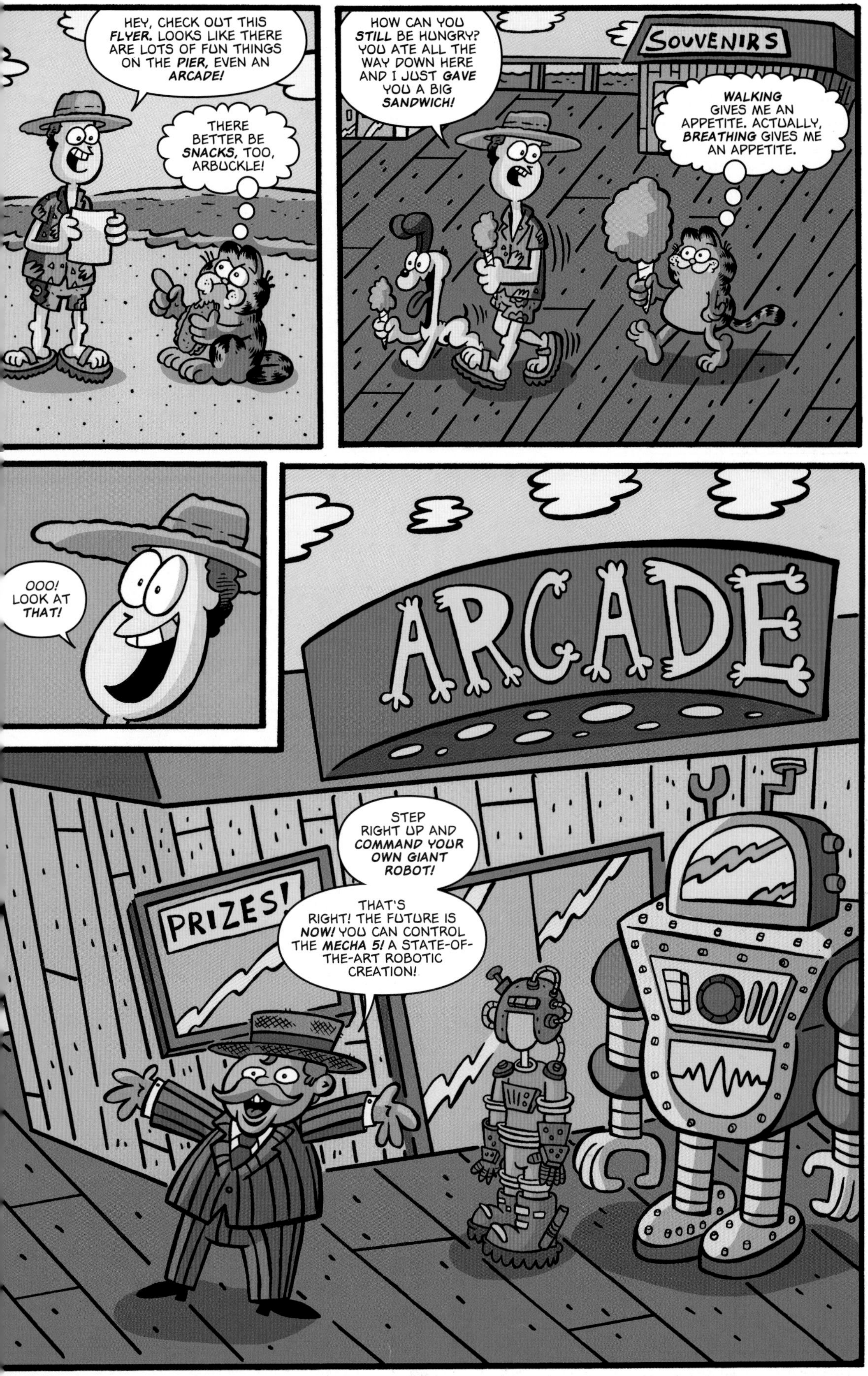
HEY, CHECK OUT THIS FLYER. LOOKS LIKE THERE ARE LOTS OF FUN THINGS ON THE PIER, EVEN AN ARCADE!
THERE BETTER BE SNACKS, TOO, ARBUCKLE!
HOW CAN YOU STILL BE HUNGRY? YOU ATE ALL THE WAY DOWN HERE AND I JUST GAVE YOU A BIG SANDWICH!
SOUVENIRS
WALKING GIVES ME AN APPETITE. ACTUALLY, BREATHING GIVES ME AN APPETITE.
OOO! LOOK AT THAT!
ARCADE
STEP RIGHT UP AND COMMAND YOUR OWN GIANT ROBOT!
PRIZES!
THAT'S RIGHT! THE FUTURE IS NOW! YOU CAN CONTROL THE MECHA 5! A STATE-OF-THE-ART ROBOTIC CREATION!

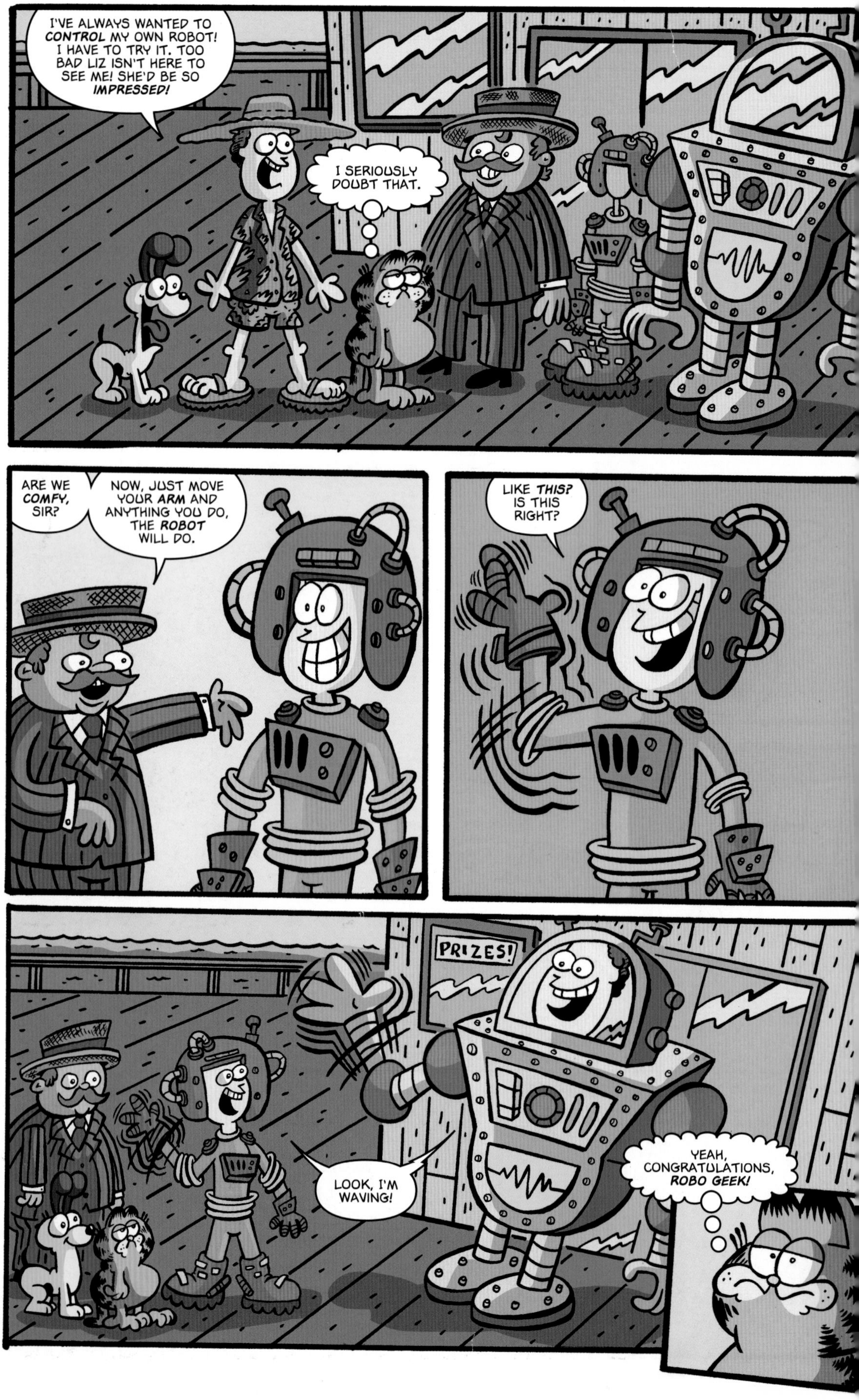
I'VE ALWAYS WANTED TO CONTROL MY OWN ROBOT! I HAVE TO TRY IT. TOO BAD LIZ ISN'T HERE TO SEE ME! SHE'D BE SO IMPRESSED!
I SERIOUSLY DOUBT THAT.
ARE WE COMFY, SIR?
NOW, JUST MOVE YOUR ARM AND ANYTHING YOU DO, THE ROBOT WILL DO.
LIKE THIS? IS THIS RIGHT?
PRIZES!
LOOK, I'M WAVING!
YEAH, CONGRATULATIONS, ROBO GEEK!

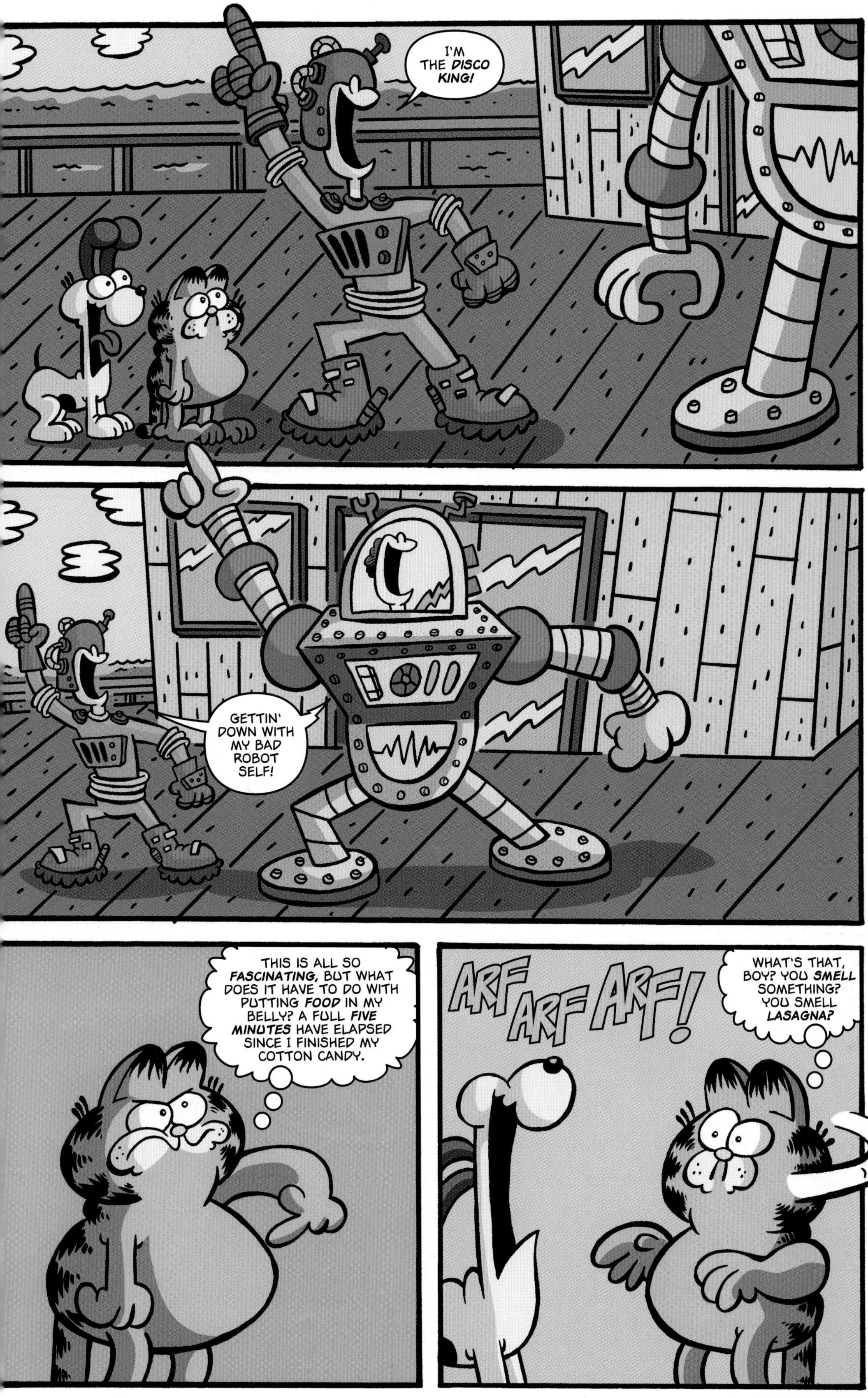
I'M THE DISCO KING!
GETTIN' DOWN WITH MY BAD ROBOT SELF!
THIS IS ALL SO FASCINATING, BUT WHAT DOES IT HAVE TO DO WITH PUTTING FOOD IN MY BELLY? A FULL FIVE MINUTES HAVE ELAPSED SINCE I FINISHED MY COTTON CANDY.
ARF ARF ARF!
WHAT'S THAT, BOY? YOU SMELL SOMETHING? YOU SMELL LASAGNA?

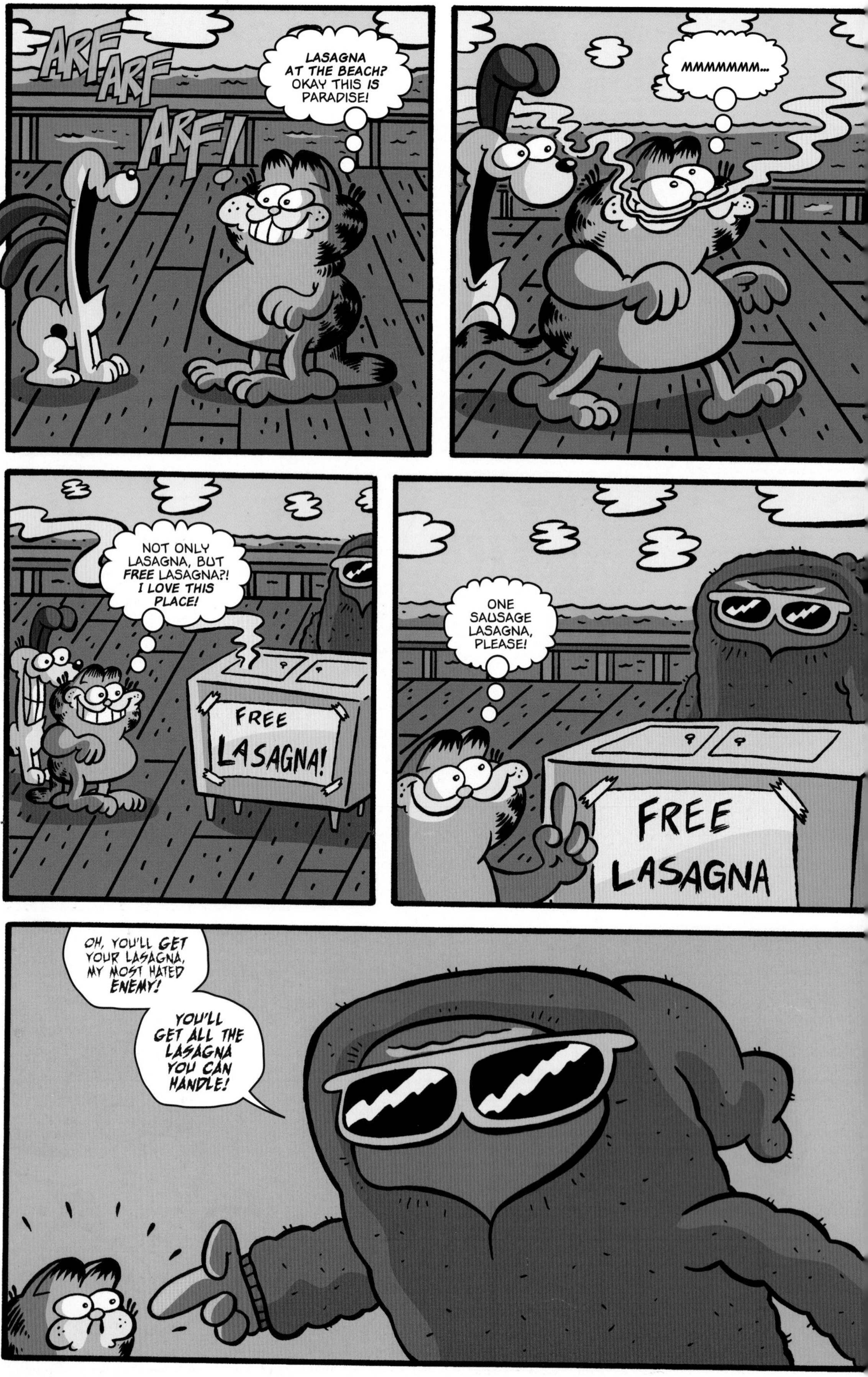
ARF ARF ARF!
LASAGNA AT THE BEACH? OKAY THIS IS PARADISE!
MMMMMMM...
NOT ONLY LASAGNA, BUT FREE LASAGNA?! I LOVE THIS PLACE!
FREE LASAGNA!
ONE SAUSAGE LASAGNA, PLEASE!
FREE LASAGNA
OH, YOU'LL GET YOUR LASAGNA, MY MOST HATED ENEMY!
YOU'LL GET ALL THE LASAGNA YOU CAN HANDLE!

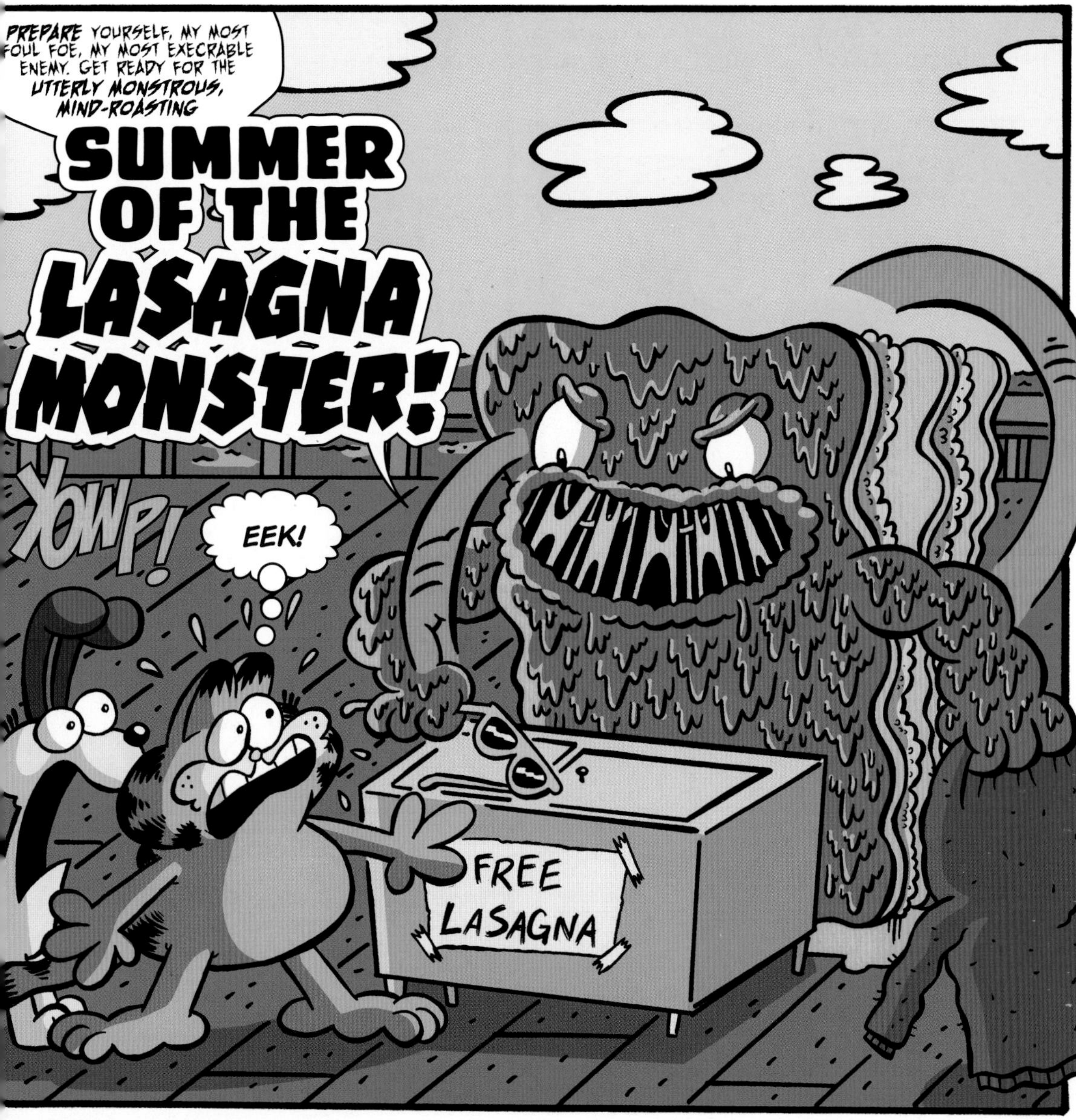
PREPARE YOURSELF, MY MOST FOUL FOE, MY MOST EXECRABLE ENEMY. GET READY FOR THE UTTERLY MONSTROUS, MIND-ROASTING
SUMMER OF THE LASAGNA MONSTER!
YOWP!
EEK!
FREE LASAGNA

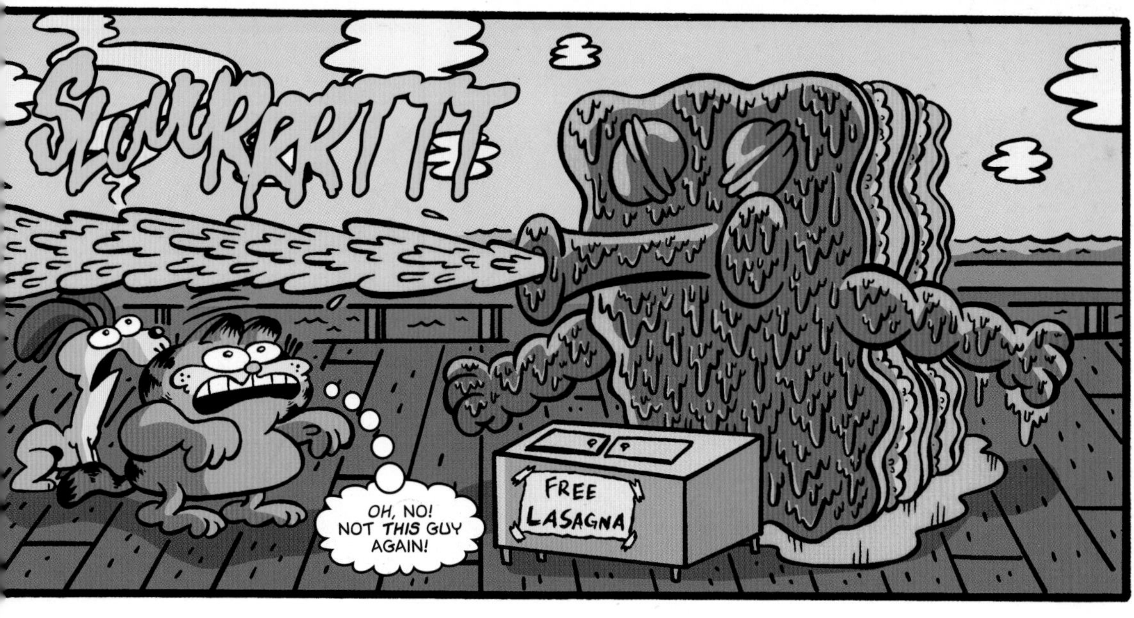
SLOURRRTTT
OH, NO! NOT THIS GUY AGAIN!
FREE LASAGNA

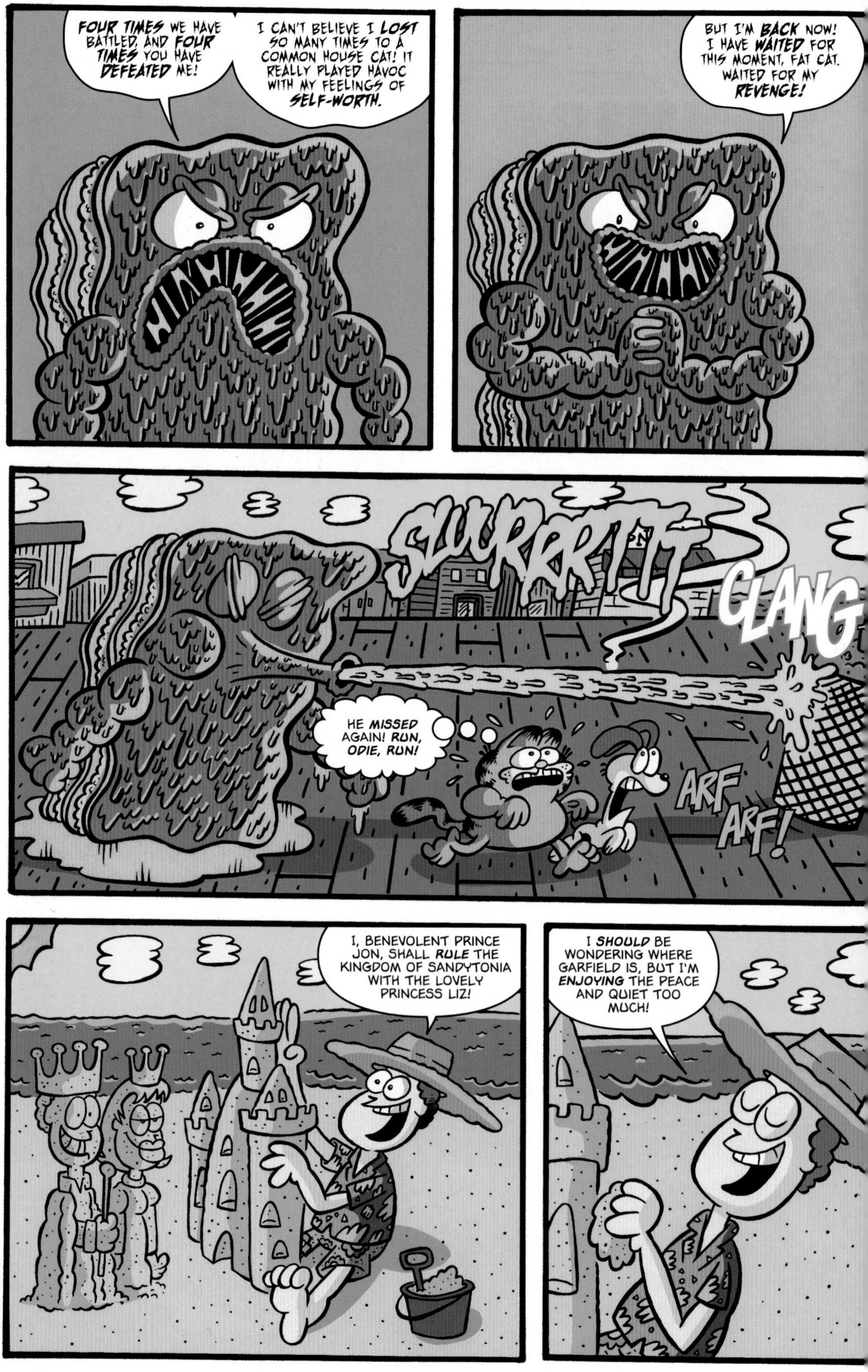
FOUR TIMES WE HAVE BATTLED, AND FOUR TIMES YOU HAVE DEFEATED ME!
I CAN'T BELIEVE I LOST SO MANY TIMES TO A COMMON HOUSE CAT! IT REALLY PLAYED HAVOC WITH MY FEELINGS OF SELF-WORTH.
BUT I'M BACK NOW! I HAVE WAITED FOR THIS MOMENT, FAT CAT. WAITED FOR MY REVENGE!
SLURRRTTT
CLANG
HE MISSED AGAIN! RUN, ODIE, RUN!
ARF ARF!
I, BENEVOLENT PRINCE JON, SHALL RULE THE KINGDOM OF SANDYTONIA WITH THE LOVELY PRINCESS LIZ!
I SHOULD BE WONDERING WHERE GARFIELD IS, BUT I'M ENJOYING THE PEACE AND QUIET TOO MUCH!

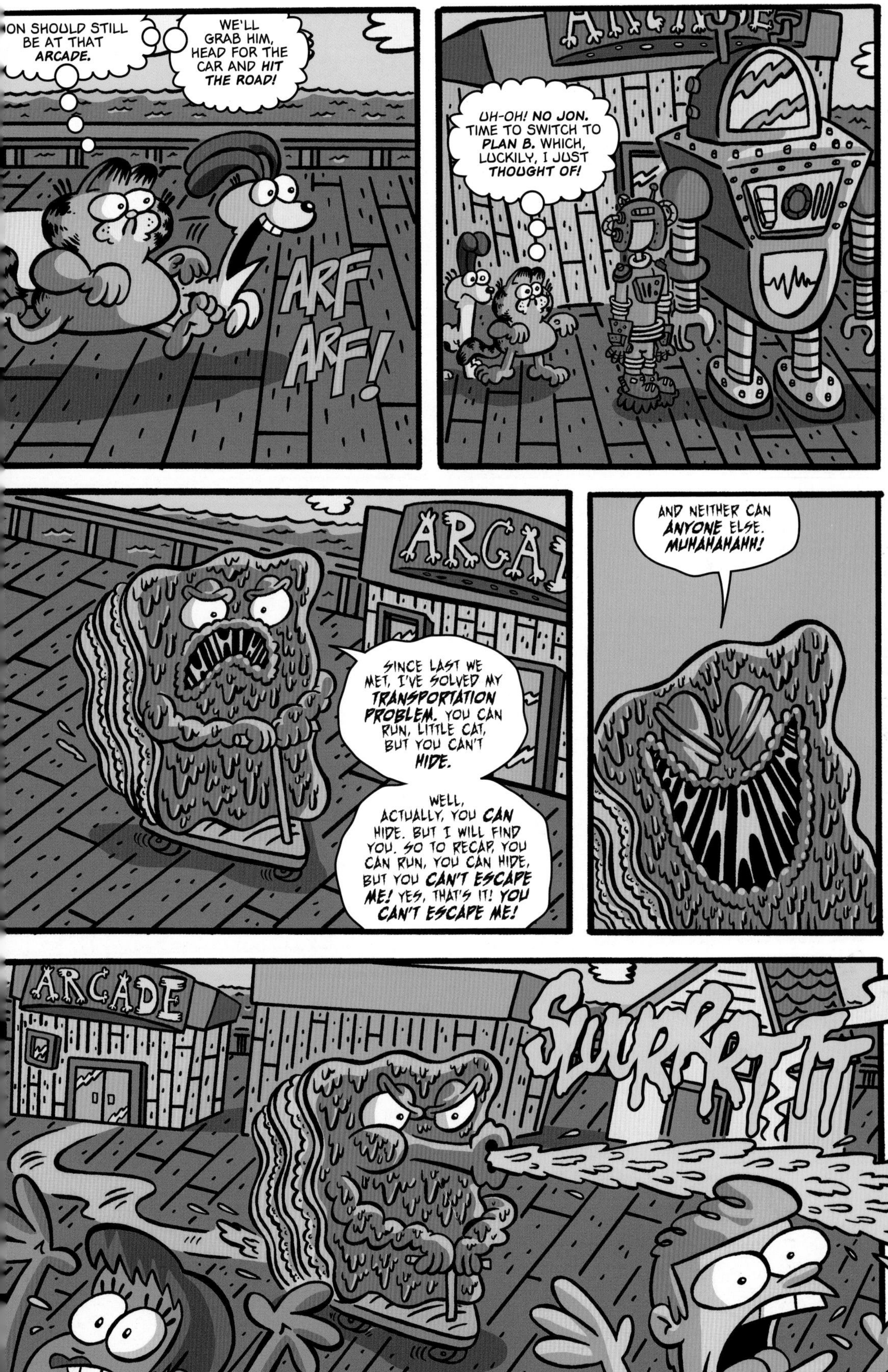
ON SHOULD STILL BE AT THAT ARCADE.
WE'LL GRAB HIM, HEAD FOR THE CAR AND HIT THE ROAD!
ARF ARF!
UH-OH! NO JON. TIME TO SWITCH TO PLAN B. WHICH, LUCKILY, I JUST THOUGHT OF!
SINCE LAST WE MET, I'VE SOLVED MY TRANSPORTATION PROBLEM. YOU CAN RUN, LITTLE CAT, BUT YOU CAN'T HIDE.
WELL, ACTUALLY, YOU CAN HIDE. BUT I WILL FIND YOU. SO TO RECAP, YOU CAN RUN, YOU CAN HIDE, BUT YOU CAN'T ESCAPE ME! YES, THAT'S IT! YOU CAN'T ESCAPE ME!
AND NEITHER CAN ANYONE ELSE. MUHAHAHAHH!
ARCADE
SLURRRTTT

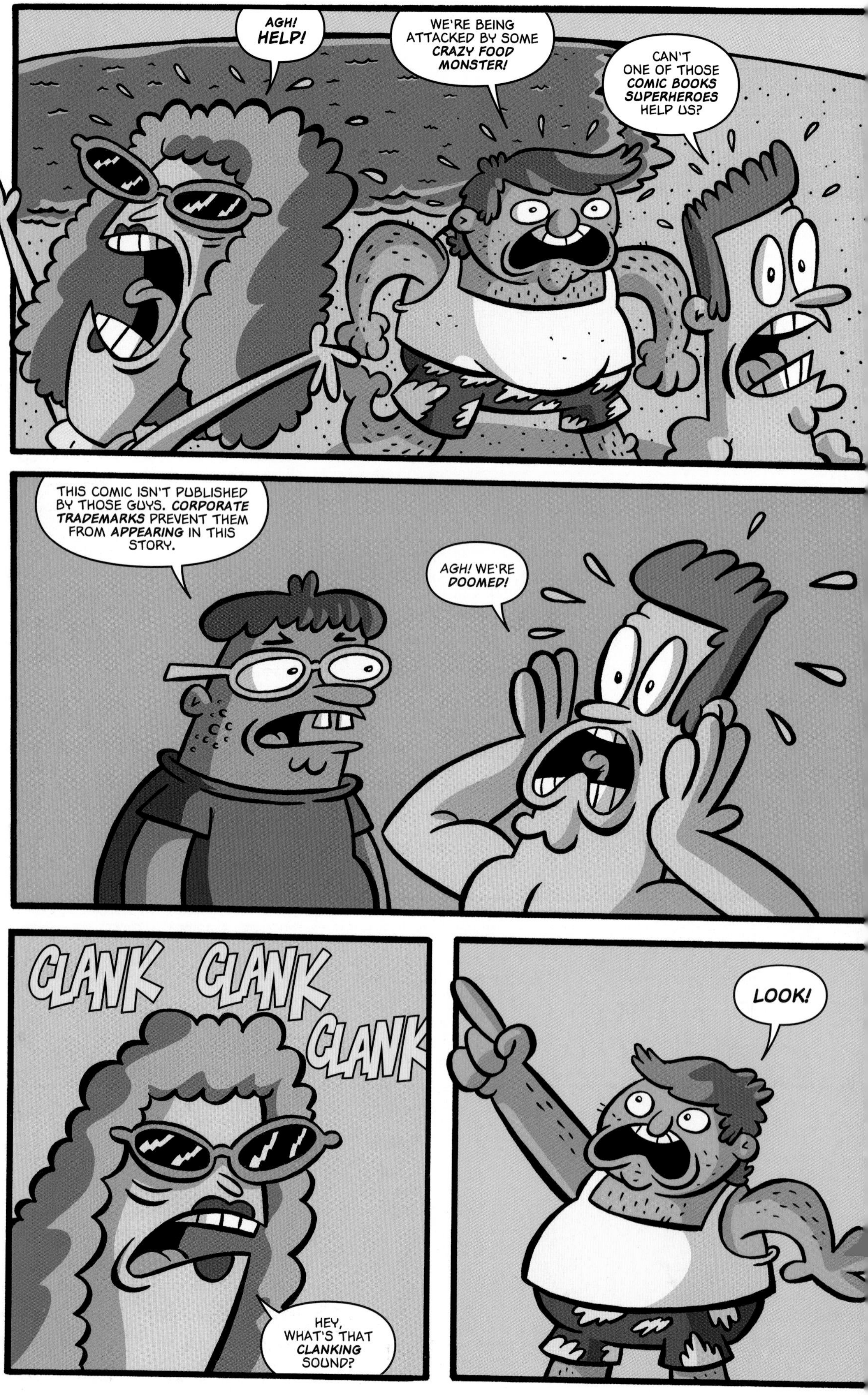
AGH! HELP!
WE'RE BEING ATTACKED BY SOME CRAZY FOOD MONSTER!
CAN'T ONE OF THOSE COMIC BOOKS SUPERHEROES HELP US?
THIS COMIC ISN'T PUBLISHED BY THOSE GUYS. CORPORATE TRADEMARKS PREVENT THEM FROM APPEARING IN THIS STORY.
AGH! WE'RE DOOMED!
CLANK CLANK CLANK
HEY, WHAT'S THAT CLANKING SOUND?
LOOK!

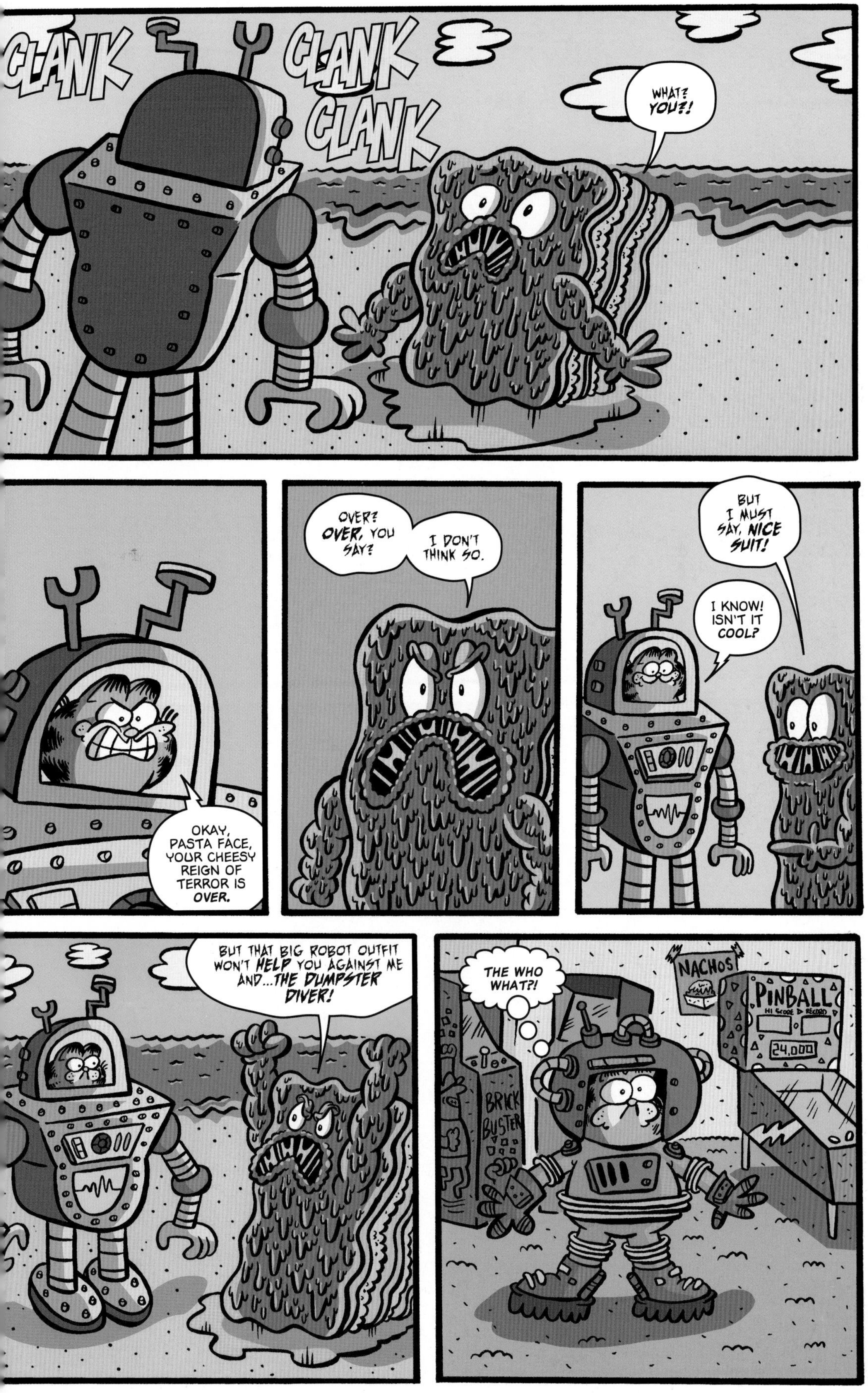
CLANK
CLANK
CLANK
WHAT? YOU?!
OKAY, PASTA FACE, YOUR CHEESY REIGN OF TERROR IS OVER.
OVER? OVER, YOU SAY?
I DON'T THINK SO.
BUT I MUST SAY, NICE SUIT!
I KNOW! ISN'T IT COOL?
BUT THAT BIG ROBOT OUTFIT WON'T HELP YOU AGAINST ME AND...THE DUMPSTER DIVER!
THE WHO WHAT?!
NACHOS
PINBALL
HI SCORE
RECORD
24,000
BRICK BUSTER

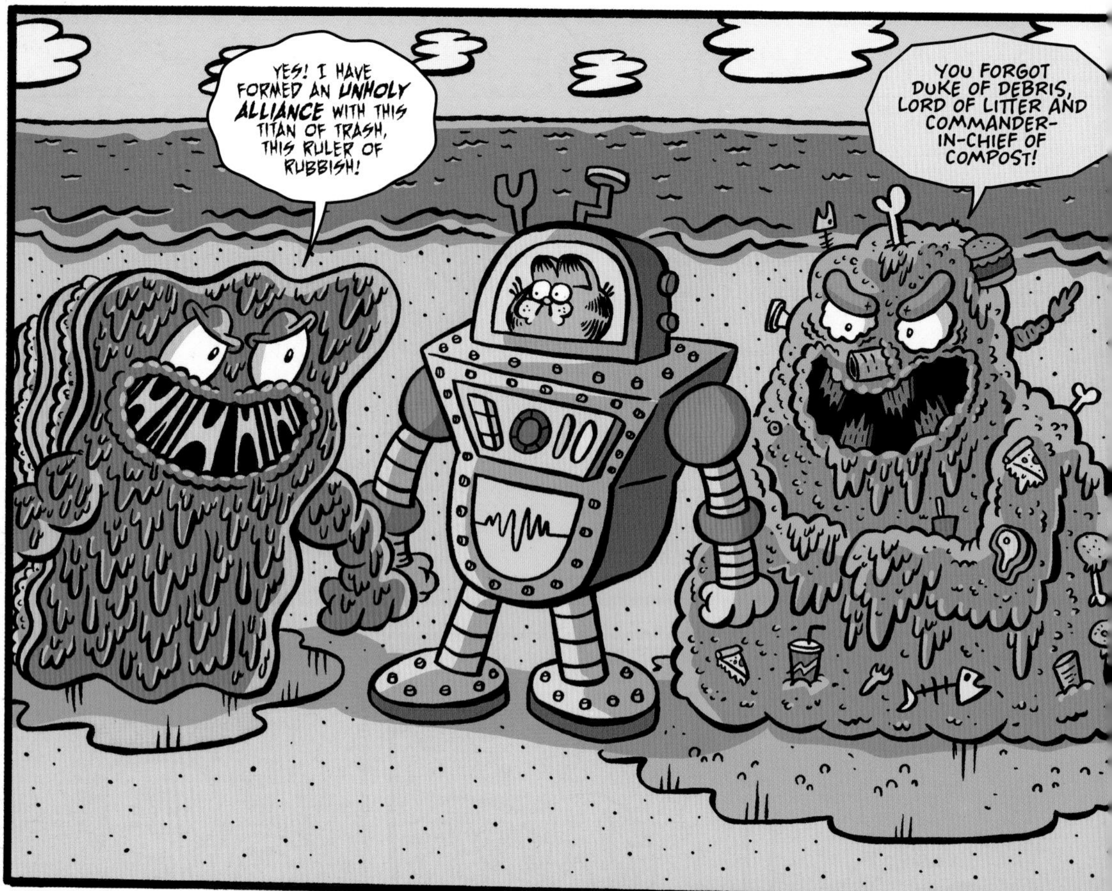
YES! I HAVE FORMED AN UNHOLY ALLIANCE WITH THIS TITAN OF TRASH, THIS RULER OF RUBBISH!
YOU FORGOT DUKE OF DEBRIS, LORD OF LITTER AND COMMANDER-IN-CHIEF OF COMPOST!

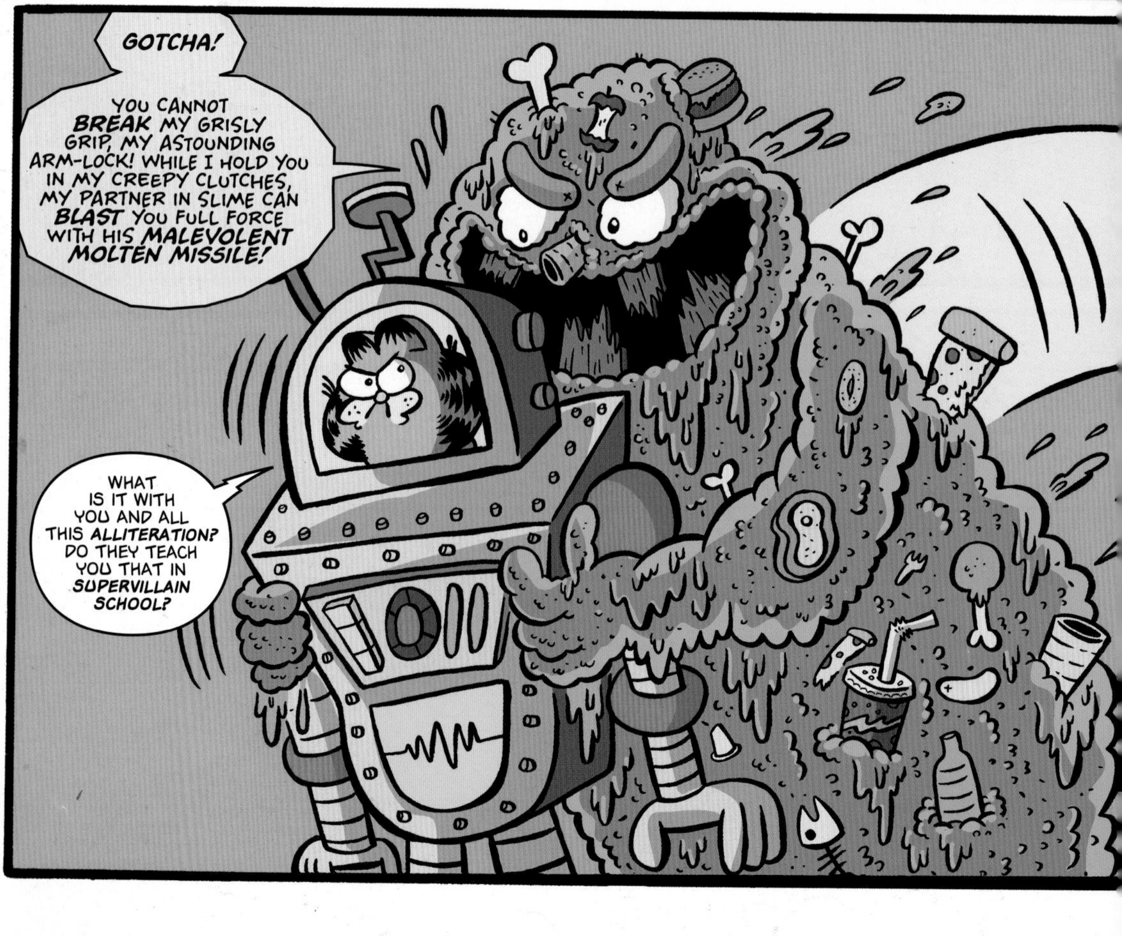
GOTCHA!
YOU CANNOT BREAK MY GRISLY GRIP, MY ASTOUNDING ARM-LOCK! WHILE I HOLD YOU IN MY CREEPY CLUTCHES, MY PARTNER IN SLIME CAN BLAST YOU FULL FORCE WITH HIS MALEVOLENT MOLTEN MISSILE!
WHAT IS IT WITH YOU AND ALL THIS ALLITERATION? DO THEY TEACH YOU THAT IN SUPERVILLAIN SCHOOL?

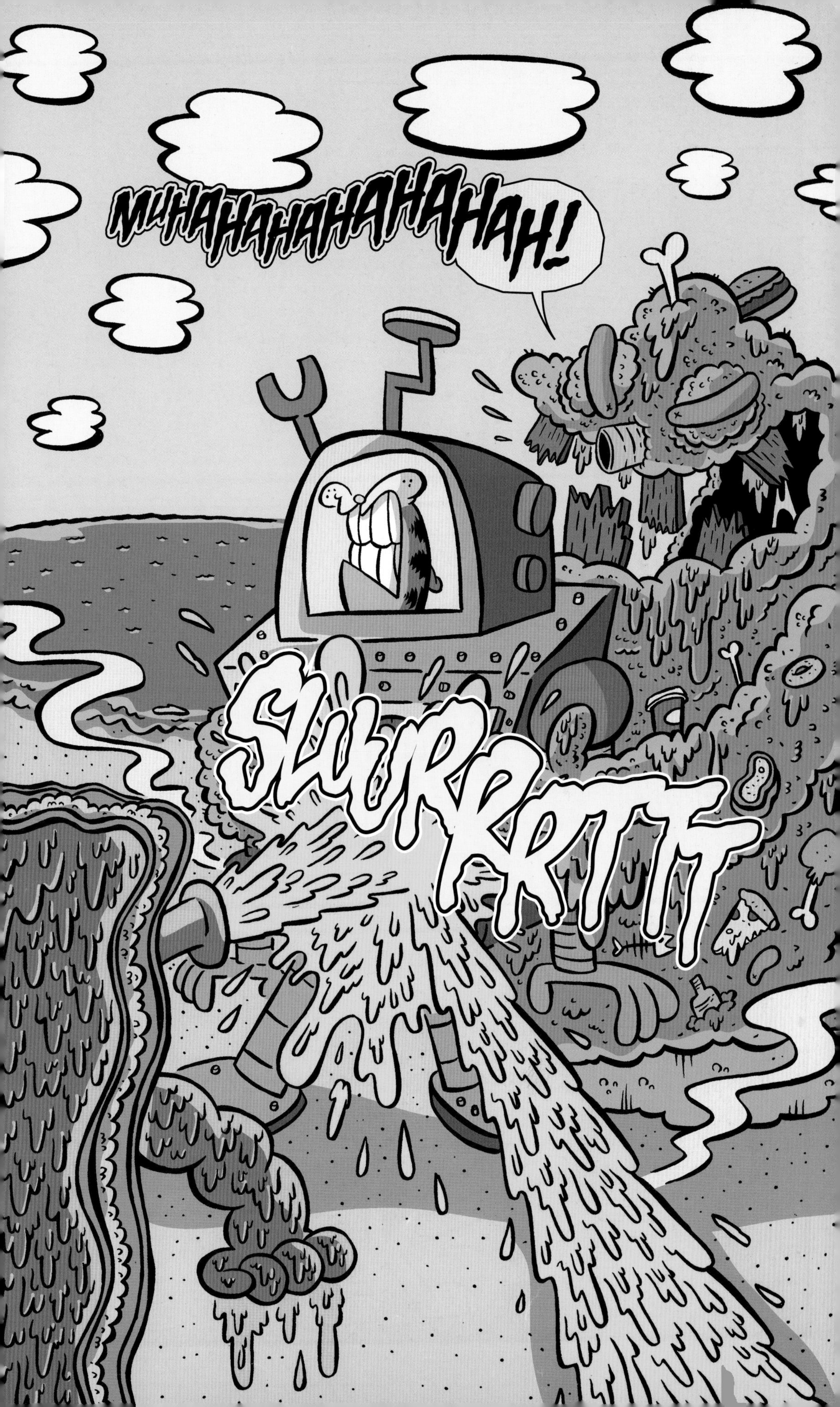
MWHAHAHAHAHAHAHAHAH!
SLURRRTTT

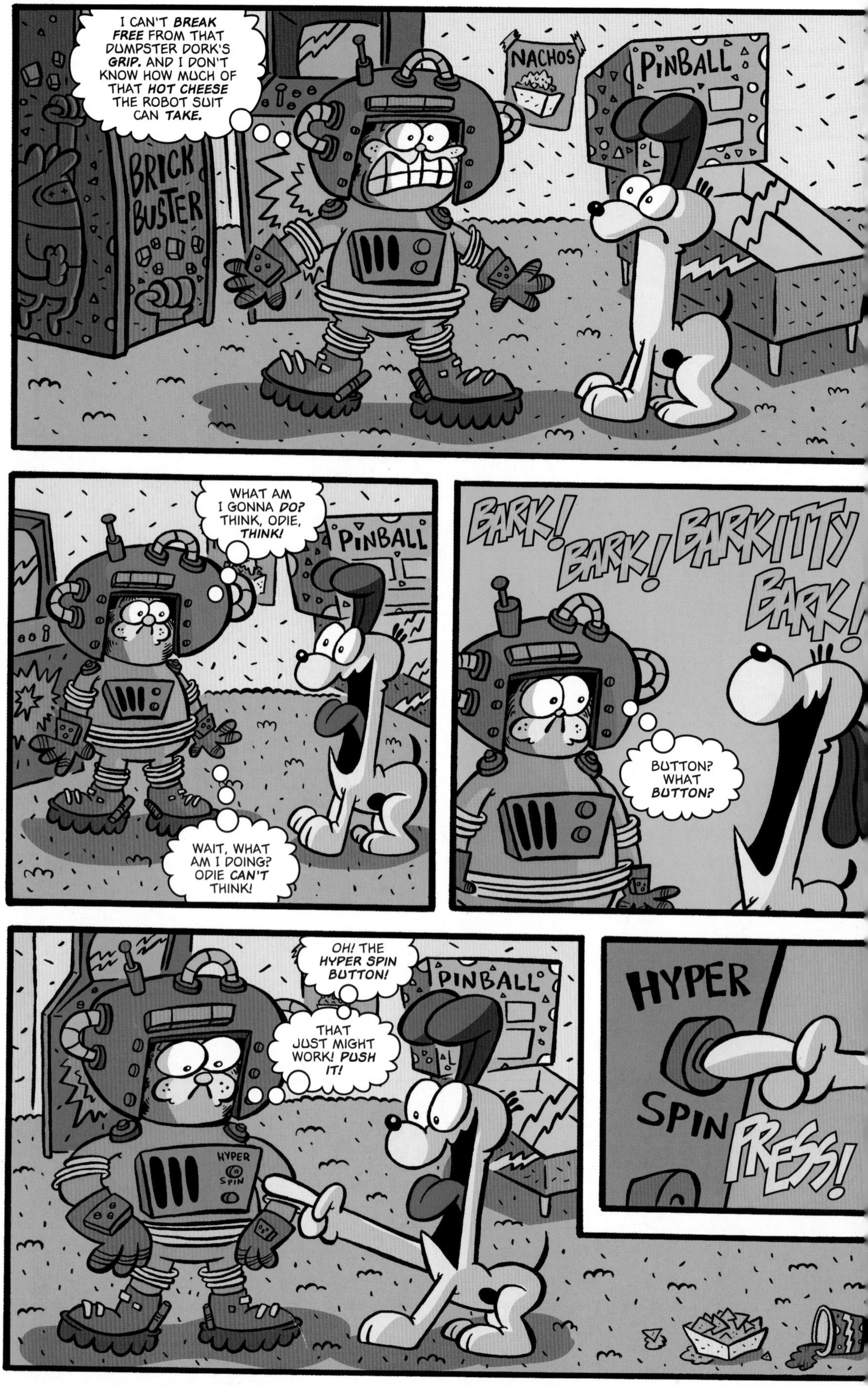

I CAN'T BREAK FREE FROM THAT DUMPSTER DORK'S GRIP. AND I DON'T KNOW HOW MUCH OF THAT HOT CHEESE THE ROBOT SUIT CAN TAKE.
NACHOS
PINBALL
BRICK BUSTER
WHAT AM I GONNA DO? THINK, ODIE, THINK!
PINBALL
WAIT, WHAT AM I DOING? ODIE CAN'T THINK!
BARK! BARK! BARKITTY BARK!
BUTTON? WHAT BUTTON?
OH! THE HYPER SPIN BUTTON!
PINBALL
THAT JUST MIGHT WORK! PUSH IT!
HYPER SPIN
HYPER
SPIN
PRESS!

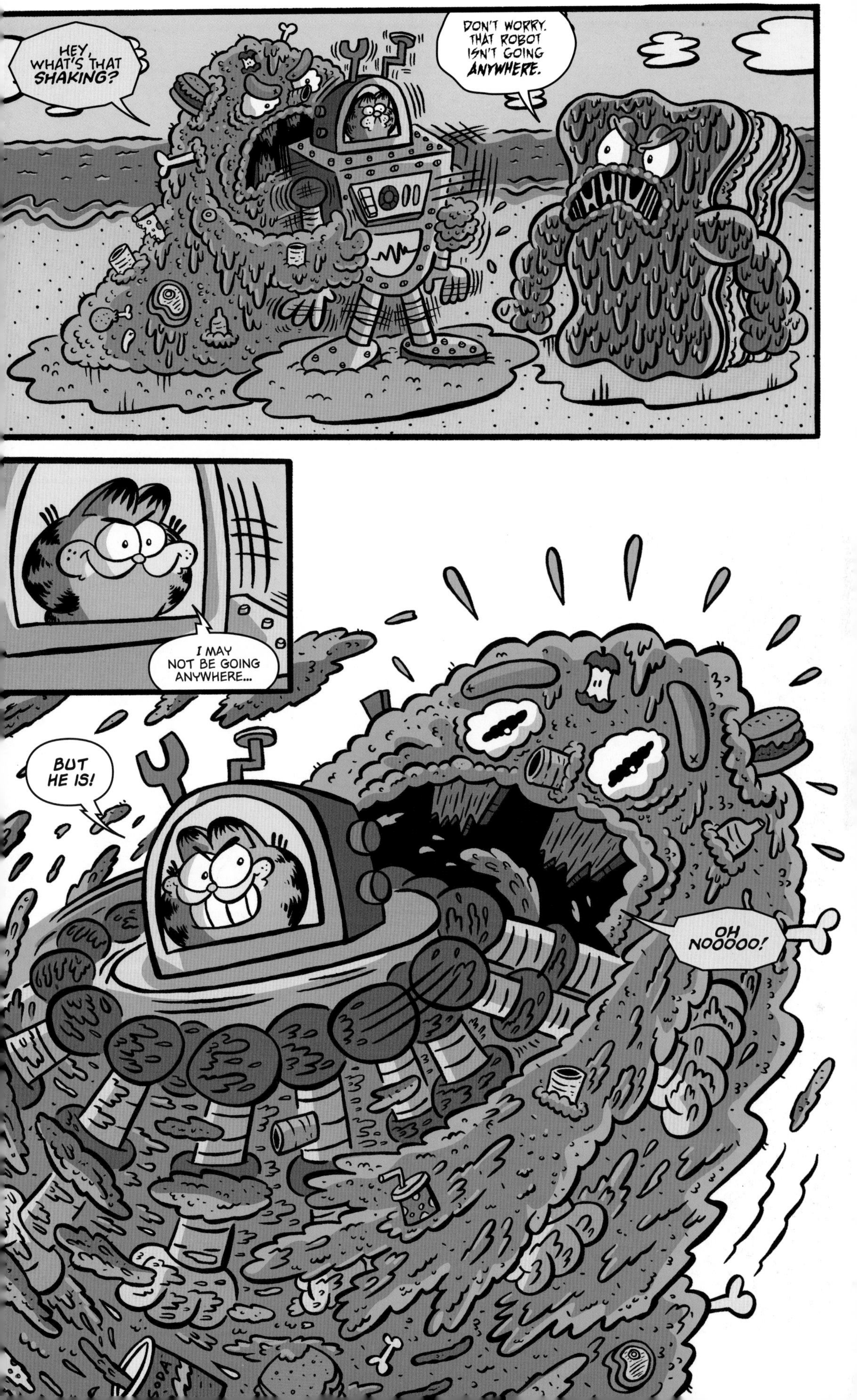
HEY, WHAT'S THAT SHAKING?
DON'T WORRY. THAT ROBOT ISN'T GOING ANYWHERE.
I MAY NOT BE GOING ANYWHERE...
BUT HE IS!
OH NOOOOO!
SODA

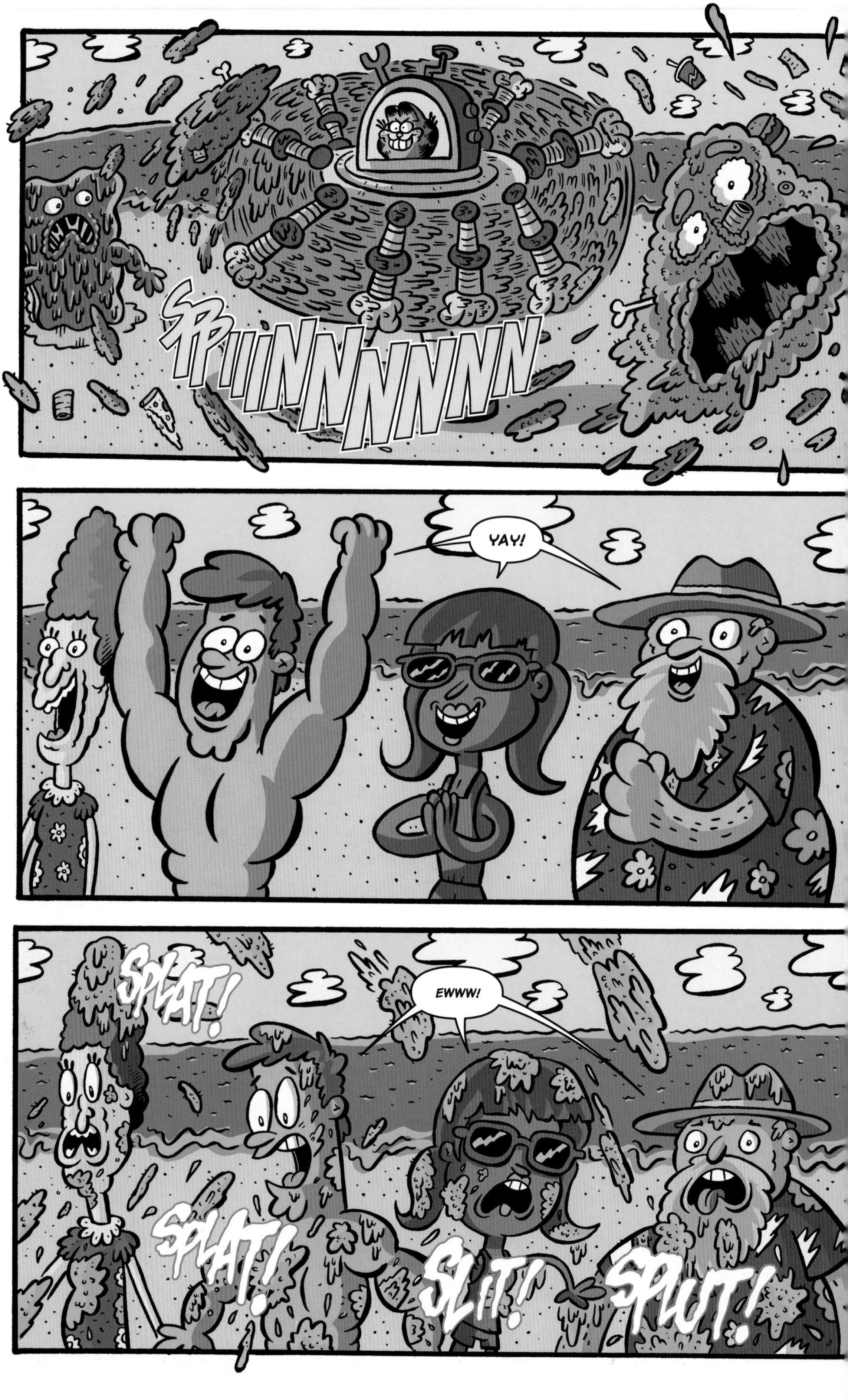
SPIIIINNNNNNNN
YAY!
SPLAT!
EWWW!
SPLAT!
SLIT!
SPLUT!

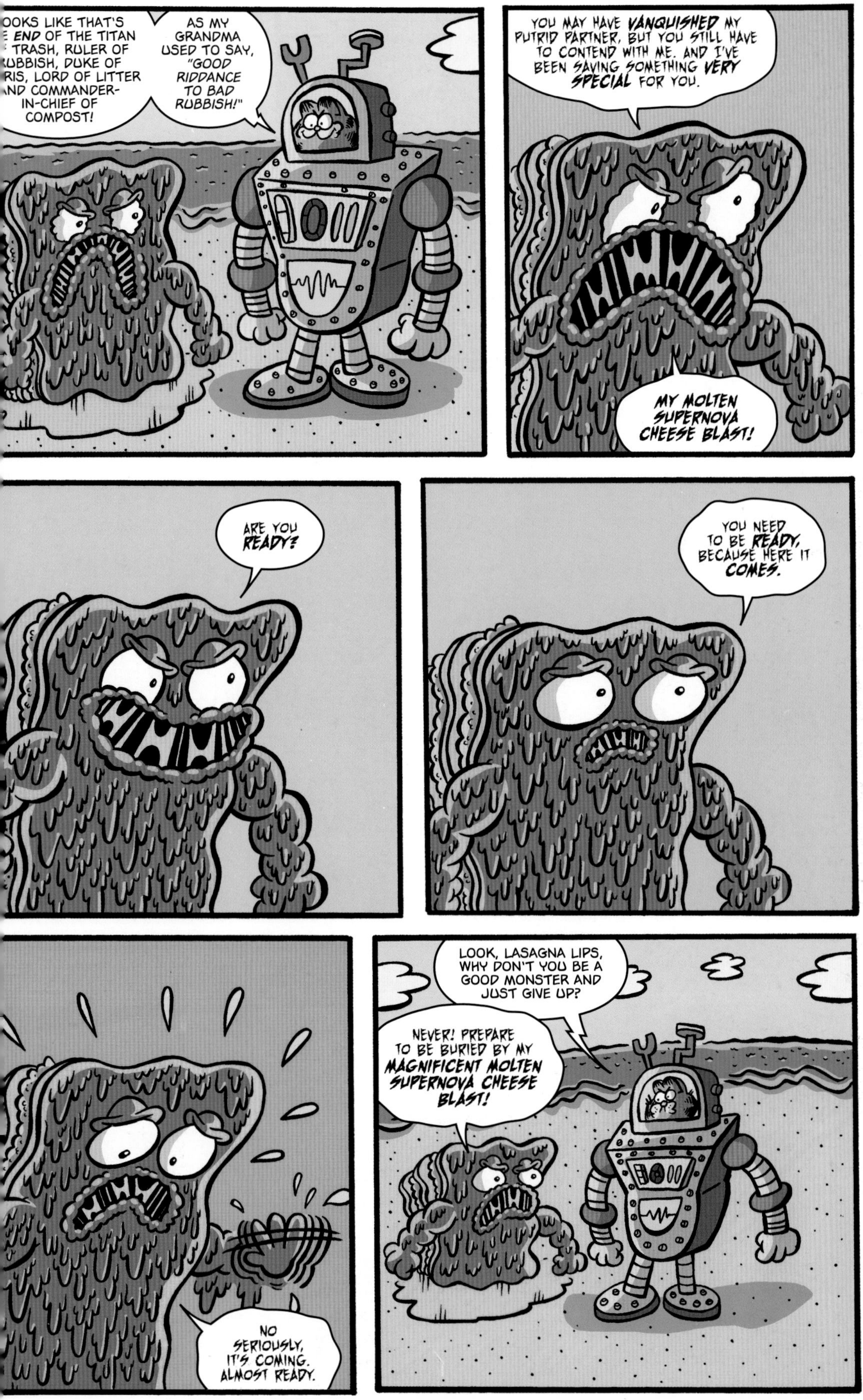
OOKS LIKE THAT'S
E END OF THE TITAN
TRASH, RULER OF
UBBISH, DUKE OF
RIS, LORD OF LITTER
ND COMMANDER-
IN-CHIEF OF
COMPOST!
AS MY GRANDMA USED TO SAY, "GOOD RIDDANCE TO BAD RUBBISH!"
YOU MAY HAVE VANQUISHED MY PUTRID PARTNER, BUT YOU STILL HAVE TO CONTEND WITH ME. AND I'VE BEEN SAVING SOMETHING VERY SPECIAL FOR YOU.
MY MOLTEN SUPERNOVA CHEESE BLAST!
ARE YOU READY?
YOU NEED TO BE READY, BECAUSE HERE IT COMES.
NO SERIOUSLY, IT'S COMING. ALMOST READY.
LOOK, LASAGNA LIPS, WHY DON'T YOU BE A GOOD MONSTER AND JUST GIVE UP?
NEVER! PREPARE TO BE BURIED BY MY MAGNIFICENT MOLTEN SUPERNOVA CHEESE BLAST!

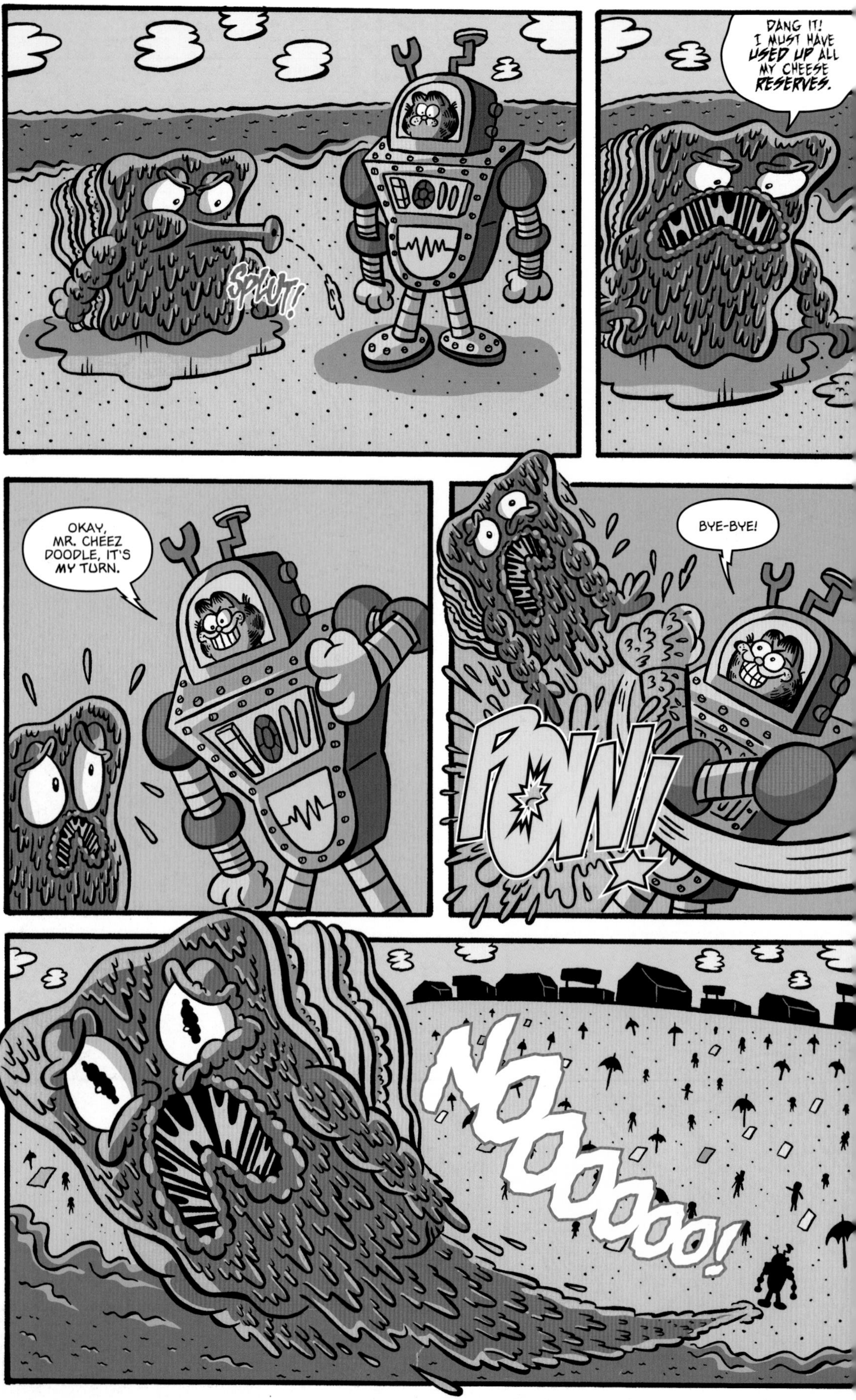
SPLUT!
DANG IT! I MUST HAVE USED UP ALL MY CHEESE RESERVES.
OKAY, MR. CHEEZ DOODLE, IT'S MY TURN.
BYE-BYE!
POW!
NOOOOOOO!

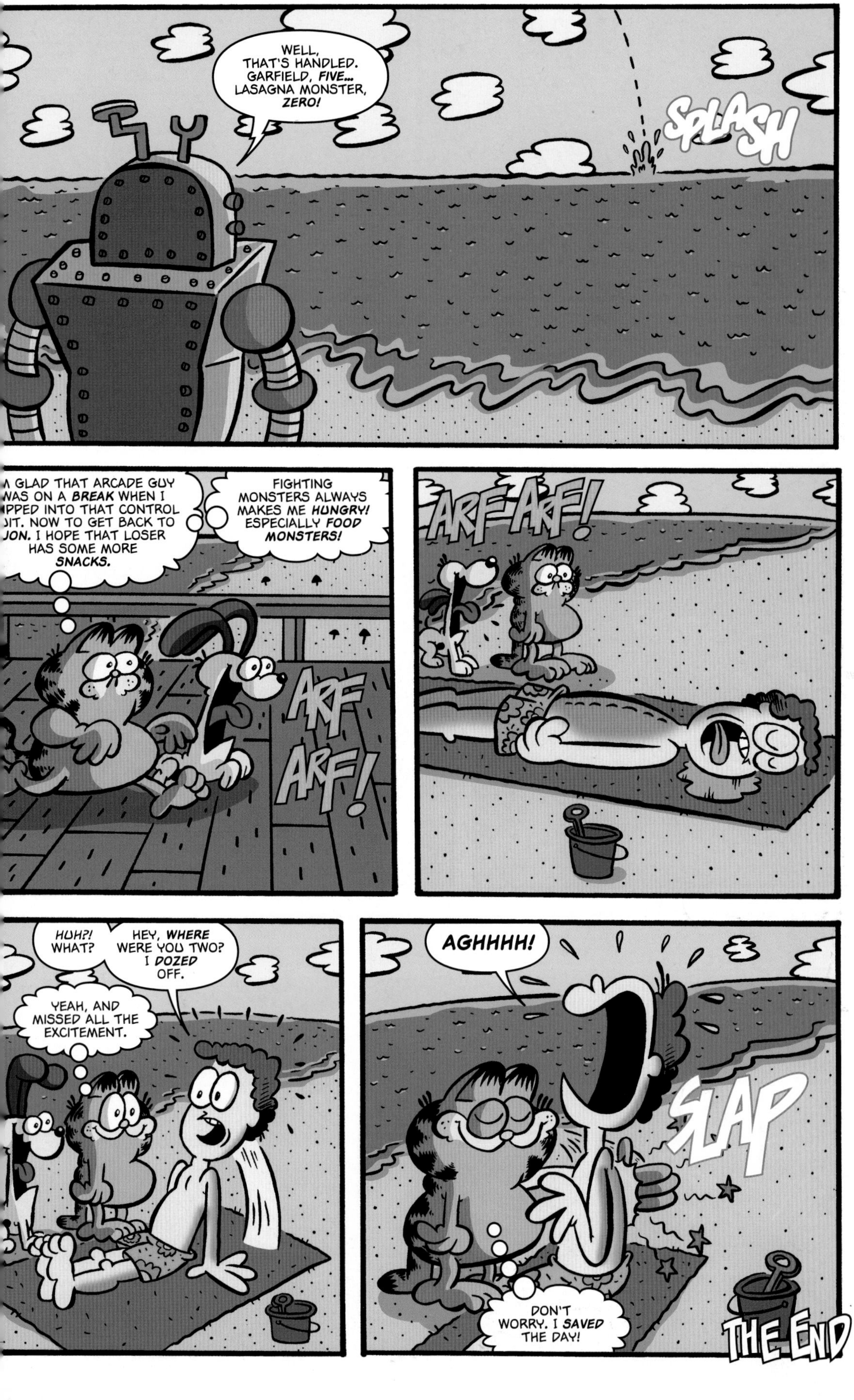

WELL, THAT'S HANDLED. GARFIELD, *FIVE*... LASAGNA MONSTER, *ZERO!*
SPLASH
M GLAD THAT ARCADE GUY WAS ON A *BREAK* WHEN I PPED INTO THAT CONTROL IT. NOW TO GET BACK TO JON. I HOPE THAT LOSER HAS SOME MORE *SNACKS.*
FIGHTING MONSTERS ALWAYS MAKES ME *HUNGRY!* ESPECIALLY *FOOD MONSTERS!*
ARF ARF!
ARF ARF!
*HUH?!* WHAT?
HEY, *WHERE* WERE YOU TWO? I *DOZED* OFF.
YEAH, AND MISSED ALL THE EXCITEMENT.
AGHHHH!
SLAP
DON'T WORRY. I *SAVED* THE DAY!
THE END

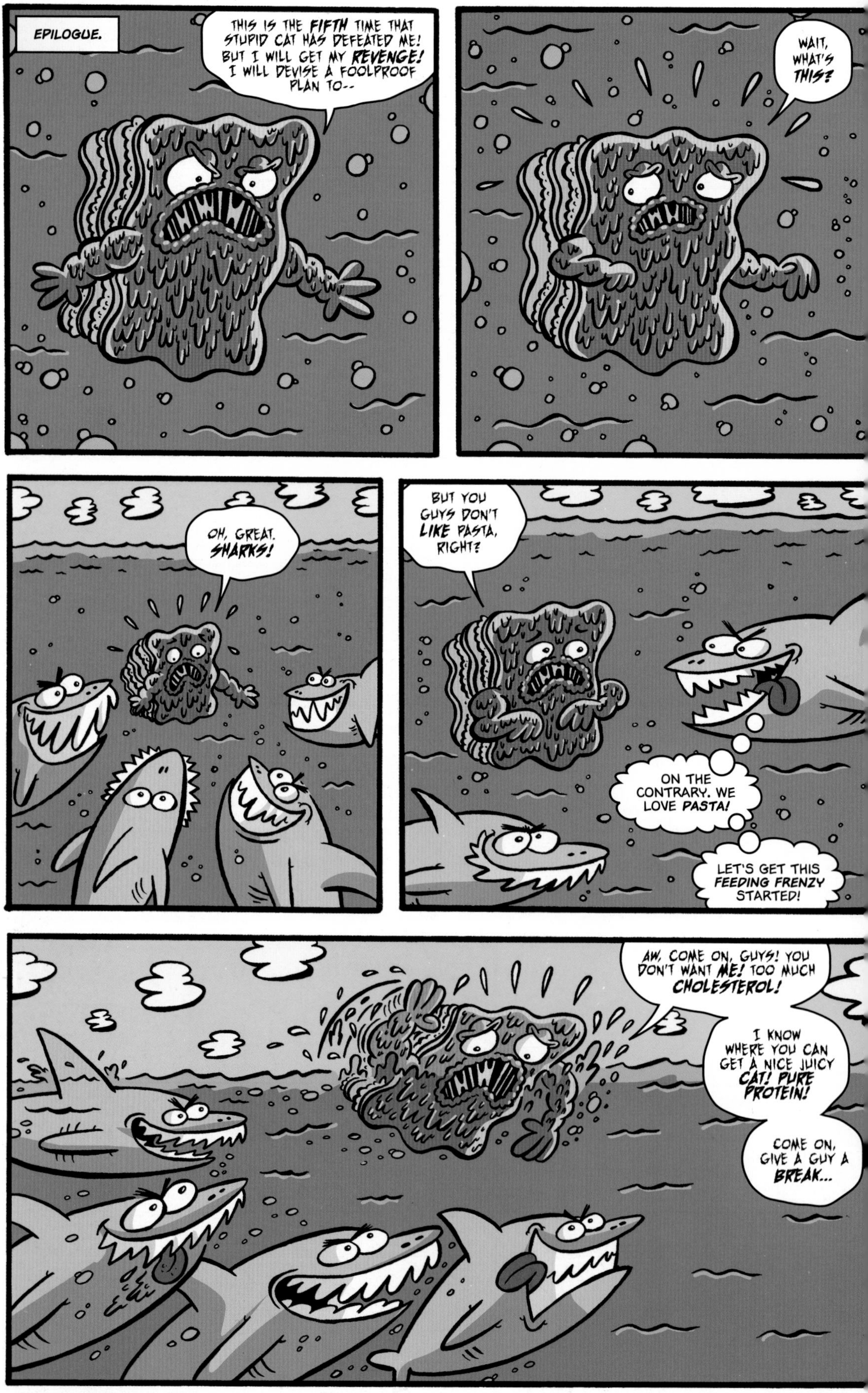
EPILOGUE.
THIS IS THE FIFTH TIME THAT STUPID CAT HAS DEFEATED ME! BUT I WILL GET MY REVENGE! I WILL DEVISE A FOOLPROOF PLAN TO--
WAIT, WHAT'S THIS?
OH, GREAT. SHARKS!
BUT YOU GUYS DON'T LIKE PASTA, RIGHT?
ON THE CONTRARY. WE LOVE PASTA!
LET'S GET THIS FEEDING FRENZY STARTED!
AW, COME ON, GUYS! YOU DON'T WANT ME! TOO MUCH CHOLESTEROL!
I KNOW WHERE YOU CAN GET A NICE JUICY CAT! PURE PROTEIN!
COME ON, GIVE A GUY A BREAK...

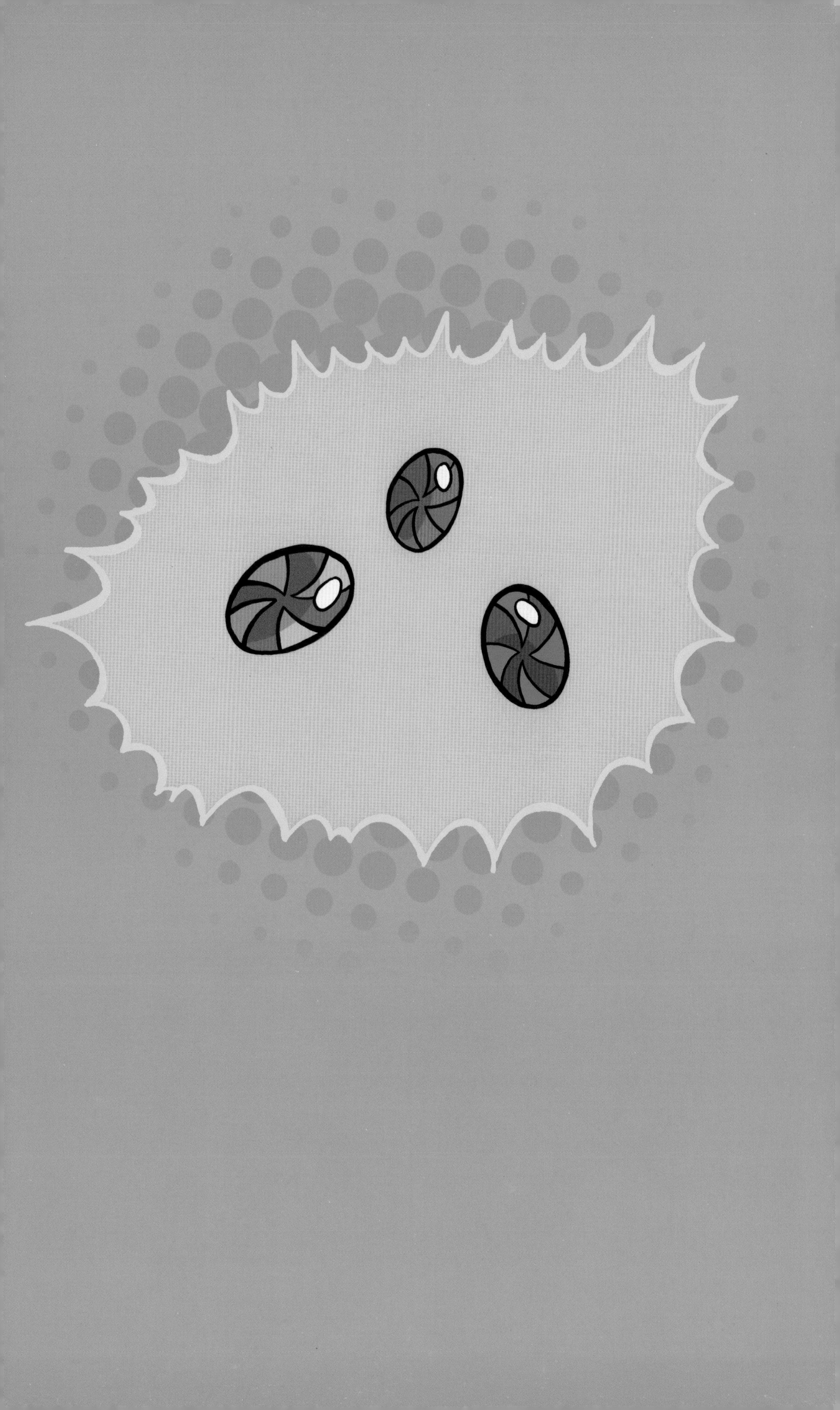

# The Fall
# Season

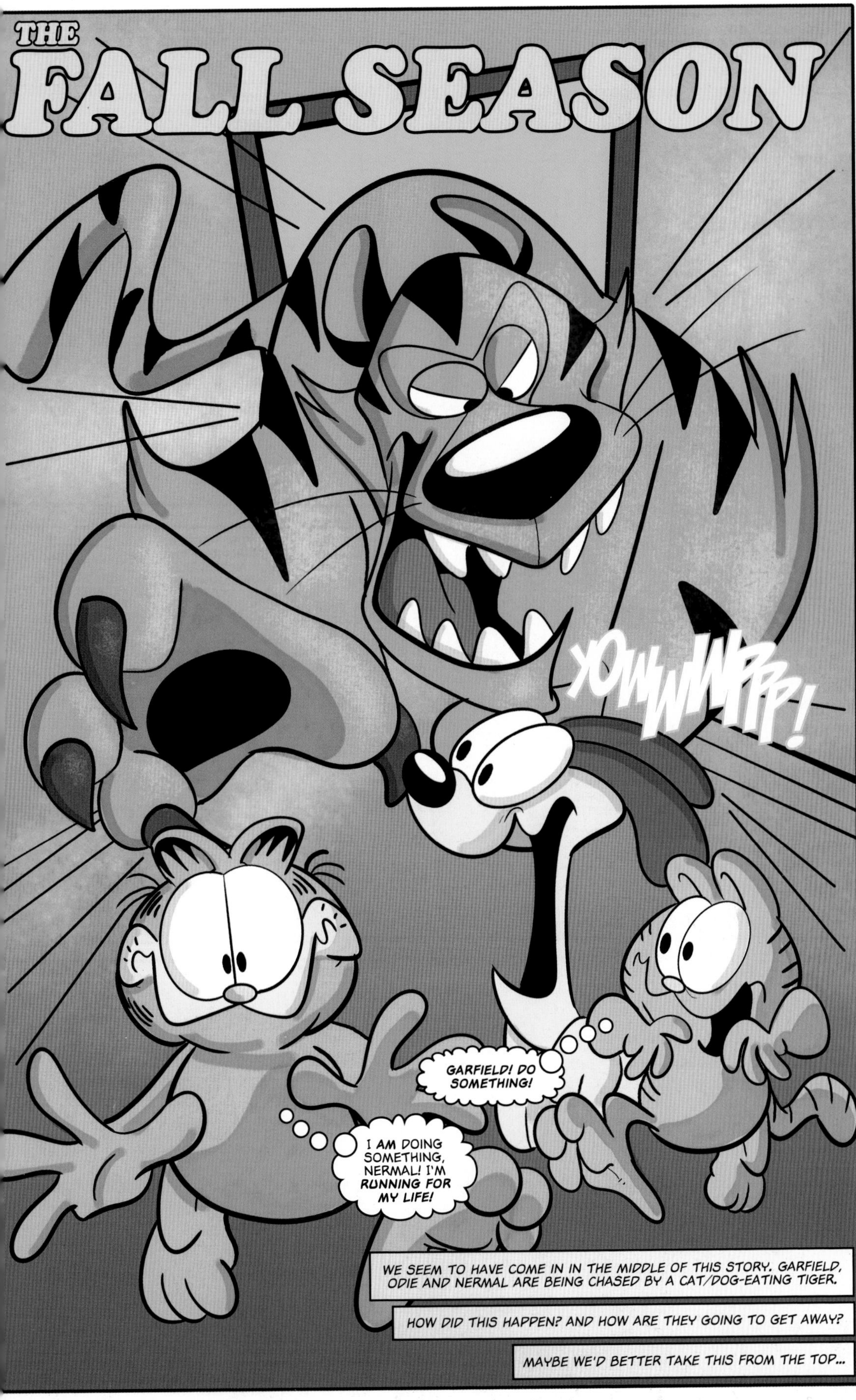
THE FALL SEASON
YOWWWRRR!
GARFIELD! DO SOMETHING!
I AM DOING SOMETHING, NERMAL! I'M RUNNING FOR MY LIFE!
WE SEEM TO HAVE COME IN IN THE MIDDLE OF THIS STORY. GARFIELD, ODIE AND NERMAL ARE BEING CHASED BY A CAT/DOG-EATING TIGER.
HOW DID THIS HAPPEN? AND HOW ARE THEY GOING TO GET AWAY?
MAYBE WE'D BETTER TAKE THIS FROM THE TOP...

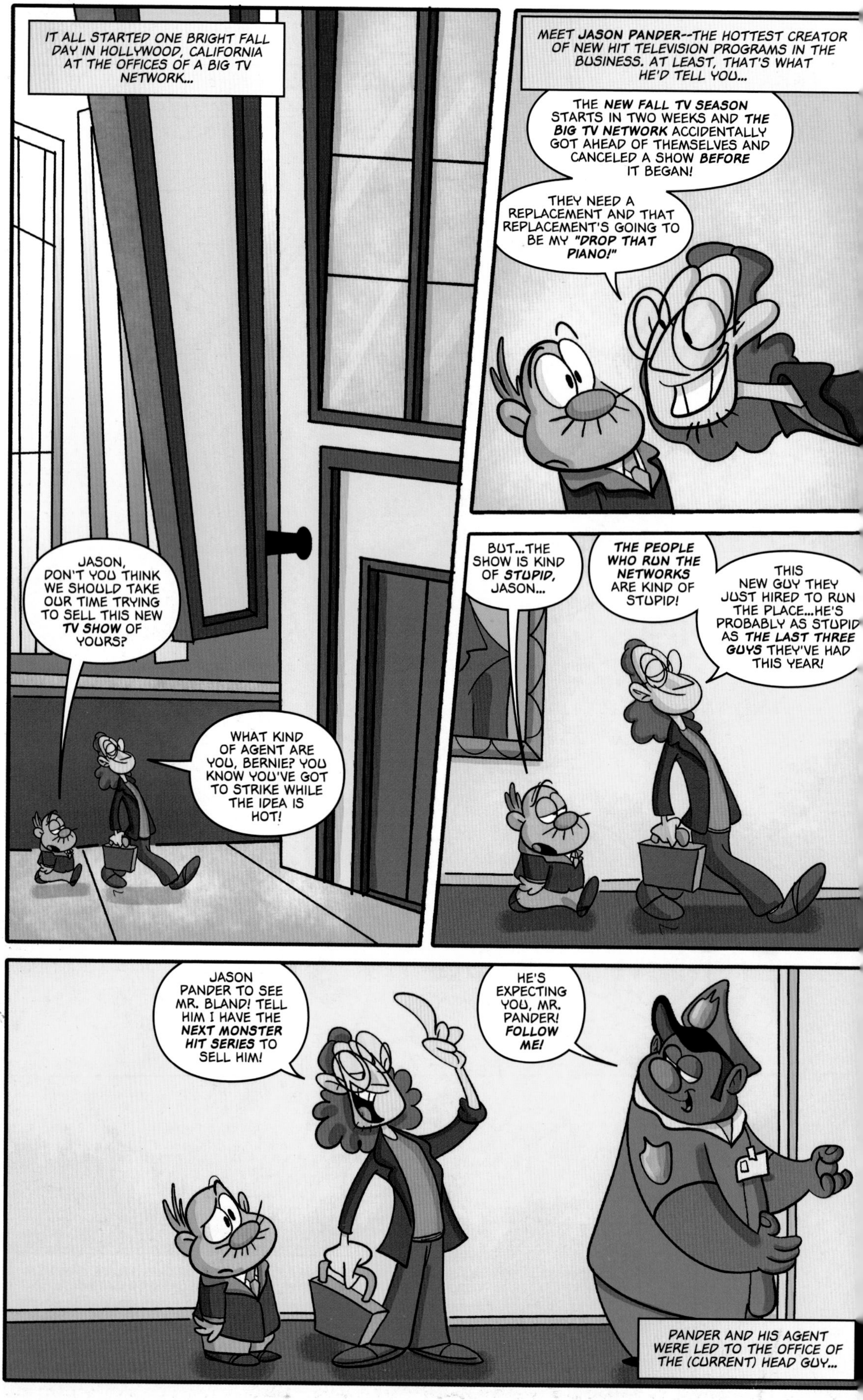
IT ALL STARTED ONE BRIGHT FALL DAY IN HOLLYWOOD, CALIFORNIA AT THE OFFICES OF A BIG TV NETWORK...
JASON, DON'T YOU THINK WE SHOULD TAKE OUR TIME TRYING TO SELL THIS NEW TV SHOW OF YOURS?
WHAT KIND OF AGENT ARE YOU, BERNIE? YOU KNOW YOU'VE GOT TO STRIKE WHILE THE IDEA IS HOT!
MEET JASON PANDER--THE HOTTEST CREATOR OF NEW HIT TELEVISION PROGRAMS IN THE BUSINESS. AT LEAST, THAT'S WHAT HE'D TELL YOU...
THE NEW FALL TV SEASON STARTS IN TWO WEEKS AND THE BIG TV NETWORK ACCIDENTALLY GOT AHEAD OF THEMSELVES AND CANCELED A SHOW BEFORE IT BEGAN!
THEY NEED A REPLACEMENT AND THAT REPLACEMENT'S GOING TO BE MY "DROP THAT PIANO!"
BUT...THE SHOW IS KIND OF STUPID, JASON...
THE PEOPLE WHO RUN THE NETWORKS ARE KIND OF STUPID!
THIS NEW GUY THEY JUST HIRED TO RUN THE PLACE...HE'S PROBABLY AS STUPID AS THE LAST THREE GUYS THEY'VE HAD THIS YEAR!
JASON PANDER TO SEE MR. BLAND! TELL HIM I HAVE THE NEXT MONSTER HIT SERIES TO SELL HIM!
HE'S EXPECTING YOU, MR. PANDER! FOLLOW ME!
PANDER AND HIS AGENT WERE LED TO THE OFFICE OF THE (CURRENT) HEAD GUY...

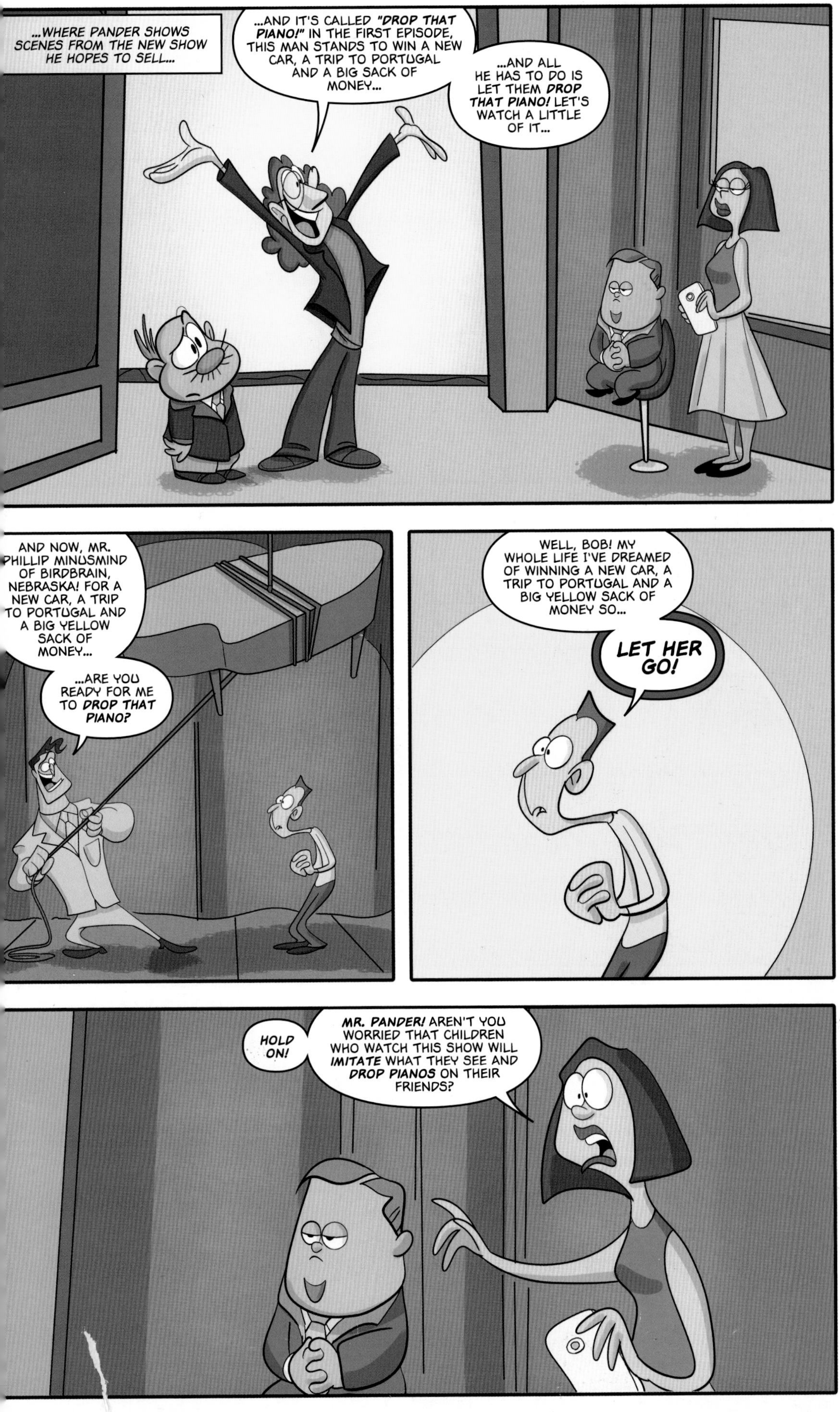
...WHERE PANDER SHOWS SCENES FROM THE NEW SHOW HE HOPES TO SELL...
...AND IT'S CALLED "DROP THAT PIANO!" IN THE FIRST EPISODE, THIS MAN STANDS TO WIN A NEW CAR, A TRIP TO PORTUGAL AND A BIG SACK OF MONEY...
...AND ALL HE HAS TO DO IS LET THEM DROP THAT PIANO! LET'S WATCH A LITTLE OF IT...
AND NOW, MR. PHILLIP MINUSMIND OF BIRDBRAIN, NEBRASKA! FOR A NEW CAR, A TRIP TO PORTUGAL AND A BIG YELLOW SACK OF MONEY...
...ARE YOU READY FOR ME TO DROP THAT PIANO?
WELL, BOB! MY WHOLE LIFE I'VE DREAMED OF WINNING A NEW CAR, A TRIP TO PORTUGAL AND A BIG YELLOW SACK OF MONEY SO...
LET HER GO!
HOLD ON!
MR. PANDER! AREN'T YOU WORRIED THAT CHILDREN WHO WATCH THIS SHOW WILL IMITATE WHAT THEY SEE AND DROP PIANOS ON THEIR FRIENDS?

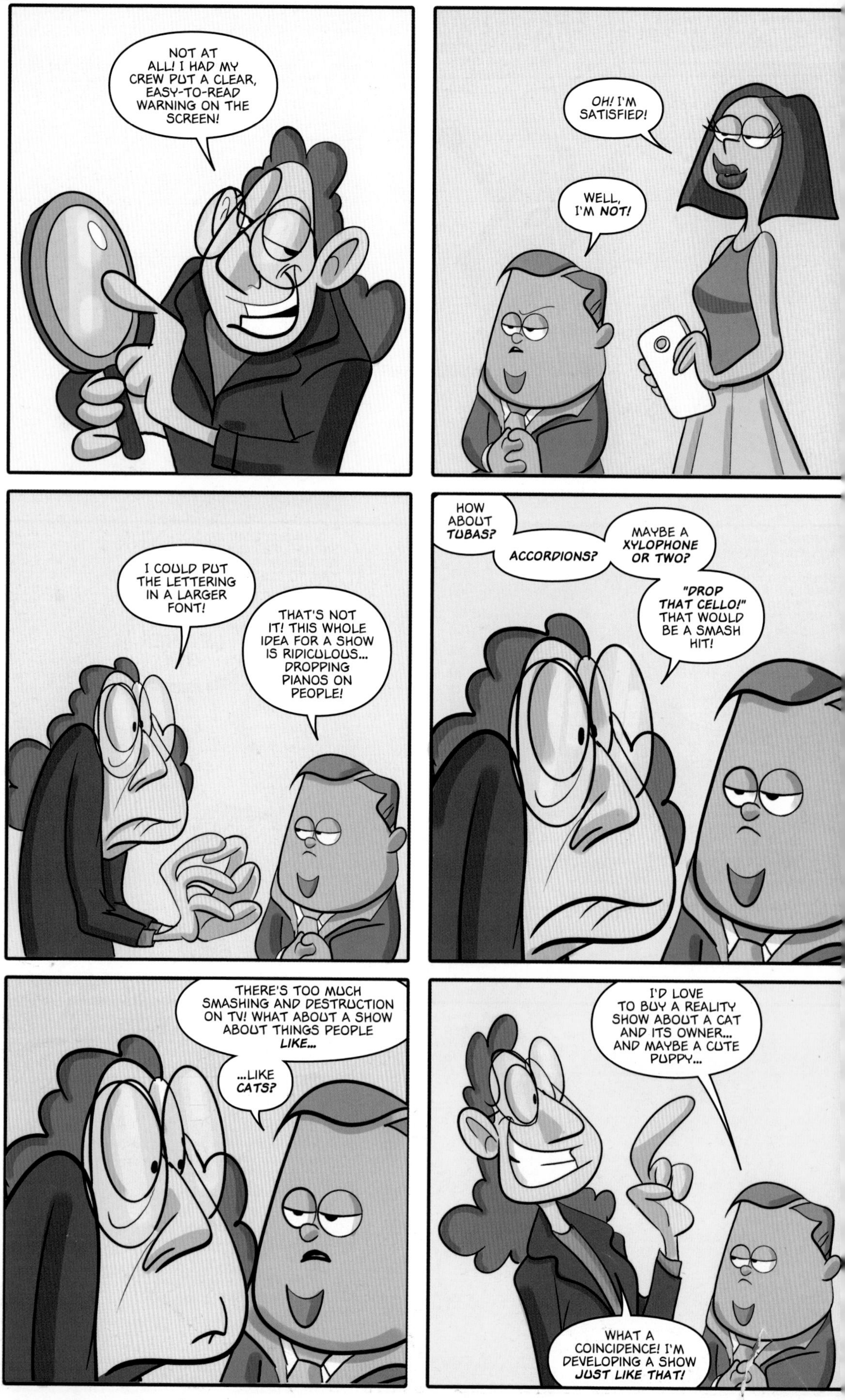
NOT AT ALL! I HAD MY CREW PUT A CLEAR, EASY-TO-READ WARNING ON THE SCREEN!
OH! I'M SATISFIED!
WELL, I'M NOT!
I COULD PUT THE LETTERING IN A LARGER FONT!
THAT'S NOT IT! THIS WHOLE IDEA FOR A SHOW IS RIDICULOUS... DROPPING PIANOS ON PEOPLE!
HOW ABOUT TUBAS?
ACCORDIONS?
MAYBE A XYLOPHONE OR TWO?
"DROP THAT CELLO!" THAT WOULD BE A SMASH HIT!
THERE'S TOO MUCH SMASHING AND DESTRUCTION ON TV! WHAT ABOUT A SHOW ABOUT THINGS PEOPLE LIKE...
...LIKE CATS?
I'D LOVE TO BUY A REALITY SHOW ABOUT A CAT AND ITS OWNER... AND MAYBE A CUTE PUPPY...
WHAT A COINCIDENCE! I'M DEVELOPING A SHOW JUST LIKE THAT!

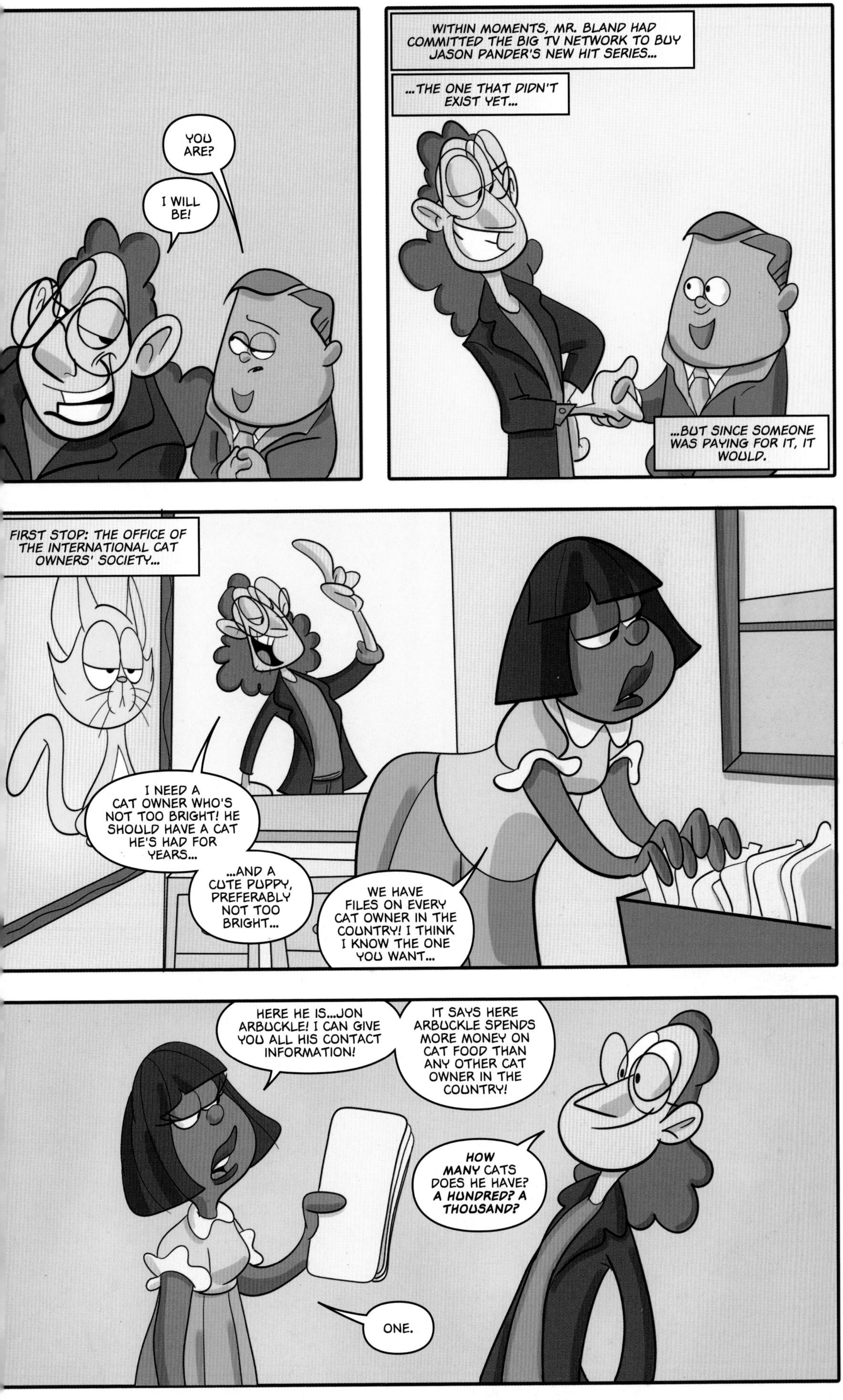

YOU ARE?
I WILL BE!
WITHIN MOMENTS, MR. BLAND HAD COMMITTED THE BIG TV NETWORK TO BUY JASON PANDER'S NEW HIT SERIES...
...THE ONE THAT DIDN'T EXIST YET...
...BUT SINCE SOMEONE WAS PAYING FOR IT, IT WOULD.
FIRST STOP: THE OFFICE OF THE INTERNATIONAL CAT OWNERS' SOCIETY...
I NEED A CAT OWNER WHO'S NOT TOO BRIGHT! HE SHOULD HAVE A CAT HE'S HAD FOR YEARS...
...AND A CUTE PUPPY, PREFERABLY NOT TOO BRIGHT...
WE HAVE FILES ON EVERY CAT OWNER IN THE COUNTRY! I THINK I KNOW THE ONE YOU WANT...
HERE HE IS...JON ARBUCKLE! I CAN GIVE YOU ALL HIS CONTACT INFORMATION!
IT SAYS HERE ARBUCKLE SPENDS MORE MONEY ON CAT FOOD THAN ANY OTHER CAT OWNER IN THE COUNTRY!
HOW MANY CATS DOES HE HAVE? A HUNDRED? A THOUSAND?
ONE.

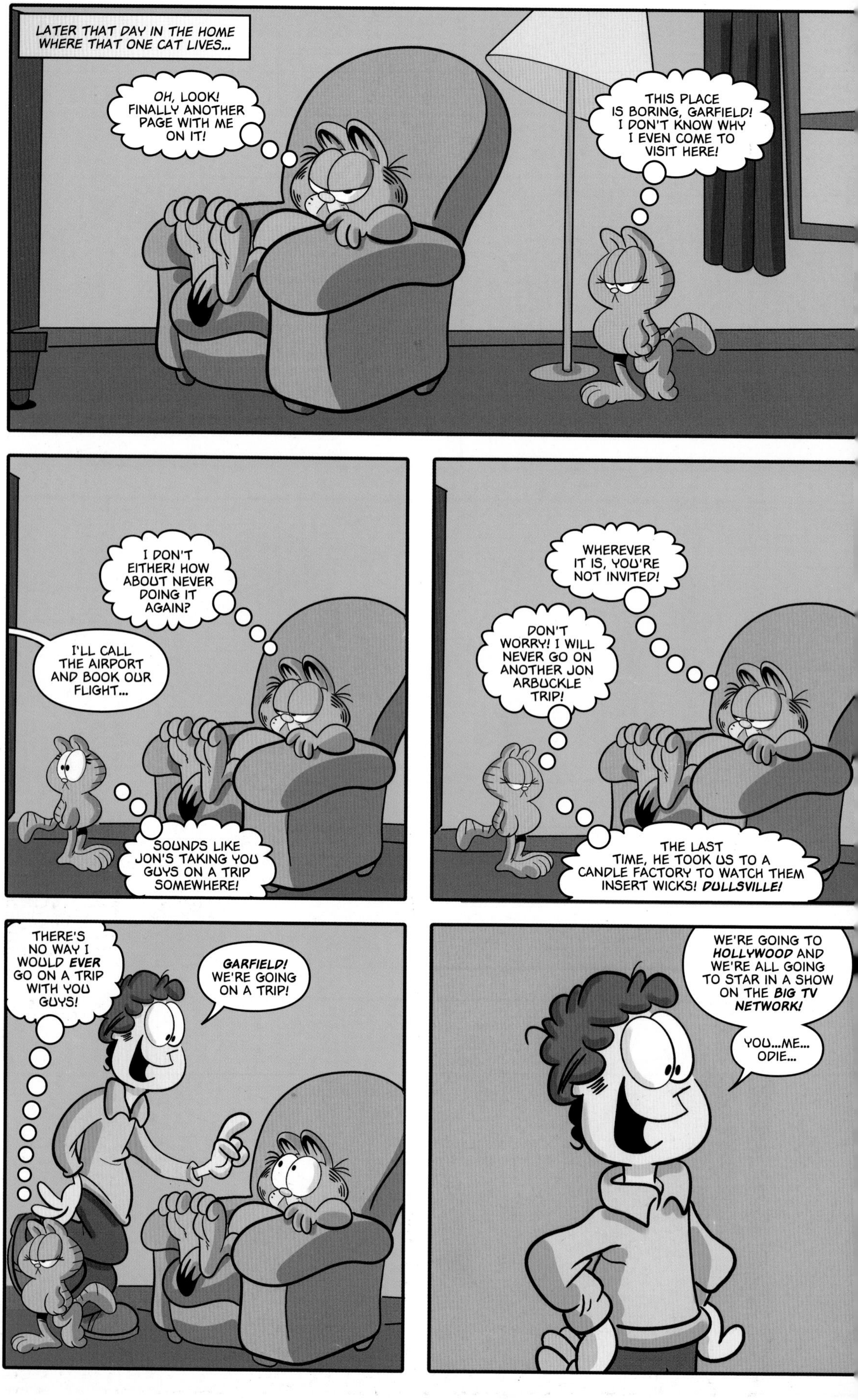
LATER THAT DAY IN THE HOME WHERE THAT ONE CAT LIVES...
OH, LOOK! FINALLY ANOTHER PAGE WITH ME ON IT!
THIS PLACE IS BORING, GARFIELD! I DON'T KNOW WHY I EVEN COME TO VISIT HERE!
I DON'T EITHER! HOW ABOUT NEVER DOING IT AGAIN?
I'LL CALL THE AIRPORT AND BOOK OUR FLIGHT...
SOUNDS LIKE JON'S TAKING YOU GUYS ON A TRIP SOMEWHERE!
WHEREVER IT IS, YOU'RE NOT INVITED!
DON'T WORRY! I WILL NEVER GO ON ANOTHER JON ARBUCKLE TRIP!
THE LAST TIME, HE TOOK US TO A CANDLE FACTORY TO WATCH THEM INSERT WICKS! DULLSVILLE!
THERE'S NO WAY I WOULD EVER GO ON A TRIP WITH YOU GUYS!
GARFIELD! WE'RE GOING ON A TRIP!
WE'RE GOING TO HOLLYWOOD AND WE'RE ALL GOING TO STAR IN A SHOW ON THE BIG TV NETWORK!
YOU...ME... ODIE...

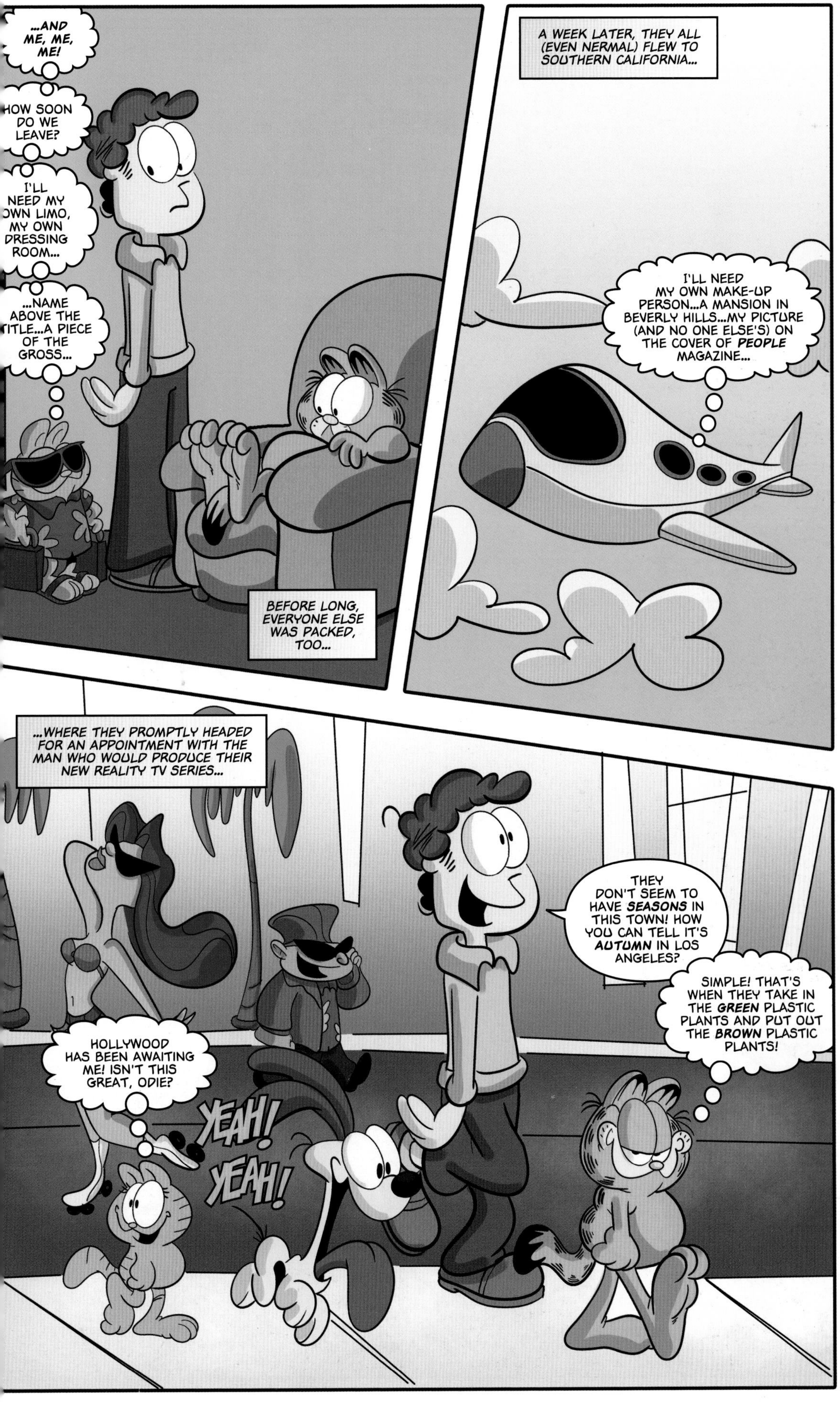
...AND ME, ME, ME!
HOW SOON DO WE LEAVE?
I'LL NEED MY WN LIMO, MY OWN DRESSING ROOM...
...NAME ABOVE THE ITLE...A PIECE OF THE GROSS...
BEFORE LONG, EVERYONE ELSE WAS PACKED, TOO...
A WEEK LATER, THEY ALL (EVEN NERMAL) FLEW TO SOUTHERN CALIFORNIA...
I'LL NEED MY OWN MAKE-UP PERSON...A MANSION IN BEVERLY HILLS...MY PICTURE (AND NO ONE ELSE'S) ON THE COVER OF PEOPLE MAGAZINE...
...WHERE THEY PROMPTLY HEADED FOR AN APPOINTMENT WITH THE MAN WHO WOULD PRODUCE THEIR NEW REALITY TV SERIES...
THEY DON'T SEEM TO HAVE SEASONS IN THIS TOWN! HOW YOU CAN TELL IT'S AUTUMN IN LOS ANGELES?
SIMPLE! THAT'S WHEN THEY TAKE IN THE GREEN PLASTIC PLANTS AND PUT OUT THE BROWN PLASTIC PLANTS!
HOLLYWOOD HAS BEEN AWAITING ME! ISN'T THIS GREAT, ODIE?
YEAH!
YEAH!

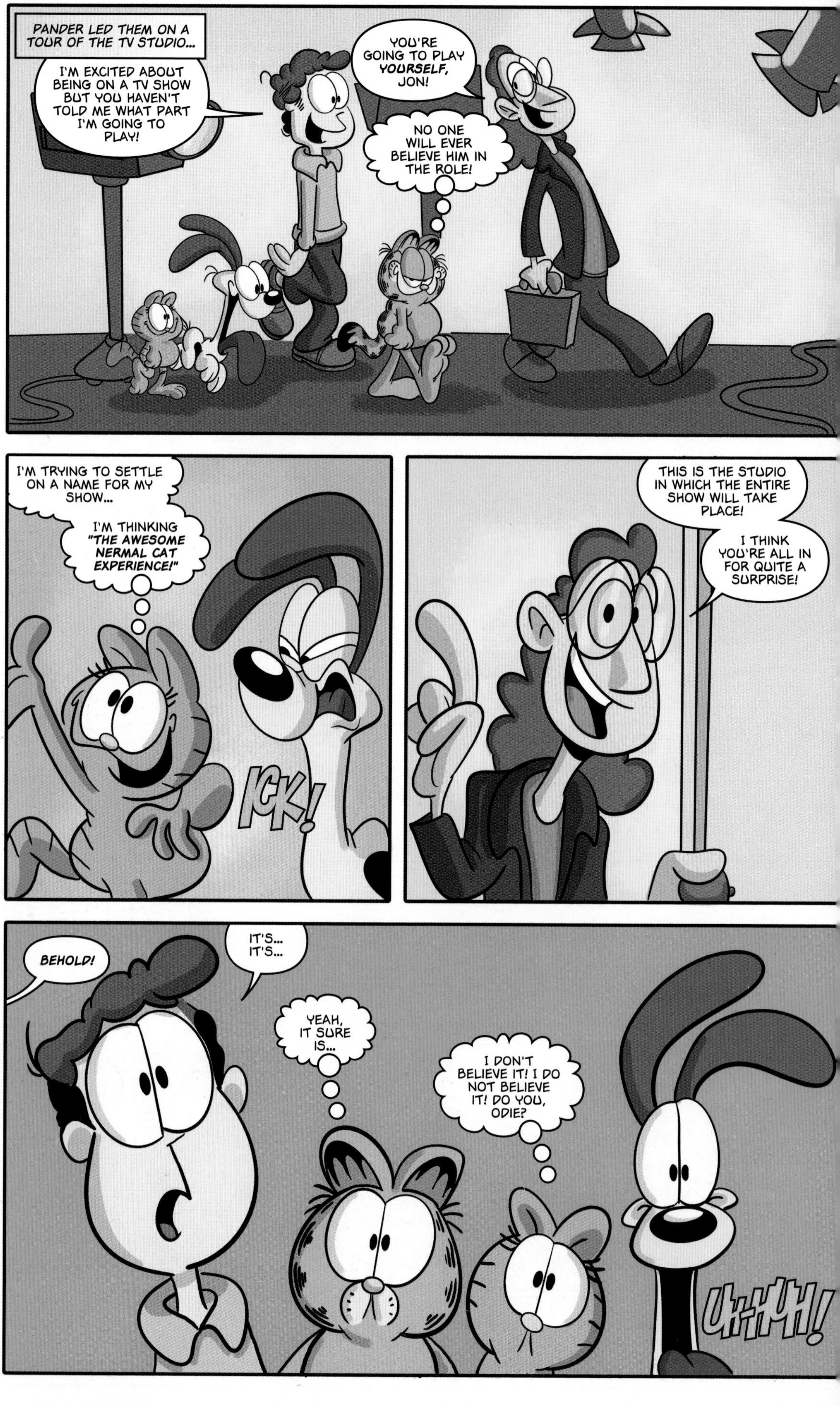
PANDER LED THEM ON A TOUR OF THE TV STUDIO...
I'M EXCITED ABOUT BEING ON A TV SHOW BUT YOU HAVEN'T TOLD ME WHAT PART I'M GOING TO PLAY!
YOU'RE GOING TO PLAY YOURSELF, JON!
NO ONE WILL EVER BELIEVE HIM IN THE ROLE!
I'M TRYING TO SETTLE ON A NAME FOR MY SHOW...
I'M THINKING "THE AWESOME NERMAL CAT EXPERIENCE!"
ICK!
THIS IS THE STUDIO IN WHICH THE ENTIRE SHOW WILL TAKE PLACE!
I THINK YOU'RE ALL IN FOR QUITE A SURPRISE!
BEHOLD!
IT'S... IT'S...
YEAH, IT SURE IS...
I DON'T BELIEVE IT! I DO NOT BELIEVE IT! DO YOU, ODIE?
UH-HUH!

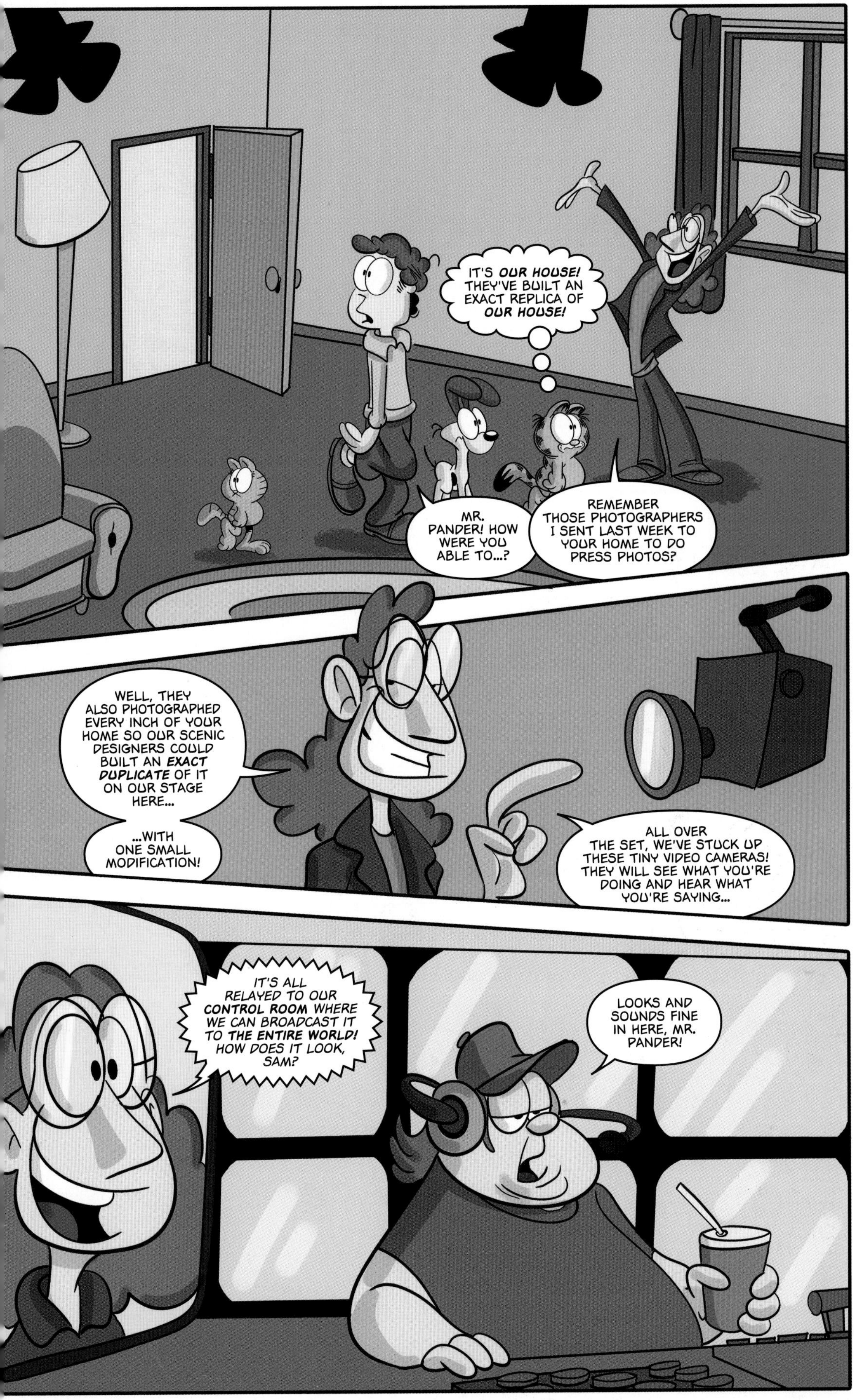
IT'S OUR HOUSE! THEY'VE BUILT AN EXACT REPLICA OF OUR HOUSE!
MR. PANDER! HOW WERE YOU ABLE TO...?
REMEMBER THOSE PHOTOGRAPHERS I SENT LAST WEEK TO YOUR HOME TO DO PRESS PHOTOS?
WELL, THEY ALSO PHOTOGRAPHED EVERY INCH OF YOUR HOME SO OUR SCENIC DESIGNERS COULD BUILT AN EXACT DUPLICATE OF IT ON OUR STAGE HERE...
...WITH ONE SMALL MODIFICATION!
ALL OVER THE SET, WE'VE STUCK UP THESE TINY VIDEO CAMERAS! THEY WILL SEE WHAT YOU'RE DOING AND HEAR WHAT YOU'RE SAYING...
IT'S ALL RELAYED TO OUR CONTROL ROOM WHERE WE CAN BROADCAST IT TO THE ENTIRE WORLD! HOW DOES IT LOOK, SAM?
LOOKS AND SOUNDS FINE IN HERE, MR. PANDER!

BUT WHAT ARE WE SUPPOSED TO DO?

JUST BE YOURSELVES! FORGET ABOUT THE CAMERAS AND GO ABOUT YOUR LIVES AS YOU ALWAYS DO HERE!

I'LL HAVE YOUR LUGGAGE SENT OVER! ENJOY YOUR NEW HOME FOR A WHILE!

AND IF THE SHOW'S A HIT, YOU'LL BE HERE SEVERAL YEARS WHILE I GET VERY, VERY RICH!

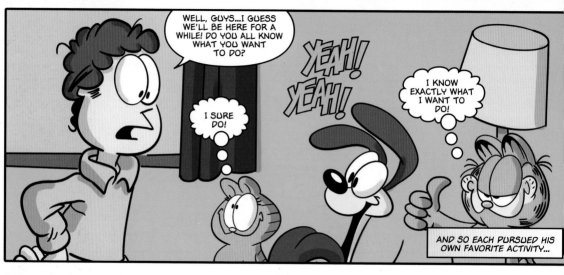

WELL, GUYS...I GUESS WE'LL BE HERE FOR A WHILE! DO YOU ALL KNOW WHAT YOU WANT TO DO?

I SURE DO!

YEAH! YEAH!

I KNOW EXACTLY WHAT I WANT TO DO!

AND SO EACH PURSUED HIS OWN FAVORITE ACTIVITY...

...ODIE CHASED HIS TAIL...

ARF ARF!

...NERMAL AUDITIONED...

ALAS, POOR YORICK! I KNEW HIM, HORATIO...A FELLOW OF INFINITE JEST, OF MOST EXCELLENT FANCY...

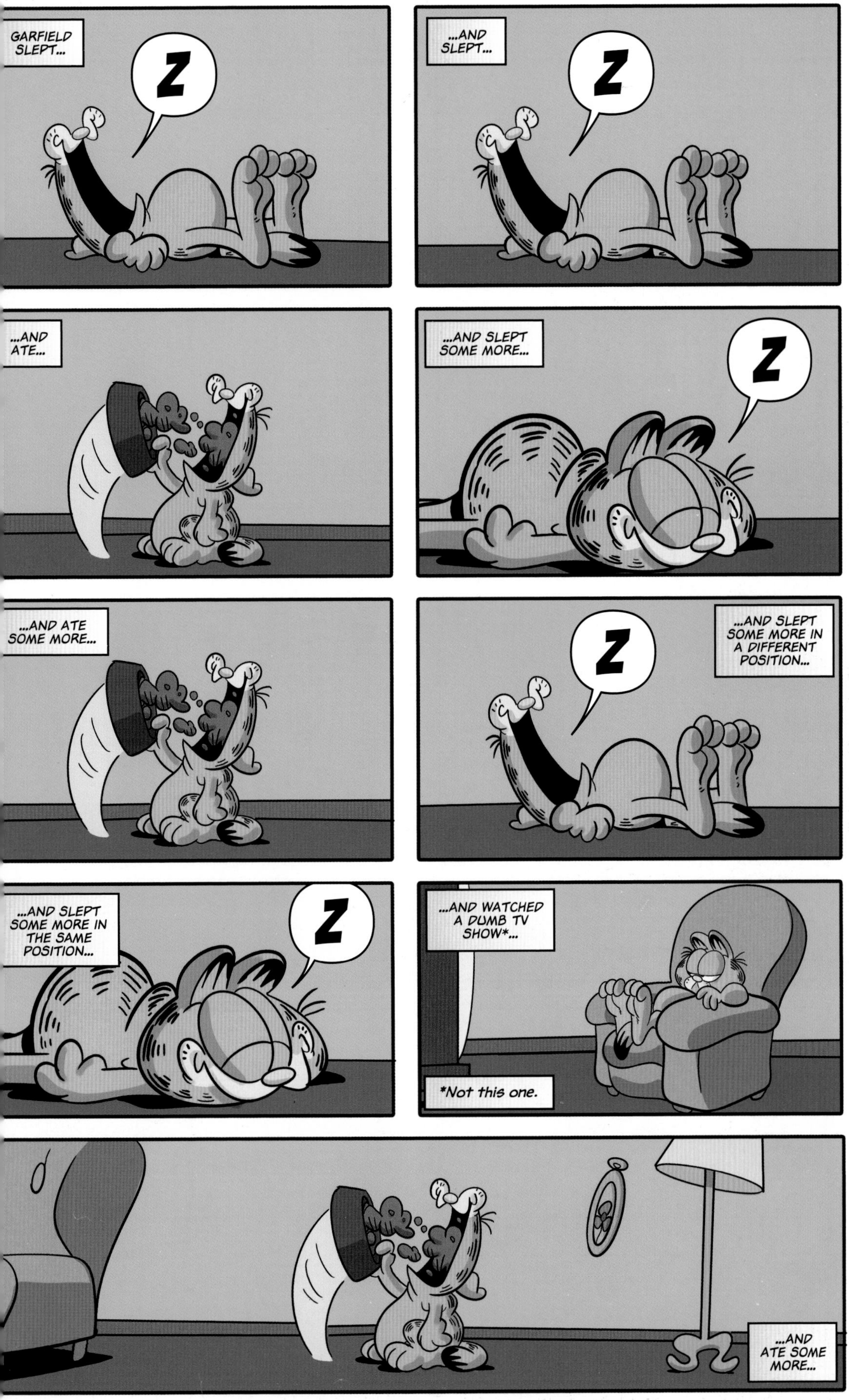
GARFIELD SLEPT...
Z
...AND SLEPT...
Z
...AND ATE...
...AND SLEPT SOME MORE...
Z
...AND ATE SOME MORE...
...AND SLEPT SOME MORE IN A DIFFERENT POSITION...
Z
...AND SLEPT SOME MORE IN THE SAME POSITION...
Z
...AND WATCHED A DUMB TV SHOW*...
*Not this one.
...AND ATE SOME MORE...

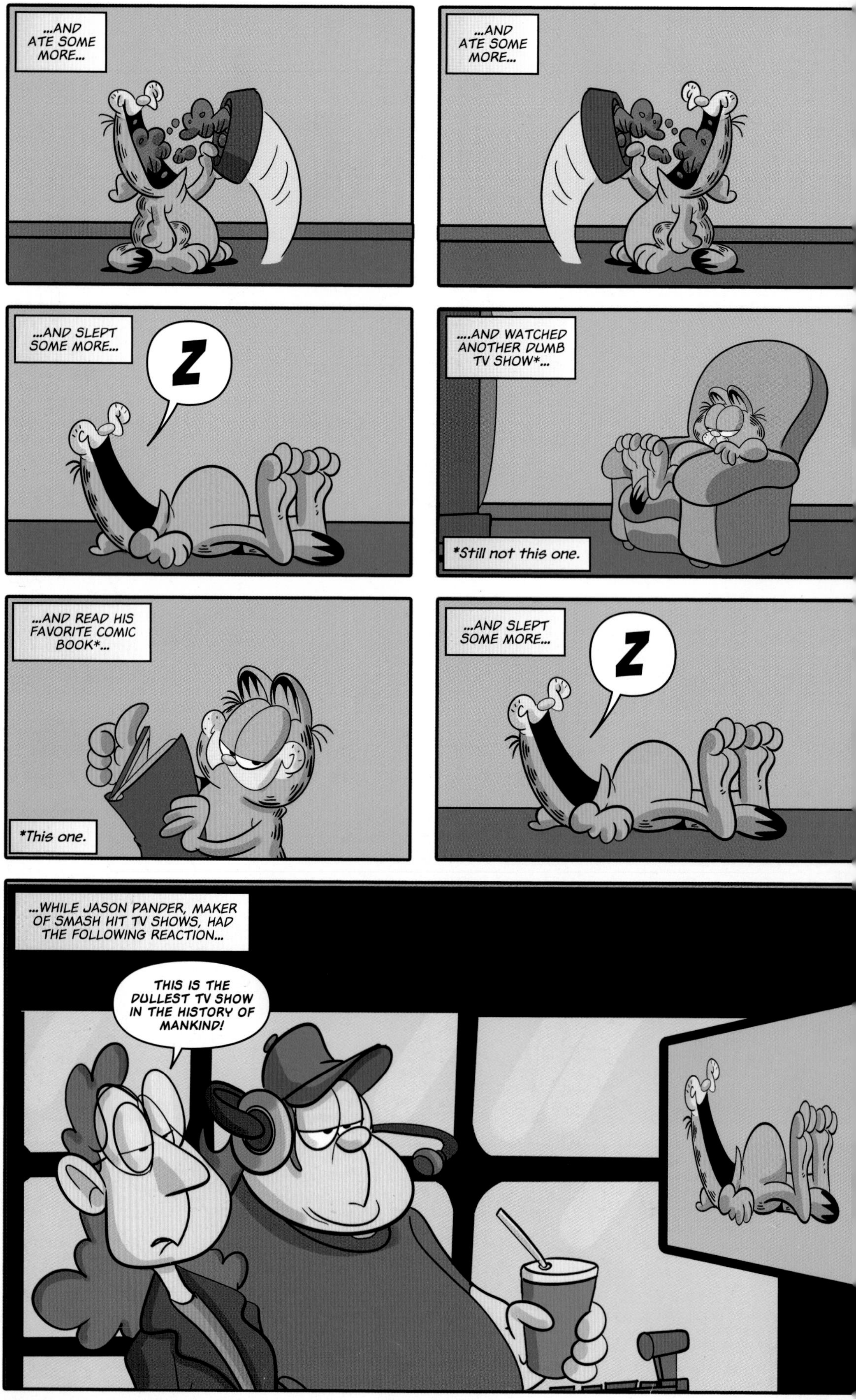
...AND ATE SOME MORE...
...AND ATE SOME MORE...
...AND SLEPT SOME MORE...
Z
....AND WATCHED ANOTHER DUMB TV SHOW*...
*Still not this one.
...AND READ HIS FAVORITE COMIC BOOK*...
*This one.
...AND SLEPT SOME MORE...
Z
...WHILE JASON PANDER, MAKER OF SMASH HIT TV SHOWS, HAD THE FOLLOWING REACTION...
THIS IS THE DULLEST TV SHOW IN THE HISTORY OF MANKIND!

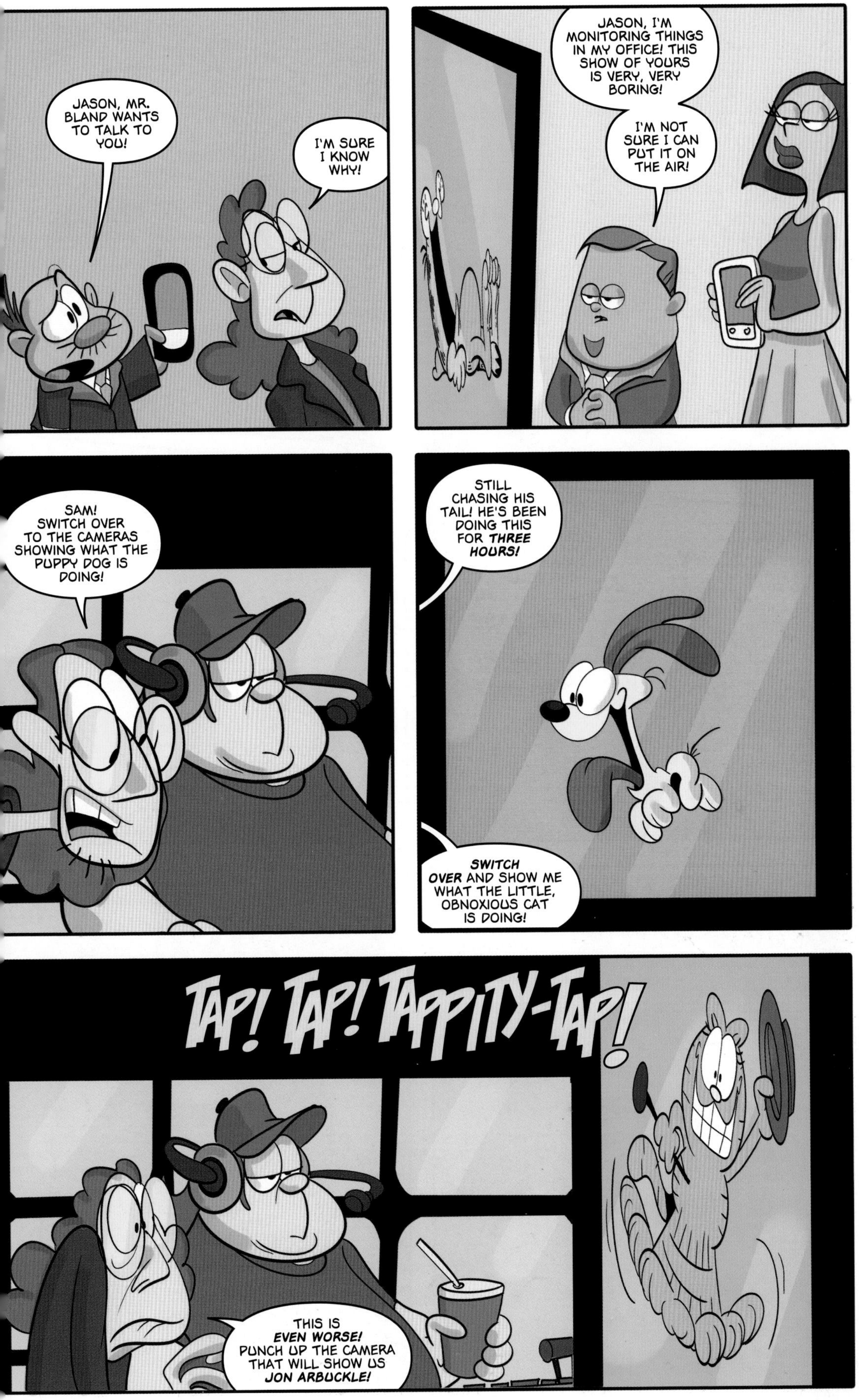
JASON, MR. BLAND WANTS TO TALK TO YOU!
I'M SURE I KNOW WHY!
JASON, I'M MONITORING THINGS IN MY OFFICE! THIS SHOW OF YOURS IS VERY, VERY BORING!
I'M NOT SURE I CAN PUT IT ON THE AIR!
SAM! SWITCH OVER TO THE CAMERAS SHOWING WHAT THE PUPPY DOG IS DOING!
STILL CHASING HIS TAIL! HE'S BEEN DOING THIS FOR THREE HOURS!
SWITCH OVER AND SHOW ME WHAT THE LITTLE, OBNOXIOUS CAT IS DOING!
TAP! TAP! TAPPITY-TAP!
THIS IS EVEN WORSE! PUNCH UP THE CAMERA THAT WILL SHOW US JON ARBUCKLE!

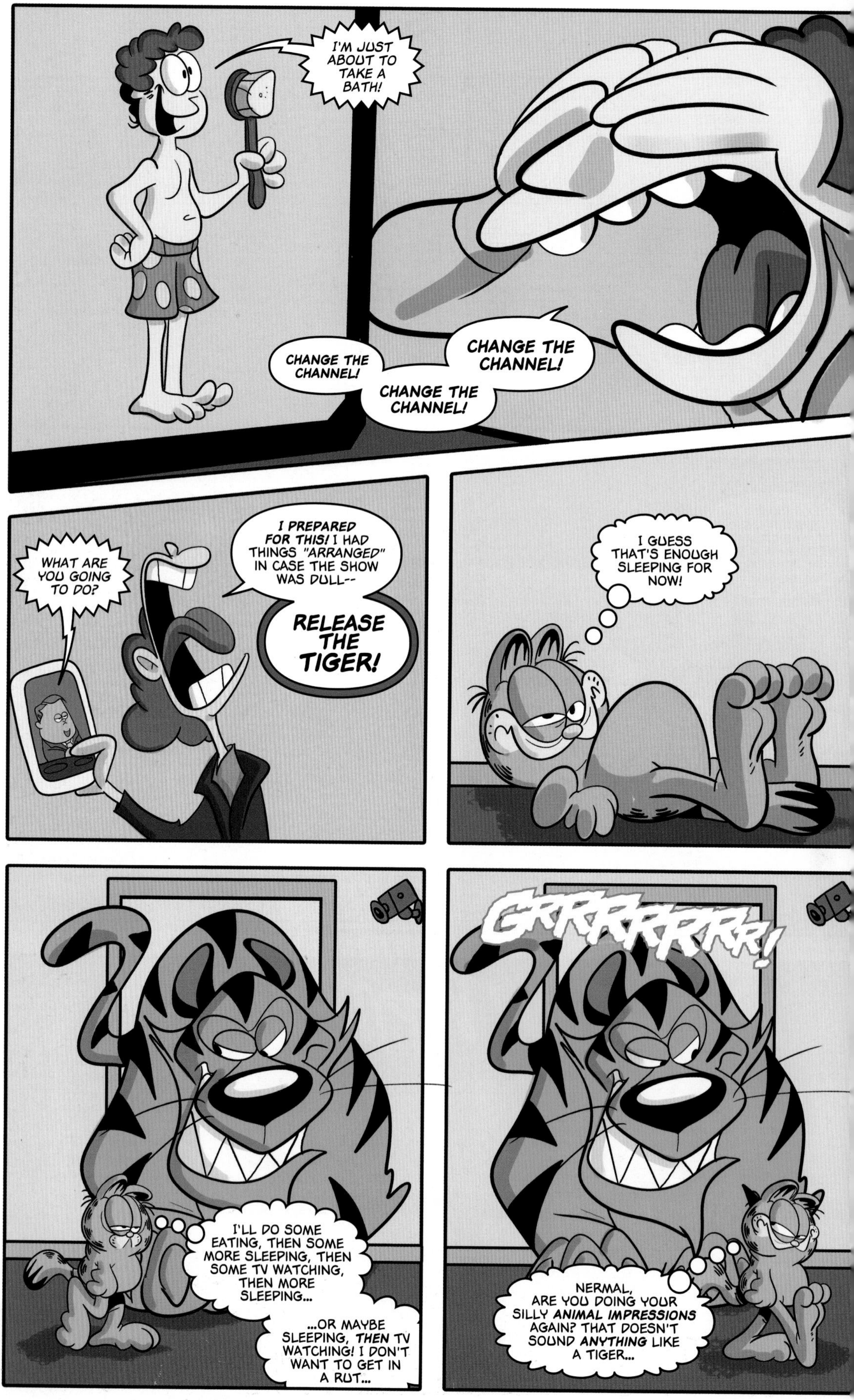
I'M JUST ABOUT TO TAKE A BATH!
CHANGE THE CHANNEL!
CHANGE THE CHANNEL!
CHANGE THE CHANNEL!
WHAT ARE YOU GOING TO DO?
I PREPARED FOR THIS! I HAD THINGS "ARRANGED" IN CASE THE SHOW WAS DULL--
RELEASE THE TIGER!
I GUESS THAT'S ENOUGH SLEEPING FOR NOW!
I'LL DO SOME EATING, THEN SOME MORE SLEEPING, THEN SOME TV WATCHING, THEN MORE SLEEPING...
...OR MAYBE SLEEPING, THEN TV WATCHING! I DON'T WANT TO GET IN A RUT...
GRRRRRRRR!
NERMAL, ARE YOU DOING YOUR SILLY ANIMAL IMPRESSIONS AGAIN? THAT DOESN'T SOUND ANYTHING LIKE A TIGER...

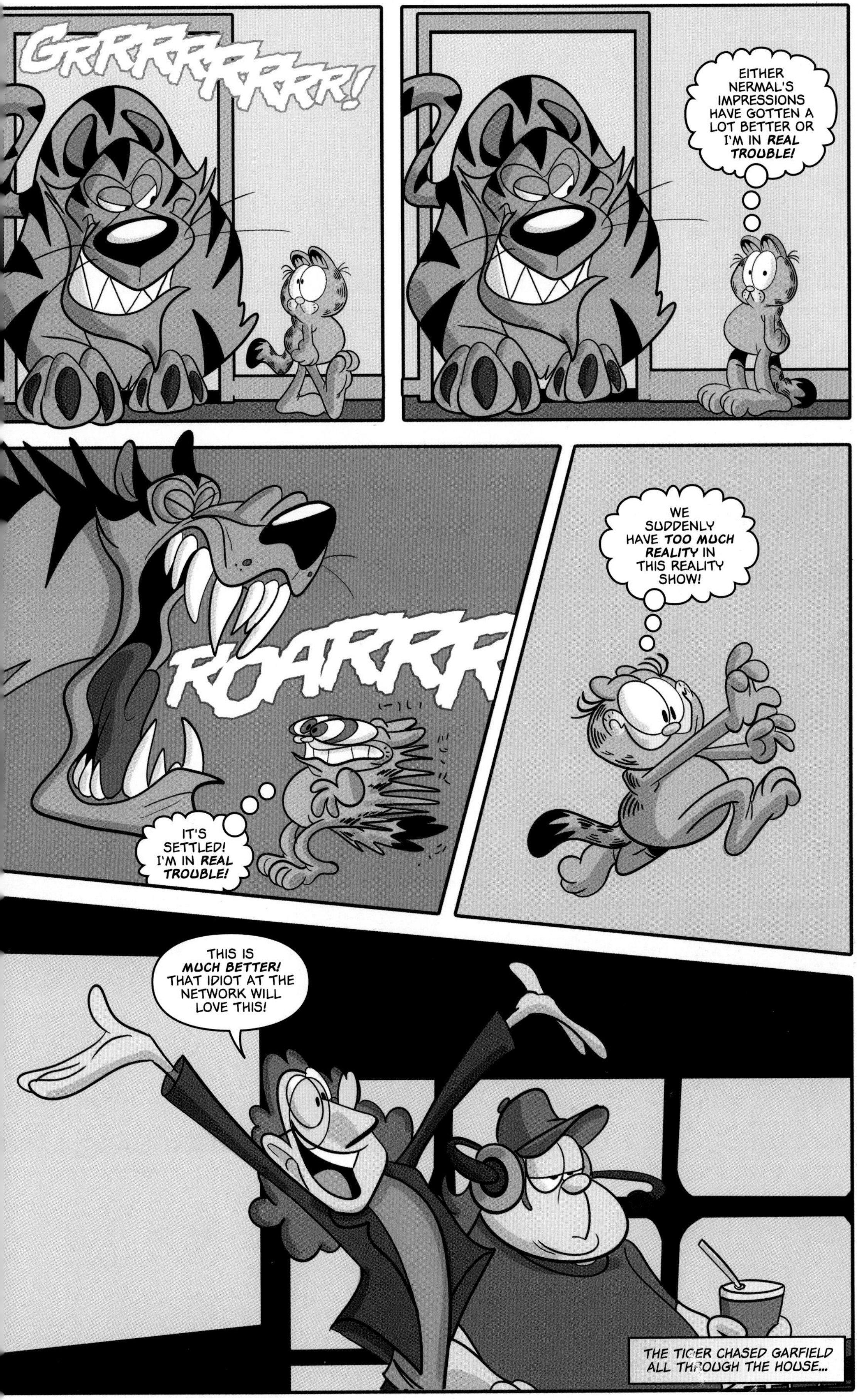
GRRRRRRRRRR!
EITHER NERMAL'S IMPRESSIONS HAVE GOTTEN A LOT BETTER OR I'M IN REAL TROUBLE!
ROARRR
IT'S SETTLED! I'M IN REAL TROUBLE!
WE SUDDENLY HAVE TOO MUCH REALITY IN THIS REALITY SHOW!
THIS IS MUCH BETTER! THAT IDIOT AT THE NETWORK WILL LOVE THIS!
THE TIGER CHASED GARFIELD ALL THROUGH THE HOUSE...

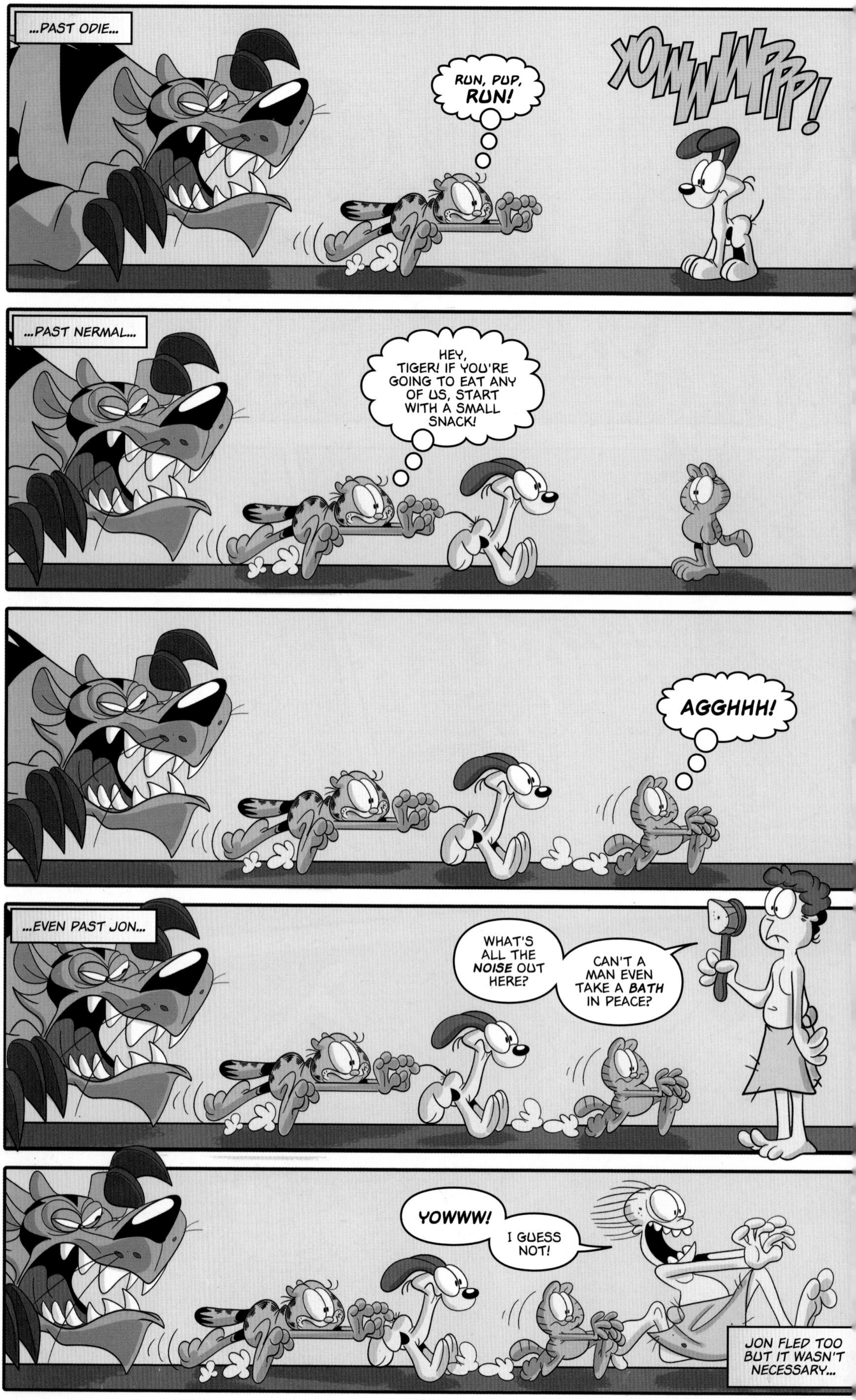

...PAST ODIE...
RUN, PUP, RUN!
YOWWWRRR!
...PAST NERMAL...
HEY, TIGER! IF YOU'RE GOING TO EAT ANY OF US, START WITH A SMALL SNACK!
AGGHHH!
...EVEN PAST JON...
WHAT'S ALL THE NOISE OUT HERE?
CAN'T A MAN EVEN TAKE A BATH IN PEACE?
YOWWW!
I GUESS NOT!
JON FLED TOO BUT IT WASN'T NECESSARY...

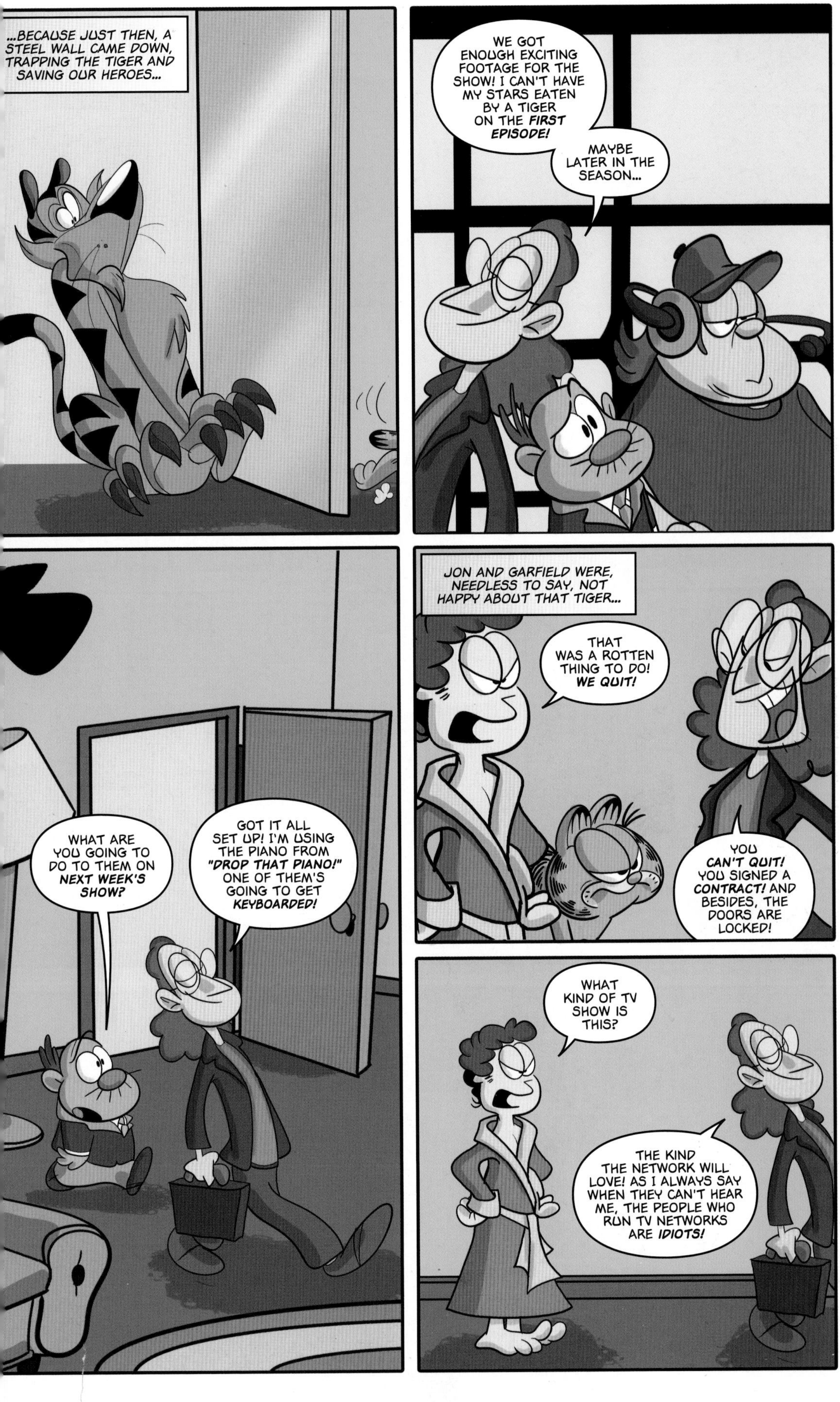
...BECAUSE JUST THEN, A STEEL WALL CAME DOWN, TRAPPING THE TIGER AND SAVING OUR HEROES...
WE GOT ENOUGH EXCITING FOOTAGE FOR THE SHOW! I CAN'T HAVE MY STARS EATEN BY A TIGER ON THE FIRST EPISODE!
MAYBE LATER IN THE SEASON...
WHAT ARE YOU GOING TO DO TO THEM ON NEXT WEEK'S SHOW?
GOT IT ALL SET UP! I'M USING THE PIANO FROM "DROP THAT PIANO!" ONE OF THEM'S GOING TO GET KEYBOARDED!
JON AND GARFIELD WERE, NEEDLESS TO SAY, NOT HAPPY ABOUT THAT TIGER...
THAT WAS A ROTTEN THING TO DO! WE QUIT!
YOU CAN'T QUIT! YOU SIGNED A CONTRACT! AND BESIDES, THE DOORS ARE LOCKED!
WHAT KIND OF TV SHOW IS THIS?
THE KIND THE NETWORK WILL LOVE! AS I ALWAYS SAY WHEN THEY CAN'T HEAR ME, THE PEOPLE WHO RUN TV NETWORKS ARE IDIOTS!

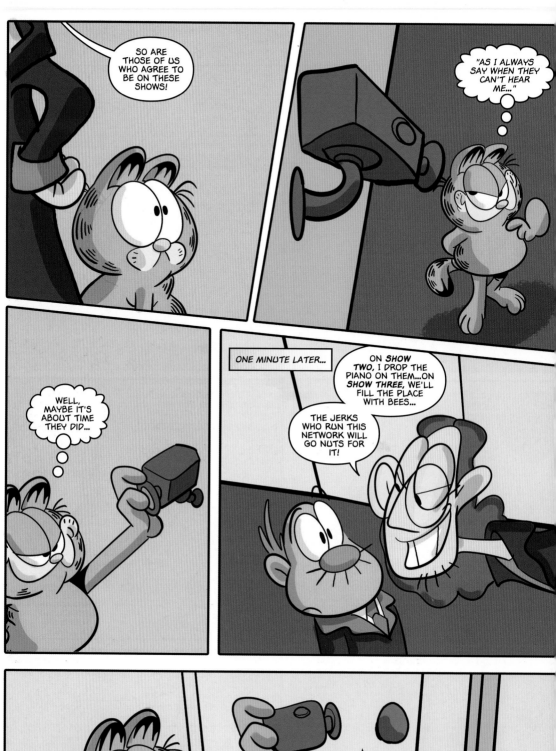

SO ARE THOSE OF US WHO AGREE TO BE ON THESE SHOWS!

"AS I ALWAYS SAY WHEN THEY CAN'T HEAR ME..."

WELL, MAYBE IT'S ABOUT TIME THEY DID...

ONE MINUTE LATER...

ON *SHOW TWO*, I DROP THE PIANO ON THEM...ON *SHOW THREE*, WE'LL FILL THE PLACE WITH BEES...

THE JERKS WHO RUN THIS NETWORK WILL GO NUTS FOR IT!

I DON'T KNOW WHERE THEY FIND SUCH DUMB PEOPLE...

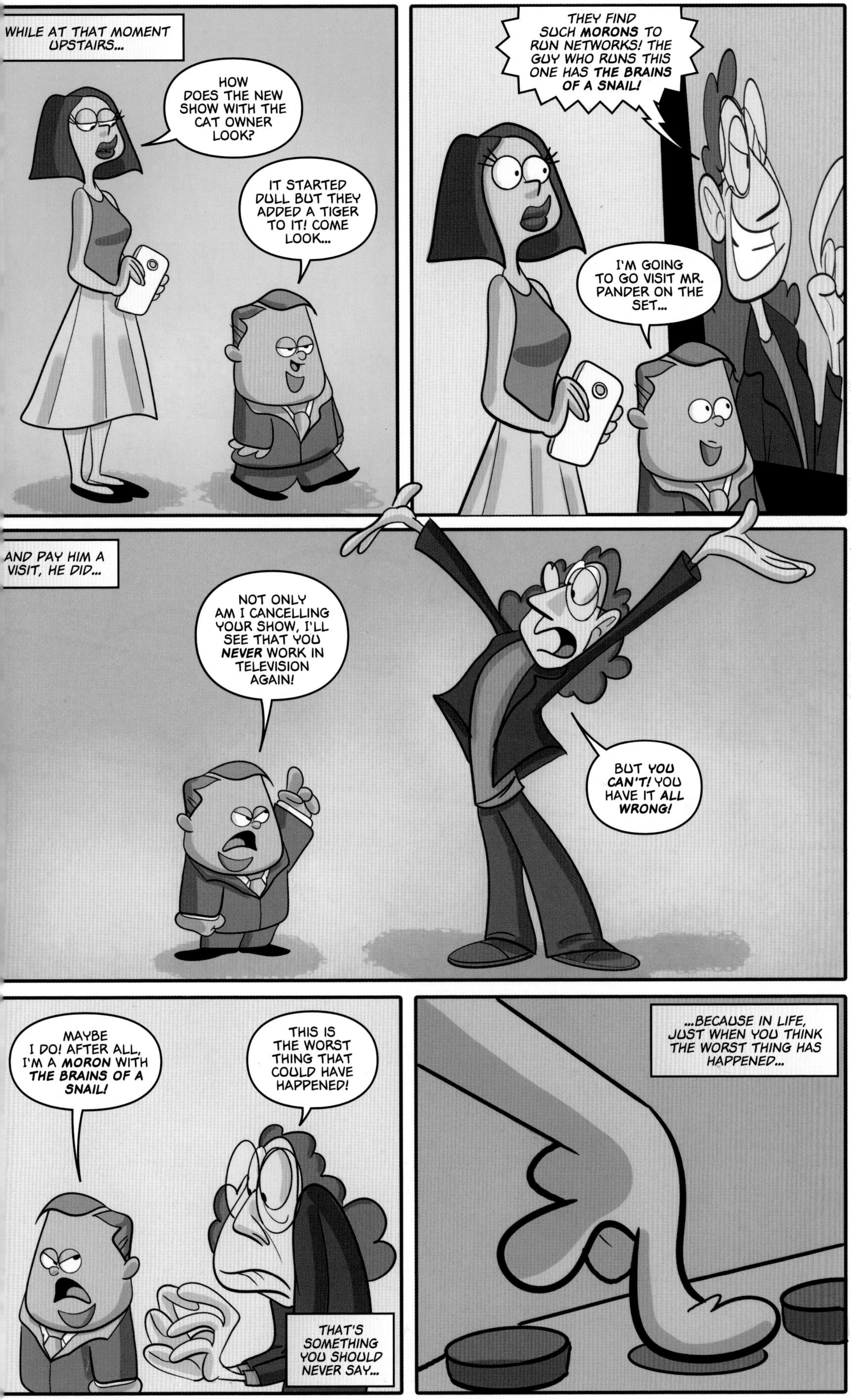

WHILE AT THAT MOMENT UPSTAIRS...
HOW DOES THE NEW SHOW WITH THE CAT OWNER LOOK?
IT STARTED DULL BUT THEY ADDED A TIGER TO IT! COME LOOK...
THEY FIND SUCH MORONS TO RUN NETWORKS! THE GUY WHO RUNS THIS ONE HAS THE BRAINS OF A SNAIL!
I'M GOING TO GO VISIT MR. PANDER ON THE SET...
AND PAY HIM A VISIT, HE DID...
NOT ONLY AM I CANCELLING YOUR SHOW, I'LL SEE THAT YOU NEVER WORK IN TELEVISION AGAIN!
BUT YOU CAN'T! YOU HAVE IT ALL WRONG!
MAYBE I DO! AFTER ALL, I'M A MORON WITH THE BRAINS OF A SNAIL!
THIS IS THE WORST THING THAT COULD HAVE HAPPENED!
THAT'S SOMETHING YOU SHOULD NEVER SAY...
...BECAUSE IN LIFE, JUST WHEN YOU THINK THE WORST THING HAS HAPPENED...

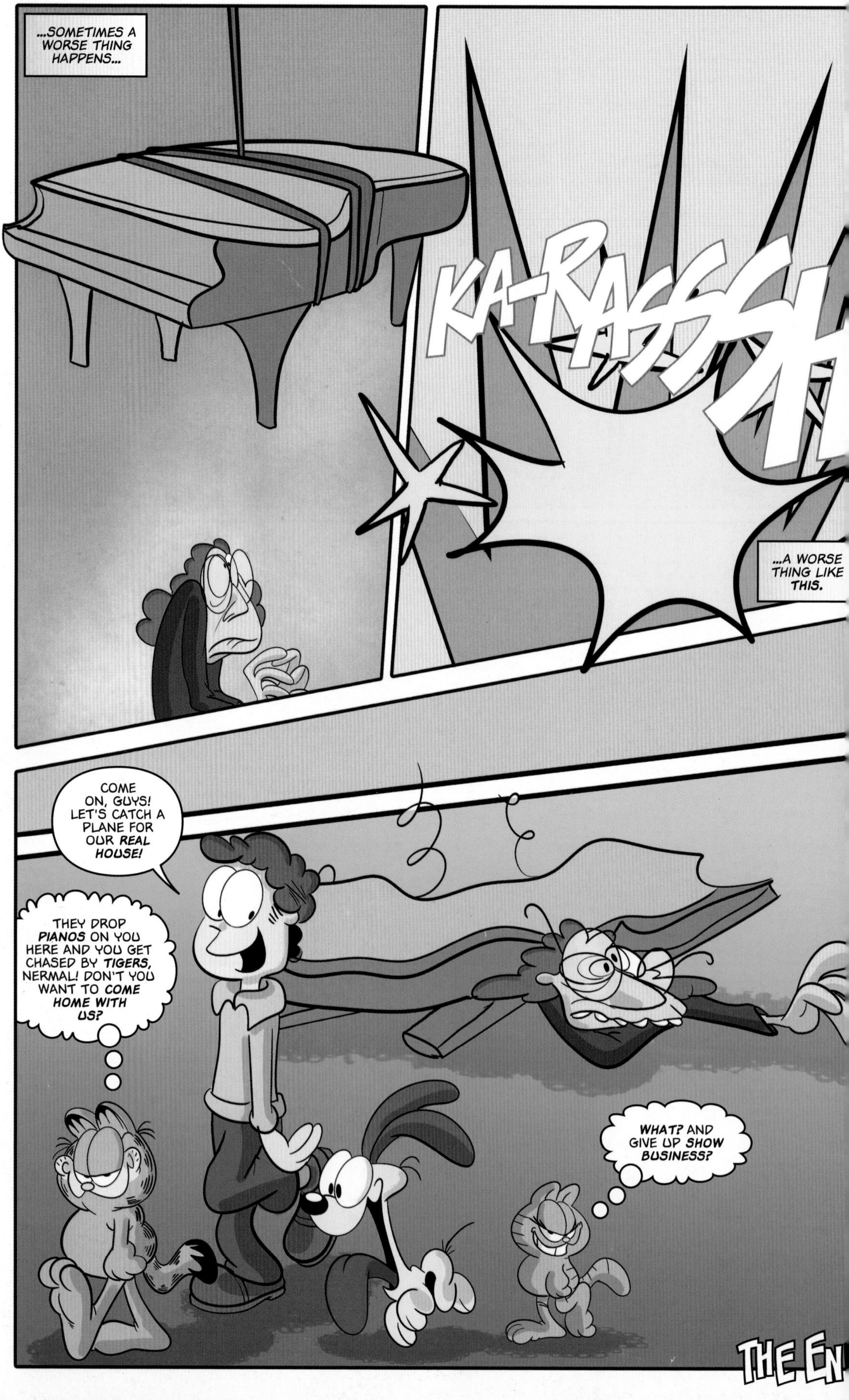
...SOMETIMES A WORSE THING HAPPENS...
KA-RASSSH
...A WORSE THING LIKE THIS.
COME ON, GUYS! LET'S CATCH A PLANE FOR OUR REAL HOUSE!
THEY DROP PIANOS ON YOU HERE AND YOU GET CHASED BY TIGERS, NERMAL! DON'T YOU WANT TO COME HOME WITH US?
WHAT? AND GIVE UP SHOW BUSINESS?
THE EN

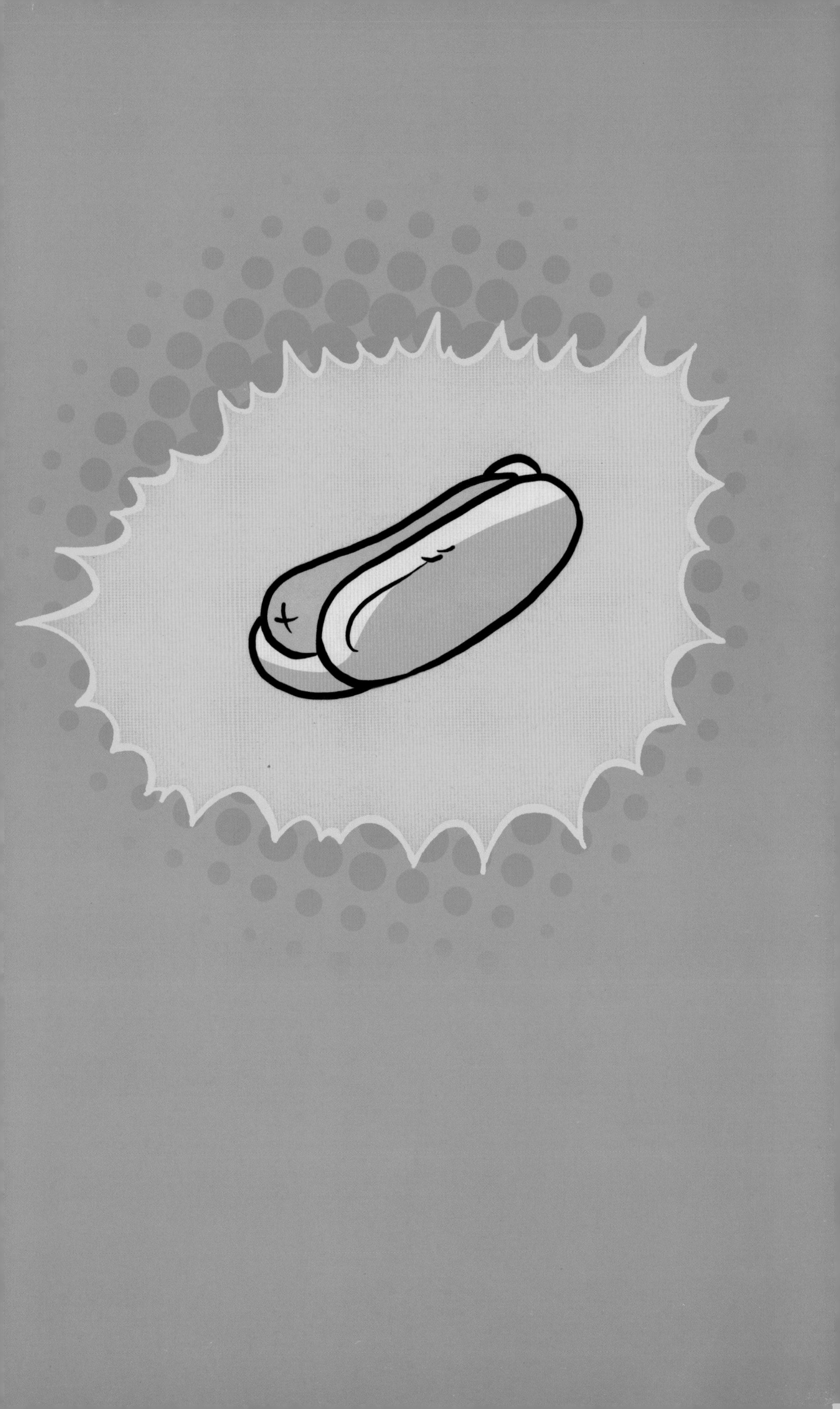

# Comedy of Terrors

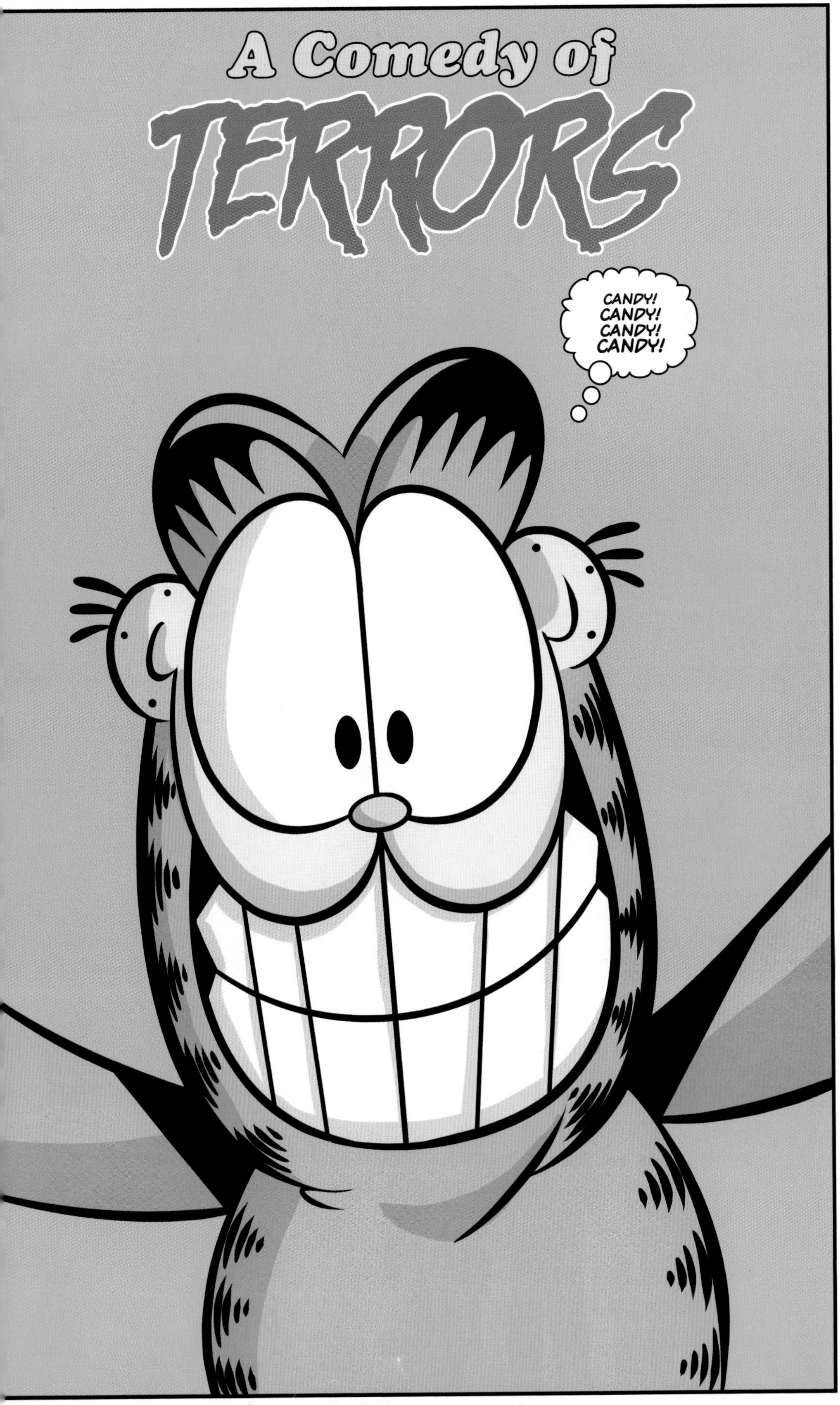
A Comedy of
TERRORS
CANDY!
CANDY!
CANDY!
CANDY!

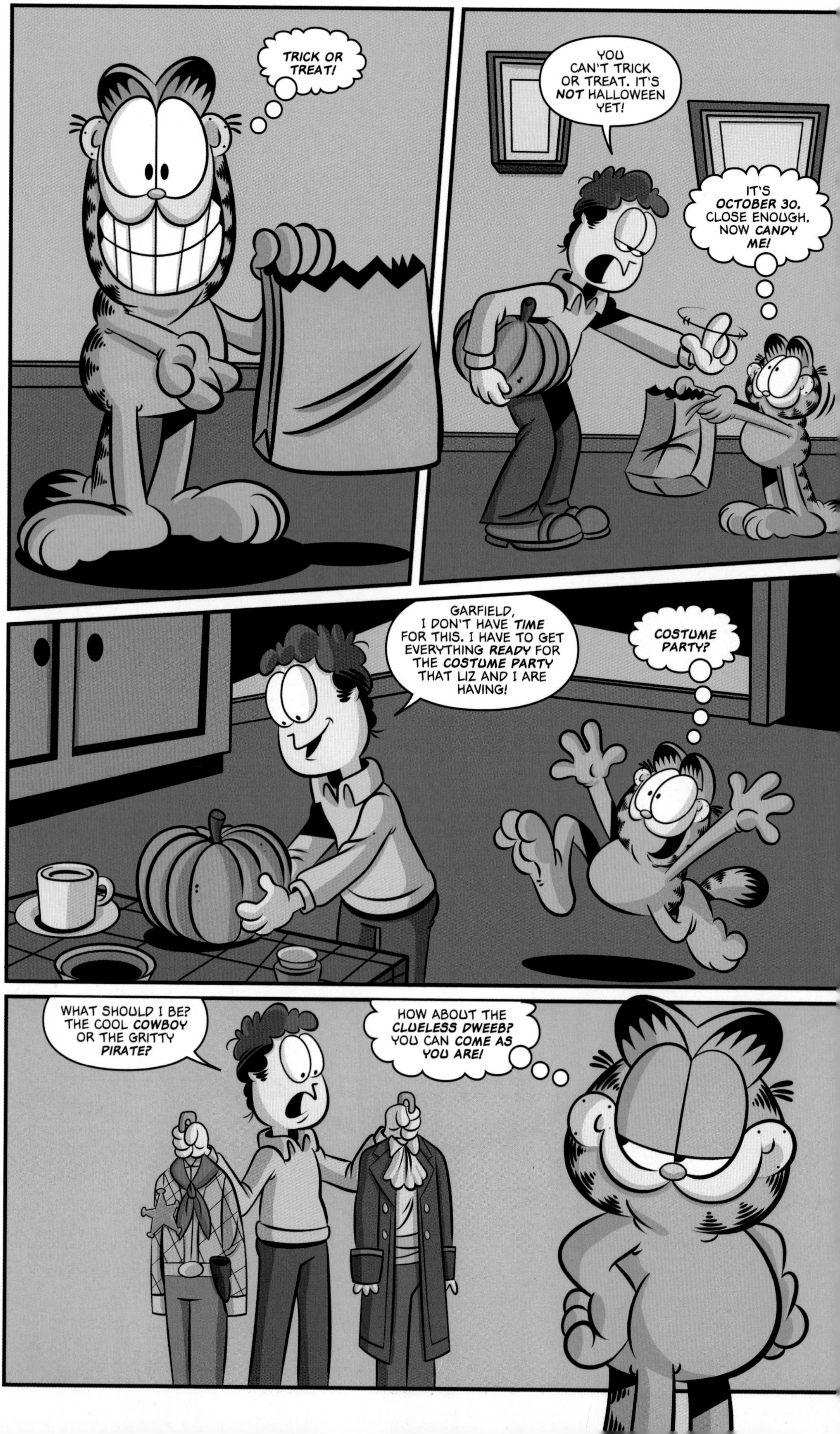
TRICK OR TREAT!
YOU CAN'T TRICK OR TREAT. IT'S NOT HALLOWEEN YET!
IT'S OCTOBER 30. CLOSE ENOUGH. NOW CANDY ME!
GARFIELD, I DON'T HAVE TIME FOR THIS. I HAVE TO GET EVERYTHING READY FOR THE COSTUME PARTY THAT LIZ AND I ARE HAVING!
COSTUME PARTY?
WHAT SHOULD I BE? THE COOL COWBOY OR THE GRITTY PIRATE?
HOW ABOUT THE CLUELESS DWEEB? YOU CAN COME AS YOU ARE!

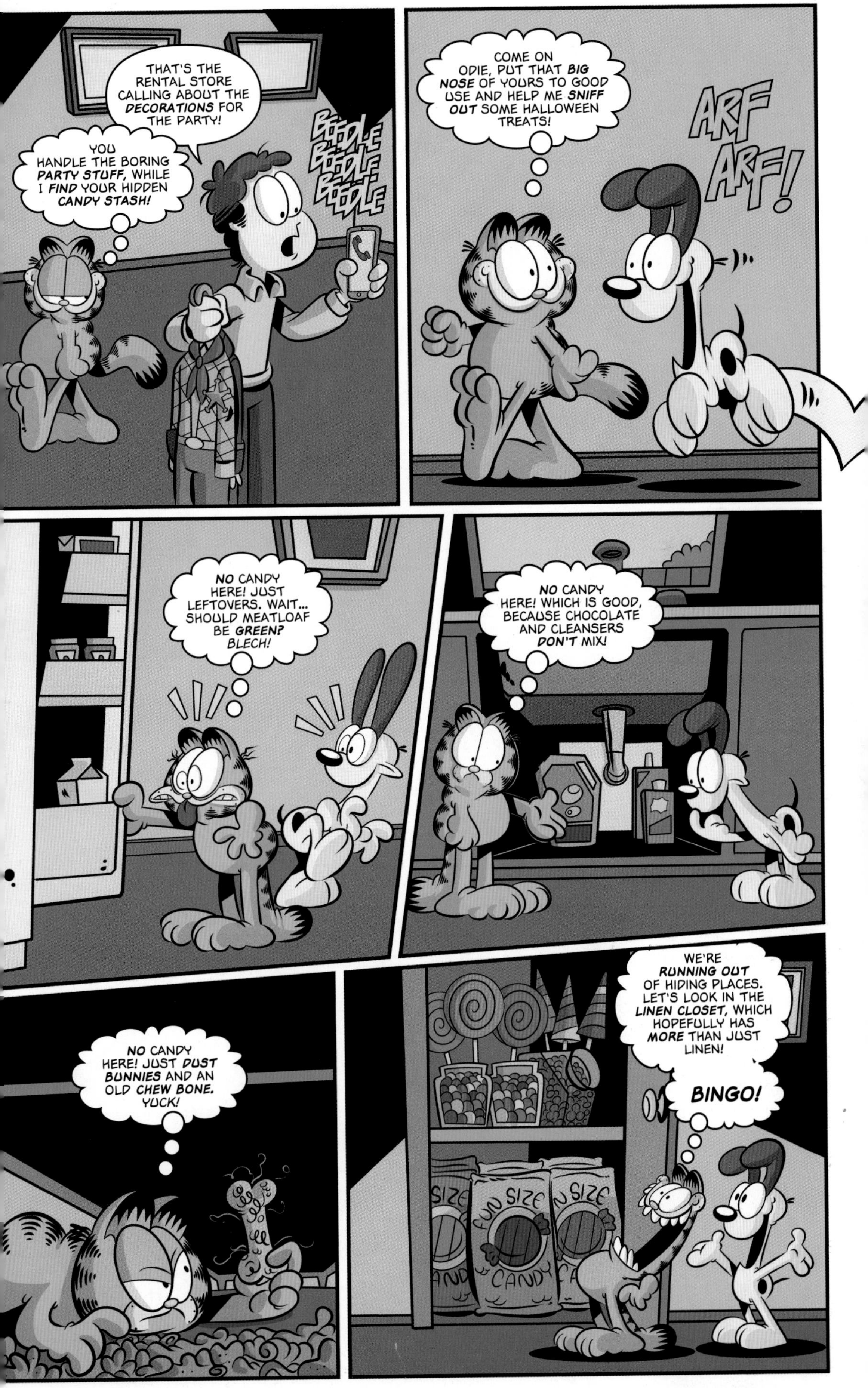
THAT'S THE RENTAL STORE CALLING ABOUT THE DECORATIONS FOR THE PARTY!
YOU HANDLE THE BORING PARTY STUFF, WHILE I FIND YOUR HIDDEN CANDY STASH!
BEEDLE BEEDLE BEEDLE
COME ON ODIE, PUT THAT BIG NOSE OF YOURS TO GOOD USE AND HELP ME SNIFF OUT SOME HALLOWEEN TREATS!
ARF ARF!
NO CANDY HERE! JUST LEFTOVERS. WAIT... SHOULD MEATLOAF BE GREEN? BLECH!
NO CANDY HERE! WHICH IS GOOD, BECAUSE CHOCOLATE AND CLEANSERS DON'T MIX!
NO CANDY HERE! JUST DUST BUNNIES AND AN OLD CHEW BONE. YUCK!
WE'RE RUNNING OUT OF HIDING PLACES. LET'S LOOK IN THE LINEN CLOSET, WHICH HOPEFULLY HAS MORE THAN JUST LINEN!
BINGO!
FUN SIZE CANDY

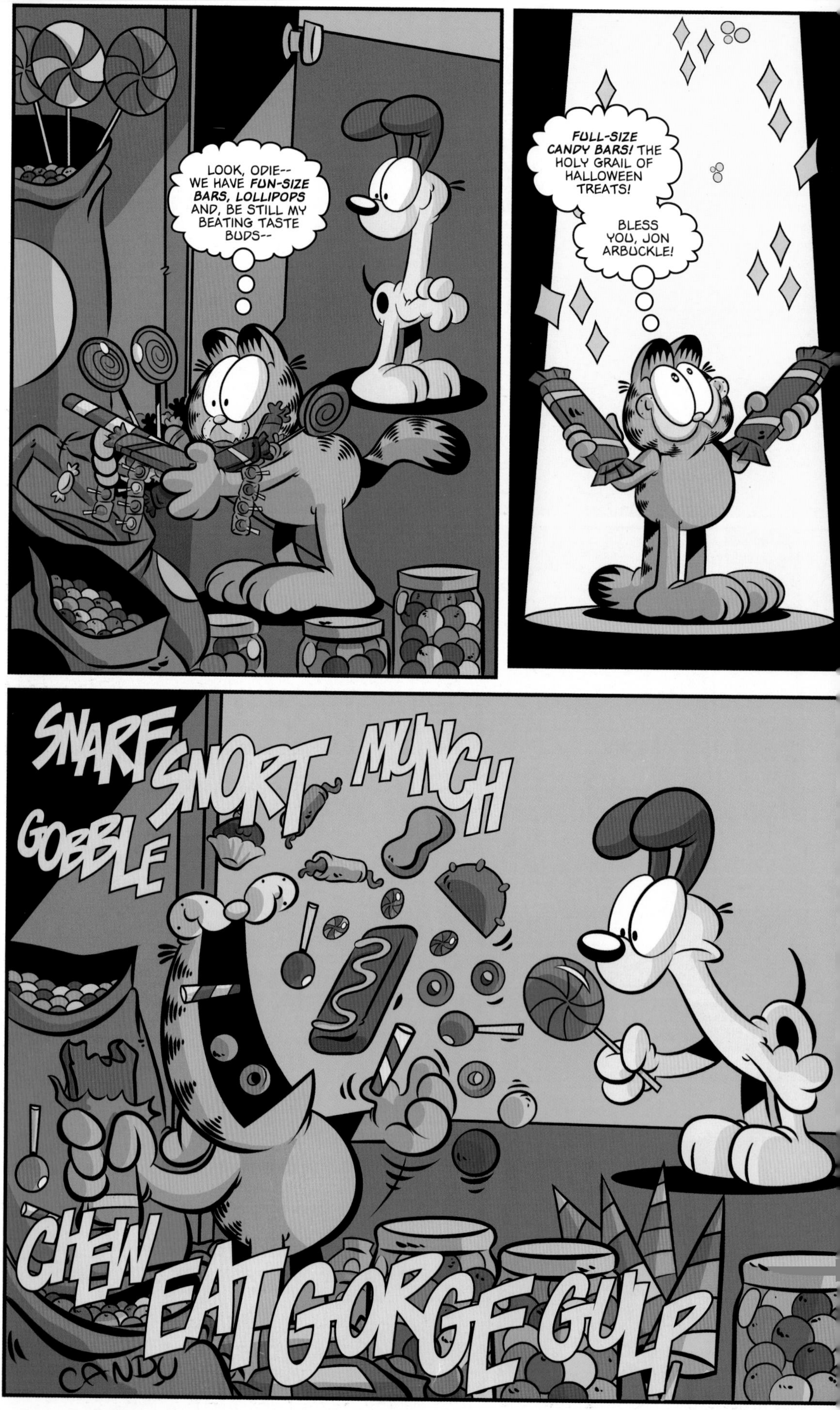
LOOK, ODIE-- WE HAVE FUN-SIZE BARS, LOLLIPOPS AND, BE STILL MY BEATING TASTE BUDS--
FULL-SIZE CANDY BARS! THE HOLY GRAIL OF HALLOWEEN TREATS!
BLESS YOU, JON ARBUCKLE!
SNARF
SNORT
MUNCH
GOBBLE
CHEW
EAT
GORGE
GULP
CANDY

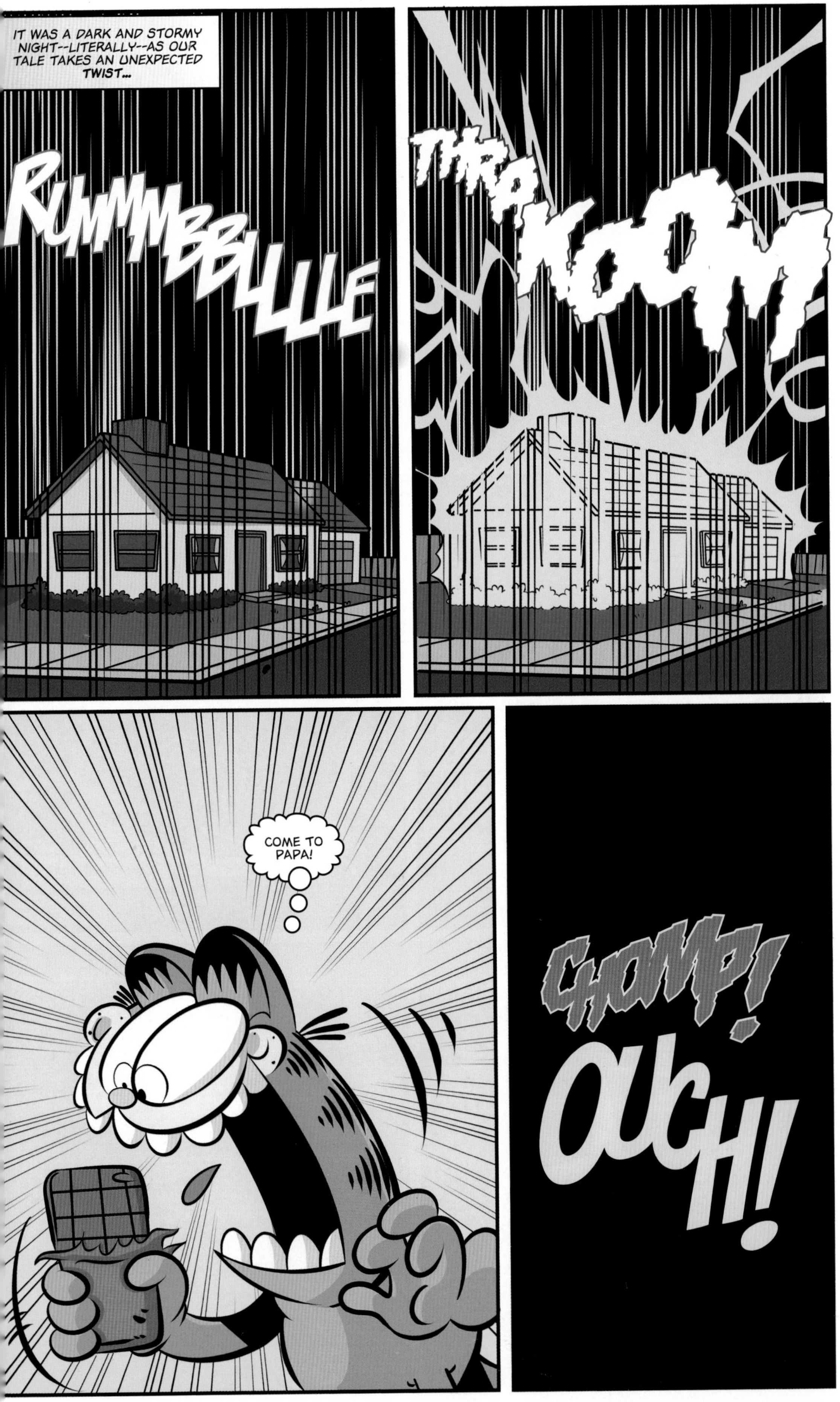
IT WAS A DARK AND STORMY NIGHT--LITERALLY--AS OUR TALE TAKES AN UNEXPECTED TWIST...
RUMMMBBLLLLE
THRA KOOM!
COME TO PAPA!
CHOMP!
OUCH!

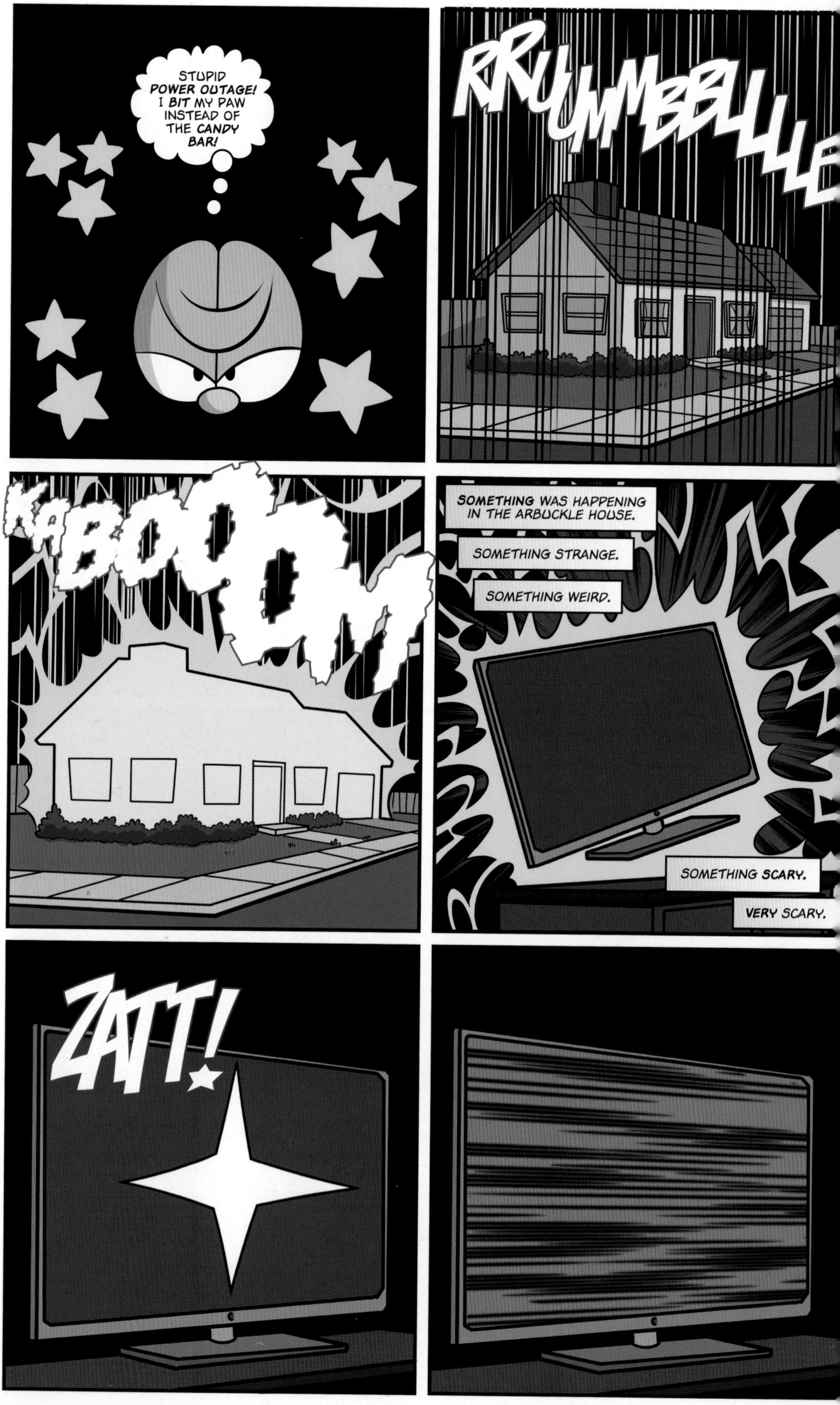
STUPID POWER OUTAGE! I BIT MY PAW INSTEAD OF THE CANDY BAR!
RRRUUMMBBLLLLE
KABOOOM
SOMETHING WAS HAPPENING IN THE ARBUCKLE HOUSE.
SOMETHING STRANGE.
SOMETHING WEIRD.
SOMETHING SCARY.
VERY SCARY.
ZATT!

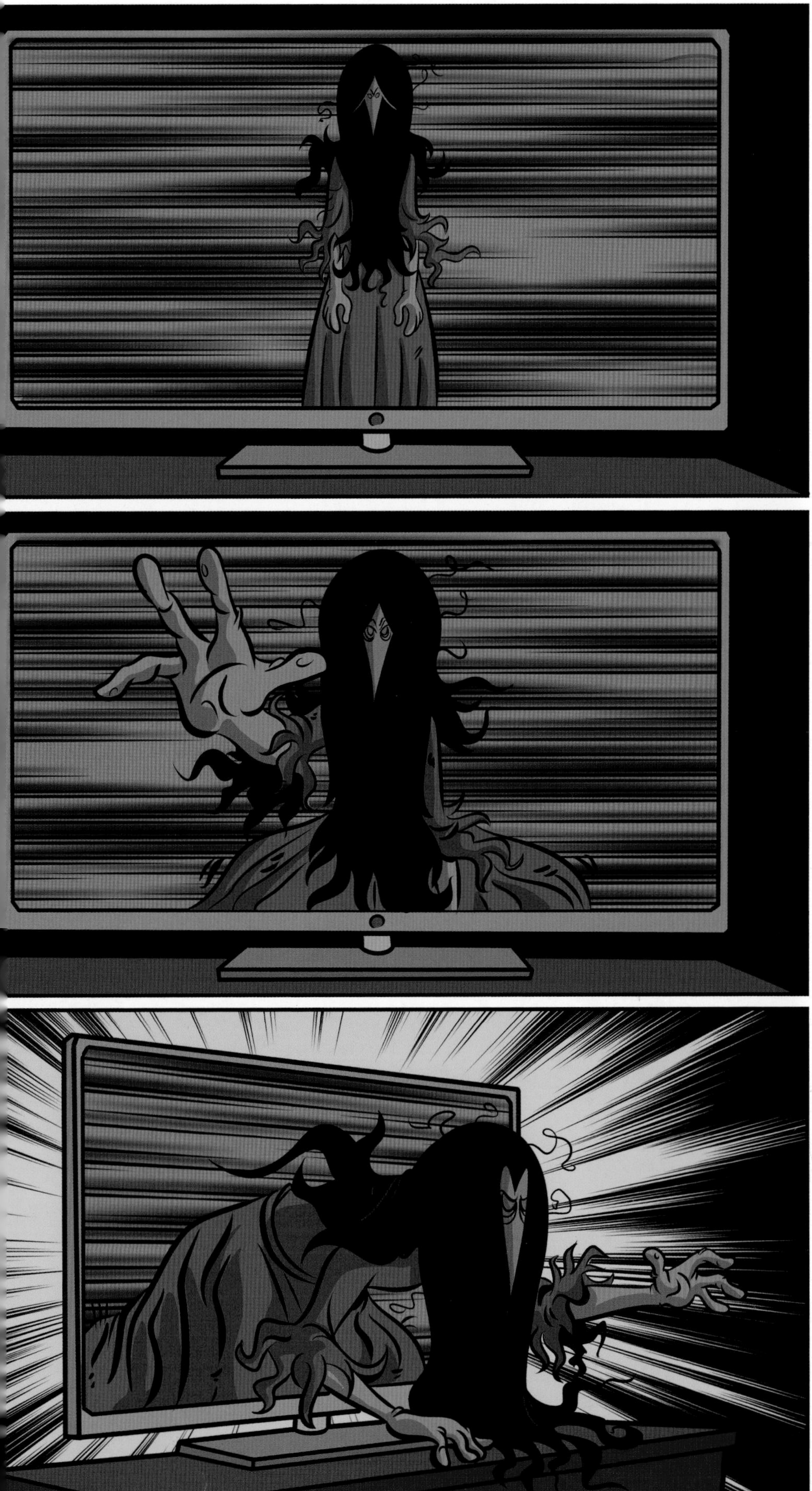

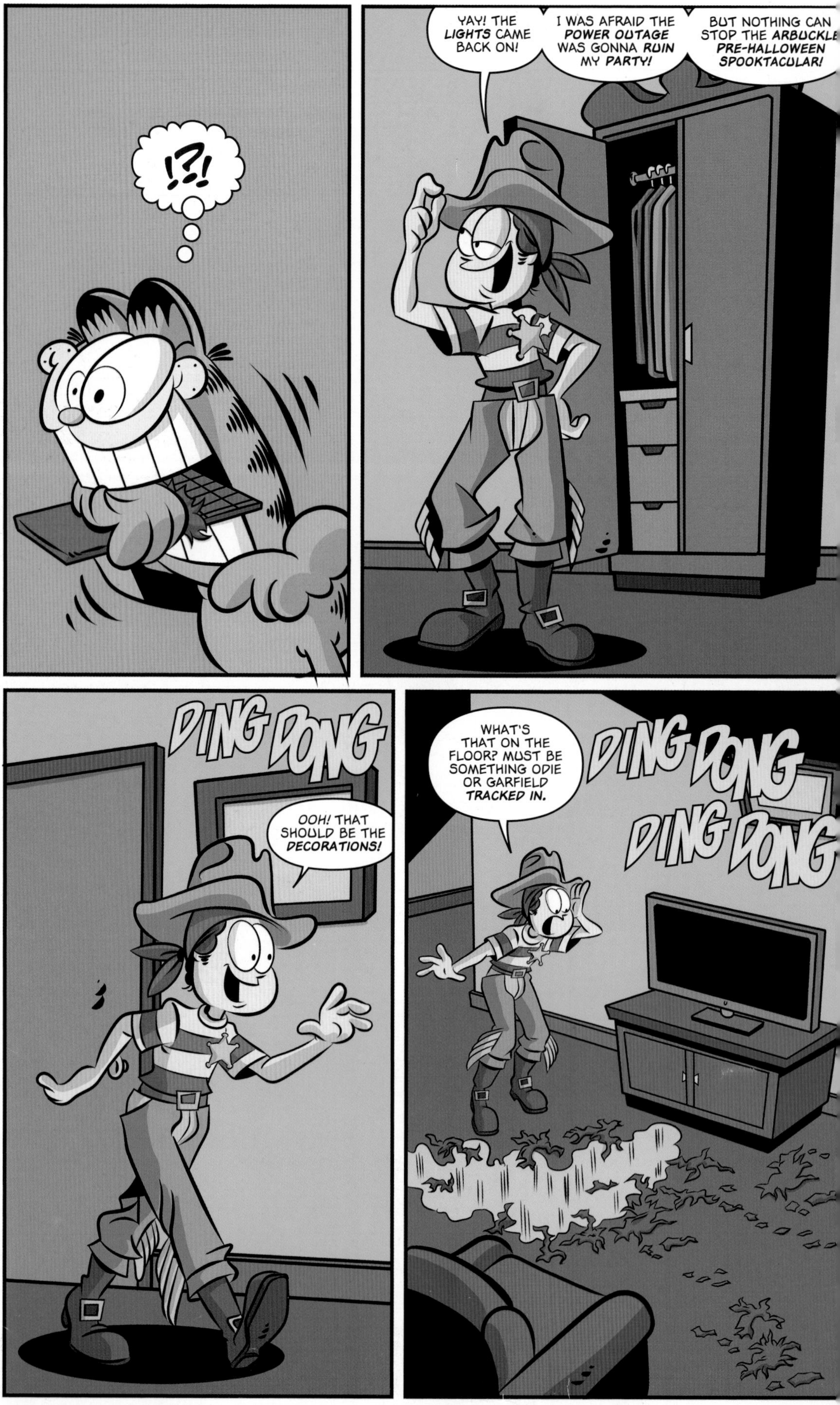
!?!
YAY! THE LIGHTS CAME BACK ON!
I WAS AFRAID THE POWER OUTAGE WAS GONNA RUIN MY PARTY!
BUT NOTHING CAN STOP THE ARBUCKLE PRE-HALLOWEEN SPOOKTACULAR!
DING DONG
OOH! THAT SHOULD BE THE DECORATIONS!
WHAT'S THAT ON THE FLOOR? MUST BE SOMETHING ODIE OR GARFIELD TRACKED IN.
DING DONG
DING DONG

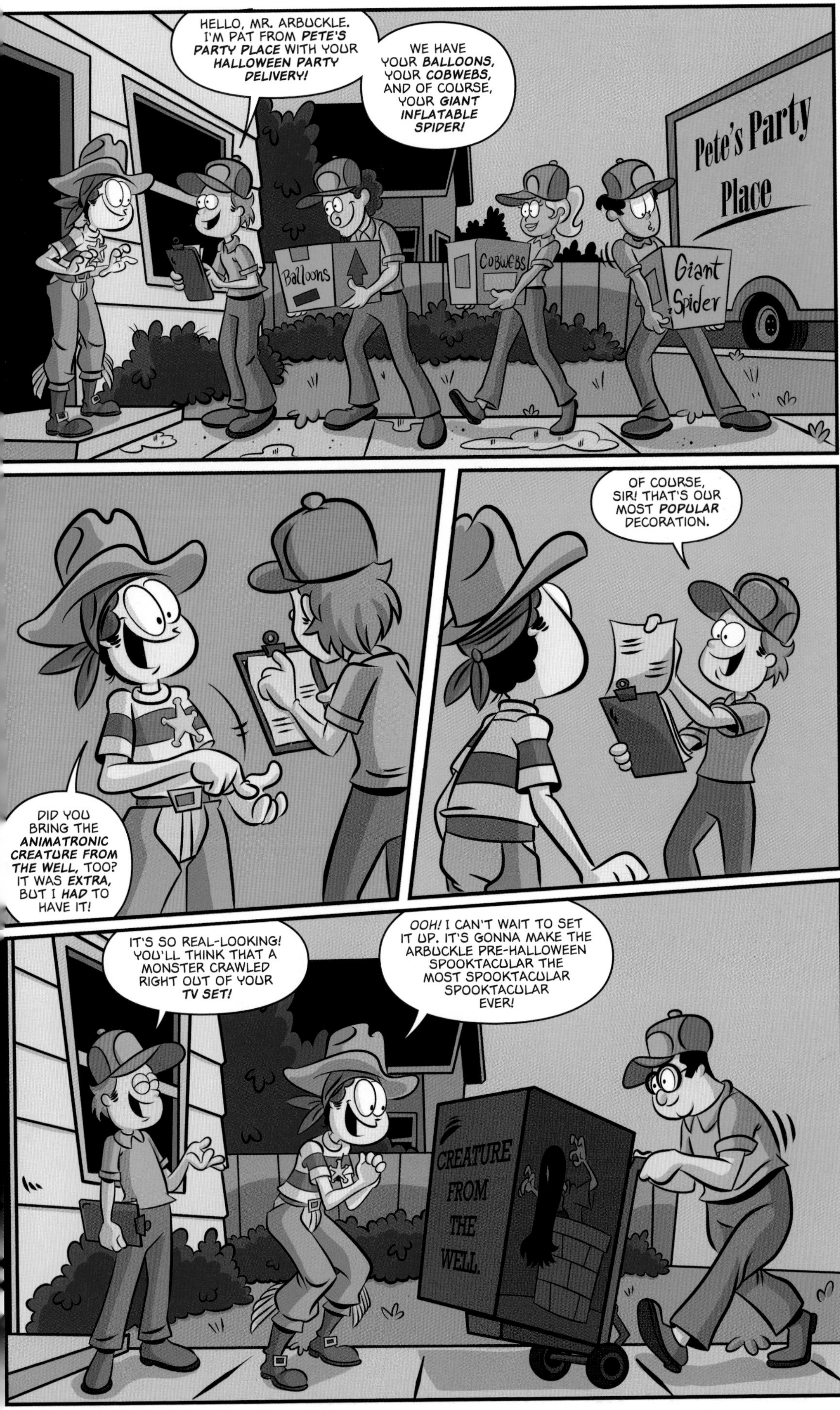
HELLO, MR. ARBUCKLE. I'M PAT FROM PETE'S PARTY PLACE WITH YOUR HALLOWEEN PARTY DELIVERY!
WE HAVE YOUR BALLOONS, YOUR COBWEBS, AND OF COURSE, YOUR GIANT INFLATABLE SPIDER!
Pete's Party Place
Balloons
COBWEBS
Giant Spider
DID YOU BRING THE ANIMATRONIC CREATURE FROM THE WELL, TOO? IT WAS EXTRA, BUT I HAD TO HAVE IT!
OF COURSE, SIR! THAT'S OUR MOST POPULAR DECORATION.
IT'S SO REAL-LOOKING! YOU'LL THINK THAT A MONSTER CRAWLED RIGHT OUT OF YOUR TV SET!
OOH! I CAN'T WAIT TO SET IT UP. IT'S GONNA MAKE THE ARBUCKLE PRE-HALLOWEEN SPOOKTACULAR THE MOST SPOOKTACULAR SPOOKTACULAR EVER!
CREATURE FROM THE WELL.

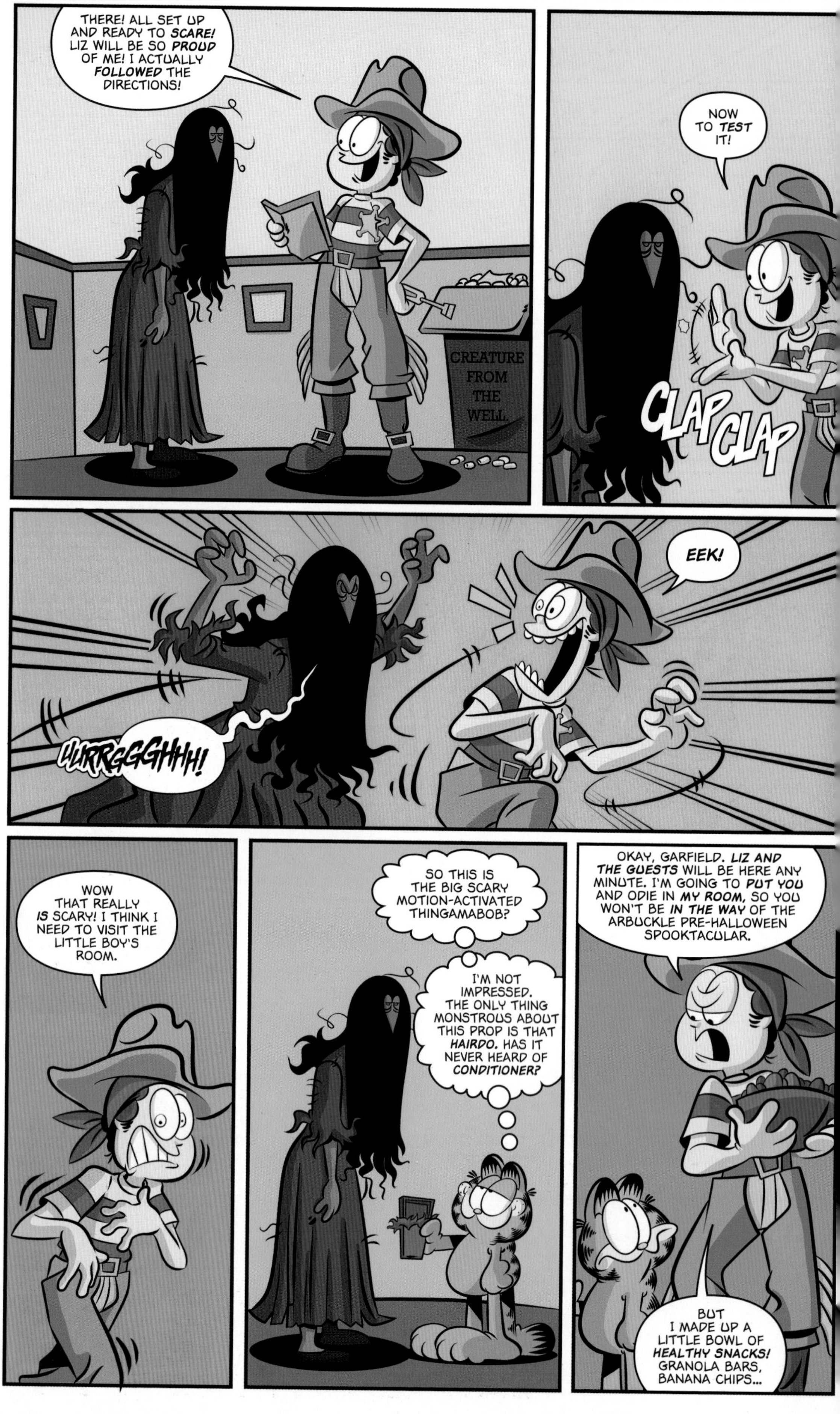
THERE! ALL SET UP AND READY TO *SCARE!* LIZ WILL BE SO *PROUD* OF ME! I ACTUALLY *FOLLOWED* THE DIRECTIONS!
CREATURE FROM THE WELL.
NOW TO *TEST* IT!
CLAP CLAP
EEK!
UURRGGGHHH!
WOW THAT REALLY *IS* SCARY! I THINK I NEED TO VISIT THE LITTLE BOY'S ROOM.
SO THIS IS THE BIG SCARY MOTION-ACTIVATED THINGAMABOB?
I'M NOT IMPRESSED. THE ONLY THING MONSTROUS ABOUT THIS PROP IS THAT *HAIRDO.* HAS IT NEVER HEARD OF *CONDITIONER?*
OKAY, GARFIELD. *LIZ AND THE GUESTS* WILL BE HERE ANY MINUTE. I'M GOING TO *PUT YOU* AND ODIE IN *MY ROOM,* SO YOU WON'T BE *IN THE WAY* OF THE ARBUCKLE PRE-HALLOWEEN SPOOKTACULAR.
BUT I MADE UP A LITTLE BOWL OF *HEALTHY SNACKS!* GRANOLA BARS, BANANA CHIPS...

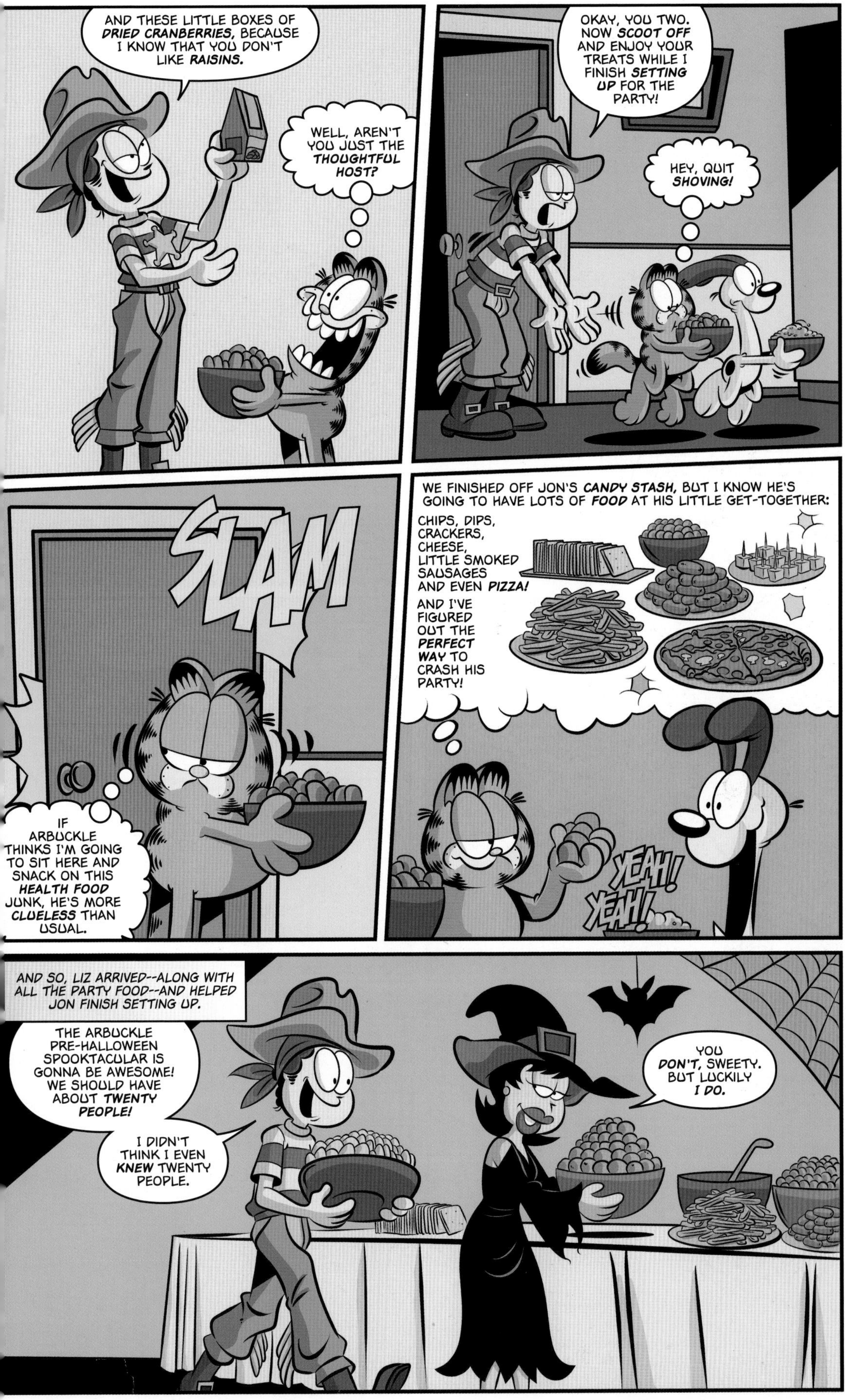
AND THESE LITTLE BOXES OF DRIED CRANBERRIES, BECAUSE I KNOW THAT YOU DON'T LIKE RAISINS.
WELL, AREN'T YOU JUST THE THOUGHTFUL HOST?
OKAY, YOU TWO. NOW SCOOT OFF AND ENJOY YOUR TREATS WHILE I FINISH SETTING UP FOR THE PARTY!
HEY, QUIT SHOVING!
SLAM
IF ARBUCKLE THINKS I'M GOING TO SIT HERE AND SNACK ON THIS HEALTH FOOD JUNK, HE'S MORE CLUELESS THAN USUAL.
WE FINISHED OFF JON'S CANDY STASH, BUT I KNOW HE'S GOING TO HAVE LOTS OF FOOD AT HIS LITTLE GET-TOGETHER:
CHIPS, DIPS, CRACKERS, CHEESE, LITTLE SMOKED SAUSAGES AND EVEN PIZZA!
AND I'VE FIGURED OUT THE PERFECT WAY TO CRASH HIS PARTY!
YEAH! YEAH!
AND SO, LIZ ARRIVED--ALONG WITH ALL THE PARTY FOOD--AND HELPED JON FINISH SETTING UP.
THE ARBUCKLE PRE-HALLOWEEN SPOOKTACULAR IS GONNA BE AWESOME! WE SHOULD HAVE ABOUT TWENTY PEOPLE!
I DIDN'T THINK I EVEN KNEW TWENTY PEOPLE.
YOU DON'T, SWEETY. BUT LUCKILY I DO.

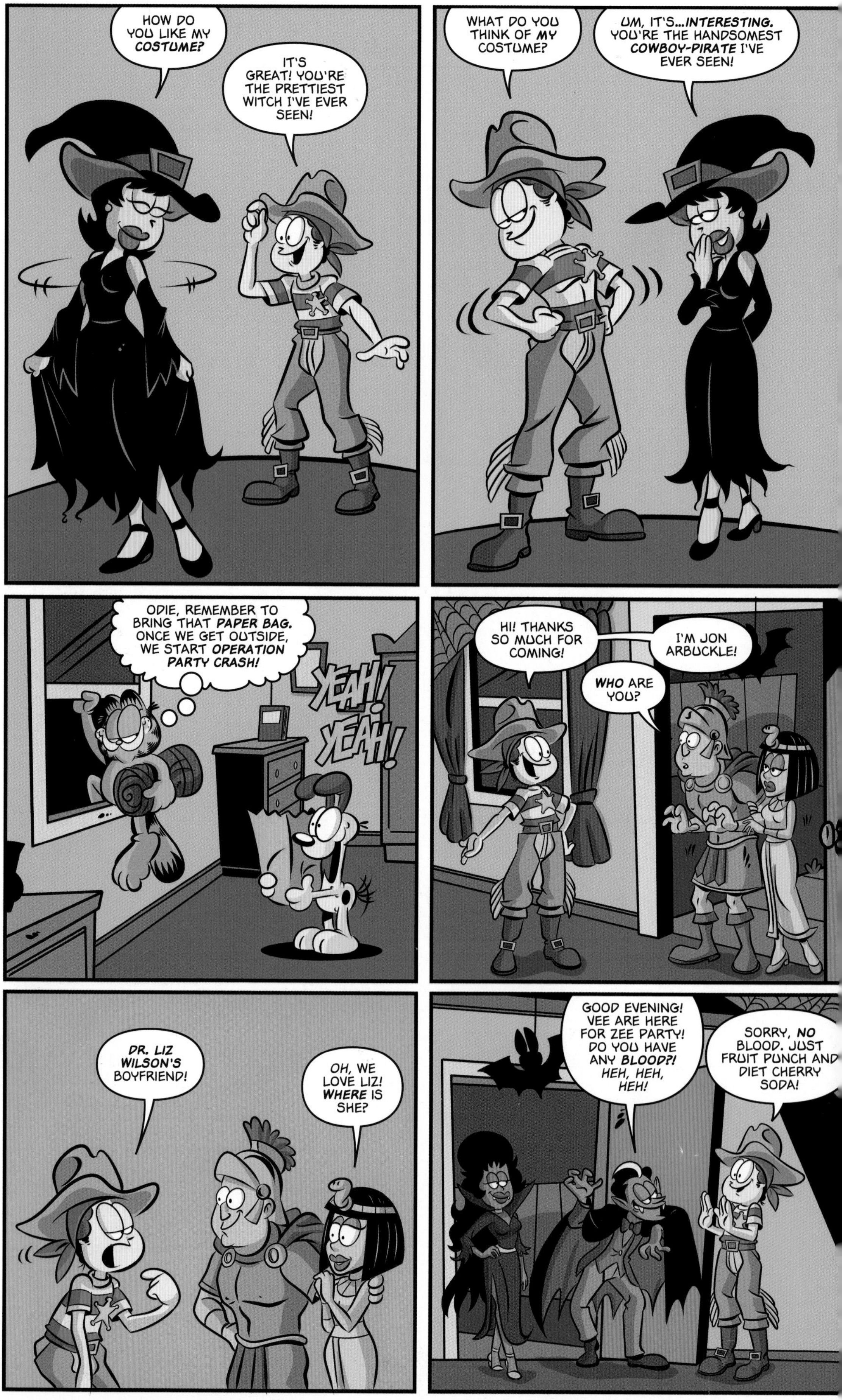
HOW DO YOU LIKE MY COSTUME?
IT'S GREAT! YOU'RE THE PRETTIEST WITCH I'VE EVER SEEN!
WHAT DO YOU THINK OF MY COSTUME?
UM, IT'S...INTERESTING. YOU'RE THE HANDSOMEST COWBOY-PIRATE I'VE EVER SEEN!
ODIE, REMEMBER TO BRING THAT PAPER BAG. ONCE WE GET OUTSIDE, WE START OPERATION PARTY CRASH!
YEAH! YEAH!
HI! THANKS SO MUCH FOR COMING!
I'M JON ARBUCKLE!
WHO ARE YOU?
DR. LIZ WILSON'S BOYFRIEND!
OH, WE LOVE LIZ! WHERE IS SHE?
GOOD EVENING! VEE ARE HERE FOR ZEE PARTY! DO YOU HAVE ANY BLOOD?! HEH, HEH, HEH!
SORRY, NO BLOOD. JUST FRUIT PUNCH AND DIET CHERRY SODA!

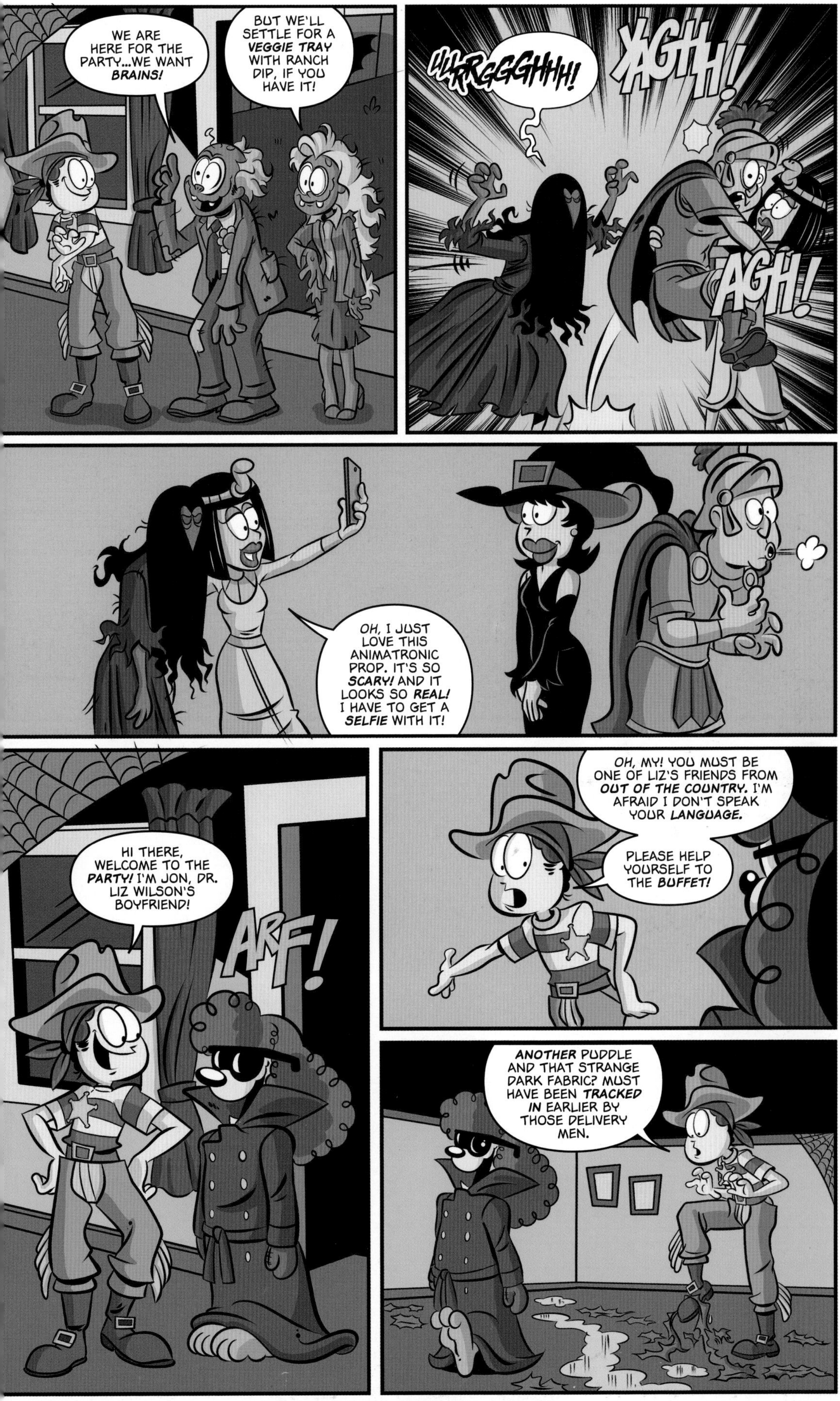
WE ARE HERE FOR THE PARTY...WE WANT BRAINS!
BUT WE'LL SETTLE FOR A VEGGIE TRAY WITH RANCH DIP, IF YOU HAVE IT!
UURRGGGHHH!
YAGHH!
AGH!
OH, I JUST LOVE THIS ANIMATRONIC PROP. IT'S SO SCARY! AND IT LOOKS SO REAL! I HAVE TO GET A SELFIE WITH IT!
HI THERE, WELCOME TO THE PARTY! I'M JON, DR. LIZ WILSON'S BOYFRIEND!
ARF!
OH, MY! YOU MUST BE ONE OF LIZ'S FRIENDS FROM OUT OF THE COUNTRY. I'M AFRAID I DON'T SPEAK YOUR LANGUAGE.
PLEASE HELP YOURSELF TO THE BUFFET!
ANOTHER PUDDLE AND THAT STRANGE DARK FABRIC? MUST HAVE BEEN TRACKED IN EARLIER BY THOSE DELIVERY MEN.

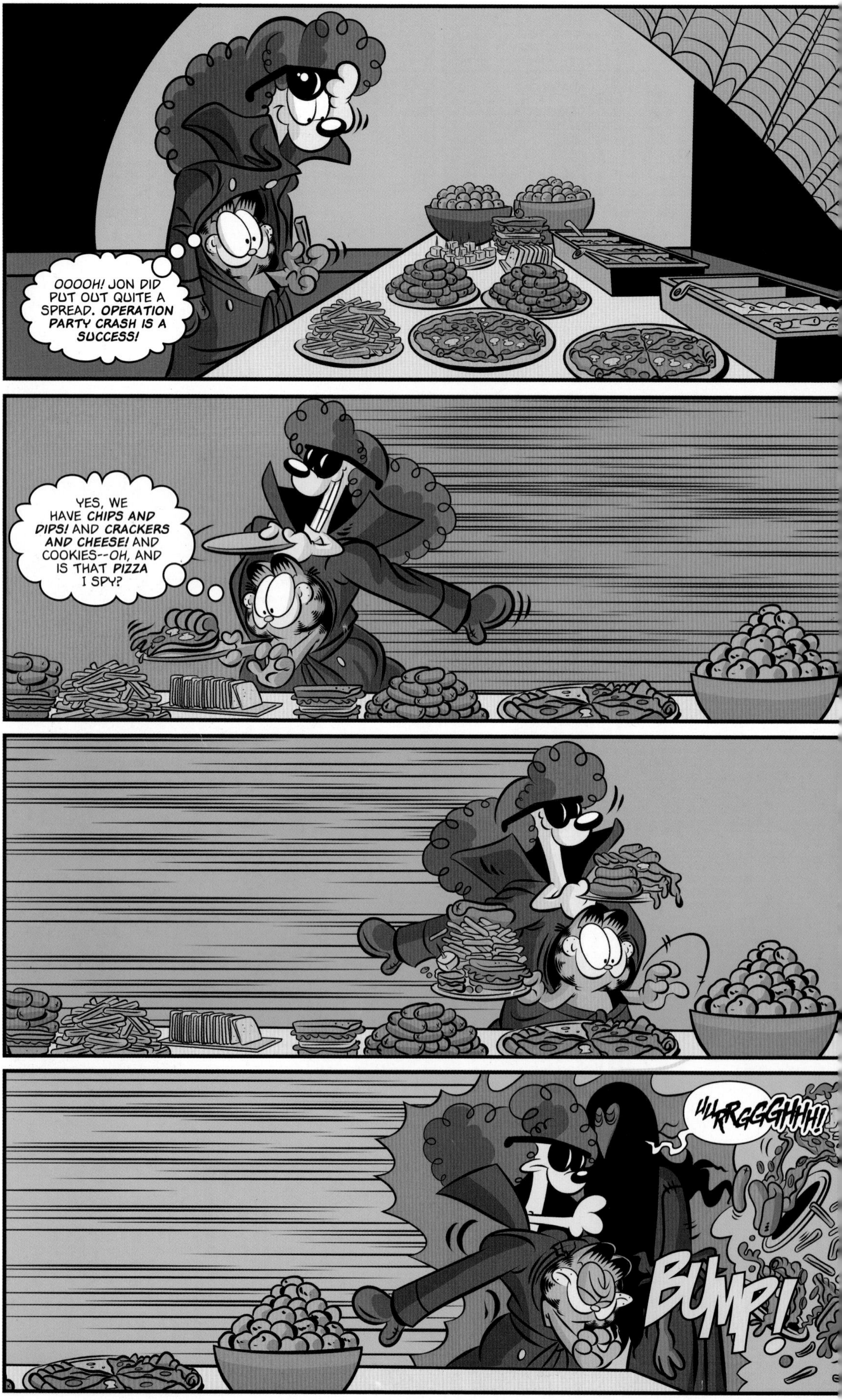
OOOOH! JON DID PUT OUT QUITE A SPREAD. OPERATION PARTY CRASH IS A SUCCESS!
YES, WE HAVE CHIPS AND DIPS! AND CRACKERS AND CHEESE! AND COOKIES--OH, AND IS THAT PIZZA I SPY?
ULLRRGGGHHH!
BUMP!

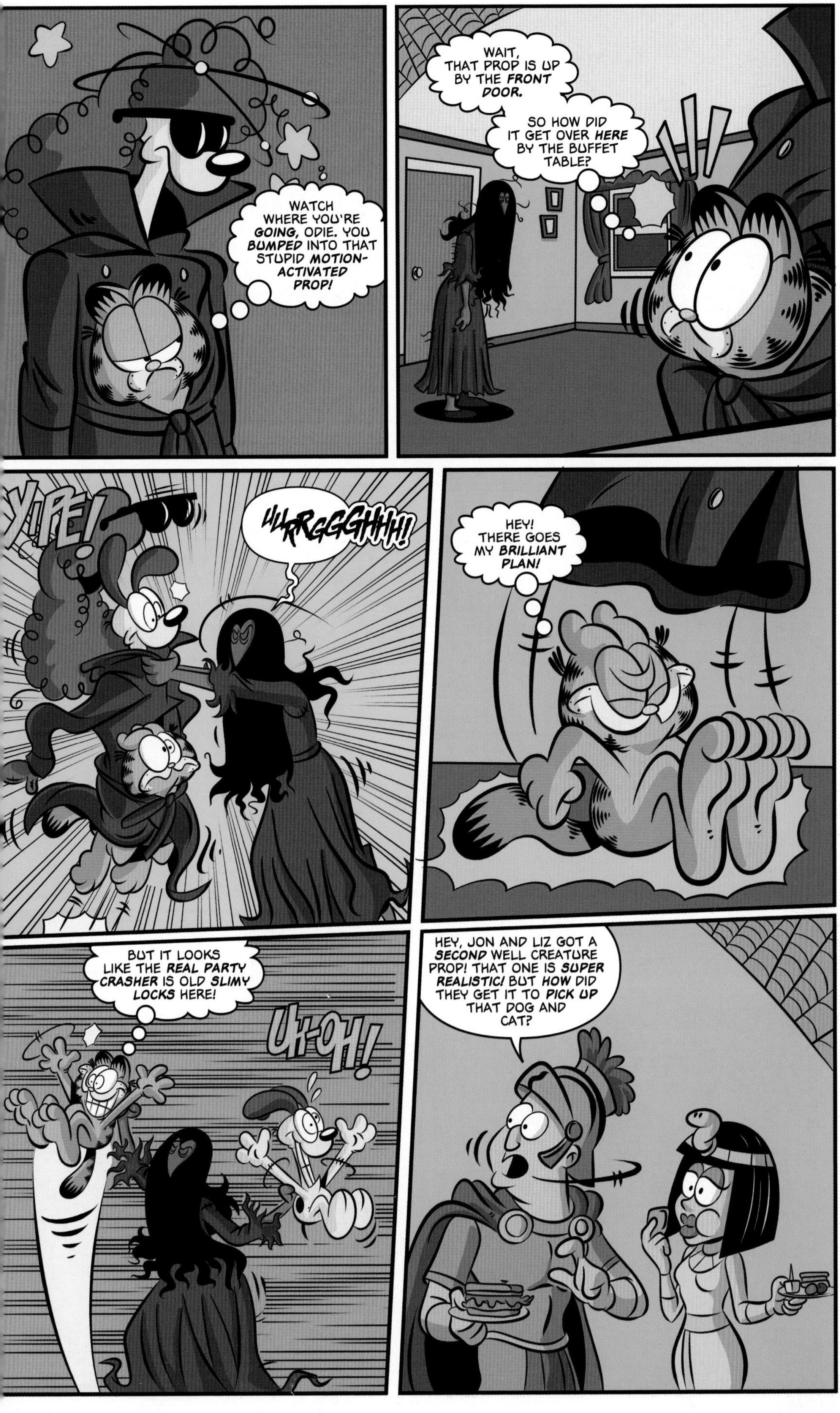
WATCH WHERE YOU'RE GOING, ODIE. YOU BUMPED INTO THAT STUPID MOTION-ACTIVATED PROP!
WAIT, THAT PROP IS UP BY THE FRONT DOOR.
SO HOW DID IT GET OVER HERE BY THE BUFFET TABLE?
YIPE!
UURRGGGHHH!
HEY! THERE GOES MY BRILLIANT PLAN!
BUT IT LOOKS LIKE THE REAL PARTY CRASHER IS OLD SLIMY LOCKS HERE!
UH-OH!
HEY, JON AND LIZ GOT A SECOND WELL CREATURE PROP! THAT ONE IS SUPER REALISTIC! BUT HOW DID THEY GET IT TO PICK UP THAT DOG AND CAT?

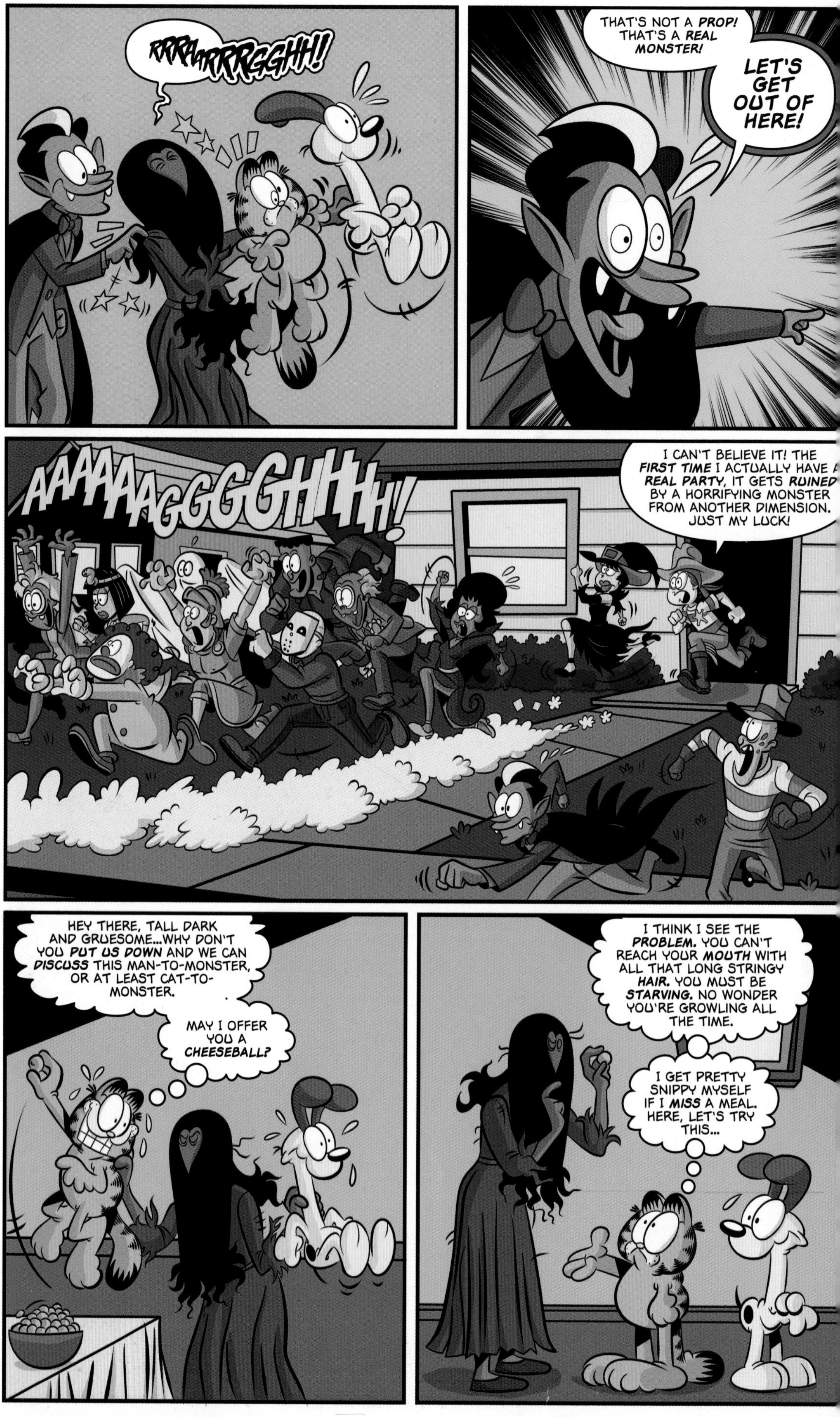

RRRAWRRRGGHH!
THAT'S NOT A PROP! THAT'S A REAL MONSTER!
LET'S GET OUT OF HERE!
AAAAAAAGGGGHHHHH!
I CAN'T BELIEVE IT! THE FIRST TIME I ACTUALLY HAVE A REAL PARTY, IT GETS RUINED BY A HORRIFYING MONSTER FROM ANOTHER DIMENSION. JUST MY LUCK!
HEY THERE, TALL DARK AND GRUESOME...WHY DON'T YOU PUT US DOWN AND WE CAN DISCUSS THIS MAN-TO-MONSTER, OR AT LEAST CAT-TO-MONSTER.
MAY I OFFER YOU A CHEESEBALL?
I THINK I SEE THE PROBLEM. YOU CAN'T REACH YOUR MOUTH WITH ALL THAT LONG STRINGY HAIR. YOU MUST BE STARVING. NO WONDER YOU'RE GROWLING ALL THE TIME.
I GET PRETTY SNIPPY MYSELF IF I MISS A MEAL. HERE, LET'S TRY THIS...

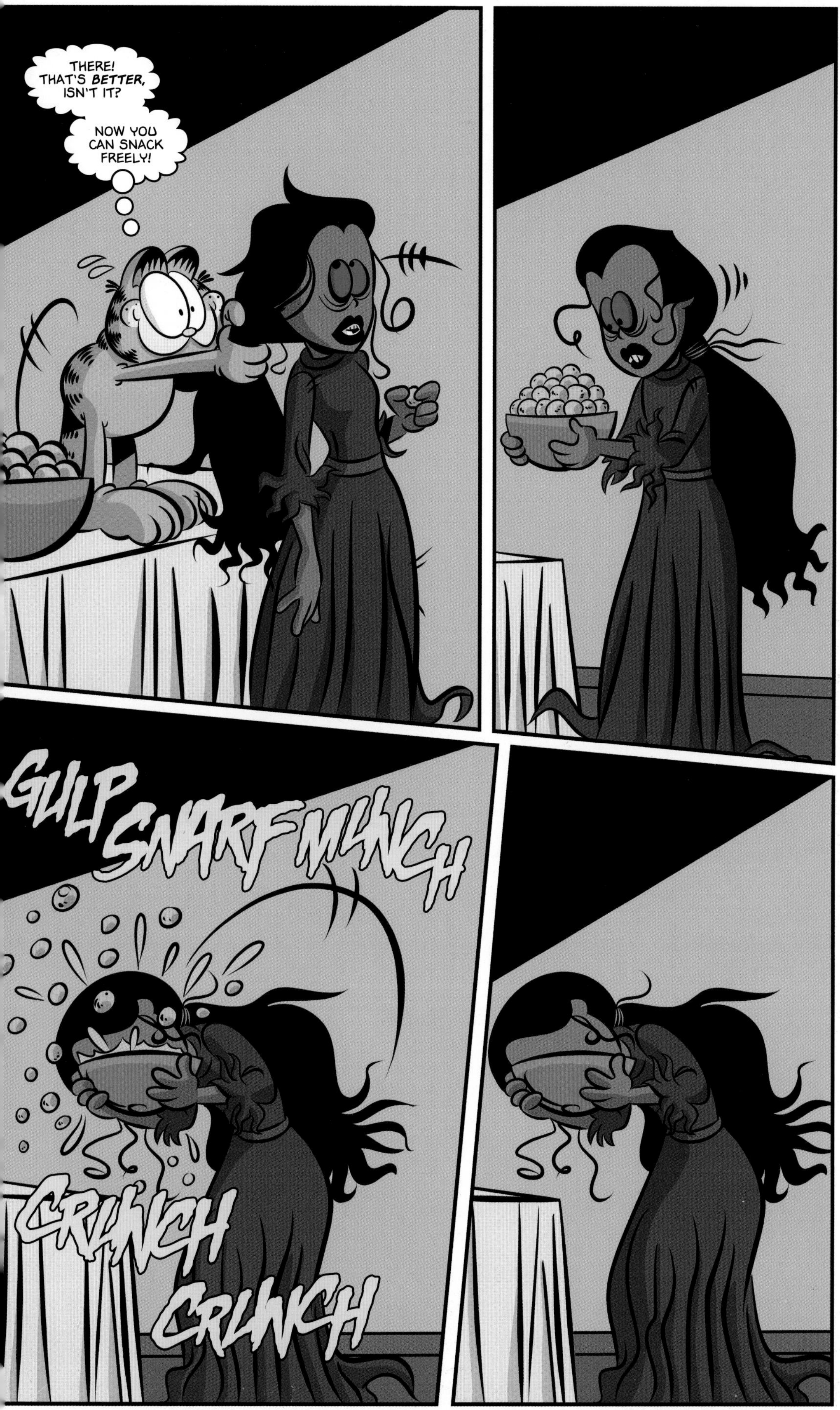
THERE! THAT'S *BETTER,* ISN'T IT?
NOW YOU CAN SNACK FREELY!
GULP
SNARF
MUNCH
CRUNCH
CRUNCH

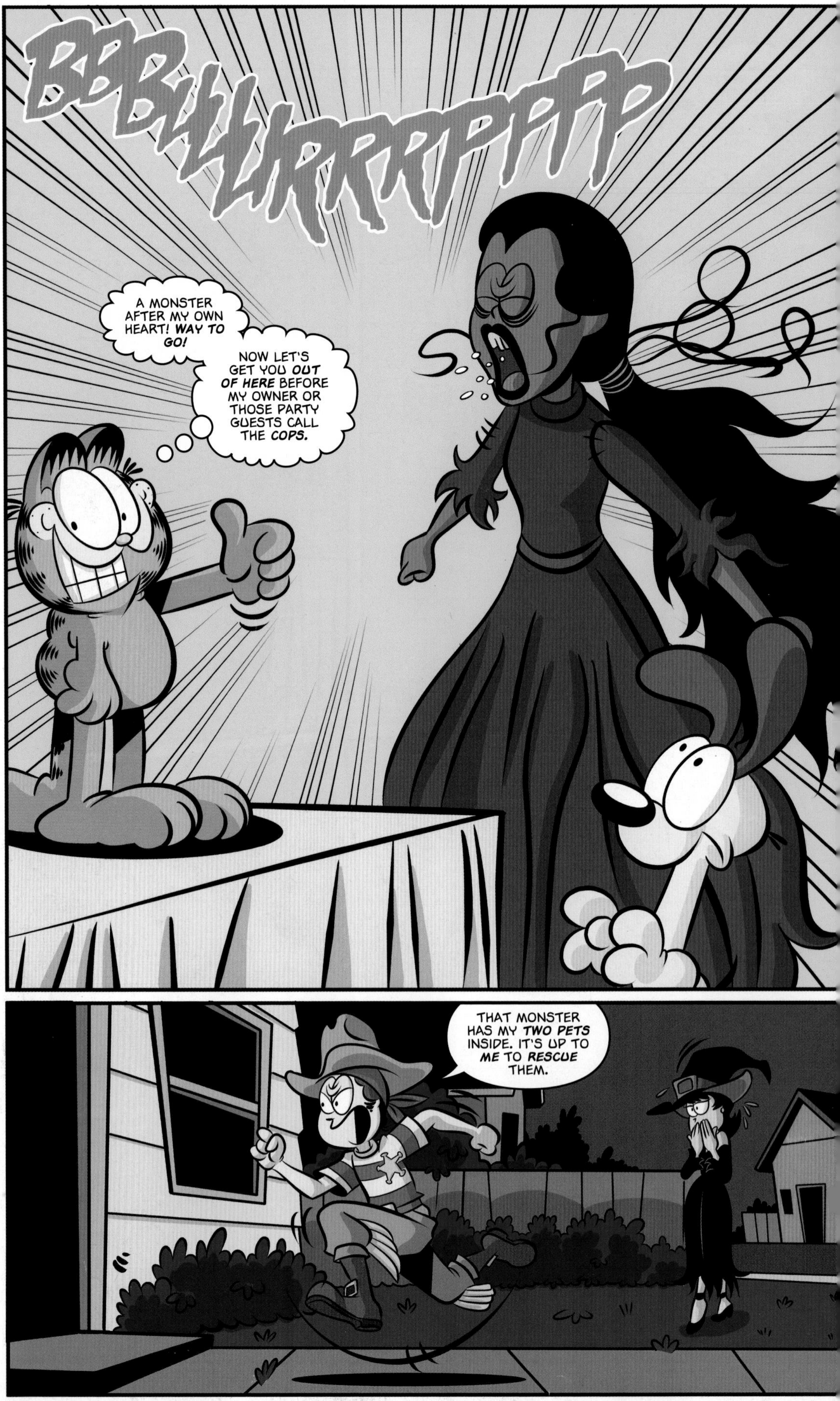
BBBLLLRRRRPPPP
A MONSTER AFTER MY OWN HEART! WAY TO GO!
NOW LET'S GET YOU OUT OF HERE BEFORE MY OWNER OR THOSE PARTY GUESTS CALL THE COPS.
THAT MONSTER HAS MY TWO PETS INSIDE. IT'S UP TO ME TO RESCUE THEM.

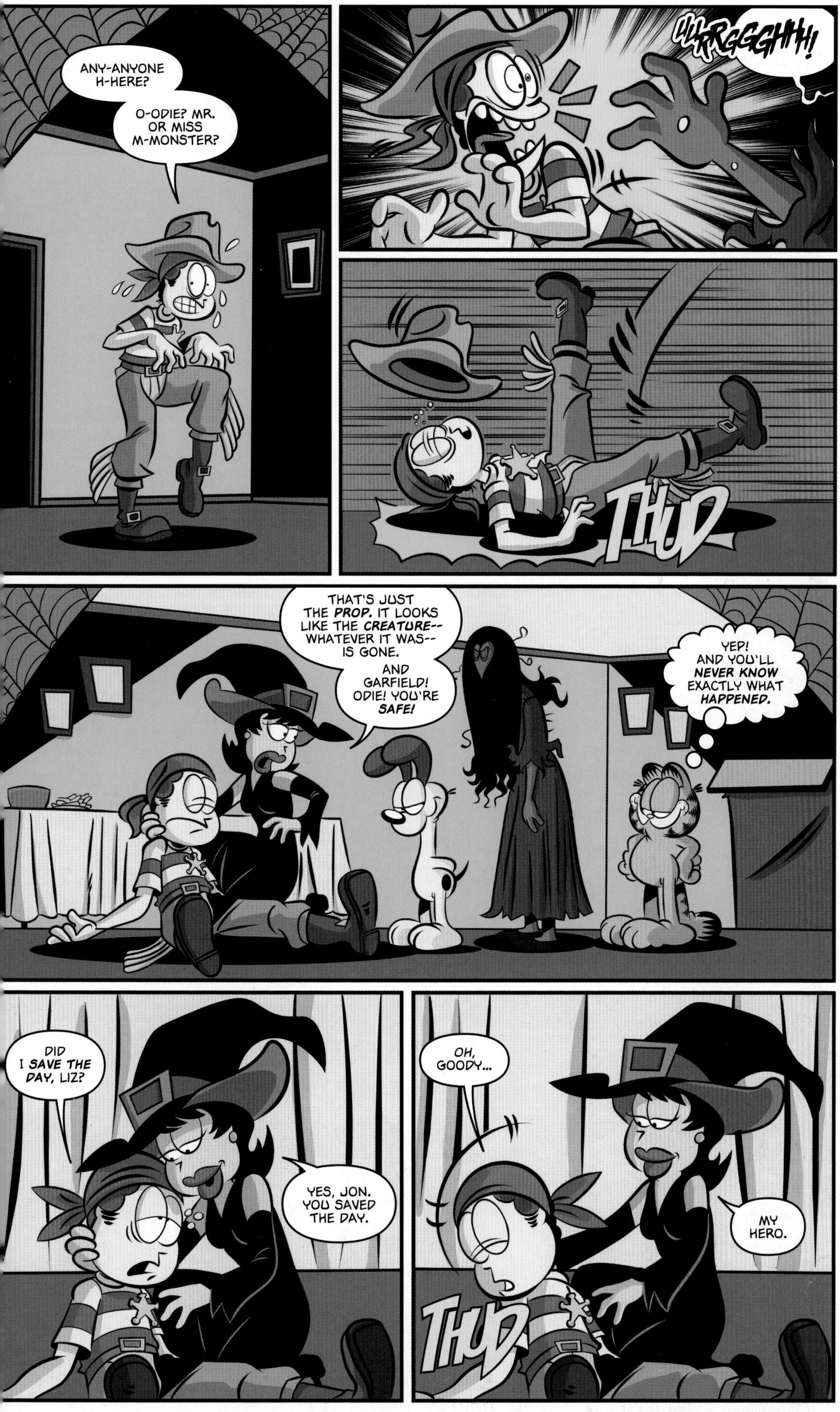
ANY-ANYONE H-HERE?
O-ODIE? MR. OR MISS M-MONSTER?
ULLRRGGGHHH!
THUD
THAT'S JUST THE **PROP.** IT LOOKS LIKE THE **CREATURE--** WHATEVER IT WAS-- IS GONE.
AND GARFIELD! ODIE! YOU'RE **SAFE!**
YEP! AND YOU'LL **NEVER KNOW** EXACTLY WHAT **HAPPENED.**
DID I **SAVE THE DAY,** LIZ?
YES, JON. YOU SAVED THE DAY.
OH, GOODY...
THUD
MY HERO.

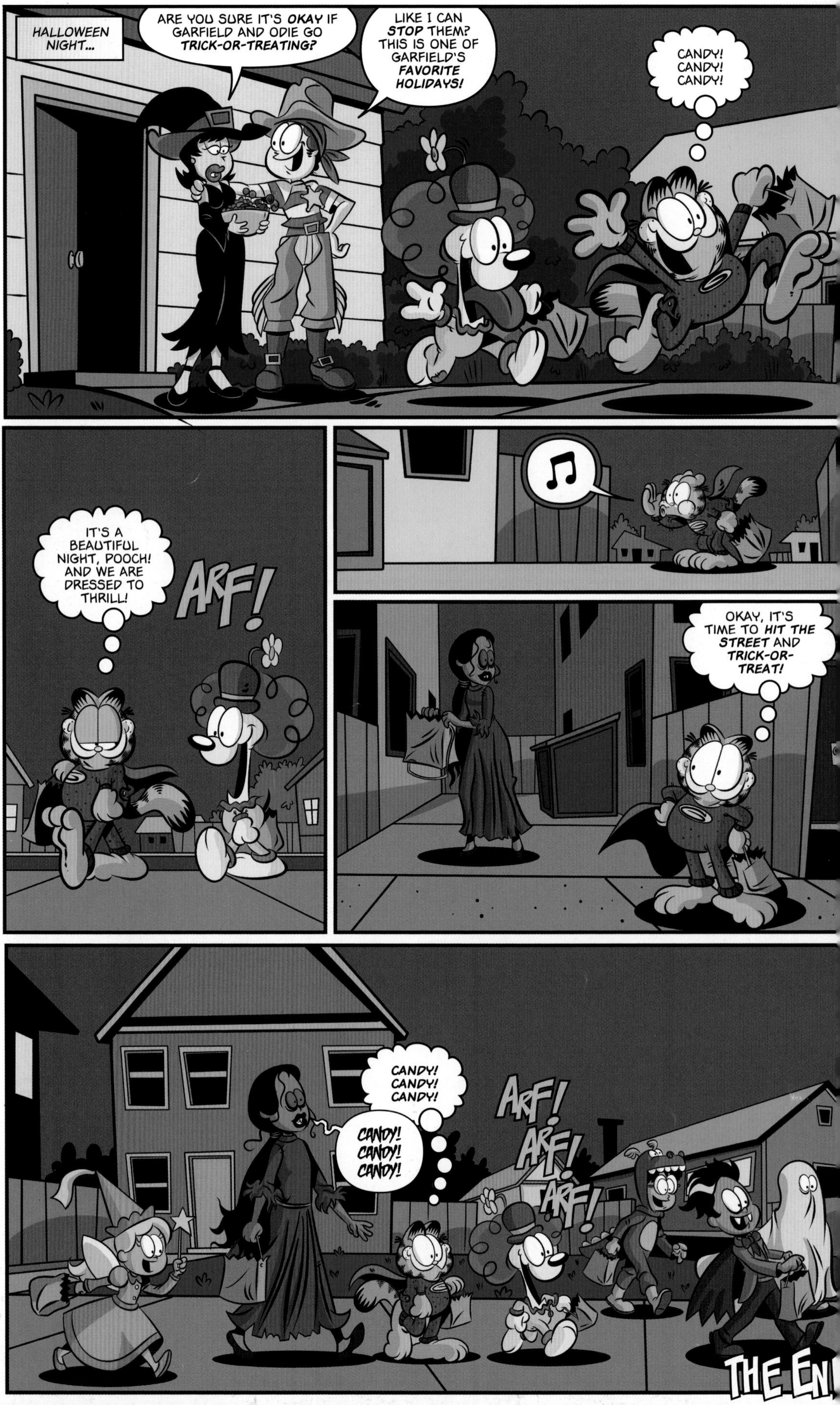
HALLOWEEN NIGHT...
ARE YOU SURE IT'S OKAY IF GARFIELD AND ODIE GO TRICK-OR-TREATING?
LIKE I CAN STOP THEM? THIS IS ONE OF GARFIELD'S FAVORITE HOLIDAYS!
CANDY! CANDY! CANDY!
IT'S A BEAUTIFUL NIGHT, POOCH! AND WE ARE DRESSED TO THRILL!
ARF!
OKAY, IT'S TIME TO HIT THE STREET AND TRICK-OR-TREAT!
CANDY! CANDY! CANDY!
CANDY! CANDY! CANDY!
ARF! ARF! ARF!
THE EN

# Cover
# Gallery

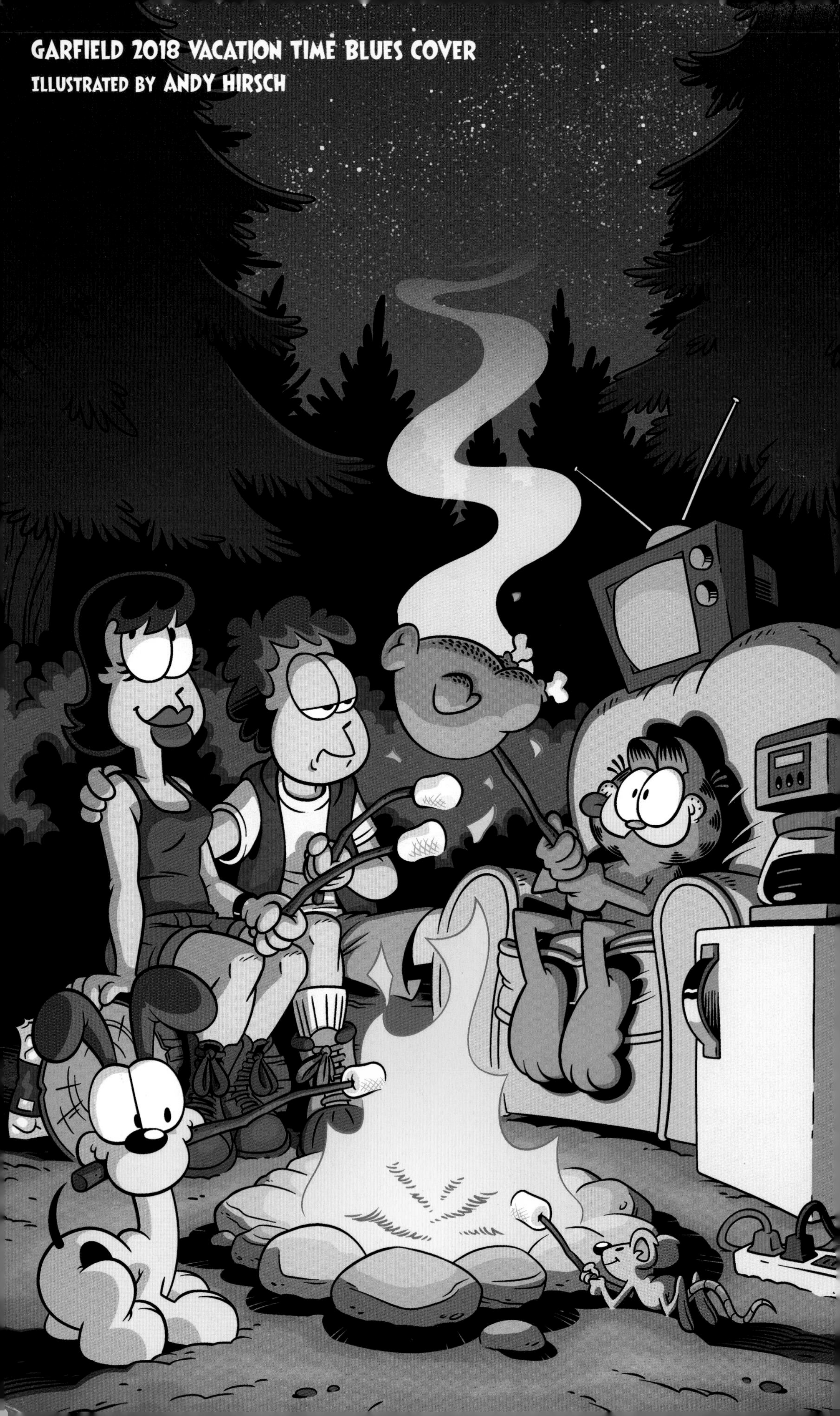
GARFIELD 2018 VACATION TIME BLUES COVER
ILLUSTRATED BY ANDY HIRSCH

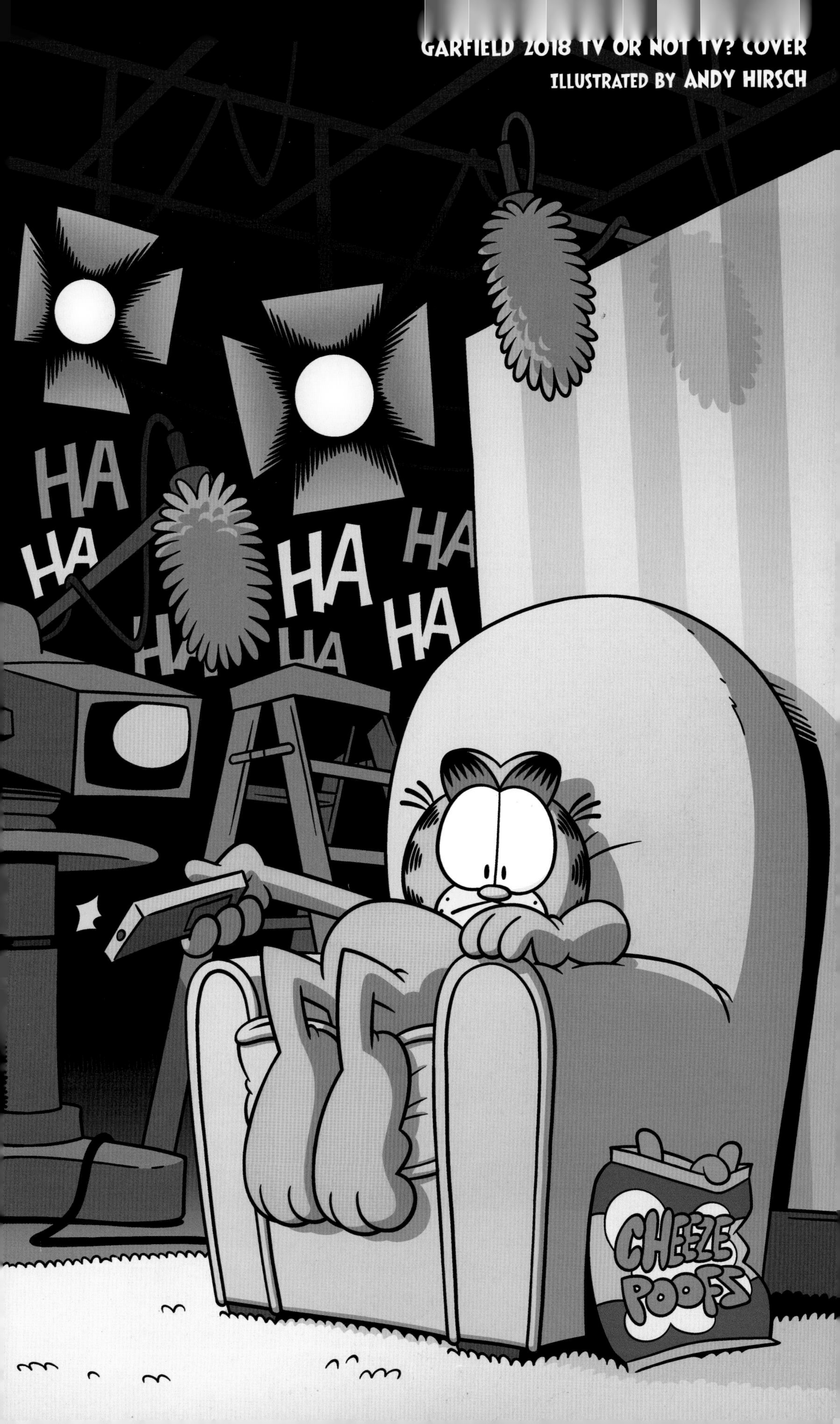
HA
HA
HA
HA
HA
CHEEZE POOFS

GARFIELD 2018 TV OR NOT TV? COVER
ILLUSTRATED BY ANDY HIRSCH

# Food Fun

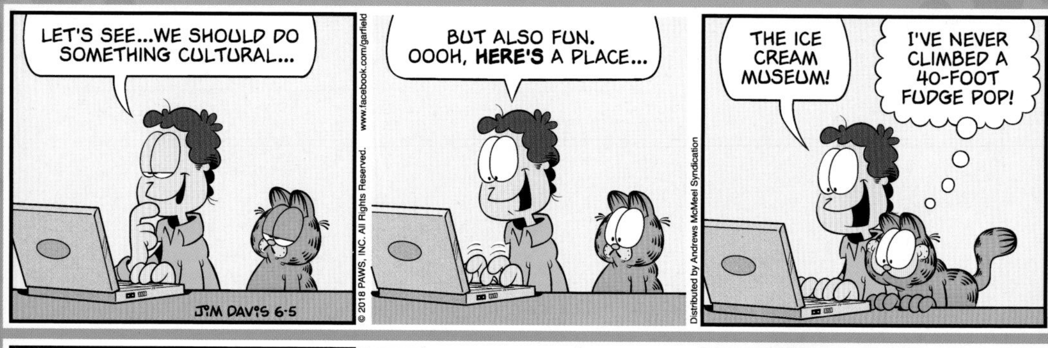

LET'S SEE...WE SHOULD DO SOMETHING CULTURAL...
JIM DAVIS 6-5
BUT ALSO FUN. OOOH, HERE'S A PLACE...
THE ICE CREAM MUSEUM!
I'VE NEVER CLIMBED A 40-FOOT FUDGE POP!
© 2018 PAWS, INC. All Rights Reserved. www.facebook.com/garfield
Distributed by Andrews McMeel Syndication


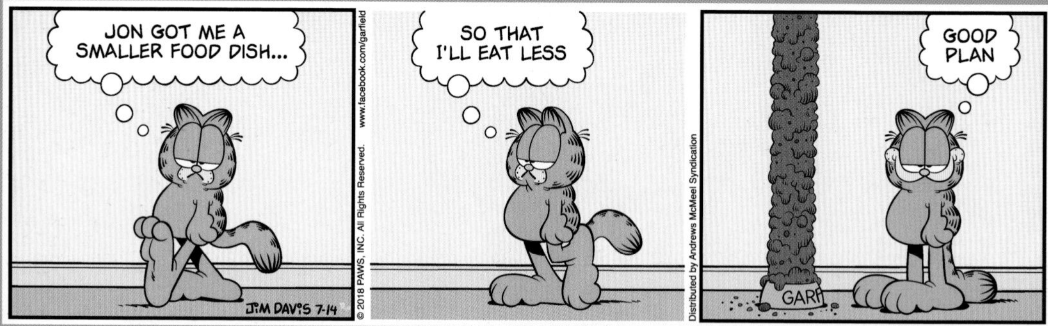

JON GOT ME A SMALLER FOOD DISH...
JIM DAVIS 7-14
SO THAT I'LL EAT LESS
GOOD PLAN
GARF
© 2018 PAWS, INC. All Rights Reserved. www.facebook.com/garfield
Distributed by Andrews McMeel Syndication


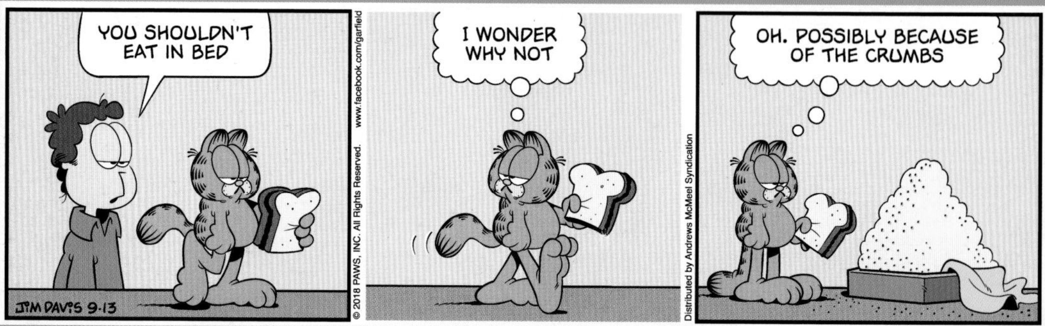

YOU SHOULDN'T EAT IN BED
JIM DAVIS 9-13
I WONDER WHY NOT
OH. POSSIBLY BECAUSE OF THE CRUMBS
© 2018 PAWS, INC. All Rights Reserved. www.facebook.com/garfield
Distributed by Andrews McMeel Syndication


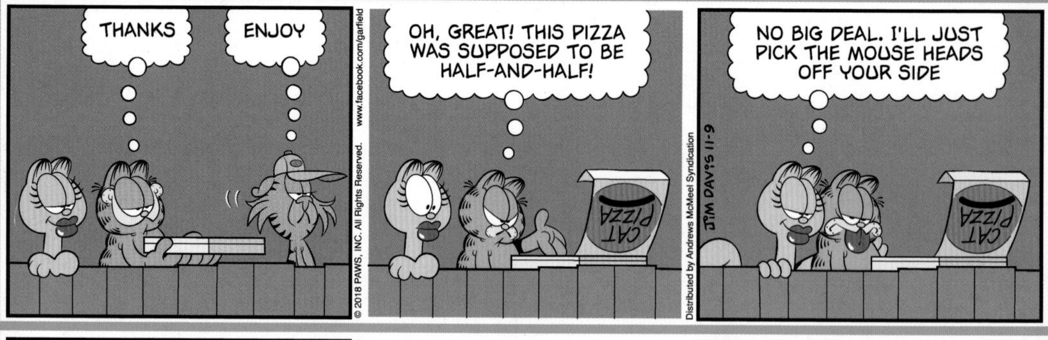

THANKS
ENJOY
OH, GREAT! THIS PIZZA WAS SUPPOSED TO BE HALF-AND-HALF!
CAT PIZZA
NO BIG DEAL. I'LL JUST PICK THE MOUSE HEADS OFF YOUR SIDE
CAT PIZZA
JIM DAVIS 11-9
© 2018 PAWS, INC. All Rights Reserved. www.facebook.com/garfield
Distributed by Andrews McMeel Syndication


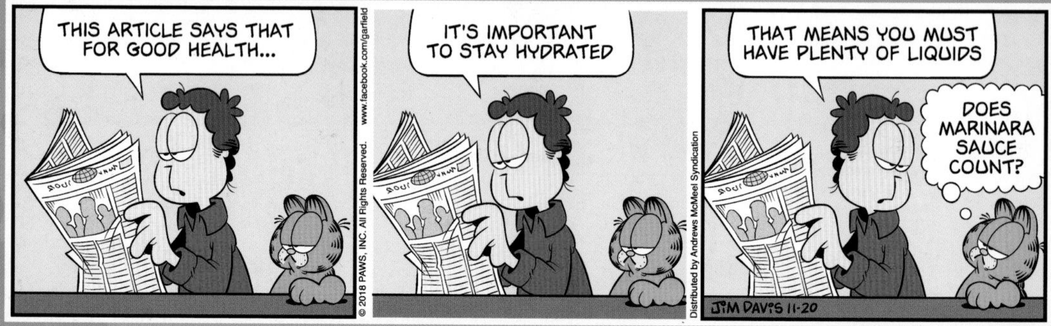

THIS ARTICLE SAYS THAT FOR GOOD HEALTH...
IT'S IMPORTANT TO STAY HYDRATED
THAT MEANS YOU MUST HAVE PLENTY OF LIQUIDS
DOES MARINARA SAUCE COUNT?
JIM DAVIS 11-20
© 2018 PAWS, INC. All Rights Reserved. www.facebook.com/garfield
Distributed by Andrews McMeel Syndication

# Lasagna: Nature's Most Perfect Food

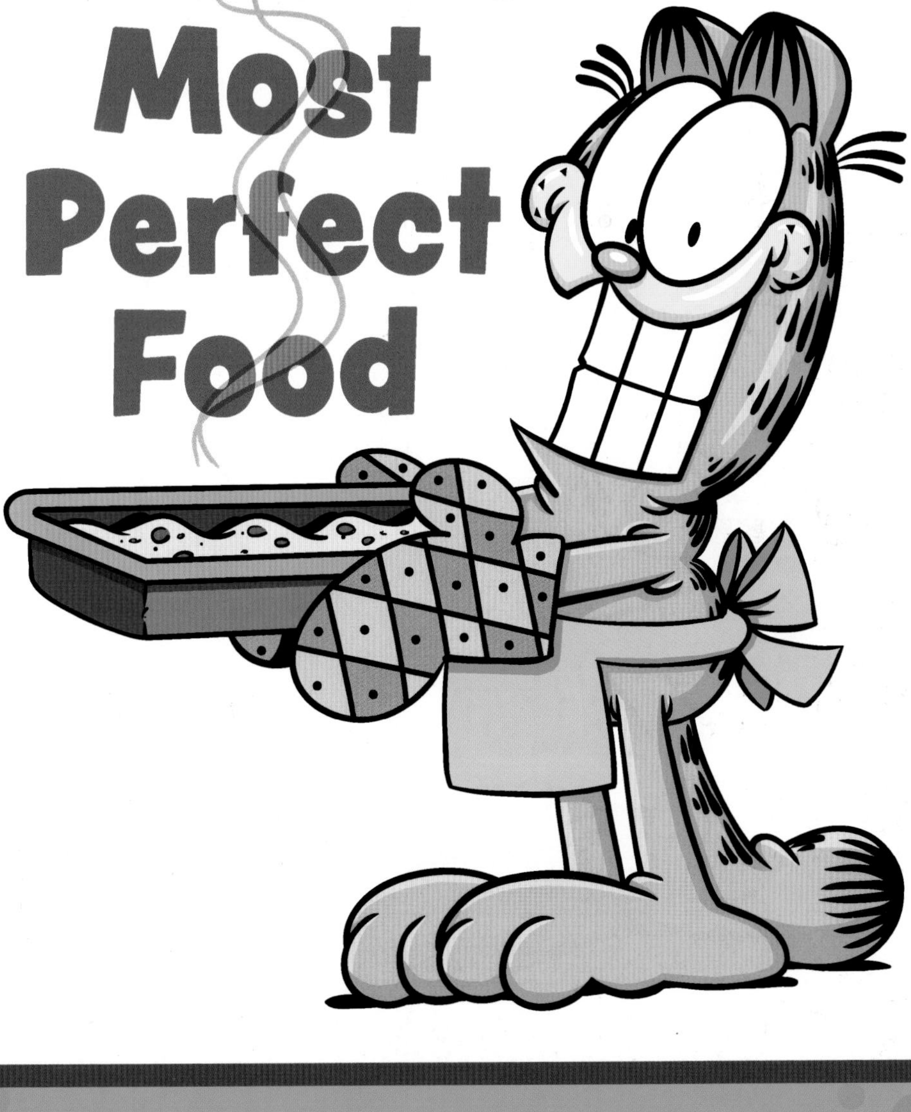

# I'll rise but I won't shine

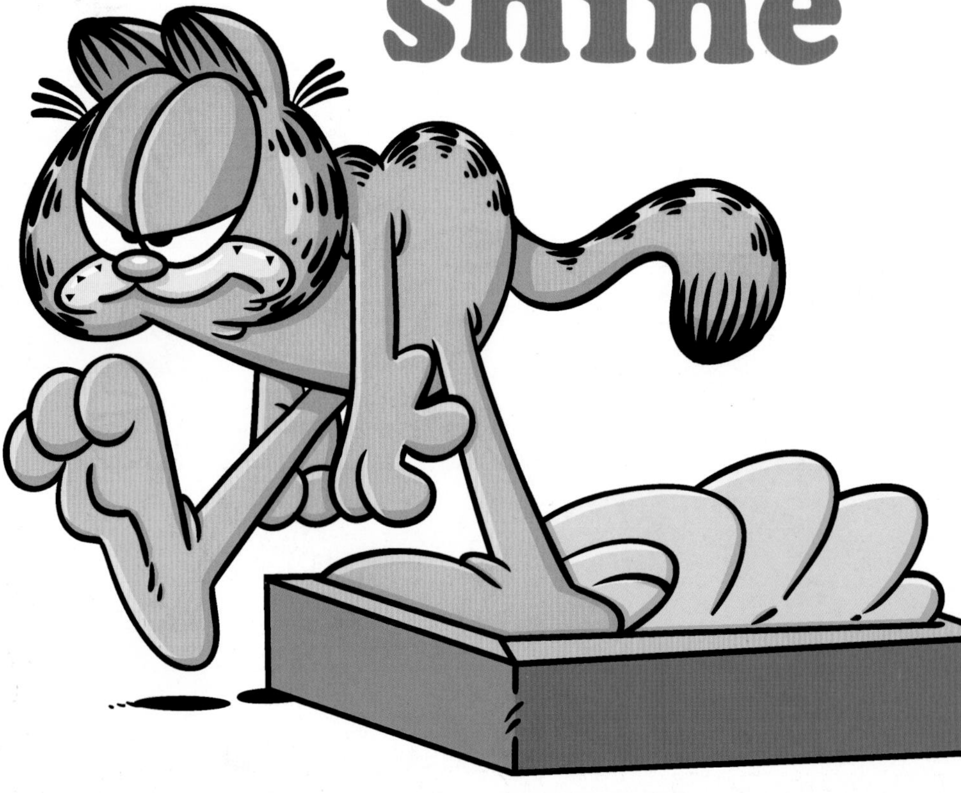

# Garfield Sunday Classics

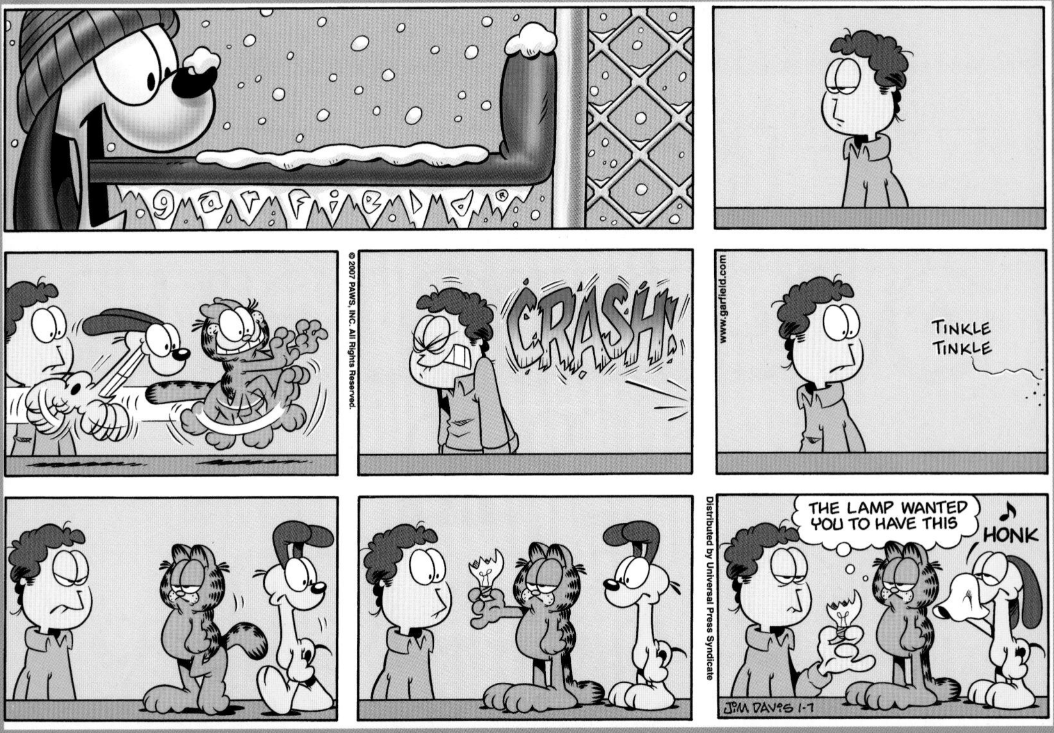
garfield®
© 2007 PAWS, INC. All Rights Reserved.
CRASH!
www.garfield.com
TINKLE TINKLE
Distributed by Universal Press Syndicate
THE LAMP WANTED YOU TO HAVE THIS
HONK
JIM DAVIS 1-7

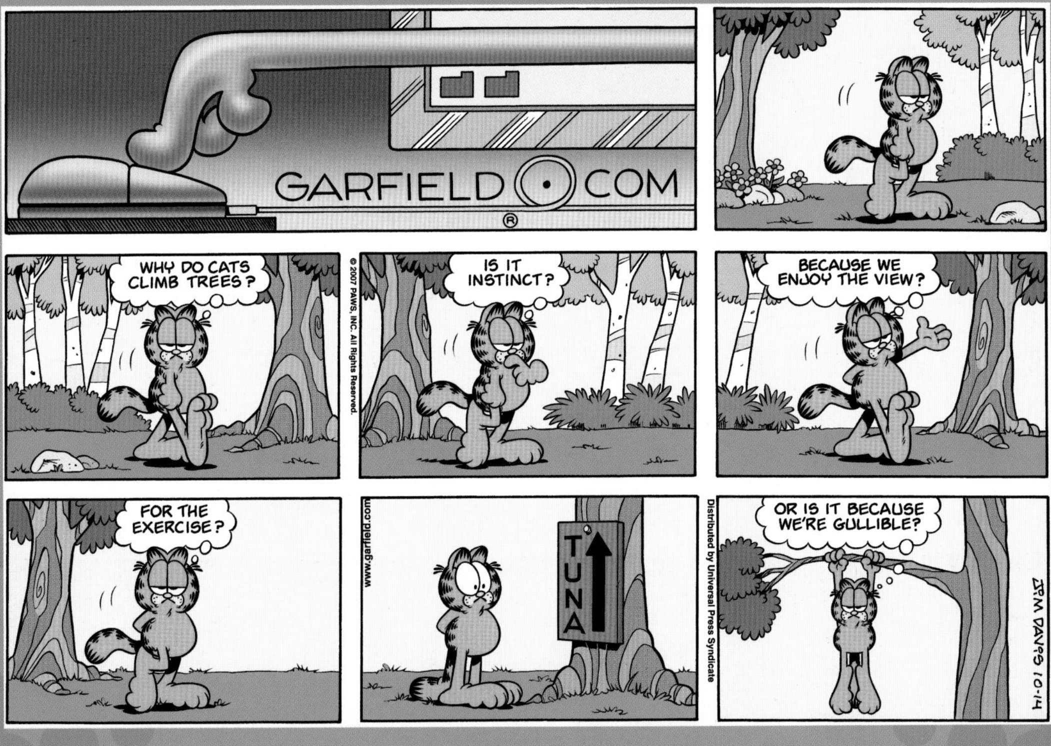
GARFIELD.COM®
© 2007 PAWS, INC. All Rights Reserved.
WHY DO CATS CLIMB TREES?
IS IT INSTINCT?
BECAUSE WE ENJOY THE VIEW?
FOR THE EXERCISE?
www.garfield.com
TUNA
Distributed by Universal Press Syndicate
OR IS IT BECAUSE WE'RE GULLIBLE?
JIM DAVIS 10-14

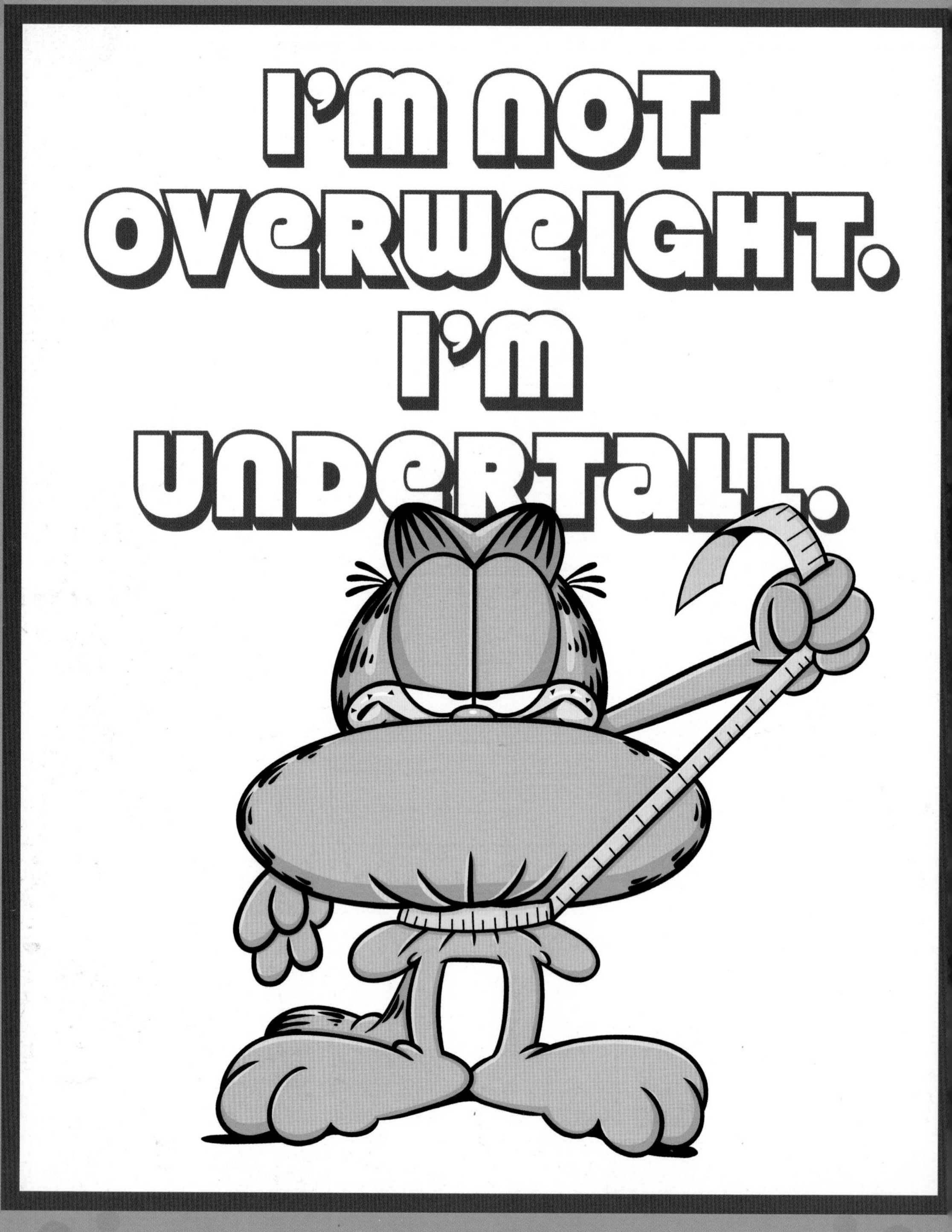
I'M NOT OVERWEIGHT. I'M UNDERTALL.

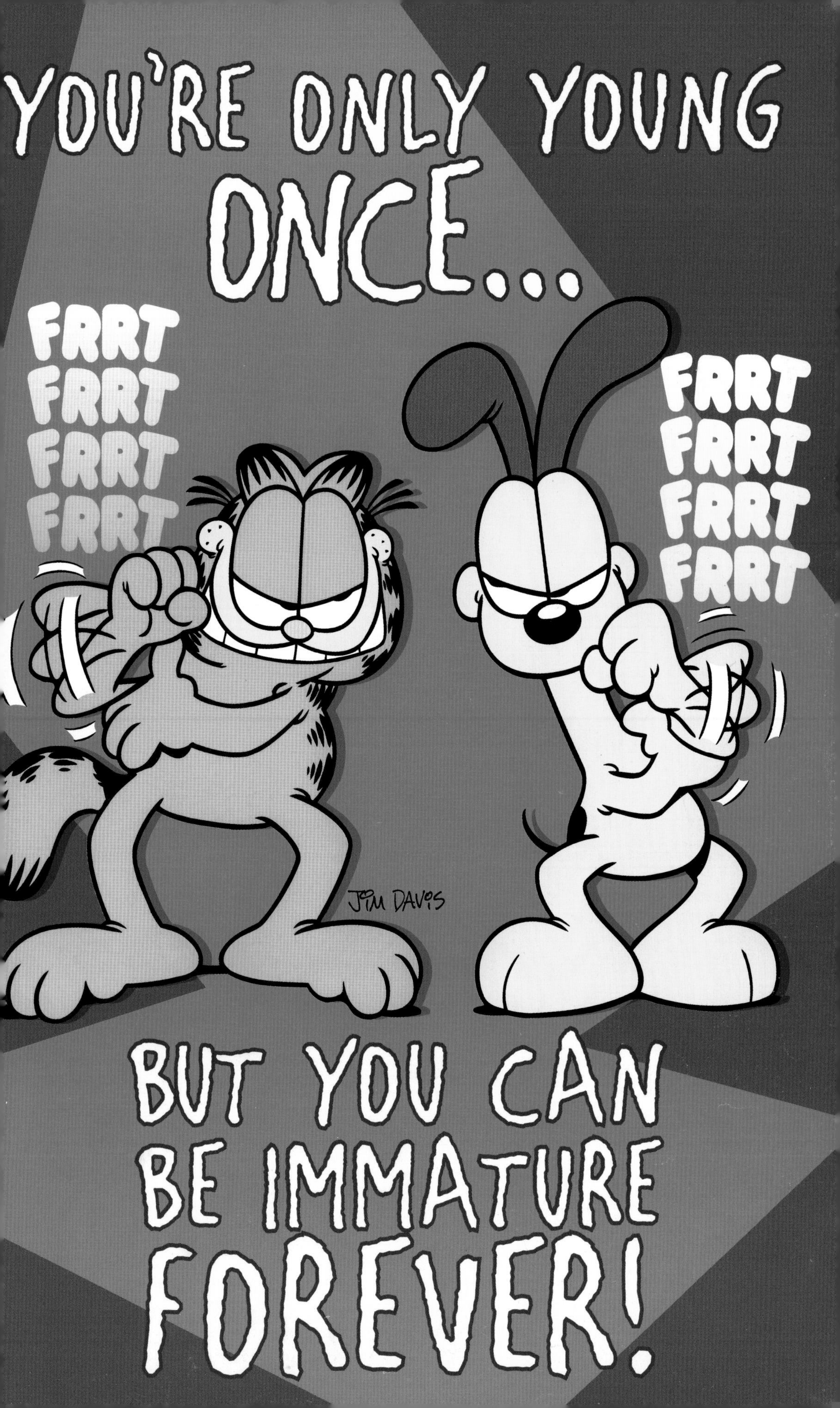
YOU'RE ONLY YOUNG ONCE...
FRRT FRRT FRRT FRRT
FRRT FRRT FRRT FRRT
JIM DAVIS
BUT YOU CAN BE IMMATURE FOREVER!

# Snack Attack

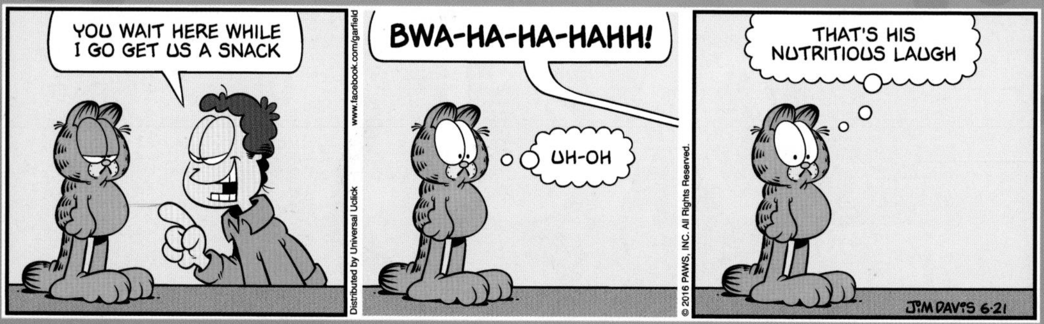
YOU WAIT HERE WHILE I GO GET US A SNACK
BWA-HA-HA-HAHH!
UH-OH
THAT'S HIS NUTRITIOUS LAUGH
JIM DAVIS 6-21
© 2016 PAWS, INC. All Rights Reserved. Distributed by Universal Uclick www.facebook.com/garfield

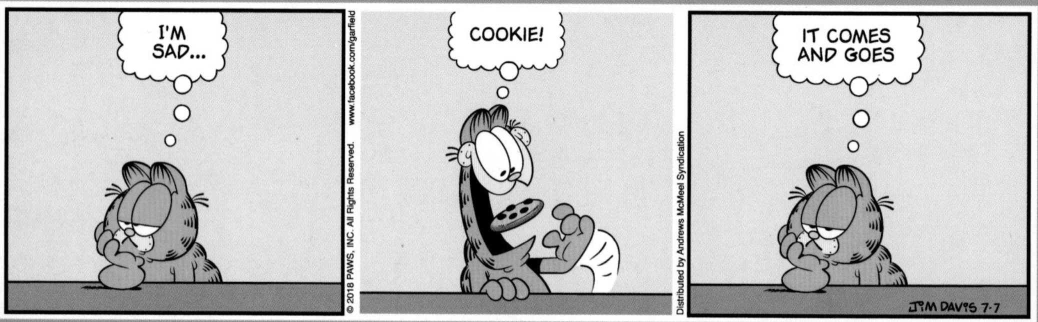
I'M SAD...
COOKIE!
IT COMES AND GOES
JIM DAVIS 7-7
© 2018 PAWS, INC. All Rights Reserved. www.facebook.com/garfield
Distributed by Andrews McMeel Syndication

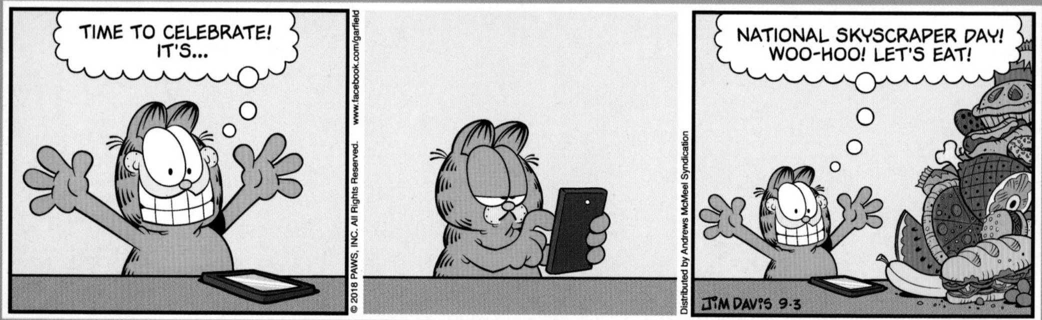
TIME TO CELEBRATE! IT'S...
NATIONAL SKYSCRAPER DAY! WOO-HOO! LET'S EAT!
JIM DAVIS 9-3
© 2018 PAWS, INC. All Rights Reserved. www.facebook.com/garfield
Distributed by Andrews McMeel Syndication

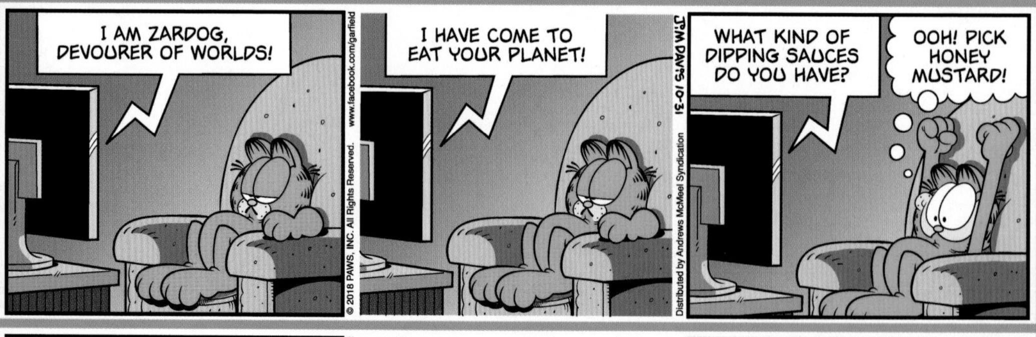
I AM ZARDOG, DEVOURER OF WORLDS!
I HAVE COME TO EAT YOUR PLANET!
WHAT KIND OF DIPPING SAUCES DO YOU HAVE?
OOH! PICK HONEY MUSTARD!
JIM DAVIS 10-31
© 2018 PAWS, INC. All Rights Reserved. www.facebook.com/garfield
Distributed by Andrews McMeel Syndication

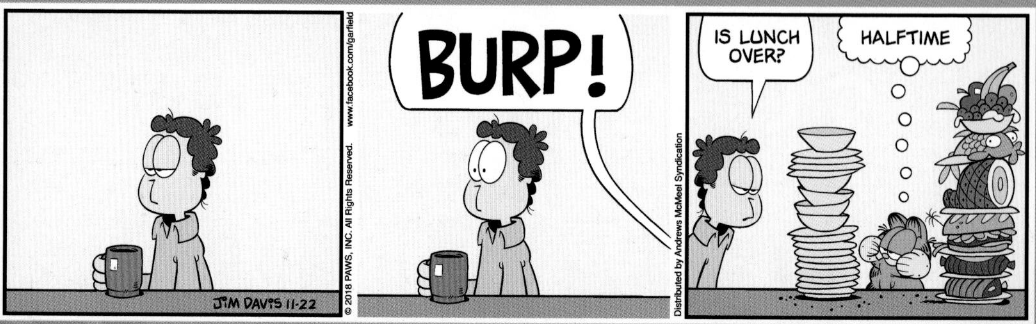
BURP!
IS LUNCH OVER?
HALFTIME
JIM DAVIS 11-22
© 2018 PAWS, INC. All Rights Reserved. www.facebook.com/garfield
Distributed by Andrews McMeel Syndication

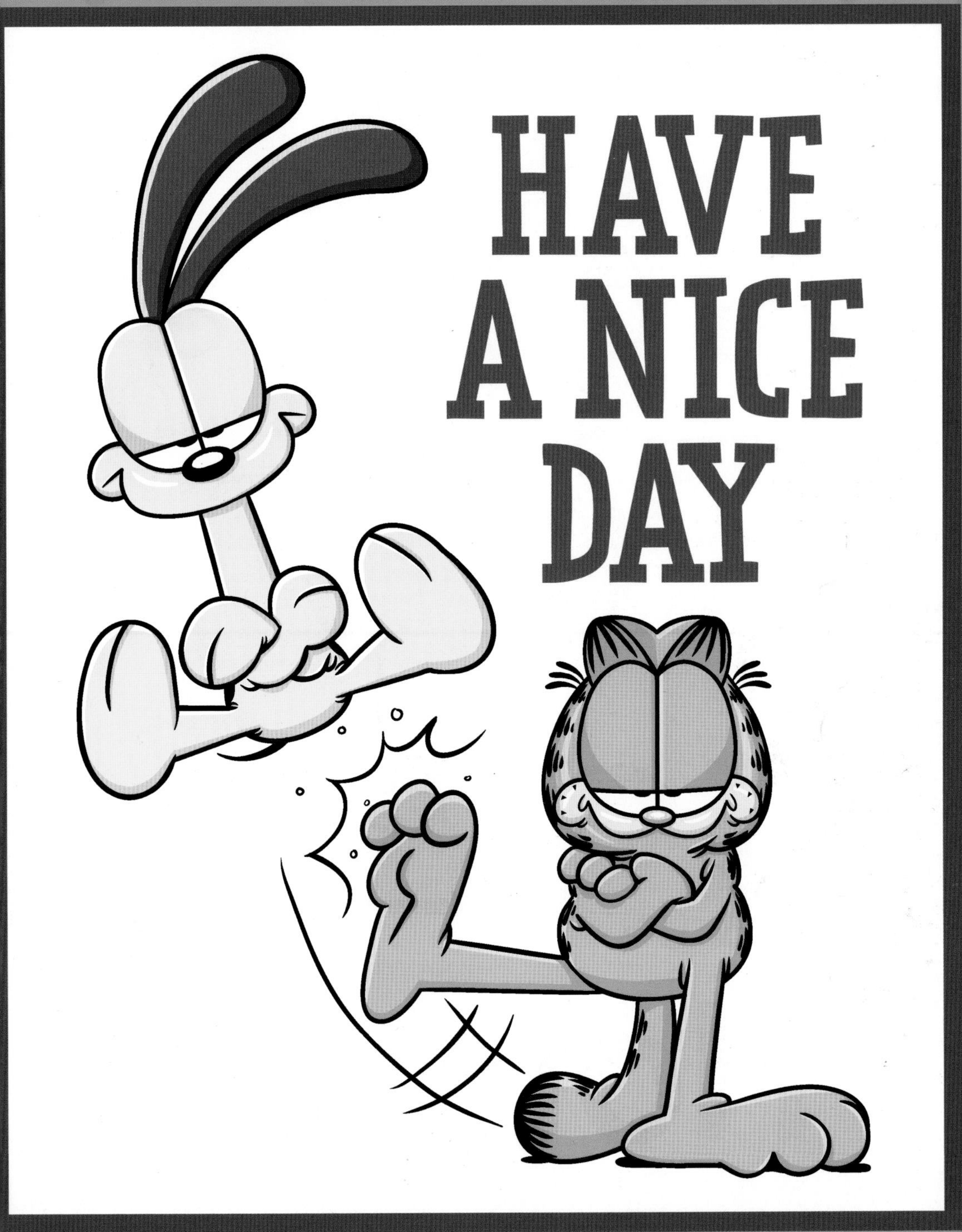
HAVE
A NICE
DAY

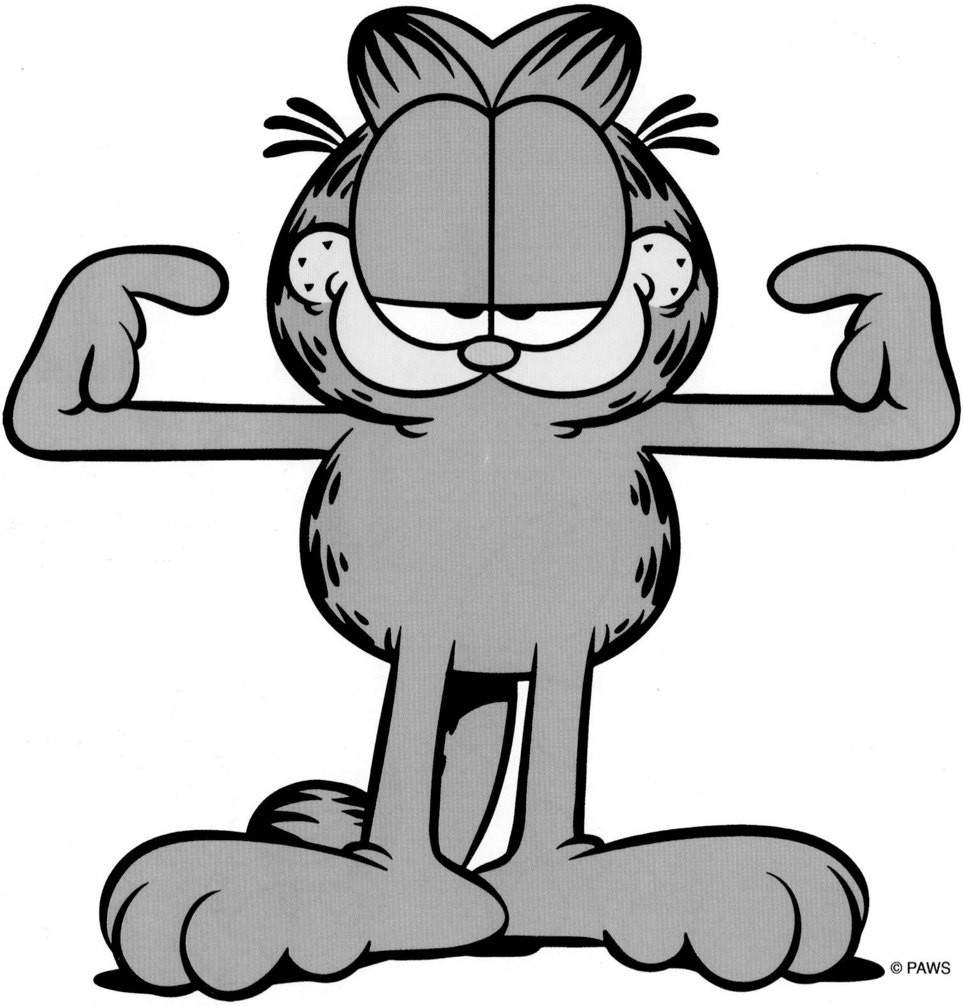
© PAWS

# Hotspot

# Garfield Sunday Classics

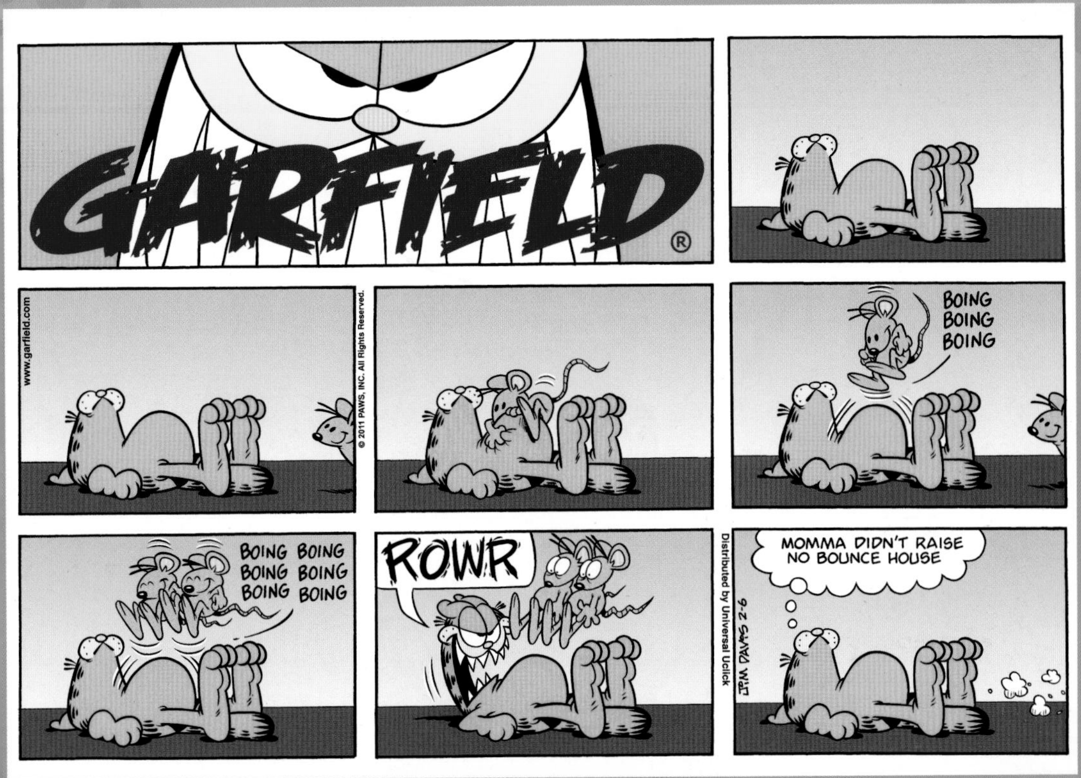
GARFIELD ®
www.garfield.com
© 2011 PAWS, INC. All Rights Reserved.
BOING
BOING
BOING
BOING BOING
BOING BOING
BOING BOING
ROWR
JIM DAVIS 2-6
Distributed by Universal Uclick
MOMMA DIDN'T RAISE NO BOUNCE HOUSE

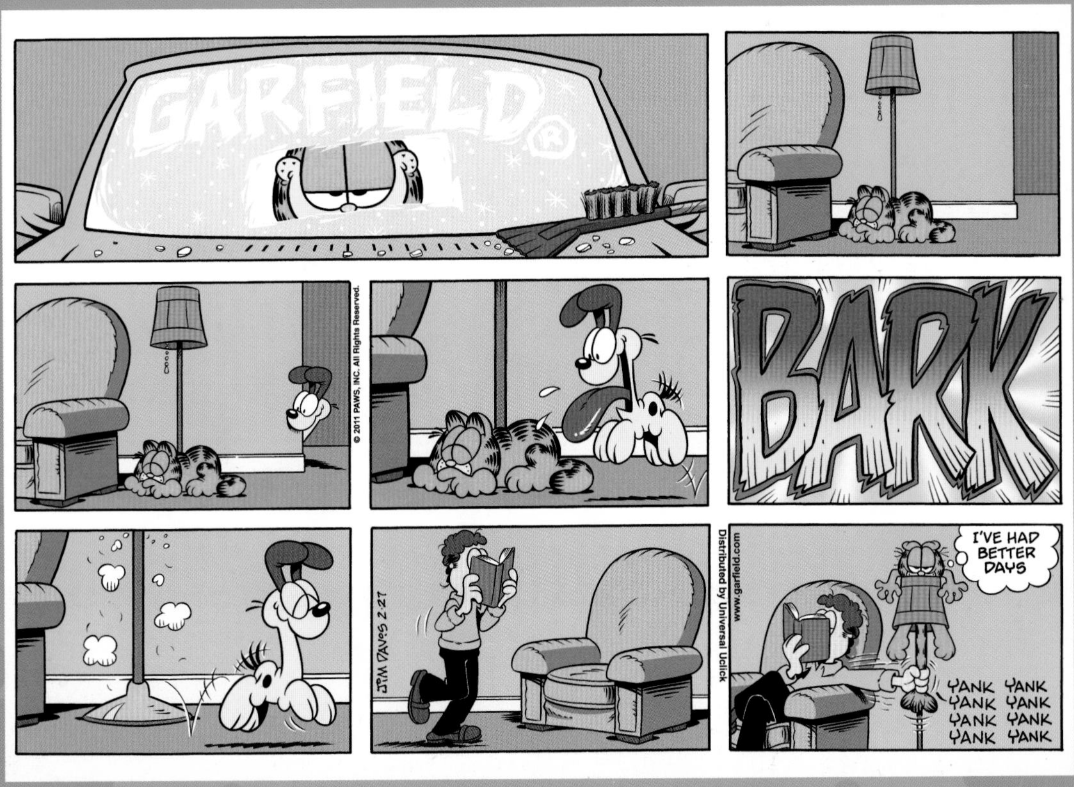
GARFIELD ®
© 2011 PAWS, INC. All Rights Reserved.
BARK
JIM DAVIS 2-27
Distributed by Universal Uclick
www.garfield.com
I'VE HAD BETTER DAYS
YANK YANK
YANK YANK
YANK YANK
YANK YANK

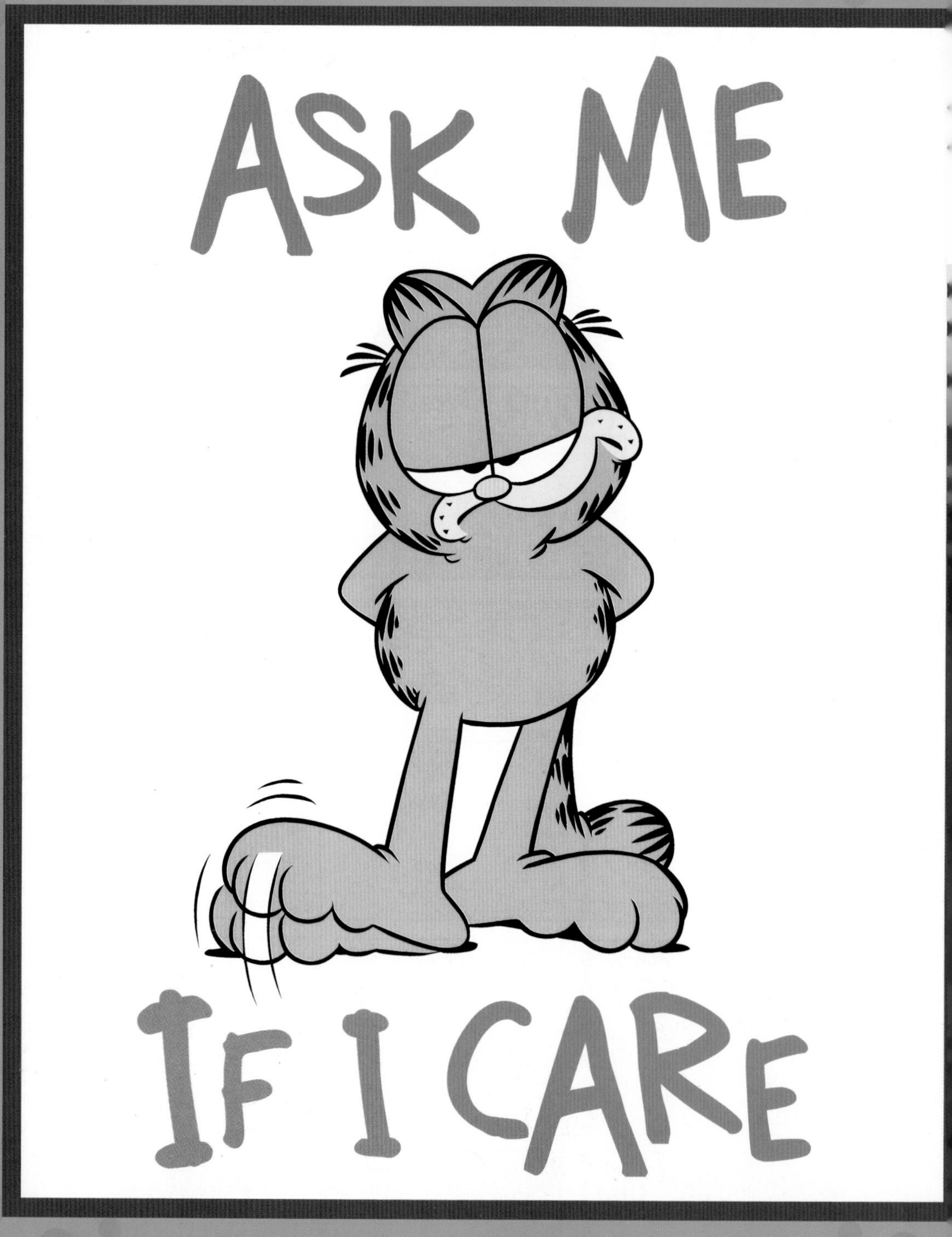
ASK ME
IF I CARE

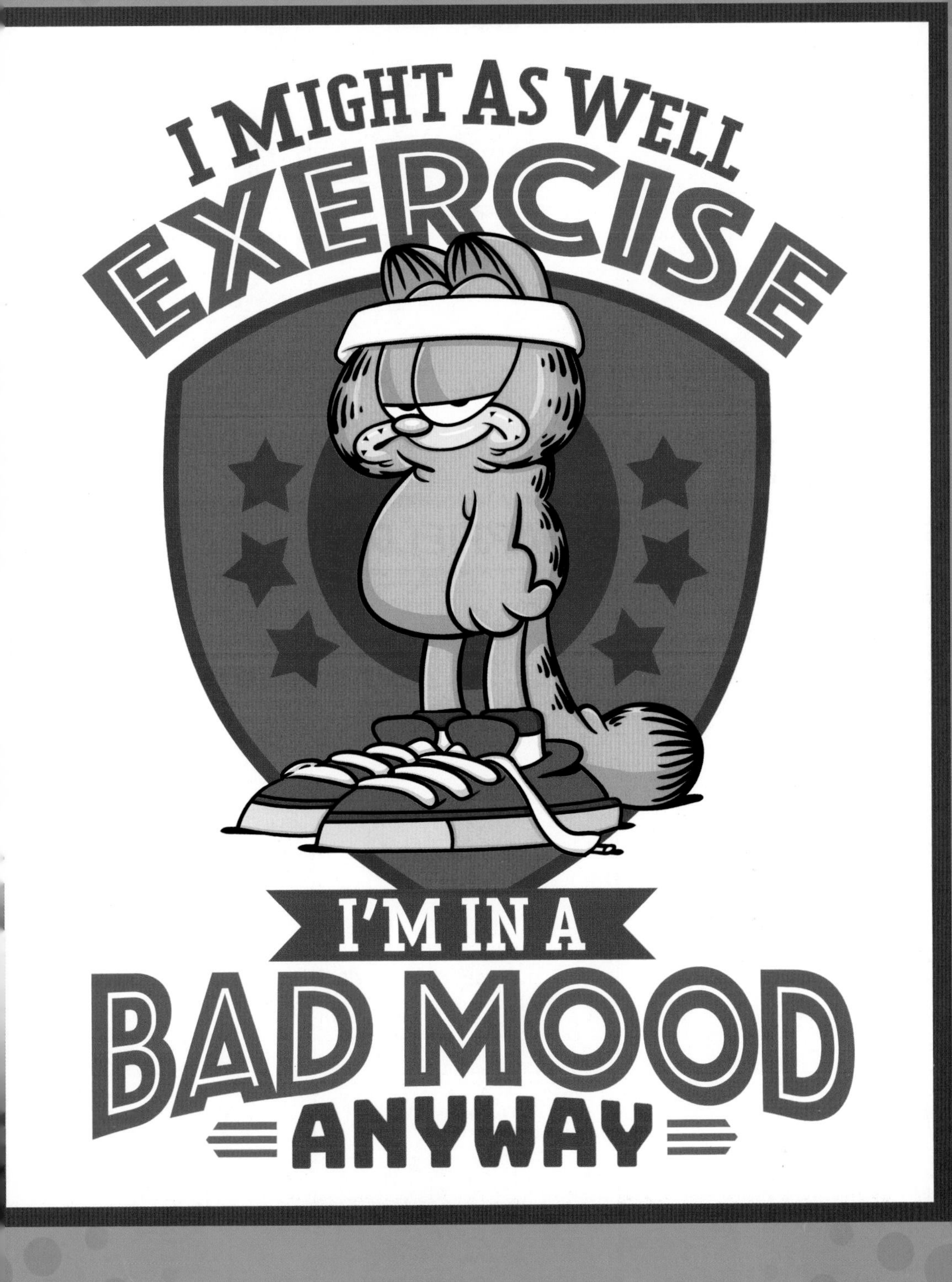
I MIGHT AS WELL
EXERCISE
I'M IN A
BAD MOOD
ANYWAY

# Coffee Cat

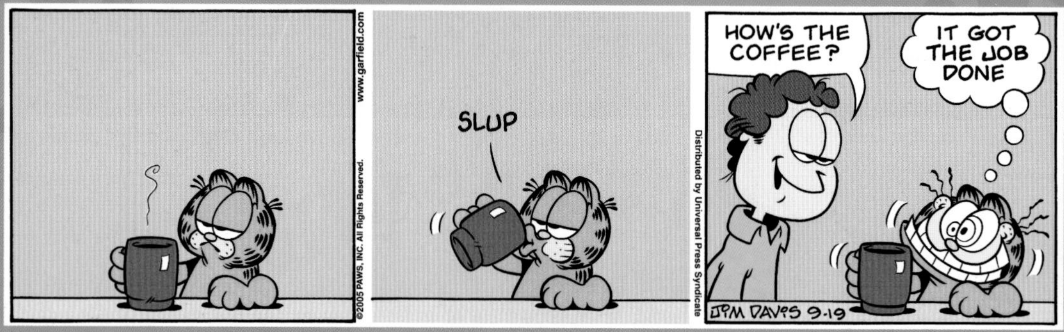
SLUP
HOW'S THE COFFEE?
IT GOT THE JOB DONE
www.garfield.com
©2005 PAWS, INC. All Rights Reserved.
Distributed by Universal Press Syndicate
JIM DAVIS 9-19

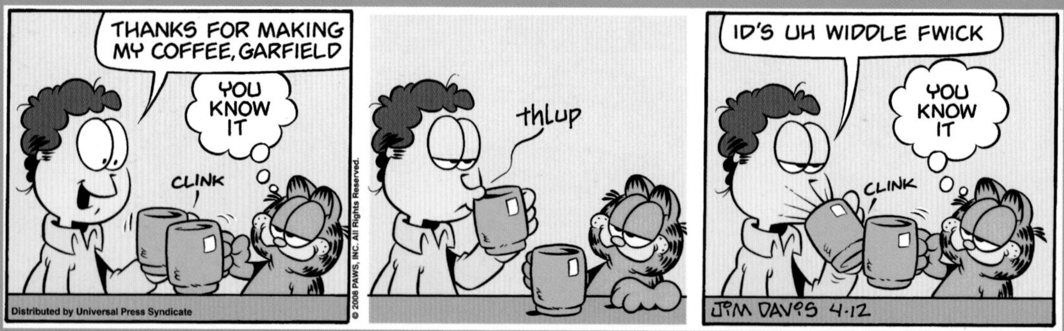
THANKS FOR MAKING MY COFFEE, GARFIELD
YOU KNOW IT
CLINK
thlup
ID'S UH WIDDLE FWICK
YOU KNOW IT
CLINK
Distributed by Universal Press Syndicate
© 2008 PAWS, INC. All Rights Reserved.
JIM DAVIS 4-12

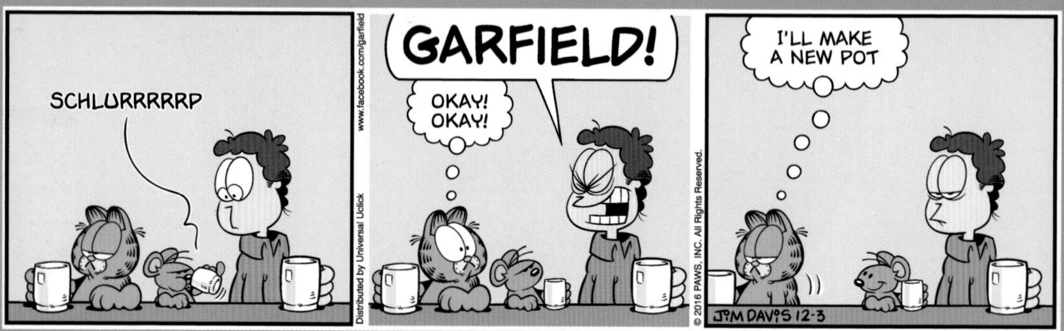
SCHLURRRRRP
www.facebook.com/garfield
Distributed by Universal Uclick
GARFIELD!
OKAY! OKAY!
I'LL MAKE A NEW POT
© 2016 PAWS, INC. All Rights Reserved.
JIM DAVIS 12-3

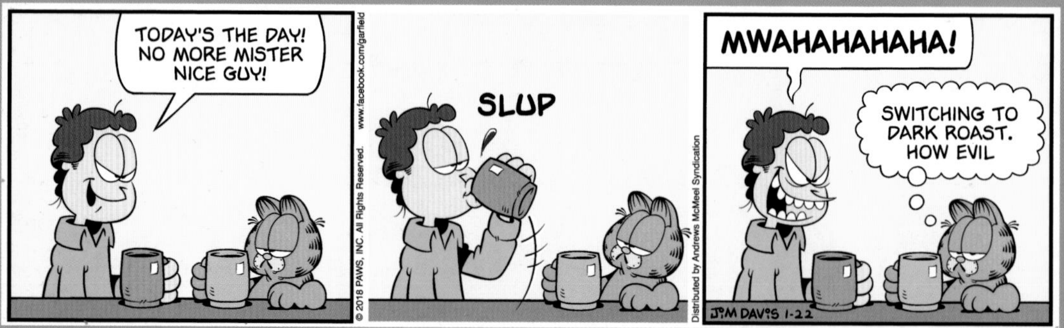
TODAY'S THE DAY! NO MORE MISTER NICE GUY!
© 2018 PAWS, INC. All Rights Reserved. www.facebook.com/garfield
SLUP
Distributed by Andrews McMeel Syndication
MWAHAHAHAHA!
SWITCHING TO DARK ROAST. HOW EVIL
JIM DAVIS 1-22

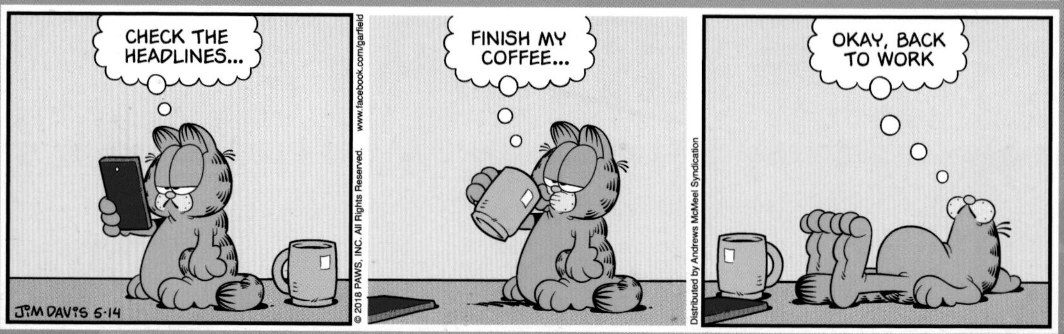
CHECK THE HEADLINES...
JIM DAVIS 5-14
© 2018 PAWS, INC. All Rights Reserved. www.facebook.com/garfield
FINISH MY COFFEE...
Distributed by Andrews McMeel Syndication
OKAY, BACK TO WORK

# CATS ARE POETRY IN MOTION.

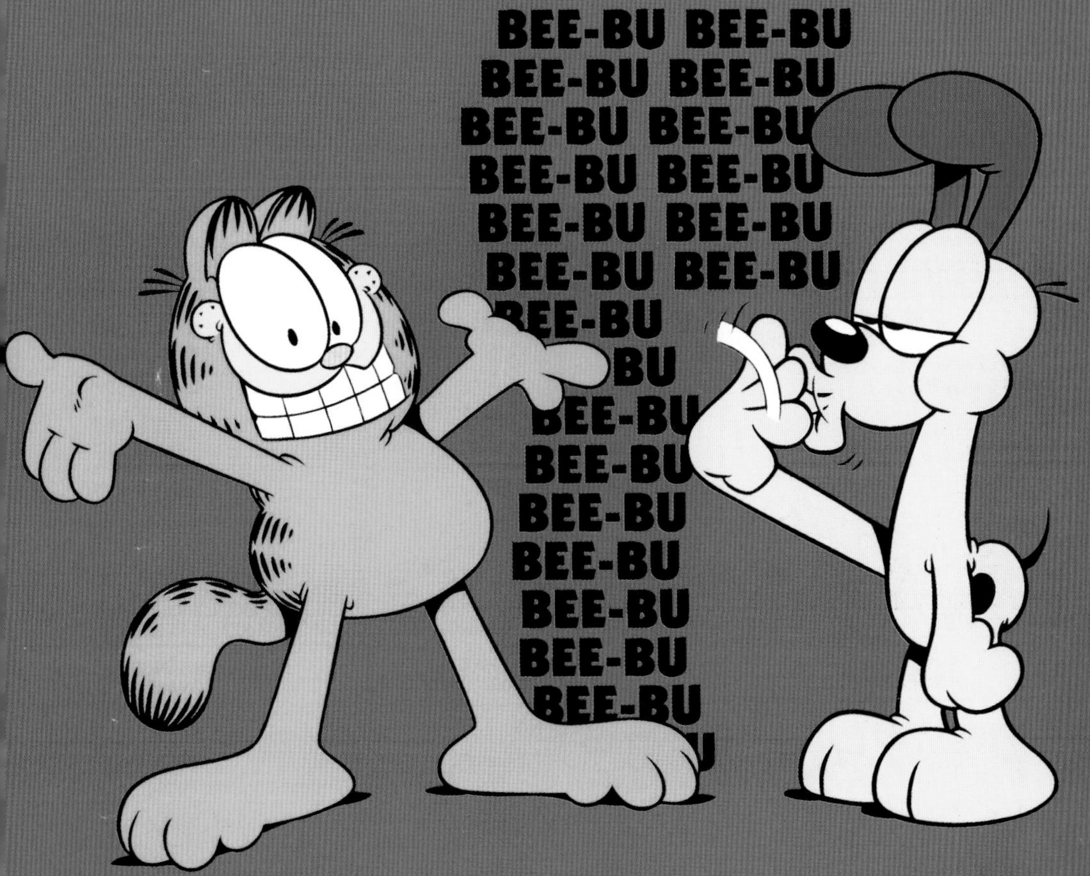

BEE-BU BEE-BU
BEE-BU BEE-BU
BEE-BU BEE-BU
BEE-BU BEE-BU
BEE-BU BEE-BU
BEE-BU BEE-BU
BEE-BU
BEE-BU
BEE-BU
BEE-BU
BEE-BU


# DOGS ARE GIBBERISH IN NEUTRAL.

# Donut Run

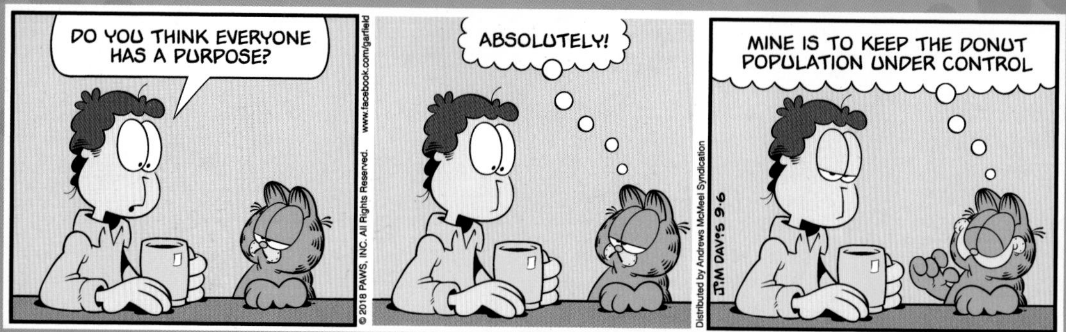
DO YOU THINK EVERYONE HAS A PURPOSE?
ABSOLUTELY!
MINE IS TO KEEP THE DONUT POPULATION UNDER CONTROL
JIM DAVIS 9-6
© 2018 PAWS, INC. All Rights Reserved. www.facebook.com/garfield
Distributed by Andrews McMeel Syndication

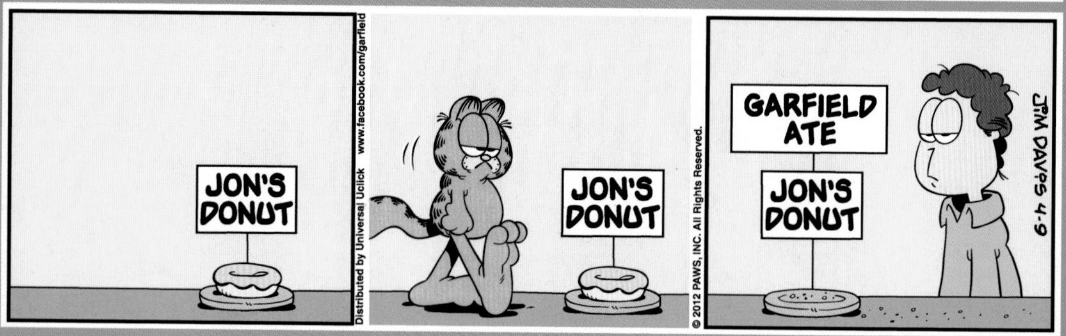
JON'S DONUT
JON'S DONUT
GARFIELD ATE
JON'S DONUT
JIM DAVIS 4-9
Distributed by Universal Uclick www.facebook.com/garfield
© 2012 PAWS, INC. All Rights Reserved.

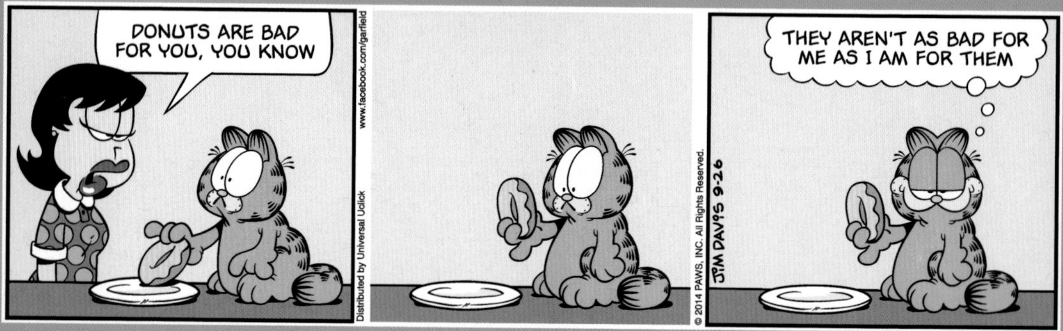
DONUTS ARE BAD FOR YOU, YOU KNOW
THEY AREN'T AS BAD FOR ME AS I AM FOR THEM
JIM DAVIS 9-26
Distributed by Universal Uclick www.facebook.com/garfield
© 2014 PAWS, INC. All Rights Reserved.

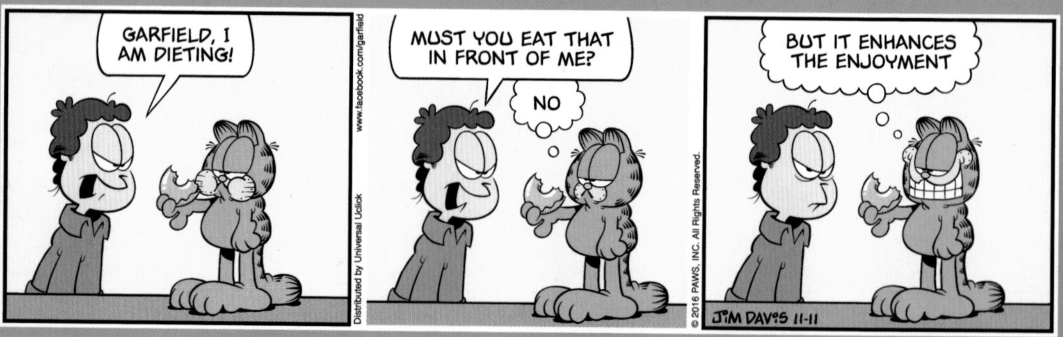
GARFIELD, I AM DIETING!
MUST YOU EAT THAT IN FRONT OF ME?
NO
BUT IT ENHANCES THE ENJOYMENT
JIM DAVIS 11-11
Distributed by Universal Uclick www.facebook.com/garfield
© 2016 PAWS, INC. All Rights Reserved.

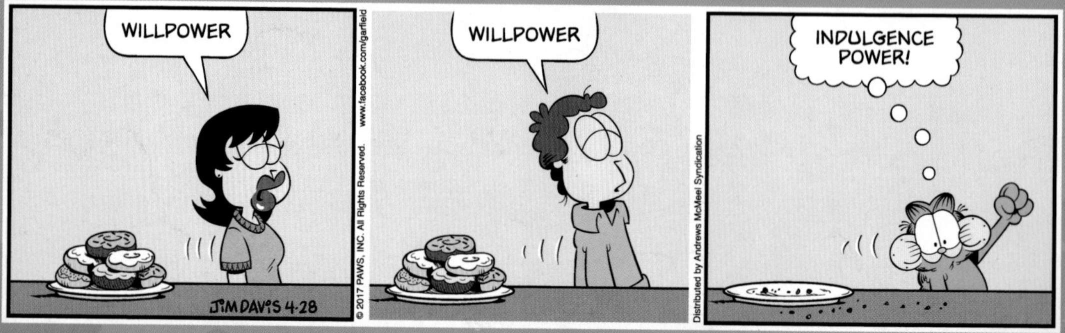
WILLPOWER
WILLPOWER
INDULGENCE POWER!
JIM DAVIS 4-28
© 2017 PAWS, INC. All Rights Reserved. www.facebook.com/garfield
Distributed by Andrews McMeel Syndication

# BIG FAT HAIRY DEAL!

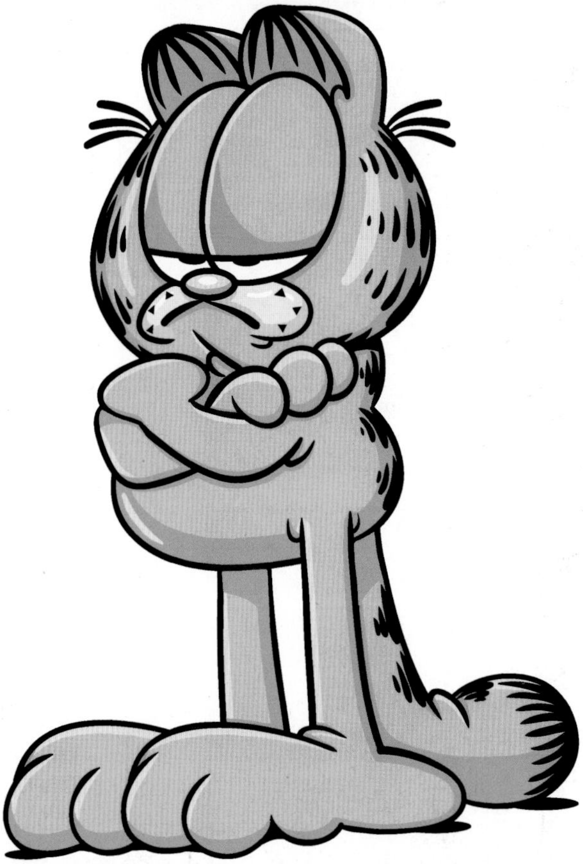

DISCOVER
# EXPLOSIVE NEW WORLDS

ADVENTURE TIME

sam sykes · selina espiritu · sarah stern
Brave Chef Brianna

KELLY THOMPSON BRIANNE DROUHARD M. VICTORIA ROBADO
MEGA PRINCESS

THE NOT-SO SECRET SOCIETY
DALEY · CRAFTS · CLARK · BRUNI

OVER THE GARDEN WALL

STEVEN UNIVERSE
VOLUME ONE

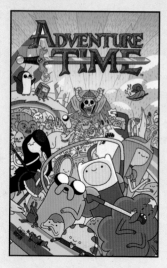

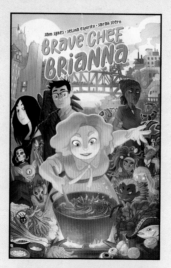

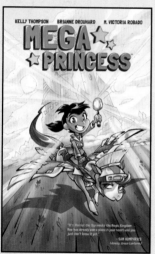

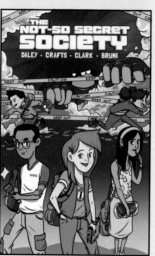

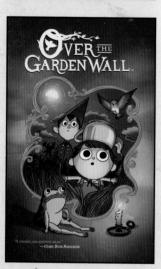

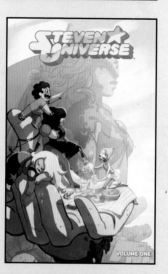

**Adventure Time**
*Pendleton Ward and Others*
**Volume 1**
ISBN: 978-1-60886-280-1 | $14.99 US
**Volume 2**
ISBN: 978-1-60886-323-5 | $14.99 US
**Adventure Time: Islands**
ISBN: 978-1-60886-972-5 | $9.99 US

**The Amazing World of Gumball**
*Ben Bocquelet and Others*
**Volume 1**
ISBN: 978-1-60886-488-1 | $14.99 US
**Volume 2**
ISBN: 978-1-60886-793-6 | $14.99 US

**Brave Chef Brianna**
*Sam Sykes, Selina Espiritu*
ISBN: 978-1-68415-050-2 | $14.99 US

**Mega Princess**
*Kelly Thompson, Brianne Drouhard*
ISBN: 978-1-68415-007-6 | $14.99 US

**The Not-So Secret Society**
*Matthew Daley, Arlene Daley, Wook Jin Clark*
ISBN: 978-1-60886-997-8 | $9.99 US

**Over the Garden Wall**
*Patrick McHale, Jim Campbell and Others*
**Volume 1**
ISBN: 978-1-60886-940-4 | $14.99 US
**Volume 2**
ISBN: 978-1-68415-006-9 | $14.99 US

**Steven Universe**
*Rebecca Sugar and Others*
**Volume 1**
ISBN: 978-1-60886-706-6 | $14.99 US
**Volume 2**
ISBN: 978-1-60886-796-7 | $14.99 US

**Steven Universe & The Crystal Gems**
ISBN: 978-1-60886-921-3 | $14.99 US

**Steven Universe: Too Cool for School**
ISBN: 978-1-60886-771-4 | $14.99 US

kaboom!™

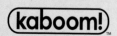

**AVAILABLE AT YOUR LOCAL COMICS SHOP AND BOOKSTORE**
To find a comics shop in your area, visit www.comicshoplocator.com
WWW.**BOOM-STUDIOS**.COM